Praise for *New York Times* bestselling author

ELIZABETH LOWELL

"I'll buy any book with
Elizabeth Lowell's name on it!"
—*New York Times* bestselling author Jayne Ann Krentz

* * *

Praise for national bestselling author

LEANNE BANKS

"When life gets tough, read a book by Leanne Banks."
—*New York Times* bestselling author Janet Evanovich

ELIZABETH LOWELL

New York Times bestselling author Elizabeth Lowell
has won countless awards, including the Romance
Writers of America Lifetime Achievement Award.
She also writes mainstream fiction as Ann Maxwell,
and mysteries with her husband as A. E. Maxwell.
She presently resides with her husband and family
in California.

LEANNE BANKS

Leanne Banks is a national number-one bestselling
author of romance. She lives in her native Virginia
with her husband, son and daughter. Recognized for
both her sensual and humorous writing with two
Career Achievement Awards from *Romantic Times
Magazine,* Leanne likes creating a story with a few
grins, a generous kick of sensuality and characters
that hang around after the book is finished. Leanne
believes romance readers are the best readers in the
world because they understand that love is the greatest
miracle of all. You can write to her at P.O. Box 1442,
Midlothian, VA 23113. A SASE for a reply would be
greatly appreciated.

LOVE SONG FOR A RAVEN

ELIZABETH
LOWELL

LEANNE
BANKS

THE FIVE-MINUTE BRIDE

Silhouette Books

Published by Silhouette Books

America's Publisher of Contemporary Romance

SILHOUETTE BOOKS

Copyright in the collection:
© 2001 by Harlequin Books S.A.

ISBN 0-373-48433-X

Cover illustration © Laurie Lefrance/i2i Art

The publisher acknowledges the copyright holders of the individual works as follows:

LOVE SONG FOR A RAVEN
Copyright © 1987 by Two Of A Kind, Inc.

THE FIVE-MINUTE BRIDE
Copyright © 1997 by Leanne Banks

This edition published by arrangement with Harlequin Books S.A.

Visit Silhouette at www.eHarlequin.com

Printed in U.S.A.

LOVE SONG FOR A RAVEN
by Elizabeth Lowell

* * *

For Mary Ben,
who wanted Carlson to be happy

One

The man called Raven came awake between one heartbeat and the next. He lay without moving, listening with the absolute stillness of someone whose life has depended many times on sensing shifts in wind and sea. Beneath him the *Black Star* tugged at its moorings in random motions, telling him that even within the shelter of the inlet, the water was choppy. Currents of air moaned around the boat with a wild, clean sound, the voice of a wind that hadn't touched land for thousands of miles until it reached the Queen Charlotte Islands. Now that voice spoke to mountains rising steeply from the cold ocean, mountains clad in evergreens and ferns, mountains so rugged that man had chosen to challenge the untamed sea in cedar canoes rather than to walk the cloud-wreathed, primal land.

The elemental song of wind and mountain and sea were familiar to the man who lay motionless on the oversize bunk. Raven listened for a moment longer, filed away the fact that the storm had arrived twelve hours early and fell asleep once more.

Beyond the shallow crease of the inlet, the sea was a heaving blackness churned by a reckless wind. The promise of predawn light had been reduced to a vague gloaming that barely penetrated the lowering clouds. The only relief from the seamless gray came from the pale curves of an open rowboat struggling against the wind-whipped waves.

Steering the powerful outboard engine with one hand, Janna Moran kept the bow of the boat headed on a diagonal course into the wind and waves. With the other hand she bailed out the boat, using a plastic bleach bottle whose cap had been screwed on tightly and whose bottom had been cut entirely off. Normally the half-gallon bottle with its built-in handle grip did an excellent job of keeping the boat dry. Or reasonably dry. Nothing in the islands was really *dry*. The combination of the cold northern sea and the relatively warm Kuroshio current made for nearly constant fog, mist, drizzle, rain and more rain.

Usually Janna enjoyed the liquid varieties of "Queen Charlotte sunshine," but not that morning. The wild predawn churning of water and wind had begun without warning, catching her out on the open sea. The storm that had been scheduled to arrive that evening had obviously picked up both speed and strength somewhere over the Pacific. Instead of the customary rain, brisk wind and choppy seas that had been predicted, the storm was shaping up to be a much more formidable affair.

Anxiously Janna scanned the coastline to her left.

By narrowing her gray-green eyes against the wind, she could just make out the rugged wall of land rising from the dark sea. She made a soft sound of dismay as she saw that she was still well short of the opening of Totem Inlet. The last time she had looked, just before the clouds had closed down in the east, she had needed only fifteen more minutes of running time before she could turn and head into the calmer waters of the inlet. But the wind had shifted. Now both tide and wind were running heavily against her, and waves were breaking over the bow as fast as she could bail.

Even worse, the outboard motor had been acting up. At first it had been no more than hesitations in the mechanical heartbeat that were so tiny she thought she had imagined them. By the time she had passed the halfway point to the inlet's safety, the hesitations had become noticeable, more ominous. The engine had stuttered twice in as many minutes, making her own heartbeat lurch.

Janna stared toward the coastline again, wondering if she dared go in closer to the land, shortening her distance to the inlet. The memory of huge waves battering against dark cliffs on either side of Totem Inlet's opening made her reject that possibility. The course she had chosen was longer but it was also far safer.

The motor coughed, faded, caught and then died.

Suddenly the wind sounded very loud. With her heart wedging in her throat, Janna turned, braced herself on the bench seat and pulled on the starter cord with all her strength. The engine made healthy ripping noises but didn't catch. She pulled again and again and felt an almost dizzying surge of relief when the motor finally beat steadily once more. Instantly she

turned the bow back into the wind and cranked the
speed up a notch or two. More water would come in
over the gunwale at a higher speed, but she would
also get to the inlet sooner.

For a few minutes Janna made good speed. Just as
her heartbeat had settled down again, the motor died
without warning. She dropped the bailing bottle,
grabbed the starter cord and began pulling. The motor
ripped, muttered and died. Janna yanked on the cord
again and again. Each time she pulled, the engine
stirred but didn't fully awaken.

"Damn you, *start!*"

As though it had only been waiting for the proper
encouragement, the motor ripped into life. Janna's
slim fingers wrapped around the handle again, feeding
gas steadily as she steered once more into the wind
and the waves. Sheets of wind-driven spray broke
over her, sending streamers of cold water pouring
over her yellow poncho. Most of the water drained
off into the boat, but some of it inevitably worked
beneath the poncho's hood to slide chilly fingers
down her spine and between her breasts. Inside the
midcalf fisherman's galoshes she wore, her feet were
soaked. So were her legs from midthigh on down.

Janna bailed rapidly—not out of any hope of staying dry, but to decrease the weight of the boat so that
it didn't ride so low in the heaped waves. Water was
heavier than it looked, as her left arm reminded her
with each stroke of the half-gallon bleach bottle. Yet
for every quart she threw back into the sea, the wind
delivered more across her face.

The motor shuddered and stopped. Janna dropped
the bailing bottle and pulled on the starter cord again
and again. With each pull the motor made a harsh

ripping noise but refused to catch. She threw a worried glance toward the coastline. It was closer. Too close. Enough light had seeped through the clouds so that she could see a distinct line of foam where breakers threw themselves at the feet of dark cliffs. There was no gap in the white line, nothing to indicate a safe place to moor short of Totem Inlet itself.

Janna squeezed the bulb leading from the gasoline reservoir to the motor. Liquid spurted invisibly. She could feel its resistance in the bulb beneath her palm. She wasn't out of gas. Whatever was causing the outboard to fail wasn't a lack of fuel. Grimly she yanked on the starting cord, putting everything she had into it.

Nothing happened.

The boat slewed sideways as a wave hit. Janna barely managed to stay aboard. Without the motor's power, the boat was at the mercy of the wind and tide. Now she was sideways to the incoming waves and being shoved toward shore at a frighteningly swift pace. She pulled hard on the cord twice more, but nothing greeted her efforts, not even the familiar coughing snarl as the motor tried and failed to keep running.

Suddenly Janna knew that it was futile to waste her energy any longer. There was no more time for her to spend pulling on the starting cord of a dead motor. She scrambled off the rowboat's stern seat and threw herself onto the middle seat. Working as quickly as her cold hands would allow, she unshipped the oars, jammed the pegs down into the oarlocks and began to row with all her strength. As she pulled on the oars, she brought the bow back around to meet the wind and waves. Immediately the boat began taking on less water.

Janna braced herself and put her back into her work, pulling in long, steady sweeps as her brothers had taught her years ago on a small lake in Washington. She watched the shoreline that lay diagonally off her stern, trying to gauge her progress by landmarks that were slowly condensing out of the cloud-wrapped dawn.

When the landmarks appeared not to move, Janna thought she was simply overanxious. She picked another landmark, counted fifty strokes and checked again. She was moving relative to the land, but just barely. The wind and the tide were simply too powerful for her to overcome; and every few seconds more water splashed into the boat, adding more weight to the already unwieldy craft. At this rate she wouldn't make Totem Inlet before her strength gave out and she was pushed onto the rocks or the rowboat was swamped in one of the larger sets of waves that humped up periodically out of the west.

For a few minutes Janna picked up the pace of the rowing, putting more space between herself and the dark cliffs that lined the edge of the sea. Always before now she had thought of herself as being reasonably strong and physically competent, the legacy both of a healthy body and the goading of three muscular brothers who had teased her mercilessly when she was too weak or too slow or too timid to play their rough-and-tumble games. She had learned to smile and joke as though she didn't hurt; and she had learned to work harder and longer so that the next time she played she would be better. As a result, she had gained a reputation as a good sport with a great sense of humor.

Water sloshed ankle-deep through the boat. Janna permitted herself to look at the shoreline. She had made almost no progress. If anything, she was afraid she had drifted closer to the cliffs. For an instant fear burst in her, taking the strength from her arms. Then she set her teeth, headed the rowboat straight out to sea instead of on a diagonal course and rowed hard. After a hundred strokes the shoreline had receded somewhat. The inlet, however, was no closer.

Janna changed course slightly, choosing a heading that would bring her closer to the inlet. As she rowed she thought over her choices. Rowing straight out to sea would keep her off the rocks but wouldn't get her to safety. Rowing a diagonal course would bring her closer to the inlet, but combined with the pressure of tide and wind, it would bring her closer to the shore, as well. It would be a race to see whether the tide and wind shoved her onto the rocks before she reached the relative shelter of the inlet. Frankly, she didn't think she would make it.

And if she didn't stop rowing to bail, she would sink before she reached either cliffs or inlet.

Janna dropped the oars, bailed frantically for a minute, then whipped off her waterproof poncho and dumped it at her feet. It the boat were capsized or swamped, she didn't want to be weighed down by the unwieldly slicker. As she reached for the oars her long, cinnamon hair fanned out wildly in the wind for an instant, only to be plastered darkly against her skull when an unusually big wave burst over the gunwale. She picked up the oars and brought the bow into the waves once more. As she rowed she kicked out of the fisherman's boots, knowing they would drag her down if she tried to swim in them. She left her soaking sneakers in place; she would need them if she got to the rocky shore.

"Not *if*," Janna said firmly to herself. "*When*. You're a strong swimmer. Just two weeks ago you swam for about a mile without a break. It's not even a quarter of a mile to the inlet's mouth."

What she didn't say aloud was that two weeks ago when she had been swimming, it had been a rare, calm, hot day, and she had been in a very sheltered inlet, where the sea was as flat as a mirror. Right now the sea was neither sheltered nor calm. But there was no point in dwelling on reasons to be afraid. She knew that in dangerous situations, panic killed more people than anything else.

Pushing every other thought out of her mind, Janna bent to the oars once more. As she rowed, the fluorescent orange of her life vest swayed like a flame in the postdawn gloom. She was the only spot of life and color showing on either land or sea.

Raven stood on the stern of the *Black Star*, looking as broad shouldered and powerful as the mountains that rose steeply on either side of Totem Inlet. Beneath his feet the stern shifted and bounced slightly on the inlet's choppy waters. He stood easily, swaying as necessary to compensate for the boat's restless surges, oblivious to the chilly wind that tugged at the open collar of his midnight-blue flannel shirt. Eyes closed, he strained to hear the faint ripping sound that would tell him that the distant motor had finally caught and held. Nothing came to him but the shivering moan of the wind as it curled between the inlet's rocky walls.

He stared up the inlet through powerful binoculars, his black eyes searching the water for any sign that the boat had reached safety. There was nothing ahead but the same tiny whitecaps and choppy little waves that slapped against the *Black Star*. Beyond the inlet's mouth he could see a line of churned water. The powerful binoculars brought every detail close. Whoever was out in the descending storm would have his hands full, especially if he were in a rowboat with a dead outboard motor.

On the other hand, Raven knew that the sound of the engine could have been carried away by the capricious wind. He could be standing there imagining more problems than existed in the storm-tossed dawn. Few people other than professional fishermen came to the western side of the Charlottes. The tourists who came to the forbidding cliffs and narrow inlets either came with guides or had enough skill to sail to the islands on their own boats. They didn't come in rowboats, either—and the sounds he had heard earlier had come from a single outboard engine.

That was why Raven wondered if he were imagining things. Few people had either the skill or the foolishness to take on the west side of the Charlottes in an open rowboat. Yet it was possible that one of the Haidas from Old Masset or Skidegate had chosen to make a personal pilgrimage to Totem Inlet. The descendant of people who had routinely raided as far south as Oregon in their dugout cedar canoes wouldn't hesitate to put out to sea in a rowboat in order to reach Totem Inlet at the first stirrings of dawn.

A corner of Raven's mouth curled into a faint smile. Of course it was possible that a Haida had come to the legendary inlet for personal reasons. That was what he was doing. He had come here in his season of discontent as though he could fish satisfaction from the dark veils of the past just as he had fished silver salmon from the green veils of the sea.

Yet satisfaction had eluded him.

With the ease of years of practice, Raven put his own personal needs aside and concentrated on listening to the wind's flexible voice. From the faint, fitful sounds that had awakened him, he knew that the boat was beyond Totem Inlet's mouth. Unless the motor had started again, the man would be forced to row against the wind and tide in order to reach safety.

Unconsciously Raven flexed his big work-hardened hands around the binoculars. If he were the man in the boat, he would be rowing right now, pulling hard on the long oars, feeling the power of his body sweeping down through the wood into the heaving sea. The boat would be cutting through the waves with deceptive ease, sliding closer to the inlet with each movement of the oars through the water.

But Raven was not the man rowing. If he had been, he would have been close enough by now to be spotted by someone standing in the inlet. There was nothing for Raven to see, however. Obviously the person out beyond the inlet lacked Raven's strength or his understanding of the danger of letting a small boat drift too close to the unforgiving shore while he worked over a motor that was well and truly dead.

Several times Raven thought he heard faint shivers of sound that could have come from a motor. Each time he caught his breath, willing the sound to hold, to strengthen. Each time the sound vanished before he could be sure it had been his ears rather than his imagination that had heard it.

The wind flexed, paused and then blew with a new, sustained roar from a slightly different angle. Raven moved even as the wind did, listening intently, staring out across the chop with dark eyes accustomed to all the moods of the sea. Nothing moved within the binoculars's broad sweep but waves and wind. Whoever was out there simply wasn't getting any closer to safety.

If anyone were out there at all.

Yet even as the thought came, Raven discarded it. With a certainty that transcended words, he knew that someone was out on the open sea, caught between the storm and the unyielding shore. He leaped to the deck of the powerboat with a speed and lightness that was unexpected in a man of his size. From the stern locker he pulled out a long rope. He tied one end to the stern cleat. In a continuation of the same motion he threw off the stern mooring line. A few seconds later the bow line was off. At his touch the two powerful inboard engines snarled into life.

Minutes later Raven was approaching the mouth of the inlet. Windblown spray sheeted across the bow as the *Black Star* surged out into the unprotected water. Raven handled the bucking, shuddering boat with the assurance of a man born and raised on the surface of the world's biggest ocean. Braced against the hammering waves, steering with one hand and his powerful thighs, he brought the binoculars to his eyes and swept the area where he thought the boat should be.

There was nothing but water being ripped apart by the wind.

Raven widened the search, feeling minutes slipping away, knowing intuitively that his worst fears were true: someone was out there, someone whose danger increased with every second. Raven couldn't spot him, despite the fact that the waves were barely big enough to hide a rowboat in their trough. Yet the water was more than rough enough to be coming in over the gunwales with every wave, rough enough to swamp a small boat before Raven could find it.

"Come on, come on, show me where you are," Raven muttered. "It's bad out here, but not that bad. You shouldn't have swamped this quick even if you don't have much time to spare for bailing."

After several more sweeps with the glasses showed nothing, Raven brought the *Black Star* onto a different heading, one that would take him farther from the inlet and closer to shore. The boat wallowed protestingly as it presented its stern to the wind and waves. A few minutes of that twisting, cork-screwing motion would have sent most people to the nearest rail with a bout of seasickness, but Raven noticed the motion only in that it made controlling the boat while looking through the binoculars almost impossible.

Just when he was ready to switch to a different heading, he caught a flash of color off toward shore. He frowned even as he turned slightly. The flash had been too close to shore and too far away from the inlet's mouth to be the boat he was looking for. More likely it was a fishing float or crab-pot marker that had torn loose in the storm.

The flash of color came again. Raven focused and saw someone straining over oars. The rowboat vanished from sight in the trough of a wave, then reappeared in a burst of spray. Instantly Raven realized that the man was in real trouble. He obviously wasn't strong enough to make headway against the tide, wind and waves, which had pushed him dangerously close to shore. In fact, he looked more like a teenager than a man. His shoulders weren't broad, nor were his arms muscular.

Abruptly Raven began to swear, his words as savage as the wind. He threw the binoculars aside and slammed the throttle forward, sending the *Black Star* leaping toward the smaller boat. That wasn't a man out there nor even a boy; it was a woman, and she was pulling her heart out against the relentless sea. Her rowboat wallowed and rolled sluggishly, bringing the gunwale perilously close to the water. Both the woman's fear and her determination were in every straining line of her body as she fought to keep the waterlogged boat on a safe course, away from the dangerous shore.

Raven sent the *Black Star* on a broad curve that brought him close to the rowboat. He saw the look of stunned relief on the woman's face when she spotted him. Easing closer, he cut the throttle and abandoned the wheel long enough to throw coils of the heavy towline over to the rowboat. He held his breath while the woman scrambled to the bow and made the line fast.

Only then did he notice how much water filled the rowboat. It was all but awash. He started to yell at the woman to bail, only to see the pale flash of a bleach bottle as she bent to work. Very carefully he eased the throttles up on the *Black Star*, taking slack from the towline. He felt the slight jerk as the rowboat's weight hit the end of the long line. Slowly, carefully, he began towing the rowboat toward the inlet.

Once both boats had settled into the new motion, Raven picked up the binoculars and turned toward the crippled rowboat thirty feet astern. For minutes that seemed like years, he divided his attention between steering the *Black Star* and watching the woman bail. Despite her efforts, the rowboat still rode far too low in the water for safety.

Suddenly the woman stopped bailing. Raven's mouth flattened as he watched her slump on the bench seat. Didn't she know that the danger wasn't over? The rowboat was wallowing like a pig in mud. When the time came to make the turn into the inlet, the rowboat's stern would be presented to the waves. There was no help for it, for there was no other way to get into the inlet. Unless she got to work the first wave that broke over the stern would send the rowboat right to the bottom.

And unless Raven cut the towrope as soon as the rowboat went under, he stood a good chance of going down with her.

Even as the thought came, Raven kicked out of his waterproof boots. Unconsciously his hand went to his belt for an instant. The worn, leather-wrapped hilt of his sheath knife nestled against his palm in cool reassurance.

"Bail!" Raven yelled, his voice as deep as the thunder of waves breaking over rocks.

A gust of wind ripped the word from his mouth and flung it back at him. Cursing, he stared through the binoculars. The woman seemed to be wrestling with something, but he was damned if he could figure out what it might be. Finally her struggles caused her to turn slightly, bringing her hands into the viewing field of the binoculars. She was prying at the fingers of her left hand, which were wrapped around the handle of the bleach bottle in a death grip.

Raven saw the muscles of the woman's left arm locked in a rigid spasm of protest over the demands that had been made on them. The arm was useless and would remain that way until the muscles uncramped. He saw tears of frustration welling from the woman's eyes as she fought her own body. Then he saw the brutal lines of exhaustion that had drawn her mouth into a harsh line and the blue-tinged pallor of her skin that warned of a body dangerously chilled. She was past the end of her physical strength, stripped to the core, all reserves spent.

Yet still she fought, refusing to quit.

A chill went over Raven, tightening his scalp in primal response. He had never seen anything quite so beautiful as the woman's courage. She was outmatched, overpowered, overwhelmed, yet she drove her slender body to work still harder, refusing to give up. Raven called to her as though he could give her some of his immense strength through an outpouring of words. He doubted that she understood him across the thirty feet of wind-churned sea, but he called to her anyway, wanting her to know that she wasn't alone.

When the woman finally managed to shift the bleach bottle to her right hand, Raven let out a hoarse shout of triumph. She began bailing with jerky, mechanical strokes, sending water sloshing out into the sea. He turned, adjusted the course of the *Black Star* and looked back again. Small plumes of water shoot-

ing over the rowboat's gunwale reassured him that
the woman was still bailing.

With agonizing slowness the *Black Star* pulled the
waterlogged rowboat toward the safety of the inlet.
Raven checked through the binoculars every few moments. The water level inside the boat had gone down
some, but not nearly enough for safety. He cut back
his speed as much as he could and still hold his own
against the storm. Although he wanted to reach the
inlet's shelter as soon as possible, he had to wait
while the woman bailed. If he tried to turn into the
inlet now, the rowboat would capsize and sink.

Helplessly Raven watched through the binoculars
as the woman struggled against the storm. The sight
of her made agony twist deep inside him. It was too
much like a time eight years ago, when he had
watched helplessly as the woman he loved slid further
and further into alternating bouts of rage and despair.
He had tried to reach Angel with words of comfort
and hope, tried to tell her that he loved her. He had
wanted her to shift the focus of her love from a dead
man to himself, from death to life. Later, when he
understood that Angel was slowly killing herself
rather than face life without the man she loved, Raven
had realized that he wanted Angel to live more than
he wanted her to love him. He had gone to her,
dragged her brutally from her shell of despair—and
had gotten his wish. Angel had gathered her courage
and her strength. She had lived. In time she had even
loved again.

But the man she loved was not Carlson Raven.

The sad memories flickered like distant lightning
at the edge of Raven's consciousness, memories
called up by the violence of his feelings of fury and

helplessness as he watched the unknown woman struggle against the storm and her own overwhelming exhaustion. He had spent a lifetime in a body so powerful that people automatically stepped back when they first saw him; yet that power couldn't do a damn thing to help the woman now, any more than it had helped Angel long ago. It seemed to be the story of his life. Intimidating strength, a hard face, and beneath it a yearning that was as unexpected as it was enduring.

Raven's mouth flattened making the blunt lines of his face even more pronounced. The speed of the woman's bailing had fallen to nothing. Raven knew that soon she wouldn't even be keeping up with the water coming in over the gunwale. Ready or not, safe or not, he had to make the turn for the inlet.

He eased the *Black Star* in a long, shallow curve that eventually, gently swung the rowboat in a direct line into the inlet. As soon as both boats were headed straight into the narrow opening, he turned and watched the rowboat through the binoculars. Now was the time of greatest danger, when the rowboat's broad, low stern was presented to the waves. The woman knew it, too. He could tell by her uneven, almost convulsive motions as she drove her exhausted body to bail just a few more times, just a few more minutes, just a few more yards, just...

Cold blue-green water humped up and welled over the stern as the rowboat wallowed into Totem Inlet's mouth. The gunwale was so low that the wave barely foamed as it rolled over the rowboat. The boat wavered, rocked wildly and turned over with shocking speed, trapping the woman beneath as it sank.

Raven threw the binoculars aside, slammed the

throttles into neutral and slashed the towrope. An instant later he hit the water in a long dive that took him halfway to the white swirl of sea that had once been a rowboat.

Nothing floated on the surface in front of him but a single oar.

Two

Janna had no warning. One instant she had her head down as she bent over to bail out the water that was slopping around her ankles. The next instant the world tilted wildly. She tried to throw herself clear as the boat capsized, but her cramped legs responded much too slowly. It was the same for her arms. Instinctively she flung them out as though to break a fall, but only managed to jam the steering arm of the outboard engine through the armhole of her life vest.

The bottom of the boat flipped over her, shutting out the light. Even as chilled as she was the water felt cold. She was dragged over as the motor turned with the boat. In the water and darkness she was disoriented, tangled with the engine, not knowing in which direction lay freedom. With a feeling of horror she realized that the boat was sinking deeper into the cold sea, pulling her down with it despite her struggles.

Suddenly Janna was caught from behind. Something clamped around her arm and yanked. The life vest ripped away, freeing her. She was spun around, pushed down and then jerked upward.

Where there had been only darkness beneath the boat, now Janna saw far above her a silver disk that shimmered and beckoned. Feebly she tried to swim upward, for instinct and intelligence both told her that if she broke through that silver light there would be air and warmth on the other side. Even as she struggled, she realized dimly that she was going up far faster than her own efforts could account for.

Janna burst through the radiant disk and began to drag air into her aching lungs, breathing in great rasps of sound. Gradually she realized that she wasn't alone. She was being supported by a man's big hands. Eyes as dark and deep as a midnight sea were watching her. Above those unflinching eyes a thick growth of raven-black hair was slicked against a skull whose bones were as powerful and uncompromising as the hands that were holding her above the inlet's choppy waves.

As though her eyes focusing on him were the signal he had been waiting for, the man turned Janna gently in his hands and brought her shoulder blades across his chest. He held her in place by putting his right arm between her breasts until she was pinned to his chest. His arm was thick, almost overwhelming in its implicit strength. She sensed a stirring behind her, felt her body floating, and then a deep swirl of water boiled up as powerful legs scissor-kicked, propelling her and the man through the water.

With a feeling of vast relief, Janna stopped fighting the cold and the sea, giving herself wordlessly to the stranger's strength.

"That's it," said a very deep voice in her ear. "Relax. You're safe."

Like everything else Janna had seen of the stranger, the voice was strong, big, dark.

"We're almost to my boat."

The words growled against her ear like stones tumbled by storm waves. She tried to answer but found the effort beyond her. Words swirled around in her mind without connecting. Dimly she realized that she was no longer cold. At some point she had just gone numb all the way to her core, losing all feeling.

"I've got to climb on board. Hold on to the ladder until I pull you up. Can you do that?"

The world turned lazily around Janna. Black eyes came slowly into focus.

"Did you hear me?"

Janna stared at the man, wondering what he wanted from her. When she saw her left hand being tugged through the rungs of a sea ladder, she felt a bizarre impulse to laugh. A big, tanned hand wrapped her fingers around a rung. He reached for her right hand, only to encounter the drowned bleach bottle.

"You can let go now," he told her. "You don't need it anymore. You're safe."

The voice rumbled and reverberated down Jenna's spine like distant thunder, reaching her on a level deeper than intelligence, sinking down to touch the same instinct that had made her keep on fighting even when she had no more strength. She accepted the absolute truth of the stranger's words. She was safe. She had known she was safe from the instant she had felt his strong hands pushing her up into the life-giving air.

Slowly, painfully, Janna's fingers unlocked, letting

the bleach bottle go. It sank swiftly, a pale shadow
fading into the depths of the sea. Under the man's
urging she wrapped her fingers around the ladder and
hung on. She saw him grasp the low metal railing that
ran along the gunwale of the boat. Muscles rippled
and bunched while he pulled himself out of the water
as casually as she would have stepped from the street
to the sidewalk. Before she had a chance to absorb
the implications of that kind of strength, she felt herself lifted from the sea and carried into a small cabin
as though she weighed no more than a puff of wind.

"Hang on to me."

Janna obeyed as the world shifted again. Vaguely
she realized that her feet were resting on something
solid. In the next moment her knees gave way. Only
the strong arm around her waist kept her from pitching face-first onto the deck. She clung to the man with
numbed hands as he shifted the engines from neutral
and slapped the throttles up. A throaty roar came in
response. The boat surged forward, racing up the inlet.

For long minutes there was only the thunder of
powerful engines and the unwavering strength of the
man supporting her. Then the engines were shut off.
He let go of her just long enough to moor the boat
and then he returned. He began stripping off her
clothes with swift, casual motions. She blinked and
pushed vaguely at his hands. It was like trying to hold
back the tide with a sigh. Desperately she reached for
more strength, but every bit she had was already involved in the huge shudders that were racking her
body.

"Don't fight me, small warrior," he rumbled

gently. "You'll never get warm in those soaking clothes."

Janna looked at the man with confused, gray-green eyes, wanting to ask who he was and how she had gotten there and why she was so terribly cold. Nothing came out but an odd whimper as the last of her strength bled away and the world darkened around her.

Raven caught her against his body, peeled off the remainder of her clothes and carried her to his oversize bunk. The sight of her pulse beating against the smooth curve of her neck reassured him, but her skin was far too cold. He yanked back the blankets from her bunk and dried her as best he could before he slid her between the sheets. He pulled off his clothes with harsh sweeps of his hands, ripping cloth in his haste. Pausing only long enough to jerk a special blanket from a cupboard, he crawled into the bunk with her.

"I don't know if you can hear me," Raven said as he arranged the woman on top of his big body, "but you're going to be warm again. This survival blanket takes every bit of our heat and reflects it back to us. It wouldn't do you much good by yourself, but as long as I'm wrapped up with you it's better than a bonfire. I'm too damn big to be chilled by a few minutes in a summer ocean."

There was no response from the woman but the convulsive shuddering of a body that had been pushed too hard and now was too cold to warm itself. Raven shook out the survival blanket and wrapped both of them within its thin, flexible folds. The inner, heat-reflecting side of the blanket gleamed in shades of silver. The outer, heat-absorbing side of the blanket was a midnight blue as dark as the sodden flannel shirt that lay in shreds on the deck by the bunk.

Long shudders of the woman's body threatened to shake off the blanket. Raven's hands moved gently over her, both soothing and slowly rubbing warmth back into her clenched muscles. After a long time her body began to relax as the violence of her shivering waned. He shifted slightly, bringing her into more complete contact with the heat of his body. She murmured and instinctively burrowed closer to the abundant warmth that was radiating into her.

Raven's hands gently massaged the long, slender back to the swell of the woman's buttocks. The firm, deep muscles were still cool to his touch but no longer chilled. She was bruised, numb, exhausted, but no longer in danger of succumbing to hypothermia. He smiled and felt a sense of satisfaction that for once his body had been good for something more than drawing sideways stares from strangers. He wondered if the woman would be frightened when she awoke and saw what had fished her from the sea.

He hoped not. Even half-drowned and utterly exhausted, she had looked sleek and very feminine beneath the soggy clothes. She also felt amazingly good in his arms, fitting against his body with a perfection that would have shortened his breath in other circumstances and was threatening to do so even now. Her hips swelled smoothly beneath his hands. Her breasts were soft and her nipples were as hard as pebbles against his chest. He wondered if she would respond like that to heat rather than cold—a man's heat. Would she come to a man with the same elemental passion and courage with which she had faced the storm?

The thought chased the last of the cold from Raven's body. He felt a surge of hot, sweet heaviness in his blood. Abruptly he cast his willpower over his glittering, leaping thoughts as though they were wild salmon coming to the net. She had trusted him enough to give herself over to his keeping despite the fact that he must have looked almost as frightening as the sea to her. He would no more violate that trust than he would have let her drown before his eyes.

"Can you hear me yet?" he asked softly, feeling his own deep voice rumble in his chest. "You're going to be fine. A few hours of sleep, some warm food, a few lazy days, and you'll be ready to tackle me with one hand tied behind your back."

The thought of anyone taking him on like that made Raven smile. He was still smiling when the woman's head stirred and wide eyes studied him through dense eyelashes. At close range her eyes were the color of a cedar forest veiled by silver fog. They were deep, intelligent, exquisitely clear.

Janna blinked, trying to connect the resilient warmth beneath her with the clear, oddly gentle black eyes that were so close to her own.

"You're very warm," she said slowly, grappling with each word through a haze of exhaustion.

"You aren't," he said, amusement clear in his deep voice as he ran his palm down to her cool, naked thigh.

"I know." She sighed and let her head sag onto his chest, too exhausted to keep her eyes open any longer. "What…happened?"

"Sleep," he said softly as he pulled the survival blanket up over her wet hair. "You'll remember when you wake up."

Raven felt her breath wash over him with reassuring warmth. Her body changed subtly, taking on the heaviness of utter relaxation. Before she took another breath she was asleep. The trust implied by that simple act washed over Raven in another kind of warmth until it was a subtle radiance shimmering within the darkest reaches of his mind. His breath sighed out to mingle with hers. He fell asleep with the scent of the woman and the sea reaching out to him, surrounding him.

Janna woke slowly. With one hand, she reached out, fumbling for the control on her electric blanket. She must have been very cold when she went to bed last night; she had left the dial on high. Even her pillow was hot. Blindly her fingers began searching for the control that hung over the mattress midway down the bed. What she found was smooth, firm, resilient, as hot as satin left out in the sun. She searched the surface with sleepy curiosity, wondering if she were still dreaming. Something stirred beneath her touch.

"Careful, woman. You're fishing in rocky waters."

Janna's eyes flew open and her head came up in a rush as she propped herself on her elbow. An odd, silvery blanket slithered aside with her sudden motion, revealing an expanse of bare male chest that was frankly intimidating—or would have been if she hadn't grown up with men nearly as large. Black hair gleamed in a neat wedge that tapered swiftly to a dark line bisecting a very large, very powerful body. Farther down the hair fanned out into a black tangle. That was where her hand was. Her fingers weren't resting in that tangle of masculine hair. Not quite.

With a gasp, Janna yanked back her hand. "I'm sorry, I...I..." Suddenly she realized that she was as naked as the giant who had stirred beneath her touch. She had been lying half on, half off his body, her breasts nestled against the muscular swell of his arm. "Who...what?"

"People here call me Raven," he said in a voice so deep that it vibrated down her spine. "As for what—"

"Never mind," she interrupted quickly, feeling a blush crawl from her breasts to her cheeks. "I might have gone crazy, but I haven't forgotten eighth-grade science."

"Science?" he asked, as he reached for the survival blanket that was sliding farther away with every instant.

"Human reproduction," she said succinctly.

Raven's laughter sent odd shivers through Janna. It was such a rich sound, as warm and textured as his very masculine flesh had been beneath her fingertips.

Janna's blush deepened at the sensual direction of her own thoughts. The cold water must have frozen what passed for her brain.

Abruptly memories exploded. Cold. Storm. Water. A silver disk floating impossibly far above her head. Everything came rushing back on Janna with dizzying force. She stared at the man lying so close to her. Strong hands. Black eyes. A voice like waves breaking over rocks, yet somehow warm, caressing. She had known it instinctively. She was safe with him.

"You saved my life."

"You fought with everything you had in you and them some," Raven said. "I just gave you a little hand."

Janna looked at the broad, dark, strong hand holding the strange blanket, pulling it up over her, tucking her within its warm folds. She would have died out in the storm if it hadn't been for those strong hands. She knew it.

"Little?" she repeated softly. "There was nothing little about it."

Raven held up his hand as though he had never seen it before and nodded. "You're right. There's nothing little about it," he said, deliberately misunderstanding. As casually as though he were alone, he leaned forward until he could flip the dark blue bed sheet up over his naked hips. "Warm enough?" he asked, looking at her with concern.

"Yes. Thank you." Even as Janna spoke, more memories came. She had been so cold she could barely feel the deck beneath her feet. She had been unable to stand, to swim, even to breathe. "I...if it hadn't been for you..."

With a shrug of massive shoulders, Raven said, "I've always been bigger than the people around me. It's good to know that I'm useful for more than pulling nets and scaring children."

Janna blinked, sensing the loneliness beneath the matter-of-fact words. For all his rough looks and overwhelming male power, Raven was not an insensitive man. Impulsively she put her hand on the bunched strength of his shoulder. "I'll bet the children run toward you, not away," she said softly. "They know they'll be safe with you. I knew it," she added, gray-green eyes searching his. "Raven, I don't know how to thank—"

"You must be thirsty," he said, cutting off her words.

Janna suddenly realized two things: Raven didn't want her thanks, and she was thirsty. Her throat felt as though it were lined with sandpaper. "Yes," she said, hearing the rasp in her own voice.

"Swallowing saltwater will do it to you every time. I've got tea, coffee, water or soup."

"Tea. Please."

Janna tried not to watch as Raven rolled out of the bunk in a single coordinated movement, taking the sheet with him. She tried, but not looking at him was impossible. He was so big that he filled the cabin. On him, the navy blue cloth he wrapped casually around his hips looked the size of a beach towel rather than a bed sheet. She had come from a family of big men, and at five feet nine inches wasn't exactly small herself; but the man called Raven was a giant.

He was also compelling in the same wild, primitive way that the surrounding land was compelling. The naked strength and endurance in him tugged at her senses, as did the laughter and solitude that gleamed deep within his black eyes. Potent, vital, alone, Raven called to her at levels she hadn't even known she had until she had awakened with his life's heat radiating through her.

What a pity she didn't call to him in the same way.

Janna's mouth curved down in a sad smile. She had awakened naked in bed with the most intriguing man she had ever met, and he had treated her like a sister even after her hand had blundered into such intimate contact with his body. She was used to being treated like a sister. After all, she was one. Sister to three strapping brothers. That didn't bother her. Being treated like a sister by her ex-husband—that *had* bothered her.

Wryly Janna conceded that she shouldn't be surprised that Raven hadn't been physically intrigued by her. She blew a limp, damp string of hair away from her nose and sighed. She had no illusions as to how she looked under the best of circumstances. Striking was what her family said. Privately, Janna had decided that was what people told tall women they liked who didn't possess the soft, blond, kittenish looks that men invariably preferred. Having just been fished from the sea half-drowned and blue with cold, Janna knew she must look about as appealing as a beached jellyfish.

No wonder Raven hadn't wanted her gratitude. The poor man must have been terrified that she would offer to pay him off in bed. Again Janna smiled wryly. He had reason to worry. He wouldn't have gotten any great bargain from accepting her offer. Experienced she was not. She could count on one hand the number of times her husband had made love to her during their short "marriage."

"Such sad eyes," Raven said. "Worrying about what happened? Don't. You're safe now. I'll take you back to civilization as soon as the storm blows over. As for your boat…" he shrugged. "I'll see that you get a new one. And a decent engine to go with it."

Janna's eyelashes swept down, concealing her emotions. Then the comment about the engine penetrated. Her eyes opened wide as she looked up at Raven. "How did you know that the engine gave me trouble?"

"Nobody rows the west side of the islands in a storm for the sheer joy of it," Raven said dryly. "One lump or two?"

"I feel like I've already taken fifty," Janna said,

rubbing her left arm. "Two lumps, please. How did you know I liked sugar in my tea?"

"You look like a woman who enjoys her senses," he said matter-of-factly. "Is your arm still cramped?"

"Was it cramped?" asked Janna, looking at her left arm with new interest and wondering what Raven had meant about her enjoying her senses.

"Don't you remember?"

Janna frowned, drawing dark cinnamon eyebrows down in soft, twin curves. "I remember that damned engine quitting and starting and quitting until finally it went dead. I remember rowing." She looked at her hands. They were red, chafed and blistered here and there from the rough oar handles. "I remember being cold."

"Do you remember bailing?"

"Sure. Every chance I got." She grimaced. "It wasn't often enough, though."

"What do you remember after you saw the *Black Star*?"

Janna looked around at the beautifully finished interior of the boat. "Is this the *Black Star*?" she asked, indicating the boat with her hand, then yanking the blanket hurriedly into place as it slithered down her breasts.

Raven nodded. With an effort of will he kept from staring at the corner of the blanket, where one nipple peeked invitingly from beneath the silver folds. The blush that had risen up Janna's clear, flawless skin when she had realized that she was naked and in bed with a stranger had told Raven that she wasn't accustomed to waking up that way. Her curious, incendiary touch as she explored his rapidly hardening flesh had told him that she wasn't accustomed to men, period. Nor was she a child. He guessed that she was in her early twenties. Most women her age would have known instantly what that particular part of a man's anatomy felt like between the sheets. She hadn't.

That had been all that had kept Raven from returning the favor, running his hand down her warm, supple body to discover the heat deep inside her. He was sure that sensual heat was there, and he was sure that she would give it to him if he asked. She was so damned grateful for being fished out of the inlet.

Raven's mouth turned down in a hard curve. He wasn't that kind of predator, despite his name and his looks. He wouldn't take advantage of her gratitude. The woman with the sad eyes and brave smile wasn't a predator, either. Once the emotions of the instant wore off, she would regret having given in gratitude what she had been born to give in love.

But not to him. Experience had taught Raven that he just wasn't the kind of man that women loved. He was too big. Too hard. Too rough. Too Indian. To make it worse, he was invariably attracted to his opposite—like the deliciously soft, wonderfully supple woman he had found fighting the sea. Usually such women proved to be disappointing in other ways, lacking the core of humor and courage that he valued far more than he valued mere looks.

Angel had been different. She had discovered in herself enough raw courage for ten people. And so had the woman he had pulled from the sea, the woman watching him now with clear, silver-green eyes. Trusting him.

Gently Raven tucked the blanket in around Janna's

shoulders, concealing the tempting pink nipple from sight. "Do you feel like breakfast?" he asked.

"Gee, I don't know. Do I look like breakfast?" she shot back, embarrassed to realize that she had been hanging out of the blanket like a ripe raspberry and all he could think of was covering her up. Then she heard her own words all but demanding that Raven notice her nakedness. She groaned at the flush climbing up her cheeks once more. "You saved the body, but I'm afraid you left the brains at the bottom of the inlet."

"I'll look for them when I fish for dinner," Raven promised blandly, but his eyes gleamed like polished jet. "Do you have a name, or are you like the shamans, giving your true name to no one?"

"Janna Moran," she said. She eased her right arm cautiously out from beneath the slippery blanket and held out her hand. "And you're—Raven?"

"Yes," he said, taking her hand.

For a moment they smiled at each other, silently recognizing the incongruity of introducing themselves after they had awakened naked in one another's arms. Janna's fingers looked slender and very feminine against the weathered toughness of Raven's hand. He remembered how those fingers had felt exploring him sleepily.

"Is that a first or a last name?" Janna asked as Raven released her hand and turned away quickly.

"When I fill out forms for the government, it's a last name, and Carlson is my first name. Otherwise, Raven is the name most people use."

He hesitated, thinking of Angel. She and Grant had called him Carlson. But Grant was dead. Only Angel called him Carlson now—and Miles Hawkins, Hawk, the man Angel loved. Hawk called him Carlson, too.

Raven smiled slightly, remembering how he had felt when he had discovered the depth of Angel's love for another man. He supposed he should have hated Hawk, but hatred was impossible. Hawk had given Angel the very heart of life. Raven loved him for that as he had never loved another man.

"But not everyone calls you Raven," Janna said softly, seeing the bittersweet smile on Raven's lips. Janna wanted to ask who the woman was who could make Raven smile with such love and sadness, but Janna said nothing. It was enough to know that there was a woman, and love and sadness. "What shall I call you?"

"Raven. It's how I think of myself, now."

Janna smiled, feeling somehow as though she had received a gift.

"Raven," Janna said, liking the feel of the name on her tongue.

Raven smiled down at Janna, wondering what thoughts moved in the shadowed depths beneath the clear silver-green of her eyes. The smile she gave him in return was open, friendly, engaging, humorous. It was also subtly different from the ones he had seen before he tucked the blanket around her shoulders. Part of Janna's personality was now concealed, the part that had shimmered just beneath the surface of her eyes when she looked at him and saw the man who had pulled her from the cold water.

Raven frowned slightly, feeling as he always did when he saw life flashing just below the green surface of the sea, life turning and diving for the cool, safe depths, life sliding away from his presence. Somehow, something beautiful and fragile had gone, and there was only the vague glimmer of reflected light to mark its passing.

"Is there anyone waiting for you?" Raven asked.

"Waiting?"

Janna's confusion told Raven more than he had asked. She lived alone, as he did, and she had lived that way for so long that the idea of people worrying about her absence simply didn't occur to her.

"A husband, a lover, family, friends," he said softly, searching gray-green eyes. "Anyone who might be worried about you being out in a small boat in a storm."

"Oh." Janna laughed lightly and shrugged. "No. I'm twenty-four and fancy-free. I haven't had a husband for years, never had kids at all, my friends don't expect me back in Seattle until September and my landlady doesn't care where I am as long as the rent is on time. She drinks, you see. I'm paid through August, so she's not going to worry if I never come back."

Raven didn't know which surprised him more, that Janna had been married or that she was utterly alone in the Queen Charlottes for the next few weeks.

"Are you on vacation?" he asked.

Janna shrugged again. "Sort of. I'm doing some line drawings for a friend's book on the Queen Charlottes. I've been trying for weeks to get to Totem Inlet, but something always happened."

"Something?"

"Rain, usually. Mist, a lot. Wind, too."

Raven smiled. "Welcome to the Queen Charlottes."

"Yeah. Welcome all to hell." Janna laughed, taking the bite out of her words.

Slowly laughter faded. For a moment her eyes seemed almost silver once more, passion and emotion shimmering just below the surface.

"I've never seen a more savage place," she said, "or one that is more beautiful. The islands are… elemental. Creation is very close to the surface here, almost close enough to touch." She hesitated, then added softly, "It's as though the Charlottes have a special understanding with time. Time comes to the islands and then divides around them and passes by on either side like the sea. Other places change, but not the Charlottes. They have always been like this, barely condensed out of the mists of creation. Here, time doesn't exist. Only creation and mist."

For the second time since Raven had seen Janna, his scalp tightened as a wave of awareness shivered through him. Other people had noted that the islands had a savage aura, but to those people savage had meant *backward, awkward, brutal, uncivilized.* They had been afraid of the islands' raw strength and mysterious core of timelessness. Janna wasn't, even though she had nearly died exploring it.

"Yes," Raven said softly. "I love these islands, too. I come to them to renew my own silences."

"And now you're saddled with a chatty tourist," Janna said, grimacing. "Sorry about that."

"No problem," he said. "You're a woman who understands silence. You won't disturb me."

Janna couldn't help wondering what it would take for a woman to disturb Raven. She had no doubt that it would take a woman rather than a man; her former husband had taught her to be very aware of the fact that there were men who dated and married women but who could only be sexually attracted to another man. Raven wasn't like that. She was sure of it.

With a hidden sigh, Janna decided that Raven was probably like most men, drawn to blondes who had big mysterious eyes and more curves than a mountain road. The old cliché about gentlemen preferring blondes was quite true. So did jocks, thugs, poets and nerds. Forget women with brown hair, no matter how great their sense of humor.

Nobody ever cared if a blonde had a sense of humor, great or otherwise.

"You never answered my question about breakfast," Raven said. He looked over his shoulder and checked the progress of the water heating in a kettle on the small galley stove that was just across the aisle from his bunk. "Are you hungry?"

"Are you kidding? That isn't thunder you're hearing, it's my stomach," she announced, waving her hand dramatically, only to have to make a wild grab for the drifting blanket.

Raven glanced away quickly, not wanting Janna to realize that she had inadvertently shown him a firmly curved breast topped by a nipple that was such a velvety pink that he had to clench his hands against reaching toward her.

The teakettle whistled, offering Raven a much-needed distraction. He lifted the kettle and poured water into two mugs, wondering how Janna would react if he told her how perfect she had felt stretched out along his body. Soft. Resilient. No hard edges or angles. But if he said anything like that to her, it would sound like the opening gambit in a bid for sex. He knew that she didn't want that anymore. He had seen the desire fade from her after he had tucked in the blanket around her shoulders. The shimmering veils of passionate emotion had gone as though they had never existed, leaving only laughter in her clear gray-green eyes.

He wondered why that made him feel both sad and very angry, as though he should have taken what she had offered when she had offered it and not had any scruples about why she wanted him. Other women had wanted or not wanted him, and it hadn't mattered in any real way. Except for Angel. Her rejection had made pain a part of his everyday life. Finally, long before Miles Hawkins had met Angel, Raven had understood that some things were not meant to be. For him, Angel was one of them. He could either accept that, or he could destroy himself over it.

In the end, he had accepted it as he accepted storms and elusive fish and the powerful body that made men and women nervous. Life was what it was. He was what he was. Love was what it was.

Beyond his reach.

Three

"Do you have a knife?" muttered Janna.

Raven heard the disgust in her muffled voice. Beneath his black mustache, his lips shifted into a smile at the picture she made. She was kneeling over the freshwater creek and wringing out her soapy hair. The long, curving lines of her body were revealed through the water-splashed flannel of one of his shirts. Below the trailing ends of cloth, her calves were pale and smooth, tautly curved, glowing in the misty light that was characteristic of the Queen Charlottes.

"Yes," Raven mumbled. "I have a knife."

"Good. Cut off this mess, would you?"

"I have a better idea."

"Shaving it off?" she retorted. "Sold!"

Janna felt as much as heard Raven's laughter when he knelt next to her on the moss-covered ground. His chest rubbed against her back as his fingers slid into the soapy, slippery mass of her hair.

"I didn't mean that you had to wash my hair."

"Your arm is still sore, isn't it? Rest. I'll take care of it."

"I've done nothing but lie around and let you take care of me since you fished me out of the inlet," Janna protested.

"A whole thirty hours," Raven said gravely. "Such laziness. I'll have to report you to the tourist bureau."

"But—"

"Hush," rumbled Raven. "I love a woman's long hair. Let me play with it."

Janna couldn't have answered if her life had depended on it. She was too caught up in the feel of Raven's big, gentle hands massaging her scalp. Chills went shivering over her flesh in response.

"Are you cold?" he asked, concerned. To him the day wasn't chilly, despite the wind that blustered and shredded clouds into sudden bursts of rain.

"I'm fine," Janna said quickly, suppressing another shiver. And it was true. She wasn't cold despite the fact that she was wearing only two layers of clothes—both of them Raven's. The soft cotton T-shirt held in her body heat and the heavy flannel shirt turned aside the occasional gusts of wind that reached the forest floor. It was Raven's touch that made her shiver, not the temperature.

"I'll hurry," he said.

Janna caught herself just before she told Raven to take his time, that she hadn't shivered because she was cold. In the end she said nothing, because she was afraid to open her mouth. If she did, she would probably whimper from the sheer pleasure of feeling his hands so strong and gentle as he washed her hair.

Your brains really must be at the bottom of the inlet, she told herself in disgust.

Her brains, yes. Her nerve endings, no.

Think of Raven as one of your brothers.

Janna tried to take her own excellent advice. It didn't work. The only times her brothers had had their hands in her hair was to give it a good yank. Never had they massaged her scalp with strong, slow, sensual motions.

So think of Raven as your hairdresser. He has his hands in your hair all the time.

Janna tried to think of Raven as her hairdresser. It was impossible.

Raven was…Raven. He was the most intriguing man she had ever met. Beneath his rough exterior he was a man capable of tenderness, laughter and the kind of silence that made her feel peaceful rather than uneasy.

And in him there was a promise of male sensuality that sent tiny streamers of fire through her. It should have frightened her. *He* should have frightened her. She hadn't been attracted to anyone since her divorce. She had been too vulnerable, too uncertain. Too afraid. Despite the assurances of her family and Mark's family, that none of it had been her fault, she still had the deep, never-spoken belief that if she had somehow been more of a woman, Mark would have been more of a man. It had taken almost two years before she could look in the mirror without silently asking herself if she had been bigger or smaller, lighter or darker, fatter or skinnier, Mark wouldn't have somehow been more attracted physically to her.

She had just gotten to the point where she could see herself in the mirror as a woman who might sexually interest a man, when she had found herself upside down and sinking fast in a cold sea. She had awakened naked in the arms of a man who was also naked. In short, she had had the best chance to attract Raven that any woman ever could, and what had happened?

He had all but chucked her under the chin, that's what.

Janna bit her lip against the thought that maybe Mark and her family and Mark's family had been wrong. Maybe there was just something lacking in her when it came to arousing a man.

Pale, slender fingers dug into the moss until Janna's knuckles went white. She forced herself to stop thinking about Mark and the sad mistake of their marriage. It was in the past. All of it. Mark had accepted what he was and was not and had made a better future for himself. She had to do the same.

Streamers of cool lather fell softly into the creek and dissolved immediately, vanishing. The lather that stayed behind on Janna's face was equally biodegradable, but it was running in the wrong direction. She swiped ineffectually at her cheek, angry at herself for fighting battles of self-esteem that she thought she had won or, at the very least, had stopped fighting herself over. She had a lot to offer a man. She could talk intelligently, cook very well, clean well enough, and identify things that crawled and swam on beaches all over the world. She was healthy, had all her own teeth, loved children and animals—and she had a great sense of humor.

Why did that list of virtues sound so depressing?

Janna sighed and squirmed unconsciously, as though trying to get away from her own thoughts.

"Hold still or you'll get soap in your eyes."

"How would I know the difference?" she mumbled, swiping at her face again.

"Sorry," Raven mumbled. "Guess I should have kept my clumsy paws out of it. You were doing fine without me."

He started to ease his fingers from the sudsy mass of Janna's hair, only to have her grab his wrists, holding him in place.

"Don't stop," she said. "Please. It feels wonderful," she said, turning her face toward Raven. It was a mistake. The weathered tan of his skin, the slashing black lines of mustache and eyebrows, and the endless mystery of his eyes all sank into her like a series of blows that took her breath away. She drew air in raggedly and tried to explain to him what she didn't understand herself. "I don't know why I'm being so snarky. I guess my usual good nature got left out in the inlet along with my brains. I'm sorry."

Raven looked down at Janna's lather-streaked face and earnest, silver-green eyes. Her moist, slightly parted lips were the same raspberry color as the tip of her breast had been. The realization made heat and heaviness sweep through Raven's body, settling in the part of him that was even now nestled against her lovely, firm bottom. He wondered what it would feel like to be naked with her right now, his hands rubbing through her hair, sliding over her body, arousing her until she opened herself and cried for him to come to her.

Even as the thought swept through Raven, he denied it, ignored it, discarded it. He had spent too many years torturing himself over a woman he couldn't have. He wasn't going to start all over now, not even in the smallest way. Janna was here by accident, not by choice. Under normal circumstances she would never have agreed to stay in the lonely inlet with a man who looked as rough as he did. Not if she had a choice. The storm had taken choice from her, stranding her with him in Totem Inlet's isolation. If he took advantage of that and of the gratitude that softened Janna's magnificent, silver-green eyes when she looked at him, he would hate himself. As soon as the storm broke, he would take her to Masset. They would stand on the dock and shake hands and smile rather uncomfortably as they parted, two people who never would have met under normal circumstances.

"Raven?"

He smiled sadly, slid one hand from Janna's hair and picked up a nearby towel. With immense gentleness he held her still and wiped the lather from her face.

"Put this over your eyes while I rinse you off."

Janna wanted to protest as Raven covered her eyes with the towel, but she didn't. She wanted to ask if it was something she had done that had made him so sad, but she wasn't going to do that, either. At least, she told herself she wasn't going to, right up to the instant when she heard her own words.

"Is something wrong?" she asked, staying Raven's hand when he would have turned her.

"Nothing new," he said simply. "And nothing wrong, really. Turn around. If you get soap in your eyes, you'll cry."

"I feel like crying right now, and I never cry," Janna said, searching Raven's midnight eyes.

His big, blunt fingertip touched her nose lightly. "That's just the last echoes of the adrenaline from yesterday. It will pass."

Gently, implacably, Raven turned Janna away from him. He stripped soap from her hair into the stream, moving with swift economy, no longer lingering to enjoy the sensual weight and texture of her hair in his hands. He rinsed her hair first with cold water from the creek, then finally with the bucket of water he had warmed on the galley stove and carried to the stream.

Janna let out a long sigh. "That feels wonderful."

Raven smiled and continued to work the warm water through her hair, rinsing away the last traces of soap. As Janna's hair lay wet between his hands, it seemed almost sable, yet it gleamed with hints of mahogany and gold. He wondered what her hair would look like in sunlight. Would the long strands be reddish brown or richly cinnamon? Would they be as straight as his own or they would curl seductively around his hands?

With a silent inward curse, Raven caught his glittering thoughts once again in the net of his will. He squeezed excess water from Janna's hair and began drying it with the towel. Her hair felt very soft, very clingy, and gleamed like wet silk in the stormy light.

"I can do that," Janna said, feeling guilty about causing Raven so much trouble. "You came here to be alone, not to be a lady's maid."

Raven removed his hands from Janna's tempting hair and stood up in a surge of controlled strength. "I'll wait for you on the shore. Do you like clams?"

"Nope. I love clams. Different thing entirely."

Raven grinned suddenly. "Raw?"

Janna stopped rubbing her hair with the towel and

looked up. Her face was flushed from bending over the creek. Her eyes had the brilliance of sun-shot mist. "Raw clams?" she asked carefully, wondering if she had understood him. She loved clams, but had never brought herself to eat them raw.

"Umm," he said.

"Is that a rumble-yes or a rumble-no?" she retorted.

Raven laughed. "Just a rumble. How about clam chowder with raw oysters on the side?"

"Sold," she said promptly, diving back into the towel, trying to ignore how she had gone weak just looking at Raven's wicked smile. From the depths of the towel, she asked, "Are they any good raw?"

"Oysters?"

"Clams."

"Raw?" he asked innocently. "I don't know. Are they?"

"Good?"

"No. Raw."

Janna's hands stilled as she heard the laughter vibrating in Raven's voice. Surrounded by a cloud of flying hair, her face emerged from the towel. "Do you know my brothers by any chance? I used to have this conversation with them all the time."

"Was it good?"

"And raw!"

"Then they weren't clams." Raven's smile flashed whitely, changing his face from brooding to amused in a single instant.

"Oh, help," Janna groaned, diving back beneath the towel.

"Thought you wanted to do that yourself," he said, reaching for the towel once more.

Janna's answer was muffled beneath strategically placed folds of towel. Raven's laugh wasn't. By the time he finished with her hair, she was laughing, too. She stood patiently while he combed out tangles with a gentleness that kept surprising her in a man of his size. In his broad hand the comb looked like a half-scale toy. It seemed impossible that such a powerful man could have such precise control of his every motion.

"Braid?" he asked.

"If I do, it will never dry. Sure you won't let me use your knife?"

"Positive. How about blow-drying it instead?"

"Sure. And a manicure, too, while you're at it," she retorted wryly, thinking Raven was teasing her again.

"Don't know about the nail polish. Angel never used it."

The way Raven's voice softened as he said the word Angel told Janna more than she wanted to know.

"I take it that this Angel is of the wingless, two-legged, earthbound variety?" Janna asked lightly.

He smiled. "So she keeps telling me. Never believed her, myself." He smoothed his palm over Janna's hair. "I should have thought of it yesterday."

"You were too busy rescuing me to think of angels."

"I meant the box."

"Help."

Raven tugged very gently at a damp stand of hair. "Quit teasing me. Angel left some stuff on the boat last summer. I'd forgotten about it until I saw your hair shining beneath my hand."

Silently Janna wondered if Angel was a summer resident like herself, here today and gone in September. Had Raven loved Angel only to lose her at the end of the summer? Was Angel coming back? Was that why she had left a box of things on his boat?

Was that why Raven wasn't attracted to Janna?

Janna bit her lip against the words crowding her tongue. If Raven wanted her to know about his Angel, he would tell her without being prodded by unsubtle questions such as: *Were you married to her? Are you married still? Are you in love? Engaged? Who are you, Carlson Raven? Why does your sadness and your laughter tear at me until I want to cry and laugh, too?*

Janna watched as Raven bent down, loaded shampoo and other items into the bucket and turned toward her. Every movement was both enormously powerful and oddly beautiful. It was like watching the tide flowing, strength both smooth and endless, supple and potent. She had been raised among big men, strong men; male strength had always thwarted and irritated her, not fascinated her. But Raven was different. She could not stop watching him.

"Ready?" Raven asked, holding the wire-handled bucket in one big hand.

Silently Janna turned and walked from the creek through a screen of windswept, mist-spangled cedar to the rocky margin where sea met land. The path she followed was overgrown, barely visible, older than the thick evergreens lifting to the sky. She wondered if Raven's people had come from the abandoned village whose rough-hewn cedar houses and savage totems were slowly being engulfed by the resurgent forest. Had his ancestors carved the eerie, powerful images that faced the sea like human cries frozen within time?

"Careful," Raven said, clutching Janna as she stumbled on a mossy rock. "We're going to have to tie up your socks."

Janna felt Raven's breathtaking, casual strength as he steadied and then released her. She looked down at her feet. Her tennis shoes had survived their dip in the inlet and their subsequent drying in the galley oven, but her socks had been kicked aside and forgotten in Raven's haste to warm her. As a result, today she was wearing a pair of his wool socks while hers decorated the galley railing. She had rolled and rolled the borrowed socks, but the heel still came above her ankle. It was the same for her shirt. Raven's shirt, actually. The cuffs engulfed her entire hand and the tail came below her knees.

With a sigh, Janna conceded that the islands had reduced her to looking like a refugee from a low-budget circus. All she needed was thick makeup and a painted-on smile.

Watching Raven didn't make her feel any better about her own appearance. He looked as elemental as the land itself. Wind and wet cedar boughs had combed his hair into an untamed black pelt that gleamed darkly with every shift of his body. It was the same for the rest of him; he was perfectly suited to the place and the time, as though he had always been here, a part of the island's savage perfection. She was a ragged urchin—and he was the mist and the rugged mountains, the wind and the wild sea. It was there in his fathomless eyes, in his immense strength, in his silences.

Shivering with reaction to Raven's elemental pres-

ence, Janna rubbed her hands up and down her arms.
The knowledge that Raven had worn the very shirt
that was warming her flesh didn't soothe her. Nothing
about him soothed her. Yet even as that thought came,
she knew it wasn't completely true. Nothing in her
life had ever felt as right as the instants before she
fell asleep with his powerful arms around her and his
big body radiating heat into her own chilled flesh. She
had never felt safer, more at peace, more cherished.

Raven looked back over his shoulder in time to see
Janna shiver and rub her arms as though trying to
warm herself. He frowned, wondering if she were
coming down with a fever. He held aside the last
evergreen barrier between himself and the beach and
motioned Janna forward. As she brushed by him he
looked intently at her. Other than the subtle sadness
that came over her face at times, there was nothing
obviously wrong with her. Her skin didn't look dry
or pale.

"Wait," Raven said, releasing the cedar bough.

Janna turned. "Is something—"

Her breath hissed in as he put one hand on her
shoulder and the other on her forehead. The fragrance
of evergreen clinging to him teased her nostrils. She
knew that she would never smell cedar again without
remembering this instant, Raven so close to her that
she couldn't take a breath without drawing in his
scent, primal man and evergreen combined.

"You were shivering," he said, his voice rumbling
gently. "You feel fine, though. No fever."

That won't last if you keep touching me.

Janna crushed her thought before it became incau-
tious words. She had learned with her husband that if
a man didn't want you, he didn't want you. Period.

She had read an entire shelf full of books whose sexual instructions were both explicit and frankly boggling. She had gritted her teeth, taken a deep breath and tried some of those "surefire" methods of arousal on Mark.

It had been about as arousing as a bucket of ice water. For both of them.

"I'm fine," Janna said with determined cheerfulness, stepping away from Raven's touch before she shivered again in response to his closeness. "Actually, I'm disgustingly healthy. No feminine fits of the vapors, no delicate squeamishness, no interesting pallor. Just hearty, wholesome American girl. All I need are gingham checks, patent shoes and a puppy dog pulling at my anklets."

Raven heard the unhappiness underlying Janna's wry words. He looked intently at her, wondering what had happened to her that she so underestimated her own appeal to men. It would take a blind man not to respond to her. Her hair was a silky wildness framing her oval face. The forest green of his flannel shirt made her skin glow like mother-of-pearl on a sunrise beach. Her eyes picked up the green of cloth and forest, changing it, silvering it with emotions the way the wind changed the surface of the sea. Even the oversize shirt couldn't hide the womanly promise of her breasts, the allure of hip and thigh, the feminine curves leading down to ankles that looked ridiculously slender rising out of his bunched socks.

Watching Janna as she stood framed against the ancient forest made Raven want to smooth away all the coarse masculine clothes, to brush her with satin and incense, to caress the essential femininity of her. He wanted to arouse her until she cried out his name and wept and left passionate marks on his body. He wanted to give her a pleasure to equal the courage and determination he had seen when she had pushed herself beyond exhaustion, driven by the bitter imperatives of survival, and, then, still in the grip of those imperatives, she had let go of fighting and given herself to him, trusting him as no one ever had, even Angel.

Emotion went through Raven like a gust of wind through the cedar forest, stirring everything, leaving restlessness in its wake. Through narrowed eyes he watched as Janna picked her way over slippery rocks toward the log he had lashed to old, rotted cedar posts jutting up from the beach. The makeshift dock bobbed unpredictably. Years ago he had been a logger; for him, the erratic motions of a log floating on water were as easy to walk on as a stairway. Janna, however, lacked the experience to know how the log would react to a push here and a nudge there. Several times she had almost come to grief.

Janna stood on the shore, eyeing the bobbing log distrustfully. She tested the dampness of her hair, hesitated and shrugged.

"It's not worth it," she muttered, turning away.

"What isn't?"

"Dry hair. I'll slip on that log and take a header into the inlet," she said in a resigned tone. She shivered again. This time it was the wind off the inlet rather than Raven's presence that drew the involuntary response. "On second thought, it's worth it for the jeans alone. If they're dry by now?" she added, looking up at Raven.

"Should be."

"I was afraid you'd say that."

"Wait," Raven said, touching Janna's arm. "I'll get your jeans for you. And a scarf," he added as the wind lifted her hair in a damp, silky cloud. A few of the flying auburn strands caressed his face. They felt cool and smelled sweet against the tangy, salt-laden wind.

"Afraid you'll have to fish me out again?" Janna asked wryly, eyeing the log.

Raven felt his body kindle at the memory of drying Janna off and wrapping her in a warm blanket. Naked. With a muffled sound of exasperation at his unruly thoughts, he walked the log to the *Black Star*. Moments later he returned with her jeans, still warm from the oven, and a scarf that was the clear blue-green color of the sea under full sunlight. Janna took one look at the fine, delicate cloth and knew that it was Angel's.

"No," Janna said, refusing the scarf. "I'll ruin it." She stared at the glorious, blue-green wisp and had a depressing thought. "I'll bet it's the same color as her eyes."

Raven's black eyebrows shot up. "How did you know?"

Janna sighed. "She's blond, too. Right? Small boned, willowy, graceful, a figure to break your heart, with a smile that hints at passion and tragedy?"

"Are you a witch?" he asked, only half joking.

"If I were, Angel would be a warthog," Janna muttered under her breath.

"What?"

"Nothing," she said brightly.

Janna glared at her jeans and looked around for a place to sit that wasn't wet. The closest one was on the boat. She muttered one of her brothers' favorite words. Life simply wasn't fair. In order to put on her jeans without getting wet, she was going to have to hop around on one foot and then the other, looking about as graceful as a pig on roller skates. Meanwhile Raven could watch and compare her with the oh-so-delicate Angel.

Mentally Janna sorted through her brothers' vocabulary of locker-room epithets. She found some truly appalling phrases and spoke them in the silence of her mind. Finally she smiled, feeling better. She'd always known her brothers were good for something.

"Here," Raven said, realizing Janna's difficulty as she tried to balance on one foot on the slick pebble beach. "Brace yourself against me."

She hesitated, then mentally shrugged. He'd had her naked in bed and hadn't turned a hair. He was hardly going to be affected if she braced her fanny against his thighs while she put the jeans on in the only way possible to mortals—one leg at a time.

Leaning against Raven wasn't quite enough to make the job easy. The jeans were a little overcooked; they had shrunk in the oven. Now they fit her the way bark fit a tree—faithful to even the tiniest curve and hollow. Wriggling into the stubborn cloth was the only way to get the jeans on. With her tennis shoes catching every inch of the way, she had to do some major wriggling to get the jeans up her legs.

Raven suffered the innocent bump and grind of Janna's sexy bottom against his thighs as long as he could before he slipped an arm around her rib cage and braced her firmly, hoping that she would have to squirm around less that way. The strategy was partially successful. She did indeed have to squirm less. On the other hand, her breasts inevitably rested on his forearm, their sweet weight swaying with every movement of her body. Raven didn't know whether to regret or applaud the fact that Janna's bra, like her socks, had been lost in the first frantic moments of undressing her and getting her warm.

He remembered finding the bra that morning. The sheer midnight-blue lace had looked incredibly fragile in his hand. The thought of undressing her again had come to him like lightning; only this time it would be the heat of his tongue that transformed her nipples into tight pink crowns. He could almost see them pushing against the delicate lace, rising to the caress of his mouth.

The sensual images glittered through Raven's mind, impossible to control, like salmon schooling in the sea's mysterious darkness, gathering for the fresh-water culmination that sang to them from their deepest instincts.

With a barely stifled groan Raven turned, using his hip to brace Janna rather than his thighs. The speed and intensity of his arousal surprised him. He told himself forcefully that he was no boy to go crazy over a woman's unconfined breasts brushing against his arm. He had solved the sexual mystery of male and female long ago. He knew his own needs, knew when to control them and when to appease them. Now was definitely not the time for appeasing.

In the most primitive analysis, Janna was helpless against him—and they both knew it. He was far stronger. He knew the land, knew the sea, knew how to survive on both. He had saved her life. She was utterly dependent on the civilized veneer that covered his elemental survival calculations. She knew that, too, at some unconscious, primitive level far deeper than language and culture.

And she was too damned vulnerable because of it. If he asked, she would give herself to him. He could see it in her eyes as she watched him almost secretly—admiration to the point of hero-worship. Or was it simply fear? Was that why she sometimes trembled when she brushed against him? Had she instinctively sensed what he had only just realized?

He wanted her with an intensity that bordered on violence.

He had wanted her since he had seen her refusal to give in against overwhelming odds. He had saved her life, and now some savage, ungovernable part of his mind insisted that she was his for the taking.

Even as the realization came he fought against it. He didn't want her like that, a woman coming to him for all the wrong reasons, gratitude and a primitive survival reflex driving her into his arms. He wanted Janna to come to him willingly, when she had all the alternatives of civilization open before her.

And if he kept telling himself that often enough, he might even believe it.

Four

The tide was out, leaving behind a damp, plant-slicked, glistening swath of shoreline for Raven and Janna to pick over in their search for dinner. Living off the land wasn't really necessary; Raven had enough emergency stores to keep both himself and Janna well fed for the days it would take for the storm to blow itself out along the coast. On the other hand, he was reluctant to use the emergency food unless he had to. Though the chance of the storm lasting more than a few days was small, it was on such small chances that survival often hinged. More people got into trouble through bad planning than bad luck.

Besides, Raven very much enjoyed walking along the shoreline with Janna in search of food. It was the time between squall lines, when the rain was little more than a sparkling edge to the wind. Janna accepted the wind and mist and rain with the same good nature she accepted having to wear sweaters and jackets that came down to her knees.

Raven could think of a lot of women who would have shut themselves up in the warm boat rather than scramble over chilly, slippery rocks in search of seashore life that only a scientist or a very hungry person could describe in terms of enthusiasm. Janna was both. She was happily crouched over a stretch of rocky tide pools that waves would bury in foam within a few hours. Slick seaweed glistened around her. Beneath the oversize jacket she wore, her legs looked very sleek and feminine encased in her jeans. Raven knew that her legs would look even better on the boat, when she would wear nothing more than one of his long shirts while her jeans toasted and dried in the oven.

The thought made Raven smile. He knew he would never again be able to smell sea-wet jeans and tennis shoes drying without remembering the days when a summer storm had given him a gift and then sealed him within Totem Inlet to enjoy the present. Raven couldn't think of a time he had had half so much fun as he had in the past three days. Janna was good company. Her quick mind and wry sense of humor had made the hours fly—at least in the daytime. Knowing that she was only a few feet away had made the nights incredibly long.

"What do you call this?" Janna asked, turning toward Raven.

He stared from the creature balanced on the palm of her hand to Janna, disbelief clear on his rugged face. "What did you say you majored in?"

Janna blinked, then began laughing. "Marine biology. If it will make you feel better, I know that what

I'm holding is phylum Echinodermata, class Echino-idea, and is known to its friends as *Strongylocentrotus purpuratus*. Now, what do you call it?''

"A purple sea urchin," Raven said dryly.

Janna looked up at the cloudy, windswept, glittering sky as though seeking aid or inspiration. "In Haida," she said carefully. "What do you call a purple sea urchin in Haida?"

Janna turned her face back to Raven, waiting for him to speak. Her head was cocked in an attitude of anticipation. She had learned from him that the Haida language was technically described as an isolate, a language totally unrelated to any other on the face of the earth. Basque was the only other living language that was an isolate. All other spoken languages belonged to one or another inter-related groups, such as the Romance languages. But not Haida. It stood alone, isolated. Unique.

Like Raven, who also fascinated her.

Raven's lips quirked as he measured Janna's eagerness. He was oddly proud that the Haida language truly intrigued her. He had always known that his native speech was different, but through Janna's eyes he was learning just how rare his language really was. Learning like that was an unusual experience. So was Janna. With her around life grew more interesting with every instant.

"Raven?"

He laughed softly before he answered her question in Haida.

Janna listened to the brief rumble of sound that was the Haida name for the purple sea urchin. "What does it mean?" she asked.

Beneath the gleaming midnight mustache, Raven smiled widely. "There's no—"

"Direct translation," interrupted Janna, groaning. It was a phrase she had heard too many times lately. "So give me an indirect one."

"Round, purple, spiny, edible, sea-rock dweller."

"See?" Janna demanded triumphantly. "No matter how unique the language, the human mind that thought it up is still wired along the same basic diagram. Descriptive. The scientific name for purple urchins tells me pretty much the same thing as the Haida name, but in more detail. Except for edible." She grinned. "Most scientists aren't interested in eating the subjects of their studies."

Raven eyed the prickly, violently purple urchin that Janna held. "I know how they feel," he said emphatically. "Takes your appetite away just to look at it."

"In Japan, the roe of the urchin is a delicacy, like caviar in Russia."

"We aren't in Japan."

"Where's your sense of adventure?"

"In the bottom of the inlet along with your brains," Raven retorted.

"No urchin soup?"

"No urchin soup."

"How about raw urchin?"

"How about raw sand?"

"Eagles eat urchins," Janna pointed out, remembering her surprise when she had seen an immature bald eagle perched on a log and eating an urchin with every evidence of enjoyment.

"My moiety is raven, not eagle."

The teasing light vanished from Janna's eyes, to be

replaced by a curiosity that was much more intense. She wanted—she *needed*—to know everything about Raven. "What?"

"Haidas are divided into two groups, eagle and raven," he explained. "My mother was a raven. Therefore, I'm a raven."

"The Haidas have a matriarchal society?"

"In some ways." He smiled crookedly. "It's just as well, since my father was a Scots sport fisherman named Carl who left as soon as the salmon run was over. So I'm Carlson Raven."

"Did he know your mother was pregnant?" asked Janna. Even as the words left her mouth, she knew that her curiosity was almost rude, but she couldn't help herself. She needed to know more about Raven with an urgency that overrode her polite upbringing.

"I doubt it," Raven said, shrugging. "And I doubt that it would have mattered if he had known." Raven hesitated, then added quietly, "He picked my mother up in a bar. She never had enough money to buy all the drinks she wanted."

Janna's eyes became even more silver as a sheen of tears unexpectedly gathered. She thought of how proud her father had been of his strong sons and lively daughter, and of how much love there had been between herself and her family. Then she thought of Raven growing up without that kind of love.

"What a waste," she whispered. "Most men would kill to have a son like you, and most women would die proud knowing that they had once carried you in their body."

For an instant Raven closed his eyes, unable to bear the depth of emotion he saw in Janna's. "Not really," he said finally, his voice almost harsh. His eyes opened black and very clear. "I'm Haida. Indian. Maybe that doesn't matter here and now in this inlet, but it matters like hell out there," he said flatly, gesturing with a broad, powerful hand to the rest of the world.

Janna started to object, then stopped. What Raven said was true. She didn't like it, but she was too realistic to deny it. She hated it, though. She hated it so intensely that her eyes became almost as dark as his. The thought of Raven being subjected to a loveless childhood and then to bigotry in adulthood made her so angry that she shook with the force of her suppressed emotion.

"I don't feel that way about you," she said distinctly. "You're a man, Carlson Raven. You're as fine a man as I've ever met. That's all that matters to me. That won't change whether I'm here in Totem Inlet or on the far side of the moon. And I can't bear the thought of you being raised without love, without someone to appreciate what you've become."

Janna's voice broke. She turned away quickly, replacing the spiky, fragile urchin in its nest of stone. Impatiently she wiped off her tears on the thick sweater that she wore. It was damp and smelled subtly of the sea and the man who had worn it before he had given it to her to keep her warm.

"Janna." Raven's voice was deep, gentle, gritty with restraint.

He pulled her to her feet and put his work-hardened palm beneath her chin, tilting her face up to his. He started to speak, saw her tears and felt breath rush out of his lungs as though at a blow. He bent and brushed her eyelashes with his lips. The effort it took to stop after those comforting, undemanding kisses shocked him. Slowly he released her chin, caressing the line of her jaw with his fingertips as he withdrew his hand.

"I wasn't unhappy," he said softly. "Among the Haida, children belong to their mother's moiety, and boys are initiated by their mother's brothers rather than by their fathers. My uncle raised me, as is the custom among my people."

"And your mother?" Janna asked unevenly, knowing that she shouldn't ask…unable to stop herself.

"By the time I was six my mother wasn't capable of caring for herself, much less for a son. She abandoned me and took up full-time drinking. My uncle adopted me under both tribal and Canadian law four years before she died. Eddy is a good man, a strong man, a kind man," Raven said deeply. "In the summer he fishes salmon and in the winter he carves argillite into images as old and unique as the Haida language. You'd like Eddy. He would love you. He has nothing but disgust for women who are too spoiled to walk the Queen Charlottes in a storm."

Janna looked intently at Raven, measuring the emotion that lay beneath his words. She sensed that he didn't talk casually about his parents—or lack of them—yet he had talked to her. As she looked up into his black, gleaming eyes, it was all she could do not to throw herself into Raven's arms and plead that he notice her as a woman. But throwing herself at him would be a disaster. Whatever Eddy might like, Raven himself was drawn to tragic, fragile blondes who wore silk scarves that exactly matched their mysterious blue-green eyes.

"Do you think Eddy's man enough to eat urchin soup?" Janna asked lightly, hoping Raven wouldn't notice that her smile quivered on the edge of turning upside down.

Raven smiled suddenly, transforming the dark, harsh planes of his face. "I can't wait to find out."

When Janna saw Raven's smile, emotion gusted over her like wind over the surface of the sea. She turned quickly and looked out at the water. Another squall line was sweeping in. "How long do we have to wait?" she asked.

"For the soup?"

"For the squall."

Raven's glance followed hers. He frowned as he saw the dense, blue-black wall of clouds advancing toward them on the back of a freshening wind. "Just long enough to get to the boat, if we're lucky. *Damn.* What the hell was I thinking of? I know better than to turn my back on the sea."

"No time for oysters?" asked Janna, thinking of the small oyster bed they had passed on their way to the mouth of the inlet.

"I'll get some. You go on to the boat and stay dry."

"What about you?"

"Getting wet will teach me to keep my mind on the weather." *And off how sexy your hips look when you bend over and sort through the contents of a tide pool,* Raven added silently.

"But you'll run out of dry clothes," Janna said.

"I'll wear a sleeping bag."

"No way," she said, shaking her head firmly, making light flicker and run through her softly curling cinnamon hair. "I'll wear a sheet and give you back your own clothes."

The thought of Janna naked but for a dark blue

sheet made Raven smile despite his promises to himself not to think of her in any way except as a friend or a sister.

Janna didn't see the very male smile because she had already turned and started up the shore toward the part of the inlet where the *Black Star* was moored. Raven watched her for a few moments, admiring the quintessentially feminine swing of her hips. With a muffled curse he admitted to himself how much he itched to trace Janna's graceful spine and the smooth, full curves of her bottom with his tongue and fingertips. She would feel so good, warm and firm, soft and womanly, filling his senses even as he filled her. Would she like that? Would she like being teased and tasted and finally taken by him?

The direction of Raven's thoughts was rapidly making walking uncomfortable for him. Cursing silently, he wondered how he was going to keep his hands off her for the two more days of rain and wind that the storm was predicted to run.

"Raven?" called Janna.

He looked up and realized that he had stopped walking while he fought his unruly thoughts and hungry body. Furiously he swore beneath his breath. Self-control had never been this much of a problem for him, even when he had been a boy in the first raw rush of sexuality.

"Is something wrong?" Janna asked.

"No," he said, his voice almost harsh. "I was just wondering how much longer we'll be shut up in this damned inlet."

"Oh."

Janna smiled brightly, meaninglessly. She turned and walked away from Raven as quickly as possible, all the pleasure gone from her day. She had been enjoying every instant of being marooned with Raven. It was deflating to realize that he was counting the minutes until the storm let up enough to permit them to leave. Deflating, but not surprising. If he had ever fantasized about being trapped in a deserted inlet, it would be Angel who filled his dreams, not a strange brunette with an off-the-wall sense of humor.

Raven, on the other hand, was the kind of man Janna had dreamed about long before he had fished her from the cold sea. His intelligence appealed to her as much as his strength, and his laughter made her feel as though she had stepped into a cataract of sunlight. The thought of being wanted by a man like that—really *desired*—made her tremble.

The squall line came ashore just as Janna scrambled into the boat's cabin. The second log that Raven had lashed to the original mooring log made it easier for her to walk along the bobbing "dock" to the boat without slipping. Even so, she was grateful that she wouldn't have to attempt crossing the erratically moving surface in the rain.

She smiled almost sadly. It had been very thoughtful of Raven to round up another one of the old, weathered logs that lined the inlet and add it to the "dock" just so that she wouldn't risk a dunking every time she came or went from the boat. She had watched in fascination as he stripped to his waist and maneuvered the log into the water. The raw strength of Raven's body had been almost frightening.

Yet she had wanted nothing more than to run her hands over that powerful flesh, savoring the male heat and strength, the textures both smooth and intriguingly furry. She wondered if his sweat would taste like the sea or would have the astringency of cedar. Or perhaps his taste would be a blend of salt and evergreen and man, a mixture as complex and elemental as Raven himself.

"He could taste like caviar and cherry pie for all you know or will know," Janna muttered to herself. "Or lightning and rain, or wine and—oh, the hell with it. Stop torturing yourself over what you can't have and make some tea. He's going to be wet and cold by the time he gathers a bucket of oysters for dinner."

While the water heated Janna put out two mugs, each with its own tea infuser. She liked her tea fairly mild, with lemon peel and sugar. Raven liked his tea strong enough to etch steel. Then he added canned milk and sugar in the British fashion. Janna had tried it. She still wasn't sure what it had tasted like. She knew what it had not tasted like, though. Tea.

As soon as the water boiled she poured it into the mugs, carefully leaving enough room in one for the generous amount of milk Raven would add. She stepped across the narrow galley aisle and sat at the custom-made dining table that filled one side of the small cabin. The table was larger than most ship's tables because Raven was larger than most men. At night the table was lowered, fitted into a groove and covered with a custom-made mattress. Normally Raven simply left the bunk made up and ate his meals sitting on one of the padded seats in the stern of the boat. Since Janna had joined him, he had insisted on setting up the table every morning and taking it down after dinner every night.

Janna looked toward the small triangular cabin in the bow of the boat where she slept. There was a narrow bunk running down either side, leaving a wedge-shaped aisle in between. One look at the bunks had told her why Raven didn't sleep there. He would have hung over everywhere. For her the bunk was quite comfortable. For him it would have been a bad joke.

Absently Janna tested her tea by pulling out the infuser and looking at the color of the liquid running back into the mug. Perfect. She cut off a bit of lemon peel with a galley knife. It was lethally sharp, as were all Raven's knives. She was grateful. Only a sharp knife held by a skilled, strong hand would have been able to slice through the tough fabric of the life vest that had bound her to the sinking rowboat.

She shivered unconsciously and added a teaspoon of sugar to her tea. Carefully she rewrapped the small piece of lemon that was all that Raven had had in his cooler. She had been grateful to find even that. Lemons on the Queen Charlotte Islands were a rare and exotic life form.

Restlessly Janna looked around the boat. Her glance fell on the small writing tablet and pencil that Raven had found for her so that she could make sketches. Even as she reached for the pad, she decided against it. The ruled lines would distract her, which simply meant that she was too edgy to sketch.

She went out to the *Black Star*'s stern. The canopy was snapped in place, keeping off both wind and rain, making another cabin out of the stern of the boat. The sound of rain was continuous, relentless. Normally she found it soothing. Now she just wanted to hear Raven's voice. She leaned forward, staring through the clear plastic windows in the canopy. There was nothing to see but rain. It was coming down so hard that she could barely see the shore.

The boat rocked gently against the fenders protecting the hull from the logs. Janna closed her eyes. For a long time she listened to the rain and the wind and the restless sea. She was used to being alone, yet she was not used to being lonely. And that was how she felt right now. Lonely.

"Hello the *Black Star*! Oysters coming on board."

Janna felt warmth flood through her. Even as she told herself that she was a fool for letting her heart and her hopes race, she set aside her tea and rushed over to unzip a section of the canopy. A bucket emerged into the opening, followed shortly by Raven himself. He fastened the canopy again and then turned toward Janna. He was as wet as a seal despite his waterproof jacket. He peeled off the jacket, shook it and hung it on a peg before he sniffed the air.

"Ahh," he rumbled, "my favorite dinner. Roast haunch of tennis shoes with a side order of baked jeans."

Laughter bubbled from Janna as though she were freshly opened champagne. Raven's whimsical sense of humor had been as unexpected and endearing to her as his gentleness. She held out her hand for the bucket, only to notice that it held a bottle of wine as well as oysters.

"You have, er, unusual oyster beds in the Charlottes," Janna observed, pulling out the wine bottle.

Raven grinned. "Old Haida secret."

"Someone must have let the French in on it, too," she retorted, reading the label. "How did you know I love Chardonnay?"

"Like I said," Raven answered, his voice muffled

as he bent down to pull off his soaking shoes, "you look like a woman who enjoys her senses."

"What did you do to your hand?" Janna asked suddenly, setting aside the wine.

He looked at the back of his left hand. There were several thin lines of blood welling. "Barnacles," he said, shrugging. What he didn't say was that he had been thinking about Janna when he should have been thinking about what he was doing. "No big deal," he added, cleaning off the skin with a quick swipe of his tongue and then examining the shallow cuts.

"It could be a big deal if you don't take care of it," she said crisply. "Barnacle cuts are notorious for getting infected."

She went back to the galley and returned in a few moments with hot water and an antibiotic salve. Before Raven could object she took his hand and bathed it carefully. She bent over his hand and turned it toward the light. The cuts were shallow, clean and should heal quickly. There was really no reason to worry about them. She should let go of his hand and get back to the cabin.

But Janna could not let go. The temptation to raise Raven's broad hand to her lips and kiss away the minor hurt was almost overwhelming. All that prevented her was the knowledge that the intent of her kiss would be more sensual than healing, more hungry than comforting. Silently calling herself a hundred kinds of fool, she prolonged the contact by bathing his hand again, touching him in the only way that she could.

Raven sat motionlessly in the stern seat, savoring the gentle warmth of Janna's hands. Her hair had come loose from the clip she wore at the nape of her neck. Tendrils of rich cinnamon curled softly across her cheeks like darkly shimmering flames. In the subdued light her hair glowed with life. He wondered what it would feel like to have that cool, silky hair falling freely over his bare arm, his chest, his thighs. Then he wondered why he was tormenting himself over a woman he would not let himself touch.

Janna dried Raven's hand with the same gentle thoroughness with which she had bathed it. She smoothed antibiotic salve over the tiny wounds, taking her time about it, doing it twice. When there was no further excuse to touch Raven, she reluctantly released his hand.

"There you are. Nearly as good as new." She heard her own voice and knew that it was too husky, almost breathless.

"Thanks."

Raven flexed his hand to keep from reaching out and burying his fingers in Janna's beautiful hair and pulling her mouth down to his. He wanted to tell her how much he had enjoyed having her concerned over his minor scrapes and having his big, work-roughened hand touched as though she cared if he were hurt even by such a small thing as barnacle cuts. Normally he disliked women who fussed over him, oohing and cooing over every tiny scrape. Janna was different. She had cared for him so quietly and deftly that she had left him feeling cherished rather than smothered.

"You should have children. You'd be a fine mother. Gentle hands and..." Raven's deep voice died into silence as he saw the sudden stiffening of Janna's body. She straightened and turned away from him so quickly that she almost stumbled. "Janna?"

"I forgot your tea," she said tightly. "It will be strong enough to dissolve steel by now."

"Sounds perfect to me," he rumbled, smiling.

There was no answer. Raven frowned, wondering what was wrong. Normally Janna enjoyed teasing him about the strength of the tea he drank, just as he enjoyed ribbing her about the "hot sugar water" that she preferred. He got up to follow her and demand to know what was wrong. In three longs steps he was in the cabin.

"Janna, what—"

"As your mother surrogate," she interrupted in clipped tones, "I feel compelled to point out that you're dripping all over the floor."

"Deck," he corrected her automatically, frowning. *"Deck."*

Raven's eyes narrowed as he took in the barely restrained anger radiating from Janna. He watched as she reached blindly into a drawer and brought out a punch for the can of condensed milk. She opened the can with a single savage stroke, spilling some of the thick, creamy fluid in the process. Carefully he reached past her, took the milk and metal punch, and set them beyond her reach.

"What's wrong?" he asked.

"Nothing." Janna heard her own cold word echo in the silence, watched a thread of milk spread thickly on the counter and hung on to the shreds of her self-control with every bit of willpower she possessed. "Sorry," she said finally. "Guess I'm like you."

"How so?"

"Wondering how much longer we'll be 'shut up in this damned inlet.' "

Hearing his own words repeated like that made

Raven flinch. "I didn't mean that the way it sounded. I've enjoyed the time here. I can't remember ever laughing so much."

"Yeah, a regular dream come true for you," Janna said with a bright, empty smile. "You never had a mother and I'm great motherhood material. Pity you're too old for me to adopt. We could have a lifetime of laughs."

"Janna—"

"Here," she said, interrupting, setting Raven's tea within his reach. "Drink this before it eats through the mug. I'll open the oysters. You change out of those wet clothes before you get cold."

"Yes, Mother," Raven said dryly, reaching for the top button of his shirt.

Janna flinched as though she had been slapped. Raven's black eyes narrowed as he saw her reaction.

"I didn't mean that as an insult," he said evenly.

"What woman could be insulted by being told she was great mother material?" Janna asked in a flat tone.

Raven started to say something, hesitated and settled for unbuttoning his shirt. After he pulled on dry clothes and draped the wet ones over anything handy, he went out to the stern. The canopy kept out wind and rain, but did little to preserve the warmth that made the cabin cosy.

"Aren't you cold?" he asked, eyeing Janna's long, bare legs gleaming beneath the tails of one of his flannel shirts.

She shrugged and continued wrestling with an oyster. The knife she used was very short, triangular and deadly. There was no guard on the hilt. So far she had managed to avoid stabbing anything but the oysters.

"I'll do that," Raven said. "Get back in the cabin where it's warm."

"Yes, Daddy," she muttered, but she didn't give up the oyster that she was struggling with.

The idea of feeling fatherly toward Janna was so preposterous that Raven couldn't do anything but laugh.

After a moment Janna looked up and smiled. It wasn't her best smile but it was all she had at the moment. She still was raw from hearing Raven praise her nice, motherly attributes at the very instant when she had been all shivery just from touching him. The difference between their reactions to one another couldn't have been greater...or more discouraging.

"Sorry," she said. "Guess it's cabin fever."

"Or hunger," he rumbled, touching her lips with his fingertip.

Janna's eyes widened with shock. She wondered whether Raven had read her mind. "How did you know?" she whispered.

"No great trick," he said, grinning. "It's been five hours since lunch."

"Lunch?"

"Yeah. You remember—the meal that comes after breakfast and before dinner?"

"Oh, that lunch."

"Is there more than one?" he asked innocently.

"Of course," she retorted, rallying. "There's lunch and then there's getting lunched. Lately I've been lunched more often than I've eaten."

Raven opened his mouth, closed it and then began

to laugh. "Has anyone ever told you that you have—"

"A great sense of humor?" interrupted Janna, opening the oyster with a vicious jab of the knife. "Yeah. As one of the all-time boring virtues, it ranks right up there with motherhood."

"Not to someone who never had a mother and who likes to laugh. They're gifts, Janna," he said quietly.

"Really?" she asked, picking up another oyster, avoiding Raven's eyes. "Too bad we're so far from the complaint counter. I'd exchange them for sex appeal."

Raven's jaw dropped in the instant before he told himself that Janna was kidding. He laughed, shaking his head, and wondered why a storm hadn't washed Janna into his life years ago.

Janna didn't find the idea of her being sexy nearly as amusing as Raven did. In fact, she discovered that her sense of humor on that subject had just run out.

"Here," Janna said, slapping the hilt of the oyster knife into Raven's broad palm. "I'll make the cocktail sauce. It's too cold out here for me."

Raven looked from the knife to the long, bare legs vanishing into the cabin. The door shut firmly. He looked back at the knife and wondered why he had the distinct feeling that Janna would have liked to stick it into him rather than an oyster.

Five

By the time Janna had finished rummaging through the galley in order to find ketchup and horseradish, she had regained some of her normal common-sense outlook and with it her usually easygoing temperament. As she reminded herself, it wasn't Raven's fault that he was drawn to tragic blond angels. Nor was it his problem that she was finding it harder and harder to be close to him without touching him in a decidedly unangelic fashion.

And the storm just kept calling wildly over land and sea.

From what Janna had been able to understand between the bursts of static that had come whenever Raven tried to pick up a station on the radio, they had at least two more days in Totem Inlet before the wind died down enough to make the ocean safer for small craft.

Just two days. Surely she could keep her yearnings

to herself and her sense of humor intact for a mere two days.

Gloomily Janna put out the box of oyster crackers she had found in the cupboard. After a moment of frowning at the innocent crackers, she decided to sort through the *Black Star*'s spare cooler. She knew there weren't any lemons in the small galley refrigerator, but she had high hopes for the storage cooler. She hadn't found a lemon there yet, but then she hadn't really looked, either. It wasn't the sort of thing you did on a whim.

The cooler was little more than a long, deep plastic container set below waterline and shaped to conform to the curve of the hull. A hinged section of the counter lifted to give access to the cooler. Janna lifted the lid and looked in. No lemons had grown there since the last time she had looked, but she could swear that she smelled fresh lemons beneath the pervasive odor of onions and oranges. She stared down into the darkness at the small bags crowding against each other. Getting to the bottom of the cooler was going to require a flashlight and an ability to hang her head down in an enclosed space while balancing her weight on the edge of the counter and bracing her feet at floor level on the opposite cabinet.

That was exactly what Janna was doing when Raven came into the cabin. The sight of her long, naked legs stretched diagonally across the aisle brought him to a complete stop. Muffled thumps came from the cooler as Janna shifted potatoes, onions, carrots, oranges and other durable fresh foods from one side of the cooler to the other in her quest for lemons.

Raven barely noticed the sounds. He was fighting to control the impulse to run his hands from Janna's

ankles to the smooth curve of her hips…and from
there to let his fingers slide into the shadowed feminine secrets he knew were waiting.

It would be easy to do, a few seconds, no more,
and he could peel away the dark blue lace briefs that
even now peeked from the edge of the oversize shirt.
Or he could take longer. Much longer. He could learn
every smooth bit of Janna with his teeth and his
tongue, nuzzling closer to her secrets as he slowly,
slowly, eased the lacy briefs down her beautiful legs.

Raven's hands were actually reaching for Janna before he realized it. "What the hell do you think you're
doing?" he muttered roughly to himself.

An answer floated up from below the counter.
"Looking for lemons."

"Lemons," he repeated thickly, watching his own
shirt climb higher and higher up Janna's body as she
wriggled backward up and out of the cooler's depths.
When he saw the sweet flex and shift of Janna's hips
beneath blue lace, his whole body tightened. "Oh
God," he gritted.

He closed his eyes for a few seconds and tried to
control his own hunger. It didn't work. Desire poured
in red-hot torrents through his blood and pooled urgently, rigidly, between his thighs.

"Lemons," Janna said, her voice becoming clearer
with each instant as she emerged from hanging upside
down in the cooler. "You know—something to
sweeten my disposition."

Raven laughed almost helplessly and then swore in
the same way, but silently. He had been expecting to
have a tense dinner with an angry woman and had
walked into the cabin to find Janna's sexy bottom
tempting him and her sense of humor restored. Now,

if he could just do something about the raw, hard desire that was riding him, they might get out of the inlet before he took her down onto his bunk and ate every sweet inch of her.

And then again, they might not, especially if he didn't stop watching her hips move. Now. Right now.

With a groan Raven forced himself to look away from the inviting curves of Janna's bottom. By memory alone he found a plate for the oysters and retreated to the stern, shutting the cabin door behind. Using great care he stacked oysters on the plate. When he looked over his shoulder through the cabin window, Janna was head down in the cooler again. Grimly he rearranged the mound of oysters on the plate. Three times.

"I found some!"

"Thank God," Raven said with real feeling, turning toward the cabin.

He opened the door and closed it, balancing the heavy oyster plate in one hand. One look told him he had come back a few seconds too soon. Janna was just now wriggling onto her feet. Her face was flushed and her hair was tousled from hanging upside down for the past few minutes.

And her shirt was bunched at her waist.

Janna noticed the cloth, too. As her hands were full of lemons, she restored the shirt to its proper place with a quick shimmy of her hips. The tantalizing motion made Raven groan.

"Raven?" She turned toward him. "What is it? Did you stab yourself with the oyster knife?"

No, but only because I wasn't holding it. God, woman, there should be a law against movements like that.

Raven had just enough control left to keep the thought to himself. He took a deep breath—and smelled hot tennis shoes.

Janna smelled them at the same instant. She dumped the lemons in the sink, yanked open the oven door and pulled out her forgotten jeans and shoes. Raven set aside the oysters just in time to snag a pair of flying jeans before they wrapped around his face. Janna tossed the shoes from hand to hand, muttering to herself.

"If I'd known you were this hungry, I'd have tried for some cod," he said, examining the jeans with deadpan distaste.

"Who was it that I heard earlier singing paeans of praise to baked jeans?" retorted Janna, dropping the hot but otherwise unhurt shoes to the deck.

Raven chuckled and folded the rapidly cooling jeans. Janna saw his big hands linger almost caressingly on the worn cloth of the seat and shivered, wishing she were wearing the jeans.

"Talk about hot pants," she muttered.

"What?"

"Er, are they cool enough to wear?" she asked quickly.

"Are you cold?"

Janna opened her mouth, thought better of it, and said, "No you don't."

Raven gave her a slow, sideways look. "No I don't what?"

"Sucker me into another one of those open-ended free-association conversations."

Smiling, Raven sat on his heels and poked cautiously at the tennies. He looked up and said gravely, "Give 'em another ten minutes while we have oysters on the half shell. The shoes should be tender by then.''

''Good idea.''

Before his astonished eyes she tossed the shoes in the oven, cranked the control up to high and slammed the oven door. She turned and began mixing cocktail sauce as though nothing had happened. He waited. And waited.

And waited.

Suddenly Raven's deep, warm laughter filled the cabin. He bent over, shut off the oven and whisked the shoes out.

''You'd have done it, wouldn't you?'' he asked, still laughing.

''Damn straight,'' she assured him, fighting the smile that insisted on shaping her lips into an amused curve. ''The first thing a little sister learns is to out-stubborn brothers who are bigger, stronger and tougher than she is.''

''Small warrior,'' Raven murmured, touching the cinnamon fire of Janna's hair so lightly that she didn't feel it. ''Did they torment you?''

Janna started to agree emphatically, then realized that it wasn't quite true. ''Sometimes, but they loved me in their own way. And I was a little witch to them. Sometimes.''

''But you loved them all the time,'' Raven said, watching the softness that memories brought to Janna's mouth.

''Yes,'' she whispered. ''They always tried to protect me. They used to drive me crazy vetting my dates, sending some of the boys running and scaring the others so that they were afraid to hold my hand. The only one they would let near me was the boy

next door. They liked Mark. He never came on
strong.''

Janna's smile slipped. If only they had known why
Mark wasn't aggressive with their nubile little sister.
But it wasn't fair to blame them. Mark hadn't known,
either. Not really.

''Mark? Your husband?''

''Once. No more.''

''Why?''

Janna's hands paused. With deliberate motions she
scraped the cocktail sauce into a small, shallow bowl.
'We were all wrong for each other.''

''What do you mean?'' Raven asked, sensing
something more than the usual things that pulled mar-
riages apart.

She hesitated, then shrugged again. ''Mark saw me
as a friend, a companion, a sister, sometimes even a
mother. But not a lover.'' Janna's voice was even, but
all the softness was gone from her face and memories.
''Do you want your lemon in the cocktail sauce or
on the side?''

Raven looked at Janna for a long moment, wanting
to ask more questions about her and the man she had
once loved enough to marry—a man who apparently
hadn't loved her.

''On the side,'' he said finally, asking none of his
questions because Janna's eyes were jade green, no
passionate silver, no emotion turning in the depths,
nothing to tell him whether she had been sad or happy
or indifferent when her marriage had ended.

A companion, a sister, a mother, not a lover.

Raven winced inwardly. No wonder Janna had
stiffened when he had praised her in terms of her
gentle hands and smile. He wondered if she had

wanted her husband as a lover rather than a child. Even as the question came, he knew the answer; she had wanted a lover and had gotten a child.

"Your husband must have been blind," Raven said flatly.

"How gallant of you to say so," Janna said. Her full lips formed a smile that was as emotionless as her eyes. "But unnecessary and untrue. Mark was a pilot. He had superb vision. Do you have a corkscrew for the wine?"

"Did you love him?"

"Of course not," she said. "I marry every man who asks me out more than twice."

"Janna…" Raven began.

"Corkscrew?" she asked, smiling at him again, a smile as cool as her voice. "My brothers showed me how to take out the cork just by hitting the bottom of the bottle with my hand, but I'm not as strong as they are. I bruise my palm every time. You'd be good at it, though. Strong and hard. Like them."

"Do you still love him?"

"Did anyone ever tell you to mind your own business?"

"Yes. Do you still love him?"

"Why does it matter to you?" Janna asked through clenched teeth, feeling her careful veneer of dispassion disintegrating.

"I won't let you waste your life looking over your shoulder," Raven said quietly.

"You won't let me." Janna's teeth clicked as she shut her mouth and stared at the big, immovable man in front of her. "You aren't responsible for my life. I already have a father and three older brothers who are almost as big and every bit as overbearing as you.''

"Do you still love Mark?'' Raven asked relentlessly.

"No! I haven't loved him since he cried himself to sleep in my arms because he couldn't bring himself to have sex with me!''

"What?" said Raven, disbelief clear in his voice.

"He married me because he had always liked me, and he wanted children and thought I'd be a great little mother. He thought if any woman could turn him on, it would be me. He was wrong. I couldn't have turned him on with a blowtorch! He was gay and hadn't been able to admit it!''

Janna heard the words echo in the small cabin and was appalled. She had never told anyone about that terrible night when she and her husband had both realized that he was living a lie. She wouldn't have said anything now if Raven hadn't pushed so hard. She took a long, ragged breath, wishing she could crawl under the counter to avoid Raven's dark, compassionate eyes.

"There. Feel better now?'' she asked, her voice shaking.

"I was just going to ask you the same question.''

"I've never felt worse in my life. Next time, leave me at the bottom of the inlet. The cost of being saved by you is too damned high.''

Raven made a low, involuntary sound, as though he had been struck. "Funny,'' he said finally, "that's the same thing Angel told me.''

Raven's lips twisted into a sad smile that tore at Janna's heart, telling her that somehow she had wounded him more deeply than she had imagined possible, far more than he had hurt her with his questions. Abruptly the anger drained out of her.

"I'm sorry," she whispered. "I didn't mean to—"

"It's all right," Raven interrupted, turning away. "You didn't know. And even if you did, I had it coming."

"If I had known, I wouldn't have said it. I'm not that cruel."

Raven turned toward Janna. "Small warrior," he said, smiling slightly as he stroked her cheek with his calloused palm. "Haven't you learned? Sometimes kindness doesn't get it done." He turned away, opened a galley drawer and pulled out a corkscrew. With a few easy, powerful motions he took the cork from the wine bottle. "Glasses are in the cupboard to your left."

Numbly Janna reached for the cupboard. She pulled two wineglasses from their restraints and faced Raven again. As he filled the glasses she could see his nostrils flare in silent appreciation of the wine's fragrance. He poured the pale golden liquid into the glasses, leaving room for the wine to be swirled by a deft movement of his wrist as he dipped his head to inhale the bouquet. The gesture spoke of a sophistication very much at odds with his rough shirt and jeans.

"What was Angel looking over her shoulder at?" Janna asked, surprising herself. She hadn't meant to ask Raven any more questions.

"A dead man."

Janna paused in the act of setting cocktail sauce on the table. "She loved him?"

"He died the night before their wedding. Her parents died in the same car crash. She survived. She was too badly injured to move. She could only lie there and listen to Grant's pain until he died.''

Raven's voice was matter-of-fact, which only made the words more terrible.

Janna closed her eyes, unable to repress the shiver that took her at the thought of what Angel must have gone through. She felt ashamed of herself for lashing out at Raven. However sad and painful the end of her marriage had been, it hadn't been like watching the man she loved die and being helpless even to touch his hand.

''Angel came out of it, finally,'' Raven continued, putting the plate of oysters on the kitchen table.

''And you comforted her,'' said Janna, thinking aloud, seeing in her mind a slender blonde taking refuge from pain and grief in Raven's strong arms.

He looked sideways at Janna's pale, tight face and wondered at the sadness he saw there. ''Angel had Derry—Grant's brother—to comfort her. She needed something tougher, something that would let her pour out all the rage she had at life for taking away the man she loved. The rage was destroying her. She had to get rid of it before she could cope with the despair that was the other side of rage.''

Janna's eyes opened wide as she understood. She faced Raven and saw echoes of pain in the tight lines bracketing his mouth. She remembered what he had said: *Sometimes kindness doesn't get it done.* Now she understood his words. ''You deliberately made yourself a target, didn't you?''

There was a heartbeat's pause before Raven's deep voice said, ''Yes.''

''And she hated you for it.''

Raven nodded.

"Didn't she ever understand why you did it?"

"She understood right away," he said, setting plates, forks and oyster crackers on the table. "Forgiveness took longer. Years."

"You loved her," Janna said. She was motionless, watching Raven intently, and she was afraid in a way that she didn't understand.

"Yes."

"You still love her."

Raven smiled gently to himself as he shifted oysters onto Janna's plate. "Of course. Angel loves me, too, now. You'd like her," he said, looking up. "Like you, she's a warrior of the heart. She fought her way against terrible odds and won life and love. A beautiful woman in every sense of the word."

Janna looked into her wineglass and wished it were a sea deep enough to drown in. The fear and despair she felt were worse than they had been at the moment she had found herself trapped beneath the sinking boat. Her body had been cold then. Now the cold went all the way to her soul.

Fear. She was very much afraid that she had fallen in love with Raven, a man who loved someone else. Knowing the source of her fear didn't make her any less afraid. It simply made her understand her fear. She had lost something before she even had a chance to win it.

"Why aren't you married to Angel?" Janna asked flatly.

Raven gave her a swift, sideways look, then smiled. "Canada takes a dim view of bigamy."

"You're married to someone else?" Janna asked, her head snapping up, shock clear on her face.

He laughed and shook his head. "No. Angel is though, and very happily." He sipped the wine before adding quietly, "Derry and I helped Angel to survive, but it was Miles Hawkins who truly healed her. As she healed him. They brought out the best in each other. They still do."

The affection and admiration in Raven's voice when he spoke of the man Angel loved puzzled Janna. "Most men in your shoes would hate Angel's husband."

Raven's massive shoulders moved in a shrug. "Hawk gave Angel something no other man had been able to give. She gave him what she had given to no other man. They are as deeply interlocked as the sea and the shore. To hate one would be to hate the other."

Janna listened and wondered deep within herself if she would ever be able to accept the loss of love as generously as Raven had. "You're an unusual man, Carlson Raven," she said huskily. "Angel must have been blind to choose someone else."

His teeth flashed in a white smile. "You haven't met Hawk. Tall, dark, handsome, sophisticated. Wherever he goes he turns heads. Women's heads. I've never seen anything like it."

Janna looked at Raven. "Pull my other leg," she said sardonically. "It's shorter."

"Believe me, Hawk is the most—"

"He can't be a patch on you," she said succinctly, interrupting. She took a drink of her wine and then stared down into it gloomily. "My God, I'll bet there's an epidemic of female whiplash every time you walk down the street."

Raven sat at the table and cocked an inquiring

black eyebrow at Janna. "Are you one of those women who can't take a sip of alcohol without getting delirious?"

With an impatient sound Janna put her wine on the table and scooped a lemon out of the sink. "Don't bother to be modest," she said, quartering the lemon with knife strokes that were just short of vicious. "Surely you've noticed the women piling up around your feet like autumn leaves."

Raven stuck his large feet out into the aisle and looked at them curiously. "Nope. Not a one."

"Of course not," she shot back. "You have two."

"More than six and a half, actually."

Janna blinked. "Help."

"Feet," he added blandly. "As in tall."

Smiling, shaking her head, Janna gave up. The last of her anger fled as she looked at Raven's dark face animated by inner laughter. For a tearing instant she wondered why life was so unfair as to give Raven everything she had ever wanted in a man—and then to place him beyond her reach. Sudden tears came in blinding counterpoint to laughter, threatening to choke her. She tried to speak, to explain, but all that came out were fragments of Raven's name.

"Hey, it wasn't that bad a pun," Raven said gently, coming to stand beside Janna and blot up her tears with a napkin.

Head down, leaning against his strength, Janna fought not to cry. After a minute she succeeded.

"Sorry," she said, drawing a deep breath. "I never cry. I don't know what's wrong." She sighed and reluctantly drew back from Raven's body.

"You had quite a scare a few days ago," Raven

said quietly. His hand hesitated before he permitted himself the luxury of stroking Janna's gleaming cinnamon hair. The smooth warmth of the crown of her head made his palm feel as though it was caressing fire. "It's not surprising you're still feeling the emotional aftershocks."

Janna felt Raven's touch all the way to the soles of her feet. She wanted to turn her head and catch his hard palm against her lips. Even as the impulse came, she had given in to it. Her lips brushed over his warm hand.

"You're very kind," she said huskily. "Whoever Hawk is, whatever he is, Angel took second best."

Raven watched as Janna turned from his arms and slid into the booth seat along the table. Her honesty and vulnerability to him made him ache with tenderness. And hunger. He knew that she wanted him. He knew how much he wanted her. Silently he cursed the circumstances that had brought them together and at the same time made it impossible for him to accept what she offered. He couldn't take a woman who came to him out of a combination of misplaced gratitude and primitive survival instincts.

And that was all Janna was feeling now—gratitude and the emotional aftershocks of almost dying. She would have been equally drawn to any man who had saved her life and then cared for her.

Too bad he wouldn't have been equally drawn to any woman he had fished out of the sea.

Grimly Raven's big hand closed around his wineglass. He took a quick swallow, then another, as though the beautiful Chardonnay were medicine. And, in a way, it was. If he drank enough of it he might sleep tonight instead of lying awake so frustrated and aroused that he could count his own pulse in the rigid stirrings of his sex.

With an abrupt movement Raven sat down, concealing his physical turmoil beneath the opaque barrier of the table. A hard smile tugged at his mouth as he eyed the oysters heaped on his plate. If folk tales were true, right now he needed saltpeter a hell of a lot more than he needed oysters.

Janna reached for the oyster crackers, shook out a handful and offered Raven the package. He took it without a word. She wondered what he was thinking that had etched such an odd smile onto his lips. When she realized that she was watching those same chiseled lips with breathless intensity, she looked away, flushing guiltily.

"What do you do when you aren't fishing tourists out of Totem Inlet?" Janna asked, seizing the first words that came into her mind.

"I used to be a commercial fisherman." Raven squeezed lemon onto an oyster and forked it into his mouth. "Not bad," he said thoughtfully, appreciating the acid tang of fresh lemon.

"The oyster?" she asked, pausing in the act of reaching for one of her own.

"The lemon."

Janna blinked. "Don't you usually have it with oysters?"

"No."

"Then why did you have all those lemons on board?"

"Angel likes fresh lemonade. We were going to cruise the east side of Moresby Island for a few days until Hawk got back from Tokyo. Hawk got in early, though.'' Raven smiled crookedly. "Married nearly four years and he still hates being away from Angel.''

"Maybe he didn't want to tempt fate by leaving Angel alone with you,'' Janna said dryly.

Raven smiled even as he shook his head. "Not a chance. Pass some of that sauce over this way,'' he said. "I'll try it next.''

"Haven't you ever had this kind of sauce on your oysters?'' she asked, nudging the dish full of cocktail sauce closer to him.

"Nope,'' Raven rumbled.

"Then why did you have ketchup and horseradish on board?''

"For my roast beef sandwiches." He dipped an oyster in the dish, chewed the succulent flesh and cocked his head thoughtfully. "Not bad. Kind of saucy.''

Janna winced at the awful pun. "How do you usually eat your oysters? Cooked in a stew?''

"Just the way I find them. In the raw.''

"Must be kind of chilly,'' she said, reaching for her third oyster.

"What?''

"Finding oysters in the raw. Most people wear shirts and jeans and...''

Janna ducked a casual swipe from Raven's massive hand. When she straightened again, his fingers returned to tuck a stray lock of hair behind her ear.

"We're going to have to find you a scarf the color of your eyes.''

The gentleness of Raven's touch made Janna's heart stop and then beat with redoubled speed even as she told herself it was just a casual gesture that meant nothing. And even though it had made her go all shivery, it certainly hadn't affected him. He was picking up his glass of wine as though nothing had happened.

Raven drained his glass in a single motion, cursing himself for touching Janna at every excuse—and knowing that he was just waiting for another tendril of silky hair to escape so that he could touch her again. He looked at his wineglass. Empty. Janna's was almost empty, too. He refilled both glasses and wished that he and Janna were as naked as the oysters gleaming within their pearly half shells.

"To oysters in the raw," Raven said, lifting his wineglass.

His slow, very male smile sent frissons of awareness through Janna. She touched her wineglass to his and drank quickly, deeply, grateful for the excuse to look away from Raven's midnight eyes. If he smiled like that again, she was afraid she would crawl right into his lap and beg to be kissed.

The thought shocked her. She took another quick swallow of wine and felt a different kind of warmth spread through her. Belatedly she realized that wine probably wasn't what she should be drinking; alcohol wasn't noted for enhancing self-control. On the other hand, the wine was absolutely delicious. Probably far too delicious.

"Do you still fish commercially?" Janna asked, firmly trading wineglass for oyster fork.

"I own several commercial boats," Raven said. "My cousins have fished them for the last three years while I took Hawk's money and saw the world."

"Hawk must be as generous as he is handsome."

Raven smiled crookedly. "Technically the money's mine, but Hawk is the one who made it for me. The

man's a bloody genius with investments and land. Not
long after he and Angel met, I gave him a few thousand dollars. A year later he gave me back a few
million.''

Gray-green eyes wide with shock, Janna reached
for her wineglass again, despite the vague light-
headedness that was stealing through her. The idea
that Raven was wealthy unnerved her, placing him
even farther beyond her reach. She drank a healthy
swallow of wine and told herself that she was a fool.
She needed more wits about her, not less.

On the other hand, wine's anesthetic properties had
never seemed more appealing. She drank again.

''I lost most of it the following year,'' Raven said
matter-of-factly. ''Storms and fickle fish. Hawk just
laughed and showed me how to make it all over
again.''

Janna waved her wineglass in a vague circle that
took in the *Black Star*. ''Looks like you're doing a
good job of it.''

Raven shrugged and dipped another oyster in the
thick sauce. ''Like Hawk says, money's just a way of
keeping score. It's nothing to build a life around. Angel is, though, and he knows it. Smart man, Hawk.''
Raven chewed the oyster thoughtfully. ''Still a bit
saucy.''

''Is that what you're doing?''

''Being saucy?'' he asked innocently.

But Janna didn't smile. Questions were crowding
her tongue, reckless questions fueled by frustration
and potent wine. ''Are you building your life around
Angel, too?'' she asked, forking up another oyster.

The smile vanished from Raven's face, leaving behind the silence and blunt strength that was his very

core. "I'm not a fool, Janna," he said quietly. "Angel will never love anyone but Hawk. He feels the same way about her."

"And so do you," Janna said bleakly.

She drank more wine, hoping that it would finish the job of numbing her brain that the first glass had already begun. Her tongue, however, wasn't yet numb. She had drunk just enough wine to say whatever came to her and let the chips hit the fan. Vaguely she realized that wasn't quite what chips were supposed to do. Well, the chips would just have to look out for themselves. She lifted her glass in a mocking toast.

"To love," she said. "The best antidote to happiness yet devised by man."

The bitterness in Janna's voice surprised Raven. His eyes narrowed as he saw the unhappiness the wine had revealed beneath Janna's humor.

"You aren't drinking," she noted.

Raven said nothing.

"Ah well," said Janna carelessly, shrugging, "not everyone likes the truth. There are times when I sure as hell don't." She drained her glass.

"And what is the truth?" he asked in a deep voice.

"You're hung up on Angel."

"There have been other women in my life."

"But only one Angel," Janna retorted recklessly. "The perfect willowy blond, green eyes full of mysteries and tragedy. Meanwhile the rest of the women in the world can forget it. Whatever they have to offer you isn't wanted."

"That's not true."

Janna muttered something succinct and contradictory beneath her breath as she reached for the wine bottle. It was empty. Startled, she looked at Raven's glass. It was also empty.

"More wine?" he asked smoothly. "This is getting interesting. *In vino veritas* to coin an old phrase."

"I have just enough brains left to know that more wine would be a really dumb idea for me," Janna said, stabbing an oyster so hard that her fork grated on the shell. "But don't let that stop you. I've been on a roll lately. One dumb thing after another. Next thing you know I'll be bleaching my hair and learning the harp and shopping for paper wings. Sure, bring on the wine. Fantastic idea. Should have thought of it sooner. Does wine make you tragic and mysterious, too?"

"What in hell are you talking about?" Raven asked in a mild tone.

"Wining and dining," Janna said, waving an oyster at him.

"Was that with or without an *h*?" he asked blandly, but his eyes gleamed with suppressed laughter.

For an instant Janna didn't understand. Then she heard the echoes of her own bitter words coming back to her. "Whining," she whispered too softly for Raven to hear.

"Of course," he continued, "most oysters do tend to complain when dining with a walrus. From their point of view…" He saw the brittle animation suddenly leave Janna's face, revealing the pain beneath. He curled his hand comfortingly over hers. "Janna? I was joking."

"Yes, of course," she said automatically. She looked at the big hand covering her own and knew that she couldn't keep up the pretense any longer. Her hand slid from beneath his.

"Excuse me," she said carefully. "I've had about all the comfort I can handle for one night. I have some sketching I should do while the images are still fresh in my mind."

Without waiting for Raven's answer, Janna grabbed the tablet and pencil from the counter. She retreated to her bunk in the bow, shutting the small door behind her, leaving her words to echo in Raven's mind.

I've had about all the comfort I can handle for one night.

Raven didn't know that his hand had clenched into a fist until he heard the sudden shattering of the wineglass. Slowly he opened his hand and let the glittering fragments fall to the table. Absently he wiped the bright dust from his palm. He should have known better than to buy such fragile glasses. He wasn't any good with fragile things. Too damned big. Too damned strong. Too damned brutal. The really fine things of life were invariably crushed within his grasp. Like Angel.

And like Janna.

Raven leaned his head back against the bulkhead, closed his eyes and swore tiredly.

Six

Raven awakened instantly, silently, completely. His senses told him that the storm was over. The wind was little more than a fading whisper. The *Black Star* lay almost motionless beneath him. Moonlight poured in silver torrents through openings in the spent clouds.

And nearby, someone was crying very softly.

Before Raven could stop himself, he was halfway out of bed and heading for Janna's bunk in the bow. With an effort of will he forced himself to lie down again. If he went to her, he would give her more than comfort. He would lie beside her and caress her until those beautiful legs opened for him. Then he would slide his hard, violently sensitive flesh into her softness, finding the sweet and wild union that he had been aching for ever since he had seen her struggling so bravely against the storm.

Even as Raven tried to tell himself that surely he could comfort Janna without making love to her, he knew that it wasn't true. His whole body was flushed with sexual heat, pulsing with the hard beating of his heart. He had never felt so close to the limit of his self-control with a woman. The need to comfort and ravish, to soothe and incite, to find wildness and peace within Janna was tearing him apart.

Grimly Raven lay very still, fighting his unruly body and his equally unruly emotions, knowing that it would be a long time before he got to sleep again. He had been a long time getting to sleep in the first place. He had waited for hours for Janna to stop sketching and come out of the bow cabin so that he could apologize to her in the relative safety of the main cabin. Finally he had been able to stand it no longer. He had knocked at the tiny door to her cabin. There had been a long hesitation before she had answered. Her tone had been subdued, almost flat. He had realized then how much life she usually had in her voice. The difference had gone into him like a knife.

Remembering the lack of music in Janna's voice did nothing to ease the restlessness in Raven's body right now. Nor did hearing the muffled, ragged sounds of her fighting not to cry out loud help him to be at peace. Finally, after what seemed far too long, the soft noises faded, merging with the subtle whisper of the wind. Raven sighed in relief and went back to counting silver salmon on the back of his eyelids.

The sound of the bow door furtively opening brought every nerve in Raven's massive body alive. He heard Janna tiptoe up the two steps into the main cabin. He sensed her crowding against the far side of the aisle that separated his bunk from the galley stove. His nostrils flared as her subtle, indefinable fragrance washed over him like moonlight while she eased past his bunk to the door leading to the stern.

Hands clenched into fists to keep from reaching out to her, Raven listened as Janna passed his bunk in an almost soundless rush of hurrying feet. The cabin door opened, letting in a gust of cool midnight air. Janna stood briefly in the luminous moonlight before she slipped through the door. Raven closed his eyes. It didn't help. He could still see the firm, moon-silvered rise of her breasts beneath one of his old T-shirts. He wondered if she was wearing the dark lace panties beneath or if nothing except night concealed her vulnerable softness.

It seemed an unreasonably long time before Janna stealthily opened and closed the stern door again and began easing past Raven's bunk on her way back down the narrow aisle to the bow cabin. He listened to the soft sounds of her approach, smelled the mixed fragrance of womanly warmth and the coolness of rain-washed night. He was congratulating himself on keeping his hands to himself when he saw the gleam of tears on her cheeks.

''Janna,'' he whispered, reaching out and wrapping his hand around her wrist with a reflexive hunger that he had denied too long. ''Janna, what's wrong? No, don't pull back. I won't hurt you. I just want to comfort you.''

And it was true, as far as it went. He did want to comfort her. He wanted it as much as he wanted her.

Janna trembled when she felt the power of Raven's hand wrapped warmly around her wrist.

''Janna?'' he said softly. ''Talk to me.''

''I just needed some air,'' she said, trying to control her ragged breathing. She felt like a prize fool. She hadn't cried in years, yet since she had met Raven, she rained as regularly as the clouds.

"You're crying."

"Think of it—" Her voice broke. She took a breath and finished in a rush, "Think of it as Queen Charlotte s-sunshine."

Raven's hand tightened almost painfully on Janna's arm, then eased to a caress as he ran his fingertips slowly over the softness of her inner wrist. Janna's breath came in with a raggedness that had nothing to do with tears.

"I'm sorry," he said, his voice so deep that it was as much felt as heard. "I didn't mean to hurt you with that crack about whining and dining. I thought you would—"

"That's all right," she interrupted hurriedly. Her words were quick, staccato, like cold rain whipped by a storm wind. "I was whining. There's no need for you to—to apologize for telling the truth."

"Damn it, that's not what I meant!" Raven snarled.

"I understand. Really." Janna felt her control dissolving again and wanted to crawl off somewhere before she humiliated herself even further. "Raven," she said brokenly, "please let go." Vainly she tried to pull her wrist free of his warm, immovable grip. "I'm sorry I woke you. I'm s-sorry I—oh, God, please let go of me!"

There was an instant of silence before Raven's powerful arm flexed and he pulled Janna onto the bunk, into his arms. He had just enough self-control not to kick back the covers and hold her along his hungry, naked length.

"It's all right," Raven said, stroking Janna's hair and her back, ignoring her struggles to free herself. "Go ahead, small warrior," he murmured. "Cry while I hold you. Hold me if you want to. Please, Janna. I would never have said anything about whining if I had thought you would take me seriously. You've been so brave, so full of laughter. I expected you to sling an oyster at me with a smart remark about the dangers of going for a walk with a walrus, but instead you believed what was meant to be a silly joke. Can you forgive me?"

Janna made a strangled sound that could have come from tears or laughter or an aching combination of both.

Raven's arms closed around her, rocking her gently against his huge chest. When her own arms finally stirred and crept around his neck, he felt both relief and a hunger whose violent intensity shocked him, telling him that he was even closer to the edge of his control than he had realized. His only consolation was that Janna was lying across his chest. As long as she didn't change position, she wouldn't know what she was doing to him.

So tell her. Better yet, show her, Raven advised himself sardonically. *She's much too generous and vulnerable to turn me away. She thinks she wants me. She's so damned grateful to me that she'd do anything I asked. She'd do everything. And it would be so hot, so good.*

The fugitive thoughts glittered within the darkness of Raven's mind, darting and gleaming like salmon trying to evade the net. All that kept him from giving in to his hunger was the knowledge that he would hate himself for taking advantage of Janna's vulnerability.

"What was that about an oyster and a walrus?" Janna asked finally, sighing and relaxing utterly against Raven's chest.

He smiled and brushed his lips so lightly over Janna's hair that she didn't feel the touch. "Didn't your brothers ever explain what happens when a tender, innocent, succulent little oyster goes out wining and dining with a walrus?" he asked.

Janna shook her head, afraid to trust her voice.

"Your education has been dangerously neglected."

Raven's deep voice vibrated through her, pervading her to her core, melting her with laughter and heat. Unconsciously she moved her cheek across his chest, snuggling even closer to his warmth. His arms tightened fractionally, shifting the softness of her breasts against him. Heat surged through him like chain lightning, setting fires in his male flesh.

"'Twas brillig and the slithy toves/Did gyre and gimble in the wabe...'" Raven quoted deeply, ignoring the hot, hard stirring of his aroused body.

This time he was sure that laughter was causing the soft sounds and softer movements that Janna made against him. He took in a long breath and told himself all the reasons why he would be an insensitive, unforgivable, contemptible, rotten son of a bitch if he took advantage of her now.

Janna lifted her head, looked Raven in the eye and said, "Frumious bandersnatch."

"Gesundheit," he said instantly.

Her lips quivered with the effort of holding back her laughter, but she gamely stuck with it. "It was the frumious bandersnatch that gyred and gimbled in the wabe,'' she explained. ''Not a walrus. If you don't believe me, ask Lewis Carroll.''

''Carroll was too busy waxing his ceilings and shoeing cabbages for kings to worry about who was or wasn't gyre-ing and gimble-ing in or out of wabes,'' Raven retorted.

Laughter and sudden tears trembled on the brink of release as Janna looked at Raven loving him, wanting him. She sighed his name and brushed her lips over his. He returned the soft kiss until the tip of her tongue traced his upper lip. Then he turned away and very gently tucked Janna's head against his shoulder.

It was the most exquisitely tender rejection that Janna could imagine; and it wounded her as no other ever could, sliding through her defenses like a silver razor, slicing her open all the way to her soul, leaving her helpless to do anything but curl up inside with pain.

Raven felt the difference in her instantly, a stillness and a withdrawal so complete that he couldn't believe he was still holding her. ''Janna?''

After a long moment she straightened and eased free of Raven's arms until she could stand in the narrow aisle between his bunk and the galley. She looked down at his powerful body swathed in the dark sheet, at moonlight caught in the transparent black clarity of his eyes, at the big hand held out to her. Even now she could feel the imprint of his warmth on her skin, taste him on the tip of her tongue. She wanted him so much that it was like dying to know that he didn't want her at all.

''What's wrong?'' he asked.

''Nothing new,'' Janna said finally, unconsciously echoing Raven's earlier words to her. She felt the heat and chills of humiliation slowly ebbing, leaving behind only pain and a determination not to make things more uncomfortable for the man who had been so terribly kind and patient with her. "I'm sorry about the kiss, Raven," she whispered. "Truly I am. I keep thinking that I have something to give a man in bed. I'm a slow learner. Really slow. Sorry."

"Janna—damn it! There's nothing wrong with you!" Raven said harshly, feeling his control evaporating. He had wanted to spare her, not to hurt her more. Yet everything he said or did only made it worse. Somehow he had to make her understand that it wasn't that she didn't turn him on; it was that she wanted him for all the wrong reasons. "It's the situation, not you. If we'd met any other way than—"

"Don't," she said, cutting across his words. Then, very gently, she said again, "Don't, Raven. You don't have to lie to me. I'm a big girl. I can stand the truth. And the truth is that I lack whatever that indefinable something is that arouses a man. I'm sorry I embarrassed you. I promise that it won't happen again." Janna forced a smile and held out her right hand. "Friends?"

"Friends?" gritted Raven. He stared up at Janna, his eyes as black as night itself. Her smile was infuriating, as brilliant and empty as the moonlight pouring over her outstretched hand. *"Friends?"* he repeated, smiling savagely as he reached for her.

There was no warning. One instant Janna was standing in the aisle with a social smile plastered on her face and the next instant she was flat on her back in Raven's bed with his powerful, naked leg across her thighs, pinning her to the mattress.

"Oh yes," he said thickly, "we're friends, Janna."

He took both her hands, and as he spoke he began dragging them down the length of his body. "I'm a great believer in friends being honest with each other."

"Raven? What...?"

The question ended in a gasp as Janna felt Raven's unmistakable male hardness beneath her hands.

"That's what," he rasped.

Raven was so aroused that she could feel the heavy beat of his pulse as he closed her fingers around him. He felt hot and tight to the point of bursting.

"It's been like that damn near all the time since I saw you fighting the storm," he said flatly. "You smile or you turn around or you lick your lips, and I get so hot all I can think about is opening your legs and burying myself in you. If you give me any more crap about not being sexy enough to turn a man on I'm going to..."

The words became a broken groan as Janna's fingers moved over Raven slowly, savoring every bit of his erect male flesh. His hips moved reflexively, stroking his hungry length between her caressing hands. He saw her looking at his body, smiling at the very visible proof of his desire for her. He shuddered heavily, moving against her warm hands, feeling a pleasure so intense that he clenched his teeth against a guttural cry.

"No more," Raven said finally, his voice ragged. He caught Janna's face between his big hands. "I won't take you. It wouldn't be fair to you. I just wanted you to know that I've never had a woman turn me on so hard, so quick. If you were any sexier to me, I'd come just looking at you. How's that for honest?"

Janna looked up at Raven's face. His eyes were narrowed, glittering, and his mouth was drawn back as though in pain. His skin was hot to her touch, gleaming with sweat, and every powerful muscle was rigid with passion and control. He stirred hungrily between her hands with each rapid heartbeat, a man more potent than she had ever dreamed. The knowledge that he wanted her so much was a searing wildness racing through her, melting her with a sensual heat that she had never before known. She shivered repeatedly, hotly, tiny convulsions that changed her body within the space of a few breaths. She tried to speak but could not, she could only moan his name as her own buried sensuality burst within her, drenching her with liquid fire..

The scent of her arousal made Raven's whole body tighten. As though in a hot dream he felt her passionate shivering while her legs shifted, opening for him, pleading for him as her hands drew him closer to her.

"Janna—no." And then Raven groaned, feeling the softness and moisture of her. "Oh God," he said through clenched teeth as she melted at the first touch of him, bathing him with her heat. "I can't do this to you. I haven't even kissed you. You deserve better than this."

"We're kissing now," Janna whispered.

She moved her hips until Raven's hot flesh nuzzled against her softness, letting him feel what the honesty of his desire had done to her. He wanted to tell Janna to stop before it was too late, but he couldn't speak. What she was doing took his breath away. His hands clenched on the T-shirt she wore as he fought not to lose control.

And then it was too late. The shirt ripped from neck to hem as he took her with a single powerful thrust of his hips, burying himself in her. She was sleek and ready and wonderfully tight. He had never felt anything half so good. He withdrew and drove into her again and then again, measuring her taut, welcoming softness with his own hard flesh. He knew he should slow down but it was too late for that, it had been too late since he had first seen her fighting the storm. He had never lost control with a woman but it was happening now, everything spinning away from him as pleasure burst repeatedly, wildly, shaking him to his soul. With a hoarse sound that was Janna's name, he poured himself into her, knowing only her and the sweet violence of the release she had given to him.

Janna felt the wild trembling of Raven's body, heard her name a ragged cry on his lips and held him fiercely, savoring every instant of his shuddering climax. The knowledge that he had wanted her so badly and that he had found such a complete release within her moved her in ways that she couldn't describe. Tears spilled down her cheeks as she held Raven, loving the feel of him in her arms and in her body, feeling love for him like a fierce, sweet agony in her soul, wanting nothing more from life but to hold him until she died.

Finally Raven's breathing settled into the slow rhythms of relaxation and he stirred as though to roll aside. Janna's arms tightened in silent protest. She didn't want it to end. Not yet. Not ever. His thick mustache brushed over her cheek in a silky caress as he kissed her gently and then kissed her again, nibbling softly until his lips met the warm trail of her tears. He stiffened and drew back until he could see the shining evidence against her cheek.

"My God," he said, his voice breaking. "I'm sorry, Janna. I didn't mean to hurt you."

"No," she said quickly, holding Raven as he tried to withdraw from her. "You didn't hurt me."

But even as she spoke, he gently eased from her body, his strength making a mockery of her attempts to hold him. As he left her she cried out softly. He stroked her hair with a hand that trembled.

"I'm sorry," he whispered, "so sorry. I've never lost control like that. I just wanted you too much. I forgot how strong I am, how I'm no good with fragile things. I'm sorry, Janna. God, I—" His voice broke again.

Raven closed his eyes and fought for the control that seemed to elude him every time he was close to Janna. She heard the raw emotion in his voice and saw the wild glitter of unshed tears in his eyes. With wondering fingertips she caressed his cheek and the thick black curve of his closed eyelashes.

"You didn't hurt me," she said huskily.

"You're crying," he said in a harsh tone. "I must have hurt like hell."

"No," she said, putting her fingers across his warm lips. "Listen to me, Raven. You didn't hurt. It was knowing how much you wanted me, having you inside me, feeling you fill me with your hunger and need." The words stopped in a ragged breath. "It was unbearably beautiful," she whispered, kissing him. "That's why I cried. That's why I'm still crying."

Raven's hand moved against a bulkhead switch. Instantly a soft golden light flooded the bunk. As though to reassure himself of the truth of her words, he went

swiftly over her body with his fingertips, searching
for any sign that he had hurt her in the violence of
his own need.

With wide eyes Janna watched Raven, trembling as
he gently parted her legs and touched her with exquisite care. Heat bloomed unexpectedly, making her
breath catch. He heard the tiny sound and touched her
again, wondering if he had hurt her despite her assurances that he had not. Very lightly he traced the
incredible softness of her, expecting her to flinch. She
made another stifled sound as he circled her again,
seeking her most tender flesh. She shivered helplessly
as she melted at his touch.

Raven's expression changed, became both gentle
and…hungry. He caressed Janna again, melting her
again, smiling as he felt the proof that he hadn't hurt
her. When his hand pressed against her leg, she
shifted unconsciously, giving herself to his touch,
watching him while his dark glance moved over her
in another kind of caress. She looked down at herself
and realized that she was wearing his torn T-shirt like
an open vest. The thin cotton clung to her breasts,
held by the dampness of her flushed body, and his
big hand was curved protectively, possessively,
around the vulnerable softness that she had given to
him.

"Small warrior," Raven whispered as his hand
rubbed slowly against Janna. "So soft, so hot, so generous."

Eyes wide and luminous, Janna lay on the rumpled
sheets, watching Raven while he caressed her, feeling
as though he were stroking her with silk and fire.
Slowly, very slowly, his fingertips smoothed up her
body, leaving heat and dampness in their wake. The

sensual contrast with the cool air of the cabin made her tremble.

Then Raven's long index finger finally slid beneath the torn cotton T-shirt, tracing and freeing a breast in the same motion. Janna's nipple tightened in a tingling rush. She watched his fingertip stroke slowly across her ribs, sliding closer to her other breast. Before he even touched it, the hard rise of her nipple was clear beneath the cotton. Raven's smile as he peeled aside the clinging cloth made her breath wedge in her throat.

"Raven?" she whispered.

He made a rumbling sound that could have meant anything as he traced her tight, velvety peak. She watched in helpless fascination when he bent and touched the dark nipple with the tip of his tongue. A ragged sound came from her that could have been his name. His answer was a husky male laugh and the tender pressure of his teeth closing over her nipple, tugging at her, unraveling her breath and her body in a few rushing instants. She called his name in what she meant to be a question but came out as a broken cry.

"Yes," Raven said, understanding the question Janna hadn't been able to ask. He nuzzled her breast and the curve of her throat, tasting her with obvious pleasure. "I'm going to eat every sweet bit of you. But first I'm going to find out if your mouth is as hot and wild and welcoming as your body is." He laughed again, a sound so low that it was more felt than heard. "I've never learned a woman's secrets in reverse order before," he murmured, holding himself back long enough to admire Janna's mouth. "Once I had learned the last secret, the others didn't interest

me. But you do, small warrior. I ache to know if
you'll open these lips as trustingly as you opened the
rest of yourself.''

Janna saw the sensual curves of Raven's mouth and
the black, silky gleam of his mustache as he slowly
lowered his head. She tried to say his name but could
not. Her lips parted for him on a husky sigh. She felt
the tiny shudder that took him as he brought his
mouth to hers, joining them as completely as he had
joined their bodies a few minutes ago.

When Janna felt the hot touch of his tongue, her
whole body tightened with a surge of pleasure. His
taste swept through her, filling her senses. The tip of
his tongue found hers and teased it as he had once
teased her breast. She made an inarticulate sound and
ran her fingers across the powerful muscles of his
shoulders, testing his resilience. As he felt the tiny
bite of her nails his tongue thrust deeply into her and
withdrew almost instantly, as though he were afraid
of hurting her.

''Again,'' Janna whispered, burying her fingers in
the thickness of Raven's hair, pulling his head down
to her. ''Oh, please, kiss me like that again.''

He took her words and her mouth with a hoarse
sound, kissing her so fiercely that her neck arched
across the muscular thickness of his forearm. With an
effort he brought himself under control again.

''You're pure hell on my good intentions,'' Raven
said huskily, looking at Janna's reddened lips with a
combination of regret and raw hunger.

She looked up at his narrowed eyes and licked her
lips uncertainly. They tingled and felt hot and sensitive, and she wanted nothing more than to feel herself
crushed within Raven's arms again.

"What do you mean?" Janna whispered, touching her tongue to her lips again.

He smiled. "Lick my lips like that and I'll show you."

Janna's eyes widened. Her hands slid up to his cheeks and she held him as she pulled herself toward his mouth. She licked his lips slowly, loving the feel of his breath rushing hotly over her as he groaned. His fingers thrust deeply into her hair, pulling her head back until her neck was a creamy offering to his mouth and he could see her pulse beat heavily beneath her skin. He bit her lips with sensual restraint even as he held her arched helplessly between his powerful hands.

Shivering, watching his eyes, she breathed his name.

"What do you like from a man?" Raven asked. "Tell me and it's yours. Whatever you want, however you want it, for as long as you can take it. Just tell me."

"I don't know," she admitted. "My husband never wanted this." Janna's breath caught, then came out with a ragged sound as Raven's teeth closed delicately over the pulse beating in her throat.

"You told me all I need to know about your husband," Raven said, nuzzling against the sensitive lobe of her ear. "Now tell me what you wanted from your lovers."

"I don't know. You're the only one I ever had."

Janna felt Raven become utterly still. Slowly his head came up until he could look into her eyes. She tried to make a joke of her inexperience but the words stuck in her throat.

"Ever?" he asked, hardly able to believe that a

woman as sensual and generous as Janna had never found a man to enjoy her.

"I didn't think anyone would want me. Not really. I even read a whole shelf of how-to manuals for Mark but it didn't help."

Her words ended in a soft, tearing sound as Raven's tongue thrust into her ear. She moaned softly, and her nails bit into the flexed muscles of his chest.

"Books, huh?" growled Raven, biting her ear sensually, teasing her with his tongue, feeling heat burst through him at her helpless response. He laughed softly and thrust his tongue into her ear as his teeth gently devoured her. "Let me know if I miss any paragraphs that intrigued you."

"What?" Janna asked, not understanding anything except the sensations marching over her skin, heat and cold and pleasure impossibly mingling until she shivered.

"I'm going to love you, Janna. All of you," Raven said in a deep voice, biting her neck with enough force to leave small marks. "I'm going to love you until you moan and cry and come apart. And then I'm going to start all over again, and then again, until you would kill or die to have me inside you. That's when I'll take you and you'll take me, all of me, and it will be so good you'll scream."

It was a sensuous threat and a sensual promise, and Janna wanted both to come true. As she reached for Raven, his fingers laced through hers and he pulled her hands above her head. His black, glittering eyes and elemental male smile made her whole body arch as she tried to reach him, wanting to know the hot penetration of his body once again. When he saw the helpless movement of her legs he smiled and then swore lightly when his body went hard in a single wild rush. He shouldn't want her again this soon, this much, as though he had never taken her at all. But he did.

And if he let himself look at her hungry softness any longer, he would take her.

Janna gasped as she felt herself picked up and turned onto her stomach as though she weighed nothing. She started to ask a question, then forgot what she had wanted to say as his hands slid beneath her, capturing her breasts. Heat shivered through her as he kneaded her sensitive flesh until her nipples were hard and her breathing was ragged. She sensed his breath on her spine in the instant before his teeth closed on her nape. Caught between his caressing hands and his mouth, Janna moaned his name softly.

"Raven, I want to hold you," she said.

She made a broken sound as strong fingers rolled her nipples caressingly, tightening them until fire burst deep in the pit of her stomach. Her leg flexed in helpless response as she tried to roll onto her side, instinctively seeking the fulfillment of his body within hers. His knee slid between her legs, pinning her, making it impossible for her to roll over.

"Don't you want me to hold you?" she said.

"Oh, I want it," he said through clenched teeth. "Too much. You're so damned sexy you make me lose control," he gritted. "Can't you feel what you do to me?"

Janna felt the rigid power of Raven against her hip. She moved slowly, caressing and enjoying him in the only way that she could. A husky groan was her reward. Then his hand moved, raking tenderly down her spine until his fingers found the warm crease between

her hips. He followed that down and down until he
could hold her in his palm once more.

"All that heat waiting," Raven whispered as his
teeth sank sensually into Janna's hip. He laughed
deep in his throat as he stroked her with his hard
palm, hardly able to believe that she wanted him so
much. He said her name against her skin again and
again, leaving sensual marks each time.

Janna barely heard. Raven's caressing palm was
stripping away her breath, her thoughts, her control.
Instinctively she shifted, making more room for him
between her legs, wanting more of the incredibly sensual touch. Callused fingertips moved slowly, seeking
out and caressing her most sensitive flesh until she
made a broken sound and her hips moved with his
touch. He rewarded her with another love bite that
made her moan. He felt her warmth seep over him at
the gently stinging caress and heard her cry of pleasure.

"God," he said hoarsely, turning Janna over so
that he could bite the soft heat of her inner thigh.
"You make me want to cover you everywhere with
loving marks." He turned and nuzzled the hot secrets
that awaited him. "Everywhere," he said huskily as
his teeth closed on her with exquisite care.

Sensations raced through Janna, making her tremble violently.

"Raven, I—"

"You taste like the sea," he said. "Salty, mysterious, wild."

When Raven parted Janna's legs with his hands,
she gave him what he asked without hesitation, aban-
doning herself to him because there was no other
choice. The tight nub of her passion was no longer

hidden from him. He had found it and his sweet, hungry caresses were making her helpless. Her back arched as something wild speared through her, tightening her whole body.

"Raven?" she cried, sinking her nails heedlessly into his shoulders because he was the only thing real in a world that was coming apart in slow motion around her. "Raven!"

His only answer was a low sound as his teeth closed around her with dark restraint, holding her captive for his loving. His name broke from her lips in fragments as tension coiled within her body more tightly with each instant. She called his name again, frightened now, wholly at the mercy of the sensations spearing through her with every hot caress.

"It's all right," he said huskily, "I won't hurt you." He kissed her very gently, cherishing her tender flesh. "Give yourself to me, small warrior. Let me love you."

"Yes," she whispered as he kissed her again. "Oh, yes."

And then the heat and hunger of Raven's loving stripped the world away, leaving ecstasy in its place. His hands gripped Janna's hips, holding her against him as he caressed her, increasing the wild pleasure sleeting through her, listening to the husky cries he had called from her.

When the last shivering finally faded from Janna, Raven moved slowly up her body, licking the mist of passion from her skin. He wanted her with a violence that shook him, but he made no move to take her. He knew that she had found her release; he didn't expect her to want him now.

"Raven," she said, blindly seeking his lips. "Hold me. Please, hold me."

He felt her tears against his cheek and wrapped his arms tightly around her, finding both relief and torment in pressing his erect flesh against her.

"Be inside me," she whispered, touching him with loving fingers. The thought of being joined with him again made her tremble. "Let me hold all of you, Raven. Let me feel you moving inside me. Please."

Raven closed his eyes and struggled for control. He knew that Janna might as well have been a virgin, that he shouldn't take her again so soon. And he knew that if he didn't feel himself sheathed within her loving softness again he would die.

"Janna—" he began, trying to explain why it would be better for her if they waited.

"You were right," Janna interrupted, whispering against Raven's mouth as her nails bit into his powerful back, urging him closer to her. "I would kill or die to have you inside me."

Emotion swept through Raven, changing everything as the world shifted and faded away, leaving only the woman who watched him with luminous silver-green eyes. "I'll hurt you," he said harshly.

"No," Janna said, moving her hips so that Raven pressed gently against her softness. "I was made for your loving."

Raven felt the spreading heat of Janna's pleasure and wanted her even more now than he had the first time.

"Are you sure?" he asked huskily, easing into her even as he asked, ready to withdraw at the least sign of her discomfort.

"Oh, yes, I'm sure," she said throatily, feeling the

secret, hot movements of her body as pleasure shimmered deep within her again.

Raven felt Janna's pleasure as clearly as she did. He made a thick sound and took her mouth, kissing her deeply, moving slowly within her, drinking her soft cries of love. She was heat and a glittering promise surrounding him, calling to him, loving him. She sank into him like the mist into the forest, inseparable, penetrating his very core, filling him even as he filled her; and then ecstasy swept through them in a wild silver wind, stirring them until they cried out and clung to each other, knowing only each other, letting everything else spin away into darkness.

Seven

Janna awoke slowly, dreaming that she was lying out in the sun with heat pouring over her in a golden cascade. She smiled and stirred slowly, arching herself into the warmth.

Raven smoothed his hand down Janna's body again, enjoying her uninhibited sensuality. When he had discovered that she had never taken a lover, he had felt both fiercely proud—and guilty. He believed that if he hadn't saved her life, if they hadn't been locked up together in the inlet's savage, beautiful Eden, Janna wouldn't have wanted him any more than she had wanted other men.

Yet he had taken advantage of their isolation and her gratitude anyway, because he had never wanted a woman so much.

It was the same right now. He wanted Janna. Right or wrong, passion or gratitude, Eden or hell. He wanted her. She was the sound of laughter on the wind and a wild silver mist glittering within his soul. She was the mysterious taste of the sea and the hot generosity of life itself. He would have given the blood from his veins to believe that she would have come to him no matter where and how they had met.

But he knew that it wasn't true. If they had met in a normal way, she would have taken one look at his intimidating size and dark, rough looks, and then she would have smiled politely and walked away from him.

Raven knew that Janna was a gift given to a lonely raven by the old Haida gods, the cruel gods who gave only that they might teach man the agony of loss by taking back the gift. Raven also knew that there was no way to fight the gods, no way to keep the gift and evade the agonizing loss. He could only cherish Janna for the time that she was his, and open his hands when the time was over, freeing her and praying that she would never regret having given herself for a time to a man she didn't love.

"You look as though someone carved you from stone," Janna murmured sleepily. Her fingertips traced the fierce lines on Raven's face, lines that faded even as he turned to kiss her palm. "What were you thinking about?"

"Eden and the old Haida gods," Raven said, smoothing his cheek into the warmth of Janna's hand. "And Eve." He lifted his head and looked at the gift of the gods lying within his arms. "You're so beautiful," he whispered. "All woman, hot and generous. A man could die trying to get enough of you." He sank his teeth into her palm with sensual precision. "And I can think of no better way to step into eternity than listening to your sweet cries."

Janna stared at Raven stretched out on the bed beside her, as naked and rugged as the mountains themselves. Sunlight streamed through the porthole, pure light washing over his powerful body. He was so completely male, so very perfect in her eyes that she couldn't even speak to tell him how much it moved her to be desired by him. She could only touch him with a hand that trembled. The knowledge that she had pleased him gleamed in her eyes, tears shining in her lashes like distant stars. With a soft sound she went into the arms that opened for her in silent invitation.

"I love you, Raven," Janna said, holding him close. "I think I've loved you since the moment you pulled me out of the sea."

Raven closed his eyes as pain twisted through him. He kissed Janna very gently when she would have whispered her love again. Then he sealed Janna's lips with a long, callused finger.

"Don't," he whispered, looking at her silver-green eyes, wishing that she had never spoken. He had already guessed the source of any emotion she might have for him, the reason that he was set apart from other men in her eyes; he didn't need to be reminded that it was gratitude, not love, even when the reminder came in such a sweet and gentle way.

Janna stared at Raven, understanding only the pain in his bleak eyes, not the cause. "Raven?" she asked raggedly. "Don't you want—"

His lips came down over hers in a kiss that was as warm as sunlight and as powerful as the sea itself. He held her mouth for a long, long time, savoring her, wanting her.

"It's all right," Raven whispered finally against

Janna's lips. "You don't have to love me. I know that you're grateful to be alive. I'm grateful, too. Without you I wouldn't have known what it was like to die inside you and then to live again with you inside me. I wouldn't have known what it was like to be in Eden, to find myself in a place out of time where no one exists but a single man and a single woman who were created for each other."

With a swift movement Raven took Janna's mouth. He felt a fierce elation when she opened willingly for the tender penetration of his tongue. He drank from her deeply and felt himself taken from in return before he lifted his head and looked down into eyes as enigmatic as mist veiling the primeval forest.

"Let's take this time, this savage Eden, this gift," Raven said huskily, kissing Janna between each word. "Take it without labels or promises that will haunt you when Eden is a memory and the rest of your life is very real. I want you to remember me with joy, for that's how I will remember you."

Janna closed her eyes and tried very hard not to cry out with the mingled pain and pleasure of being with the man she loved, a man who laughed with her and wept with her—and did not love her. Yet he made love to her as though she were the only woman on earth.

But she was not. There was one other woman for Raven. The woman he loved and could not have. Angel.

Do you still love her?

Of course. And she loves me, too, now.

Janna knew that she couldn't change that; she could only envy it. And she could take the bittersweet gift that was Raven, take him and understand that love was like Eden—savage, innocent, knowing only its own existence, its own needs, a law unto itself, a primeval island set in an endless sea of time.

"Yes," Janna whispered, holding on to Raven until she ached, giving him all of herself that he would allow. "Yes, I want to be remembered with joy. Remember me, love. Remember that I loved you in a place out of time."

Raven tried to look into the green depths of Janna's eyes to the soul beneath, but he saw only the darkness of her long eyelashes and the silken swirl of her hair as her mouth caressed his chest. He started to speak but his breath caught. Her tongue was a dark, sweet flame burning over his skin and her cinnamon hair was wildfire caressing his arms.

He tried to slide his hands into her unbound hair. Before he could touch her, his whole body clenched and a hoarse sound was torn from his throat as her hands found his aroused flesh. She was woman and she was fire burning him all the way to his soul. With an inarticulate cry he found her softness, caressed her until she came to him and he could bury himself in her sweet, consuming fire, burning both of them alive.

The second time Janna woke up that morning, she was still locked within Raven's arms. She nuzzled the resilient chest hair that had been tickling her nose. He tightened his arms around her, silently telling her that he was awake. Smiling, she smoothed her cheek against his warm chest. Soundlessly she whispered *I love you* and accepted the stab of sadness that came with the knowledge that she wasn't loved in return. She was cherished, though, and enjoyed as a woman in a very elemental way. Every deliciously sensual ache in her body reminded her of that, as did her breast nestled warmly in Raven's big hand.

He might not love her, but he had given her a passion that grew greater each time they made love. For that alone, she would have stayed with him. When passion was joined with his gentleness and strength, his laughter and intelligence, Raven was revealed to her as the man she had always dreamed of and never truly believed she would find.

And she could not help hoping deep within her mind that any man who made love to her as Raven did could not be utterly lost to another woman. Surely Janna had a chance to steal his love with each kiss, each caress, each cry of ecstasy torn from him.

Janna nuzzled Raven again, realized that his flat nipple was within reach and touched it dreamily with the tip of her tongue. "Mmm. You taste good. Like an oyster. Salty."

"Want some lemon juice?"

"Raven on the half shell," Janna said, tasting him thoughtfully, then biting him with great care. "Nope. No lemon juice needed. Raw is best, the same way I found you."

Janna's stomach growled, reminding both of them that she had eaten nothing last night except a few oysters.

Smiling, Raven ran the ball of his thumb down her spine. "Want to flip to see who makes breakfast?"

"Heads," she said, then made a startled sound as she was picked up, turned over and gently placed face down on the bunk.

"Tails it is," Raven said, smoothing his palm over the supple curve of Janna's bottom. "Guess you lose.

Unless you want to flip me for it, of course,'' he added innocently.

Janna pushed hair out of her eyes, saw Raven's wicked smile and realized, ''I've been had.''

''Several times,'' he agreed, laughing. He lifted Janna, pulled her slowly across his body and set her on her feet in the galley aisle. ''And if you don't start breakfast soon,'' he added in a raspy voice as he nibbled on her thigh, ''it's lunch we'll be flipping over.'' His tongue flicked out and he smiled as he heard her breath catch. ''Or maybe dinner.''

Janna's fingers threaded into Raven's black hair. When he caressed her again, she called his name in a husky voice that made him groan.

''What am I going to do with you?'' he whispered. ''Each time I have you I want you more.''

She started to say something but all that came out was a tiny, wild sound as Raven's caresses became hotter, more intimate. ''No more oysters for you,'' she said, biting her lip against a broken sound of pleasure.

Raven's breath washed over Janna's sensitive skin as he shook his head and nuzzled her at the same time. ''If that legend were true,'' he murmured against her, ''men would have hunted oysters to extinction long ago.''

''Or women,'' retorted Janna.

He chuckled and nuzzled her soft flesh. ''Are you saying that men would have hunted women to extinction, or women would have hunted oysters?''

''Precisely,'' Janna said. ''I'm glad you understand. So many people are confused by a little straightforward ambiguity. What's for breakfast?''

He gave her body a look that made her knees weak.

''Raven,'' she breathed.

He closed his eyes. ''I think I'll take a swim in the inlet while you cook tinned ham, potatoes and powdered eggs. After we eat you can take a shower while I clean up the galley. Then we'll go for a walk in the village while we still can.''

''Still can?''

''Walk,'' Raven said succinctly. His eyes opened, and they glittered with sensual heat and laughter. ''Didn't you know, small warrior?'' he asked, his voice deep. ''We're going to kill each other in bed.'' His teeth flashed whitely beneath the black mustache as he pulled the torn remains of Janna's nightshirt from the sheets. ''Know something else?'' he asked, dangling the ripped cloth from his fingertip. ''I can hardly wait.''

Janna bit her lower lip, caught between laughter and anticipation, self-consciousness and the breathtaking memory of the instant when Raven had first taken her. She knew that her expression must have revealed her thoughts, because Raven's eyes became heavy lidded and intent as he watched. With a small sound she grabbed the shredded T-shirt and hid her flushed face in it. She wasn't used to this kind of sensual teasing any more than she was used to making love—or being in love.

''I guess you're going to insist on wearing another of my T-shirts,'' Raven said gravely.

She nodded without looking up.

He smiled gently. ''On one condition.''

Warily, Janna lifted her head. ''What's that?''

''The only thing you wear in bed is me.''

Raven didn't ask whether the strangled sound Janna made was agreement or disagreement. He simply stood up, kissed her thoroughly, grabbed a bar of soap and vanished over the *Black Star*'s railing into the chilly inlet.

Somehow Janna had managed not to burn, spill or scatter the ingredients of breakfast when Raven emerged from the inlet after his saltwater bath. Naked, powerful, he looked perfectly at ease in the wild land. He also took Janna's breath away, made her hands shake and her heart beat violently. She wished that the storm were still churning beyond the inlet, locking them in, locking the world out.

Unfortunately, by the time breakfast was eaten and Janna had taken a shower, it was obvious that the storm was definitely over. She dressed gloomily, wishing that she weren't going to be kicked out of Eden quite so quickly. She wondered if Raven had business waiting for him, business that couldn't wait, or if perhaps he wouldn't mind staying in Eden for a few days longer, giving her a chance to steal just a little bit more of his love.

"Janna, I found it!"

She pulled another one of Raven's dark, huge T-shirts over her head and called, "What?"

"A real sketchbook for you to use. I knew Angel had left it around here somewhere, but I couldn't remember where."

Janna zipped up her jeans and opened the door to the cubicle that was both shower stall and head.

"Sketchbook?" Janna asked, pushing a curtain of cinnamon hair aside. The thick, silky strands ignored her fingers, falling forward again as soon as she lifted her head. She pushed at the softly curling hair again, trying to ignore the emptiness in the pit of her stomach that came every time Angel's name was mentioned. "Is Angel an artist?"

"One of the best," Raven said, smiling as he remembered the stunning stained glass panel that Angel had done for his home on Vancouver Island. The panel showed the *Black Moon*, his longline trawler, skimming over a mysterious sea while salmon gathered below in a seething silver storm. "Galleries are lined up begging for her stained glass."

"Oh." Janna would have said more, but the thought of competing for Raven with a woman who was not only courageous, beautiful and blond but an artist, as well, turned Janna's normally quick mind to glue. "Life really isn't fair, is it?" she muttered under her breath.

"What?"

"Stained glass, huh?" Janna said, rallying her thoughts with an effort, saying the first thing that came to her tongue. "I saw a really gorgeous piece in a Seattle gallery last year. I wanted that panel so much I used to stand in front of it and just ache." The memory made Janna smile slightly at her own longing. "The glass reminded me of the Inside Passage at twilight, that magical time when all legends are true. There was rank upon rank of mountains falling away to the horizon in every shade of blue imaginable, and the sea was luminous, alive as only a god could be alive, breathing light and life into everything it touched. I wish to hell I could have afforded even a corner of that panel."

"Angel put a huge price on it because she couldn't bear to sell it," Raven said, smiling slightly. "It was one of her favorites."

"That was Angel's work?" Janna asked in disbelief.

Raven nodded. "She understands that the sea is the source of all life. She's a remarkable woman," he added, holding out the sketchbook to Janna. "Like you."

Janna didn't know whether to laugh or cry or scream at the sheer unfairness of it all. Bad enough to envy Angel Raven's love, but to admire her artistic skill as well was more than Janna's uncertain emotions could handle. Wordlessly she took the sketchbook and flipped through it. Only three of the pages had drawings on them, studies of driftwood on a wide, sandy beach. There was a balance of elements and a subtle elegance of line that tugged at Janna's senses, telling her of the artist's understanding of opposites and unity.

"I shouldn't use this," she said. "Angel might—"

"She wouldn't mind," Raven interrupted quickly. "These were just preliminary sketches. The finished piece was a gift to my grandfather."

Janna closed the sketchbook and looked at Raven with doubt in her silver-green eyes.

"Use it," Raven urged. "That way you won't have to go all the way to Masset and then all the way back here just to sketch the totems at dawn. Now that I've found a real sketchbook, you can stay a few days longer, can't you?" He stopped abruptly. "Unless you have to get back to Masset right away for some reason?"

Janna smoothed her fingers over the sketchbook while happiness made her eyes as luminous as the sea itself. "No," she said huskily, "I don't have to be anywhere at all. I'd like to spend a few more days in Eden. With you, Raven.''

The pleased yet almost shy smile that Janna gave Raven made him reach for her and wrap her warmly in his arms. He inhaled her clean, womanly scent and closed his eyes, hardly able to believe his luck. A few more days in Eden.

And if his conscience gave him hell for taking advantage of Janna's gratitude, for keeping her away from the civilization that would take her from his arms as surely as night took the sun from the sky, then he would just point out to his conscience that it was only a few days, just a few, and Janna had so many thousands of days left in her life. Surely even after her feeling of gratitude wore off, she wouldn't look back and regret having spent those few extra days with a lonely raven.

"I found some pencils, too. Funny-looking ones," he said huskily. "Angel left them with the sketchbook. Want to see if they're the kind you need?''

"Sure," Janna said, holding Raven's big body until her arms ached, then reluctantly letting go.

The "funny looking" pencils turned out to be everything Janna would need to do finished drawings. She examined the pencils reverently, only to look up and see Raven watching her with an intensity that made her breath stop.

"You touch them as though they were magic," he said.

"They are," Janna said simply. "With them, I can draw. Without them, I'm a nightingale without a love song."

"In other words, a raven. Ravens sing love songs only in their dreams."

Janna hesitated, caught by the regret and acceptance that lay beneath Raven's words. "Then the raven's love song must be the most beautiful of all," she said softly, "for it's sung in silence."

Raven looked at her for a long moment before he smiled sadly. "You have the most beautiful eyes I've ever seen, Janna. Like the forest veiled in mist. Silver and green and radiant with life."

Not knowing what to say except *I love you*, the very words that Raven didn't want to hear, Janna smiled as sadly as he had. In silence he took the pencils from her and packed them carefully in a rucksack along with the sketchbook. She followed him to the makeshift dock. She was getting accustomed to the logs, but she still wasn't nearly as adept as Raven was. She was relieved to feel the rocky shore beneath her feet.

"There used to be paths here," Raven said.

He swept his broad hand in an arc across the shoreline. It was overgrown with salt-tolerant plants that crept above the tide line and blended into a mass of cedar, ferns and moss beds deeper than a mattress. After the first few steps Janna understood why the Haidas had depended on canoes rather than their feet for transportation.

Only where the ocean actually washed over the land could rock be seen. The rest of the inlet was covered in a seamless, multihued green blanket of life. If trees didn't grow in a given place, it was because the earth was too wet to support them. Boggy areas were common. Even in the forest itself it was rare to see bare bark or wood. Moss hung in beards and veils from every surface. Deadfalls were draped in thick blankets of deceptively solid-looking moss, making green traps that waited to be sprung by unwary feet. Often trees grew so close together that nothing could squeeze between. Animal life abounded, but was nearly invisible—and therefore safe from man. It was almost impossible to hunt even something as large as a bear or a deer for the simple reason that the hunter could see only a few feet beyond the barrel of his rifle.

On the other hand, if the land were impenetrable, the sea was not. Steep-sided inlets and deep sounds provided natural shelter from storm and wind. Fish abounded. Shellfish were always within reach. The ancient Haidas had wisely taken the sea's gifts and used only the narrow margin of land just beyond high tide mark. It was there that they built their cedar lodges and carved totem poles as tall as the tallest cedar trees. The totems stood facing the sea, their weathered faces bathed in the salt-laden wind. Raven identified the highly stylized symbols for Janna, pointing out the killer whale and the frog, the salmon and the eagle and the raven with wings spread on top of the pole.

"What are you going to do while I sketch?" Janna asked, pencil poised over pad.

"What I came here to do. Think."

She looked at Raven hastily, feeling guilty for having interrupted him. He cupped his broad palm under her chin and tipped her face up to his.

"I came here because I felt…restless. I don't feel that way anymore." Raven brushed his lips over Janna's. "If I didn't want to be here with you, we'd be on our way to Masset right now. Go ahead and sketch all you want. I'll be nearby if you need me." He started to walk away, then turned back. "Don't go into any of the old lodges. They're just waiting for an excuse to collapse.''

"I won't," Janna said. She turned to look at the cedar houses slowly dissolving back into the land from which they had come. "The lodges belong to other people. It would be like trespassing."

"You mean you don't want to take them apart looking for beads and bones?" he asked sardonically.

Janna looked at Raven's impassive face. Slowly she shook her head. "There would be no point. I'm not an archaeologist. I can't recreate a lost past from a handful of fragments. So I'd rather just sit and sketch and let the ghosts whisper to me across the years."

Raven looked at Janna for a long moment, a look as consuming as any kiss he had ever given her. Then he touched her mouth with his fingertips, turned away and stepped into the forest.

He vanished.

Janna blinked, unable to believe that a man as big as Raven could disappear so quickly. She took several steps forward and saw the moss springing back into place where Raven's footsteps had compressed it. She took two more steps and stopped suddenly. Evergreens and moss surrounded her. There was no sky, no sea, no true ground, just the forest primeval enfolding her in a scented embrace. Even as she watched, the last evidence of Raven's passage vanished, leaving her utterly alone.

For a moment she stood without moving, caught by the elemental stillness of the forest. Then through the trees came the harsh, primitive cry of a raven searching for its mate. In the distance came a sound that could have been an answer. Janna held her breath, listening, but heard no more. The raven called again, farther away now, a shimmering black shadow skimming over endless shades of green.

After a few moments Janna turned and went toward the shore, knowing that if she attempted the forest alone she would be hopelessly lost within a few steps. There were no trails, no piled stones to point the way, no blazes old or new to mark the passage of man. She walked along the margin of land and sea. For a long time she stood wrapped in silence, looking at the massive icons of another time, another race, another culture, another way of looking at the complex mystery of life. She found totems that were canted, on the edge of toppling over, and totems that had fallen long ago. She found totems in which the cedar itself had somehow survived the carving and had taken root once more, sending out fragrant branches. The sight of faces watching her from between the lacy branches made the hair stir on Janna's neck, as though gods had come and taken root in the Queen Charlottes' savage Eden.

When Janna knew she could absorb no more of the emotional currents sweeping through and around her, she found a log that was thickly encrusted with moss, sat down and was soon lost in her sketches. Several hours passed before she looked up. Raven was back. She could sense his presence as surely as she had sensed that the Queen Charlottes were islands set apart from time. She looked over her shoulder and smiled. Raven's black eyes kindled in response.

"How long have you been there?" she asked.

"Long enough to admire your stillness, your concentration, your elegance," he said in a deep, soft voice. "You're like a doe listening for danger at the edge of the forest."

Janna's eyes widened to reveal silver-green depths. She had never thought of herself as elegant or doelike. The realization that Raven saw those qualities in her was an immaterial caress shivering over her.

"Are you ready for a break?" Raven asked, glancing down at the sketch pad.

"My hand is numb," she admitted. "It's been a long time since I've drawn for that many hours. There's so much here, so many emotions, so little time to capture even the smallest echo of Eden...."

Raven took the pad and pencils from Janna and packed them carefully. "Follow me," he said, shouldering the rucksack. "I have something I want to show you."

She followed without question as he turned back to the forest that knew neither trail nor the possession of man. Within moments the sea was invisible, its sounds and scents lost. Nothing penetrated the mist-haunted silence but the distant cry of a raven.

"Stay in my footsteps," he cautioned. "We have to walk the edge of a small bog."

Soon the forest in front of them thinned dramatically, giving way to a clearing, where stunted evergreens struggled to maintain a toehold in land too wet to support them. The surface appeared solid, but Raven's footprints glistened with water squeezed from the humus by his weight. Water stood in small pools stained the color of tea by tannin leached from the surrounding forest. The water trickled away in small rills and rivulets until they came together in a creek. The water was absolutely clean, utterly unique in its amber clarity.

A small cabin stood just beyond the bog. The walls were of weathered cedar and the roof was finished with cedar shingles. Moss grew from every crevice between the shingles and clung to the walls. Yet the cabin was new rather than old; windows gleamed against the darker backdrop of the forest and the front door was finished with metal hinges.

"How did you find it?" Janna asked softly as she came up to stand beside Raven.

"I built it with my own hands."

She turned and looked at him. His eyes were very black, yet like the creek they were crystalline in their clarity. He was looking at the tiny cabin but he was seeing something else from his past, something that haunted him. His high cheekbones, straight nose and the powerful line of his jaw had never looked more solid, more elemental, a man carved from the enduring things of the earth.

"Come," Raven said quietly, turning to Janna and holding out his hand.

The hard warmth of Raven's palm sent a tremor through Janna. She laced her fingers deeply with his as he led her to the cabin. There was no lock on the door, no bolt, nothing to keep out intruders. In Eden there were no intruders, just one man and one woman and the land that knew no time.

Raven opened the door, lifted Janna into his arms and carried her into the shelter that he had built years ago. He left the door open, inviting in the fragrance of cedar and the unearthly radiance of mist-filtered light. There was little furniture in the room—a table, a chair, shelves that held shells and glass fishing floats that had drifted across the empty Pacific to be washed up on a distant shore. A fire was laid in a hearth that had been built from water-smoothed beach stones. Blankets had been folded to make a sleeping pallet close to the hearth.

"I would have brought you here sooner," Raven said as he kissed Janna's hair, "but there's only one room, only one place to sleep, and I was trying very hard to keep my hands off you." He smiled almost sadly. "I failed rather spectacularly, didn't I?"

"I'm glad," Janna said, pressing her lips against the corded muscles of his neck. "I love your hands on me, Raven."

His powerful arms flexed as he whispered her name, shifting her in his grasp until he could capture her mouth. The taste of him swept through her like a wind from the sea. She made a small sound at the back of her throat as she felt herself sliding over his hard body. With one arm he caught her hips against his own and moved slowly. She shivered and clung to his strength, knowing again the elemental pleasure of having him desire her.

Reluctantly Raven let Janna slide the rest of the way down his body until her feet touched the floor. He bit her lips in a series of tiny, hard kisses that made her breath break into a moan. When his tongue thrust slowly into her mouth she moved against him with sensual abandon. He groaned, let his mouth mate with hers for a wild moment, then lifted his head.

"No more," he said almost roughly.

"Why not?" Janna murmured, standing on tiptoe to kiss the pulse beating violently in Raven's throat.

"Because I promised myself that I would feed you first."

"What a lovely idea," she murmured, kicking out of her tennis shoes and stepping out of her jeans and panties with a few quick motions. "I thought you hadn't noticed that there were a few paragraphs you overlooked."

"Help," Raven said, but his smile said that the long, curving length of Janna's body was beautiful to him.

"You know," Janna said as she began to unbutton the big shirt that fit her like a dress.

Then she looked up and saw Raven's smile and decided that the shirt could wait. She would much rather touch him. With fingers that trembled she opened his flannel shirt, discovering the male textures of hair and hard muscle beneath.

"What paragraphs?" Raven persisted, though his pulse beat visibly, strongly, quickening with every touch of her mouth.

"That shelf of books that I read."

"Are you trying to tell me that last night I overlooked some paragraphs that intrigued you?" Raven's breath hissed in as Janna's tongue traced the flat disk of his nipple. He groaned when her teeth scraped delicately over him, bringing him to a hard point that she teased with her lips. "Did I miss something?" he asked hoarsely.

"Only the paragraphs dealing with ways to pleasure a man. An understandable oversight on your part," Janna added, smiling as she found and nuzzled Raven's other nipple into erect sensitivity. "After all," she pointed out reasonably, "I'm not a man."

Raven's big hand smoothed over her bare, silky hip and then tangled in the warm thatch of hair between her thighs. She was incredibly soft, hot, melting at his touch, and the knowledge that she wanted him as much as he wanted her made him feel heavy and very male.

"You're right," he said deeply, sliding his fingertips into Janna's utterly feminine heat. "You're definitely not a man," he groaned, loving her soft flesh with slow movements of his hand. "And I thank God for it."

Janna's fingers clenched on Raven's belt as she felt the first shimmering forerunners of ecstasy stream through her. Biting her lip against a moan, she tugged at the belt buckle until it opened. Beneath her fingers the warm metal buttons on Raven's jeans gave way with soft popping sounds.

"Janna…"

Raven's breath caught and his hips jerked reflexively against her caressing hands. His fingers closed over hers, preventing her from undressing him.

"Raven?" she asked softly, kissing the suddenly hot skin of his chest. "Don't you want me to touch you?"

He made a tearing sound that could have been laughter or a curse. "I'd die to have you touch me," he said roughly. "But if you take off my jeans, I'm going to open your legs and…" The words ended in a groan when Janna's fingers caressed Raven through the soft cotton of his underwear. "Don't undress me," he growled, dragging his open mouth across her forehead, her cheek, her lips, tasting her, needing her. "There are other ways I want to love you before I slide into you."

"Whatever you say," Janna murmured as she eased her fingers into the front opening of Raven's briefs.

She felt every muscle in his body tighten when she

discovered and freed his erect flesh, bringing it into her caressing hands.

"Janna—"

"You're still dressed," she pointed out, slowly stroking Raven with hands that were both gentle and possessive, smiling at his hot response.

"You can get arrested for being 'dressed' like this," he retorted, stifling a groan of pure sensual pleasure as she rubbed slowly over him.

"There aren't any police in paradise," Janna said dreamily, absorbed in appreciating the results of her handiwork. When Raven didn't answer, she glanced up almost guiltily. His face was drawn, and his eyes were narrow black slits. "You don't mind being—"

"Looked at the way a cat looks at cream?" offered Raven.

His smile made Janna weak. "Is that how I'm looking at you?" she whispered.

"Yes," he said huskily. "And it makes me feel ten feet tall and as hard as the mountains."

"You are."

"Only with you," he said, shuddering heavily and thrusting between her palms. "Only with you."

With a harsh sound Raven buried one hand in Janna's thick auburn hair, pulling her head back until her body arched into his. With his other hand he began unbuttoning her shirt, but the sweet fire of her fingers kept distracting him.

"You're hell on my clothes," Raven rasped.

His arm flexed and the shirt parted beneath his big hand, sending buttons flying. He rubbed his palm across the hardened tip of Janna's breast until she called his name on a broken sound of pleasure. He caught the sensitive nipple between his fingers and tugged, smiling fiercely as she moaned.

"Come closer," Raven said, his voice so deep it was a growl. "Closer, small warrior. I'll show you another way to tease me. And you. Oh God, come closer!"

Raven's fingers shifted, sliding down Janna's body until he could rub lightly over the softness hidden between her legs. When she opened to invite a deeper touch he smiled and moved his hips suddenly, sliding his hot flesh between her legs. Her eyes widened with surprised and then became heavy-lidded with pleasure as his hips moved again. She held him more tightly against herself and moved her hips in turn, stroking him, watching him, enjoying the frank sensuality of his smile. Her fingers pressed him closer and then closer still, wanting more of him, needing him in a way that shook her.

"Raven, I..."

Janna's breath caught in a moan as she felt heat spreading out from her body, heat caressing Raven's male flesh, heat pleading for him to share it as it was meant to be shared...deeply. She opened her eyes and saw his face contorted as though he were in torment. She knew then that he wanted her so much that not taking her was agony for him. Instinctively she shifted, guiding him, pressing him into her softness. But that only increased the sweet agony, reminding them with every breath what it would be like to be completely joined.

Raven's eyes opened suddenly, utterly black, nearly wild with need. The pallet was across the room. It might as well have been across the world. He had to be inside Janna. He had to have her *now*.

His arms closed around her with sudden, savage strength.

"Wrap your legs around me," he said, lifting her without warning. "Put your arms around my neck now and—yes—now!" he said hoarsely, thrusting into her welcoming body, feeling her close hotly around him.

Raven knew that his hands were probably bruising Janna with their powerful grip, but he couldn't force himself to let go. She was demanding him, every bit of him, with an abandon he could only fiercely enjoy. He drove into her again and again, watching her eyes haze with silver as she began to come apart in his arms. He felt the tiny ecstatic ripples deep within her body, the spreading satin heat of her response, and he savored her nails pricking him with each sweet cry that was torn from her lips. He fought to control himself but it was impossible, the pleasure he felt was too savage, too deep, pulse after pulse of ecstasy pouring out of him, shaking him to his soul.

Janna closed her eyes and rested her head on Raven's powerful shoulder as she whispered her love too softly for him to hear.

But he did hear. He spoke her name in the silence of his mind, apologizing for keeping her in his savage Eden, promising to release her in just one more day, giving her back to her own life. Just one more day, one among thousands.

I think I've loved you since the moment you pulled me out of the sea.

Raven brushed his lips over Janna's hair and wished bitterly that gratitude were another name for love.

Eight

Janna watched the harbor at Masset slide closer with every instant. Futilely she wished that the *Black Star*'s engines would fail or that the storm could have lasted a few more days, a few more weeks, forever. But that was a dream. Reality was Raven guiding the boat smoothly to a rest against the commercial dock to fill up on fuel. Reality was the fact that Raven had said nothing to her about seeing her again after she walked off the boat. Reality was a numbness spreading through Janna's soul, freezing her.

Raven glanced at Janna and then quickly looked away. The closer they had come to Masset, the more she had retreated from him. He wasn't surprised by her withdrawal, but he was surprised by the tearing pain that he felt because of it. He had known nothing like it, even when Angel had turned on him in her rage and her despair. He wanted to go to Janna and hold her close against his body, to hear her words of love just once more. The temptation was almost overwhelming.

Grimly Raven flexed his hands on the wheel, relaxing them. It was bad enough that he had taken Janna when she would have been vulnerable to any man. If he prolonged his own pleasure at her expense any longer, he wouldn't be able to meet his own eyes in the shaving mirror.

"Want 'em topped, Raven?" called the lanky boy running the pumps.

Raven waved his agreement without looking up.

Because it hurt too much to watch Raven, Janna turned her attention to the boy. He had black hair and dark brown eyes and a promise of future power in his long body. Janna noticed his confidence as he tied off the boat and wondered if Raven had looked like that as a teenager. The realization that she would never know was another kind of pain lancing through her.

"You seen Uncle yet?" asked the boy.

"No," Raven said, vaulting easily up onto the dock. Other men hailed him. He waved in answer, but didn't look away from the boy. "Did he want me for something? Is that gallery agent holding up payment again?"

Raven's voice sounded unusually deep, impossibly resonant, carrying across the water like the tone of a perfectly cast bell. For the first time in days Janna was conscious of Raven's sheer size. He was literally head and shoulders above the men around him. Yet to her it was the other men who looked wrong, different, out of place, unreal. Raven had become the standard against which she measured others. The realization shocked her.

"Nah," the boy muttered, jiggling the nozzle against the boat. "That agent ain't said nothing but yessir and nosir since you told him there was plenty of white galleries that'd take Uncle's carvings, pay him on time and kiss his Indian ass in the bargain."

Janna saw Raven's razor smile and realized that although he had always cherished her, even at the times of his greatest need, there was a core of cold savagery in him—and that he used it to protect those he loved.

"Glad to hear it," Raven said with satisfaction. "What's the problem, then?"

"Uncle says he's falling in love and it's all your fault." Strong white teeth gleamed in the boy's tanned face.

"Oh?" Raven grumbled. "What have I done now?"

The boy jerked his chin in the direction of the land. "You left her in Uncle's lap while she was waiting for you to get back from Totem Inlet."

Janna saw Raven turn and look up the dock toward land. Suddenly his face was transformed, all darkness gone, a broad smile flashing as he held out his arms. The slender blonde who had been sneaking down the dock to surprise Raven laughed and ran toward him openly, throwing herself into his arms with the confidence of a woman who knows she will be caught and held securely. Raven's big arms closed around her, and he whirled around and around on the dock while the woman laughed joyously and clung to him.

Feeling as though she were being spun around herself, Janna swayed and then leaned against the cabin wall, wondering where all her strength had gone. She could barely stand. Only then did she admit to herself how much she had hoped that a man as passionately and wildly aroused as Raven had been when they made love must have been at least a little bit involved with his emotions as well as his body.

Oh, he's in love, all right, Janna admitted to herself. *But not with me. I was just a temporary Eve in Raven's own savage Eden.*

Janna looked away from the slender, elegant blonde who was only now being set down on feet shod in Italian leather sandals. Glumly Janna looked at her own feet. They were covered by tennis shoes that were cracked from repeated bouts with salt water and the galley oven. The unflattering comparisons didn't stop there, either. Instead of wearing a clingy sea-green sweater, her own body was draped in an over-size man's shirt whose sleeves kept coming unrolled over her knuckles. Instead of smooth, scented hands, her own were chapped by seawater and covered by various nicks and welts that had come from wrestling with stubborn oyster shells.

No wonder Raven had only wanted a few days with her. Lord, the wonder was that he had wanted her at all. He must have been alone in that inlet for months to even look at her, much less to make love to her as though she were the last woman on earth—or the first.

Finished feeling sorry for yourself yet? Janna inquired sardonically of her frazzled reflection in the cabin window.

No. I'm just getting started. Try me in a few years. I might be finished by then.

I can't wait. Quit complaining and pull up your socks.

I'm not wearing socks.

Pull them up anyway.

Janna closed her eyes, rested her forehead against the cold glass and remembered all the times she had pulled up her socks and gotten on with life even when it hurt to breathe. She had no right to complain about the fact that Raven loved a woman he couldn't have and didn't love Janna, who loved him. Raven didn't love her, but he had given her the gift of himself for a few days. She had known what it was like to see a man's eyes kindle with laughter and desire as he watched her. She had known what it was like to evoke a fierce, elemental response from Raven's powerful body, to pleasure him and to be pleasured in turn.

She should be on her knees right now thanking him rather than trying not to cry because a few days weren't a lifetime. Nobody had promised her a lifetime. Nobody had promised her a damn thing. She could have died before she had ever known Raven.

She almost had.

"Are you all right?"

Janna's eyes flew open. The voice was deep, but not as deep as Raven's. The boat dipped beneath the man's weight as he came aboard. He was tall, but not as tall as Raven. He was strong, but he didn't have Raven's unusually powerful build. His hair was just as black, though, and in a lean, hard way he was as handsome as any man Janna had ever seen.

"Hawk," Janna said, remembering Raven's description of the man Angel loved. *Handsome as sin.*

A black eyebrow arched in silent query, giving an almost satanic cast to Hawk's face. His eyes were an odd shade of golden brown, like whiskey or the bird of prey he took his nickname from. "Have we met?"

"Only in a Raven's mind."

"A raven? Oh, Carlson." Hawk's mouth curled up

slightly beneath a black mustache as he looked at Janna wrapped so intriguingly in what was obviously not her shirt. The mismatch between the shirt's size and her own had the effect of emphasizing how different her body was from a man's. "Leave it to Carlson to go out fishing and come back with a stunning mermaid."

Janna's mouth turned down in a sad curve. She felt more stunned than stunning.

"Are you sure you're all right?" Hawk asked gently.

"Sure. Just pulling up my socks."

"You aren't wearing any."

"Yeah. That's where the real challenge comes in."

Hawk smiled suddenly.

Janna blinked. She had never seen a smile quite so unexpected, like a fire burning beneath glacial ice, a promise of warmth radiating magically through the cold.

"My God," Janna said, shaking her head, "I'll bet when you and Raven walk down a street together you can hear female hearts breaking like dropped crockery."

There was an instant of startled stillness before Hawk's smile became a warm male laugh that was every bit as unexpected and as beautiful as his smile had been.

Raven turned toward the sound, still holding Angel. "I see you've met Janna," he said, grinning. "She has the most incredible—"

"Sense of humor," Janna interrupted wearily. "With that and two quarters you can get a cup of coffee."

Raven's eyes narrowed at the flatness he heard in

Janna's voice. It reminded him painfully of the night when she had fled his heavy-handed company and locked herself in the bow to sketch. Janna didn't see his sudden scrutiny as she pushed away from the cabin's support.

"Do you need to get anything from the boat?" Hawk asked, looking between Janna and Raven with barely concealed curiosity.

She drew a deep breath, grabbed the tops of her nonexistent socks and pulled. "Not a thing," she said with forced cheer. "That's one of the joys of shipwreck—no excess baggage. No baggage of any kind, as a matter of fact. What you see is what you get."

An arched black eyebrow lifted in query again but Hawk said nothing. Enviously Janna watched as he mounted the dock in a single lithe movement. The gap between boat and dock looked enormous to her. She was certain that she would stumble and go sprawling, further separating herself in Raven's eyes from the ever-perfect, ever-unattainable Angel.

"Let me help."

Startled, Janna looked up into compassionate golden-brown eyes. She held up her arms and was lifted onto the dock as gracefully as though she were a prima ballerina.

"Thanks," she said. "With my luck I'd have taken a header into the bay."

Janna's glance slid past Hawk to where Raven and Angel stood arm in arm. Suddenly a swim in the bay seemed preferable to walking down the dock and smiling cheerfully as she said goodbye to the man she loved.

"Rough trip?" Hawk asked, following the direction of Janna's glance.

"Yeah, you could say that. Lost my boat, lost my engine, lost my camping gear, my sketchbook, my…"

"Heart," finished Hawk too softly for anyone but Janna to hear.

Her mouth flattened into a line of pain. Those odd-colored eyes saw far too much.

"An overrated organ," Janna said, shrugging. "The body seems to function quite well without it."

Hawk started to say something. Janna cut him off with an overly bright smile and a rush of words.

"I'm sure the three of you have a lot to catch up on," she said firmly. "Tell Raven that I'll leave his shirt with the gas jockey."

"Why don't you tell me yourself?" Raven asked, walking up in time to overhear Janna's words.

His voice was very deep, almost harsh. He saw Angel's swift, assessing look in his direction and realized that he wasn't concealing his anger very well. But he hadn't expected to look up and see Janna nestled trustingly between Hawk's hands, to see her watching Hawk's face as though she expected a second sunrise to take place there at any moment.

Nor had Raven expected Janna to vanish from his life without so much as a word. He had known that gratitude was a fleeting emotion, yet the idea that Janna could walk away from the past few days as though they had never happened enraged him. Before he realized what he was doing, Raven found himself pressing Janna in exactly the way that he had promised himself he wouldn't.

"You can give me the shirt tomorrow, when I pick you up," he said to Janna, and his tone said that he wouldn't take no for an answer.

"Pick me up," Janna repeated numbly, feeling her heart turn over as she tried desperately not to hope that Raven was reluctant to let her go.

"For a picnic on a north-facing beach. If it's clear. Very clear. Otherwise any beach will do," he added.

"Very clear," she said, when it was anything but.

"Right. That's the only time you can really see the illusions."

Janna took a deep breath. "Help."

The hard lines left Raven's face as he smiled. His hand snaked out, wrapped around the nape of Janna's neck and gently pulled her close, disengaging her from Hawk's grasp in the process.

"I'm glad you remembered what I'm good for," Raven growled.

"Help?"

"Among other things."

"Oh help," Janna breathed raggedly, feeling herself go soft in the head and everywhere else at the feel of Raven's big, warm hand on her sensitive nape. "You're making it very hard for me to be noble," she said, speaking before she thought. She winced. Not thinking before she spoke was a chronic condition for her around Raven.

"Noble?" he asked, his black eyes searching her face.

"I…I thought you might want to get on with the, uh, reunion without any…any outsiders to get in the way."

Raven said something succinct and harsh under his breath. "If there's anything that gives me a tired butt, it's nobility," he added, ignoring the fact that his anti-nobility statement was self-serving. Nobility required him to give up Janna right away. Suddenly he was damned if he were going to do that. She had a few more days in the Queen Charlottes before she had to go back to Seattle. There wasn't one reason on earth they couldn't spend those days together. A lot of reasons why they *shouldn't*, but none why they *couldn't*. "Unless you're too behind in your sketching to take the time to spend a few days sight-seeing with me?"

For an instant Janna closed her eyes, unable to bear the dark clarity of Raven's eyes looking at her, into her, seeing too much. Just as she was seeing too much. Whatever else Raven might feel for Angel, there was no deep, reckless current of desire beneath his obvious love for her. Yet Janna knew that Raven was capable of intense sensuality and white-hot, elemental desire, for she had been the focus of both. Raven didn't love Janna, but he wanted her.

And she wanted him in the same way. If the savage, shimmering wine of sensual ecstasy was all that he could accept from Janna, then she wouldn't withhold it. She couldn't. She loved him too much to deny him anything.

Janna didn't notice the two other people watching her—Hawk with compassion and Angel with growing surprise and delight. Janna saw only Raven, the man she had waited a lifetime to find.

And to lose.

But not yet. She had a few days left in this wild Eden. She would spend them with the man she loved.

"I don't need to sketch anymore," she said, her tone husky. "I found everything I needed in Totem Inlet." The words came back to Janna, haunting her with too many meanings. "For my work," she added quickly, tearing her glance away from Raven's. "Thanks to Angel."

"Your sketchbook," Raven explained to Angel without looking away from Janna.

Angel blinked her beautiful sea-green eyes at him, turned toward Hawk and said, "Must be those Tlingit shaman genes shorting out the brain again."

"Tlingit?" Janna asked, not looking away from Raven. "I thought you were Haida."

"Mostly. One of my grandparents was a Tlingit shaman. Angel says that's where I get my fishing luck and streak of cruelty."

"Carlson!" Angel said, dismayed. "That's not what I said and you know it!"

Janna looked at Raven's off-center smile and wanted to cry. "You're not cruel," she said.

"Oh, but I am," he countered softly, his eyes bleak. "Remember? Sometimes comfort just doesn't get the job done."

"That's not cruelty, that's just a very difficult way to be kind," Angel said, putting her hand on the thick muscle of Raven's forearm. "If you had enjoyed my pain, then it would have been cruelty. Just because I was too selfish to see your kindness at the time doesn't change reality. You helped me, Raven." She laughed suddenly, a sound that was surprisingly sad. "You did more than help me. Without you I wouldn't have made it."

Raven hesitated, then picked up Angel's hand, kissed it softly and replaced it on his arm. "I'm glad you feel that way, Angel Eyes. I hated hurting you."

"It was nothing to what I did to you. If you only knew how many times I've regretted what I said to you." Angel took a deep breath and let it out slowly. She turned toward Janna and smiled apologetically. "You must think we're all crazy."

"No," Janna said quietly. "I think that Raven is very good at saving lives, at being kind even when it hurts, at being…a man. More man than I've ever met."

She clasped her hands together and hoped no one could see that her fingers were shaking from the reaction that had come when Raven had picked Angel's hand up and kissed it so gently, so sadly. Seeing Raven with the woman he loved and couldn't have was tearing at Janna in ways that she would never have expected. It wasn't just herself that she was hurting for. It was Raven.

"He saved my life, too," Janna continued in a tight, desperately calm tone. "And he won't even let me thank him."

"Gratitude is like milk," Raven said roughly. "It's bland, coats your tongue and turns sour after a few days." He turned toward the boy who was manning the fuel pump. "You finished yet?"

"Gettin' there."

"Good," Raven growled, impatient to be off the dock. "Where do you live?" he asked, turning back to Janna.

"In a small house on the beach at the edge of the park."

Raven frowned. "The shack with the bear feet hanging on the mailbox?"

"Is that what they are? I was pretty sure, but I was afraid to ask." Janna shuddered, remembering her horror when she had encountered the mailbox in the twilight rain. "The first time I saw them I thought they were bare feet as in no shoes, no socks, nothing but bones. Human. There was no reason to think otherwise. The claws had been cut off, and the articulation of the foot bones and ankle looked just the same as I remembered from my anatomy class. I nearly turned around and ran for the RCMP.''

Almost reluctantly, Raven grinned. ''You wouldn't have been the first. The Mounties had a bad summer a few years back. Someone shot several bears, took the claws and skin and dragged the carcasses out to sea. The beachcombers who found the feet washed up with rope around the ankles felt the same way about it that you did. So did the Mounties until they figured out what had happened.'' His smile faded. ''Nadine has a grisly sense of humor. Has she fixed up that shack you're renting?''

''It only leaks when it rains,'' Janna said, shrugging.

''Like the boat,'' retorted Raven. ''It only leaked when it was floating. Now it doesn't leak at all.''

Raven's narrowed eyes told Janna that he disapproved of her summer lodging. Well, there was nothing she could do about that. The price had been right and had included the use of a boat and an outboard engine. Unfortunately, both boat and engine were at the bottom of Totem Inlet.

''Know any place to buy a used boat?'' Janna asked, then added hastily, ''Cheap.''

''I'll take care of it,'' Raven said. ''Old Nadine has gouged her last tourist.''

''That isn't necessary. I can—''

''Care to flip me for it?'' Raven interrupted smoothly.

Janna started to argue, took one look at the suddenly hard lines on Raven's face and decided that now wasn't the time to object. She had discovered that every time she mentioned Nadine's boat, Raven lost his sense of humor. Janna knew why. He kept thinking that if he had slept harder or started out to help later or never been at the inlet at all, Janna would have drowned.

The same thought had occurred to Janna more than once, usually in the small hours of the night, bringing her awake with her heart pounding. It had been very reassuring to feel Raven's warm presence by her side at those moments, to curl against his body as he gathered her close, to fall asleep knowing that she was safe.

"No, I don't care to flip you for it," Janna admitted, smiling slightly. "You use the damnedest coins."

Raven smiled in return, remembering both Janna's startled look and the creamy curves of her bottom as he had stroked it. "That leaves dinner to settle." He turned toward Hawk. "You two staying with Uncle?"

"He wouldn't hear of anything else."

"I'll bet. Uncle has an eye for beauty. Better keep Angel on a short leash. Uncle's quite the lady's man."

Hawk's mouth curved in a small smile. "Handsome devil, too. It's not hard to see where you got your pretty face."

Angel burst out laughing. "Hawk, you ought to be ashamed. Uncle is as homely as a muddy clam and you know it. Raven definitely is *not*."

"He's too small for my taste," Hawk said blandly.

Raven chuckled as he stepped forward and enveloped Hawk in the kind of hard hug that men reserve for brothers or the rare unrelated male whose friendship is uniquely valued. "I've missed you, Hawk. I'm glad you could get away for a few days."

"So am I. We don't see much of you in Vancouver anymore."

"I've been—restless."

"Yes," Hawk said softly. "I was restless, too. Once." He looked at Angel. "But no more."

Angel looked up at Hawk and smiled.

If Janna had had any lingering question about Raven's status in Angel's life, that doubt vanished. Angel's smile said silently that Hawk was as deeply rooted in her as her own soul. It was the same for Hawk. The single caressing touch of his fingertip on Angel's cheek proclaimed that she was a radiance that illuminated every darkness he had ever known.

Janna looked at Raven and saw his gentle smile as he watched the almost tangible currents of love flowing between his friends. Abruptly a feeling of sadness swept over Janna, a strange, almost overwhelming compassion for Raven. Angel and Hawk were two halves of a very beautiful, very powerful whole. Raven not only accepted that, he celebrated it, loving both of them equally, enjoying the visible evidence of their love for one another.

I'm not that generous, Janna realized bleakly. *I don't begrudge what Angel and Hawk have with each other—but I can't help wanting that kind of love for myself, too. Wanting it until I feel as though I've been turned inside out, every torn nerve exposed to salt air. Wanting it until I can't trust myself to look at Raven and not cry for me, for us.*

For him.

Because I want it for him, too. Even if it doesn't happen with me, I want him to have that kind of love,

*too. I want it even more than I want it for myself.
And I can't help him any more than I can help myself.*

"Janna? What's wrong?" Raven whispered.

Slowly Janna realized that she was leaning against
Raven's hard, warm chest and his arm was unobtru-
sively supporting her.

"Nothing new," she said, looking up, giving him
the best smile she had at the moment. It must not
have been very good. His eyes narrowed and he
looked at her closely. "I guess it's all catching up
with me," she said, waving her hand around vaguely.
"Coping with civilization and all that. Eden was…
addictive."

Raven's eyes kindled. His arms tightened around
Janna. "It doesn't have to end," he whispered. He
took a harsh breath as he heard his own words. He
was doing what he had promised he wouldn't, pressing her, using her gratitude for his own ends. "You
have a few more days, don't you? If you want?"

"I want," Janna whispered, giving in to the need
within her soul and holding on to Raven suddenly. "I
want that very much."

Both of Raven's arms went around Janna. He
straightened slowly, lifting her feet off the dock, loving the feel of her completely supported within his
arms. When he finally set her down again, he was
aware of Angel's amused, approving smile.

"It's settled," Raven said. "We'll meet for dinner
at Janna's place at five. I'll bring the food, Angel will
cook and Hawk will clean up afterward."

"That doesn't leave anything for me to do," Janna
pointed out.

"You," Raven said, touching her nose with his big
finger, "are sentenced to a long, hot bath. Then you

will sit in my lap and whisper to me about the lives and lusts of frumious bandersnatches.''

''I don't think you're old enough to hear stuff like this,'' Hawk said, covering Angel's ears with his hands.

''Dream on,'' she retorted, covering Hawk's ears with her own small hands and then tugging gently, bring his face down to hers. She whispered something that made his eyebrows climb and then he laughed out loud.

''You're on,'' he said, smiling down at her with sensual promise.

Janna had just finished undergoing the first part of her ''sentence'' when she heard a knock on the front door.

''Is that you, Raven?'' she called out, reaching for a towel.

''In the flesh,'' he said, walking in the front door and shutting it behind him. ''How about you? What are you in?''

''The same. Period. Are you early or am I late?'' she asked, peeking around the barely opened bathroom door.

Raven smiled as he nudged the door fully open. ''I'd say I was just in time.''

The breath caught in Janna's throat when she saw Raven's slow, sensual appraisal of her body.

''God,'' he said thickly, ''you're too beautiful to be real.''

The visible shivers that coursed over Janna's skin were the result of more than the cooler air coming into the steamy bathroom.

''Raven,'' she said huskily, but could say no more.

"Again," he murmured.

"What?"

"My name."

Raven's voice was so deep that Janna almost couldn't understand the words. He bent over her, tasting her flushed skin with slow, sensual movements of his tongue.

"Raven," Janna said. She tried to say his name again, but his mouth was teasing her breast into a hard ruby peak. The contrast of his hair against her skin was like black satin against pearl. "Raven," she said, trembling and threading her fingers into his hair as he knelt before her.

"Yes," he growled softly against the taut curve of her belly. "Like that. Say it like that. Say it as though it were the only word in the only language that mattered."

Janna felt the firm caress of Raven's hands as he stroked her body from her high-arched feet to her rounded hips, memorizing her. His tongue traced a hot, sensuous line from her knee to the nest of dark hair at the apex of her thighs, drawing tiny gasps and cries from her, making heat swirl through her in a glittering diamond mist.

"Raven," Janna said raggedly, feeling his tongue in slow, honeyed caresses that unraveled her. *"Raven."*

"Yes," he said as triumph flared heavily through him. "Like that. Call my name while I love you. When you say it like that it makes me want—everything. With you. Here. Now. Forever."

Janna clung to Raven and called his name in a husky, helpless litany of love while he cherished her. When she could no longer stand he lifted her in his arms and carried her to the small bedroom. Very gently he put her on the dark bedspread and then simply stood next to her, his clear black eyes watching her flushed body as though he had never seen a woman before.

"Raven?" she asked in a trembling voice.

Without looking away from Janna, Raven began to undress. "I'm going to love you," he said deeply. "I'm going to love you until I'm the only thing in the world to you, until my name is the only word you can remember, until you're crying for me with every breath you take. I'm going to watch your eyes change to silver when I slide into you and you come apart beneath me. Then I'm going to lick the tears from your face and begin all over again."

The hot, nearly savage certainty in Raven's eyes was reflected in his hard flesh as he knelt over her, touching her, loving her. Janna tried to speak but could not, for her body had been taken from her at his first intimate caress. She tried to speak again, but all that came out was a primitive sound of pleasure that made him smile.

And then the only sound in the room was Janna's voice calling his name in a husky, helpless love song for the raven who did not love her in return.

Nine

On the last day of August Janna awoke slowly, rubbing her cheek against the resilient wall of muscle that was Raven's chest. He made a sound of sleepy contentment, cuddled her even closer and fell back asleep between one breath and the next. Janna nuzzled Raven's warm skin contentedly but didn't go back to sleep herself. She hadn't wanted to sleep at all last night after they had come back from their trip to the Yakoon River. She hadn't wanted to waste a single instant of what might be her last hours with Raven.

Today she was going to tell him that she loved him. Today she hoped that he would accept her love rather than tenderly denying it. Today he would either love her in return or she would have to leave—for Janna knew if she stayed any longer with Raven she wouldn't be able to leave him. She wasn't even sure

that she could go now. She only knew that she had
to try. She loved Raven far too much to burden him
with a woman and an emotion that he didn't want.

Surely he loves me, if only a little, Janna thought,
pressing her cheek into Raven's abundant warmth. *No
man who didn't love just a little could be so gentle,
so passionate, so pleased just to be with me.*

Raven made no secret of his pleasure in Janna's
company. Even though she had pointed out that Angel
and Hawk had come to the Queen Charlottes to see
Raven, not a strange woman, he had ignored Janna's
protests. He was rarely beyond her reach and was
never beyond the sound of her voice. She fell asleep
with the taste of him on her lips and the warmth of
him within her, and she awoke to the feel of his heartbeat beneath her cheek and the heat of his body
pressed full-length against hers.

She had sat in Raven's lap and whispered frumious
nonsense in his ear and had heard his deep laughter
mingling with her own. She had gone to the legendary
Tlell River and seen fishermen pull shining salmon
from whiskey-colored water that was as clear and
wild as a hawk's eyes. She had seen gusts of wind
swirl over river and sea, brushing the water's surface
with quicksilver designs. She had heard gulls wheel
and keen on the leading edge of a storm, birds crying
their need to the careless sky. She had stood on the
banks of the Yakoon River and seen a spruce tree
burning like a golden flame against the primeval
green of the forest. There was no other tree of its kind
on earth. Not one. Unique, alone, living in an untamed Eden. Janna had wept to see Raven and the

golden spruce together, their power and their isolation complete.

And always, always, whether on the sea or in the forest, Janna had sensed in the primal silence the returning echoes of a raven's lonely cry.

She knew only one way to reach into that isolation, to answer that searching cry. Yet each time she had tried to tell Raven of her love he had taken the words from her lips, the breath from her body and he had substituted his own sensual words, his own breath in her body until he became part of her once more and she could say only his name, feel only his power within her, know only him and the elemental ecstasy he brought to her.

The thought that she might never again know that shimmering flight in Raven's arms made Janna close her eyes in silent pain. With a deep, slow breath she fought back the sadness, for she had promised herself that this day would be as perfect as she could make it. There would be no tears, no wounded dreams crying to be made whole. There would be only laughter and companionship and the haunting, bittersweet beauty of one final day in Eden.

And at the end of that day she would tell Raven that she loved him. At the end of that day she would know whether he loved her in return.

Janna kissed the muscular warmth of Raven's chest, nuzzling the vaguely curly wedge of hair that tickled her nose. She discovered the dark disk of his nipple just within reach of her tongue. She circled the sensitive flesh, enjoying the taste and texture of Raven. It was delicious to have him all to herself, to slowly awaken him as he had always awakened her—

deep within the hot, silken web of his sensuality, fully aroused by erotic sensations that were both dreamlike and very real, flying even higher as he merged with her and brought her the ecstasy that came only on the glittering black wings of a wild raven.

Now it was Janna's turn to savor the sleeping power of the man she loved. She might never have another chance to awaken Raven with slow, hot caresses. She might never again know the pleasure of bringing him from sleep into ecstasy.

Janna eased aside the bedcovers and looked at Raven's naked, beautifully masculine body. She knelt over him as her fingertips smoothed each ridge and swell of muscle, her touch soothing, encouraging him to remain within his dreams. He shifted beneath her caresses, responding even in his sleep, moving closer to the warm hands stroking him. Smiling, wondering what his dreams were like at the moment, Janna tasted Raven's skin with slow, catlike touches of her tongue while her palms savored the heat and muscular lines of his torso. As she nibbled and softly nipped her way from his chin to his hips, she sensed him awakening. The tip of her tongue circled his navel and then filled it with hot, delicate caresses.

Beneath Janna's hands Raven's thighs were hard, corded with muscle, powerful even when relaxed. The dense thatch of hair that lay between was an irresistible lure to her. She eased her fingers into it, seeking and finding all the changing textures of his masculinity. The differences between his body and her own fascinated her. She cherished those differences with her fingertips, her palms, her hands holding and caressing him as he changed to meet her touch. His potency compelled her in an elemental way. She wanted to know him with the same searing, wild intimacy with which he had known her.

"You're fishing in rocky waters again," Raven rumbled, his tone both amused and thick with arousal.

"Yes," Janna said, cradling his very different flesh in her hands, "I know. This time, I know."

Raven smiled as he remembered the first time they had awakened in bed together, when Janna hadn't recognized the distinctive male flesh rising hard and hot beneath her hand.

"I want to…touch you," she said softly, caressing him. "Do you mind?"

"Do I look like I mind?" he asked, his voice gritty.

Janna looked from the heavy-lidded sensuality of Raven's eyes to the hard flesh that she was caressing. "No," she agreed huskily, "You don't look like you mind. But there are other ways of touching, ways that appalled me before I knew you." She smiled slightly, thinking of that shelf of books she had thrown away after her divorce. "There are whole chapters I want to explore. With you, Raven. Only with you. Would you mind that?"

She felt the sudden, savage tightening of his body as he understood what she was asking.

"Whatever you want, small warrior," Raven said, his voice dark, caressing, thick with anticipation. "However you want it."

"'For as long as you can take it,'" Janna added, smiling, remembering what Raven had once said to her. "I'm glad you're an unusually strong man," she whispered, bending down to him. "Very glad."

* * *

The long, wide beach uncurled in front of Raven and Janna like an immense ribbon. The wind that had swept away clouds and mist alike had also stirred the ocean into a dark blue mass where whitecaps flashed and vanished only to reform again atop other metallic blue swells. Lines of breakers rolled toward the beach in creamy ranks, adding a rhythmic thunder to the deep baying of the wind. Neither picnic tables nor trash cans marred the sand's pristine surface. There were no footprints, no people, nothing but the wind and the sea and the distant keening of gulls.

"I feel as though I'm trespassing," Janna said, looking behind at the tracks they were leaving in the sand.

"The tide will wash it clean again," Raven said. "It will be as though we were never here." He looked at the position of the sun in the sky. "We have some time before Angel and Hawk are meeting us. Want to explore?"

Raven caught the sensual, almost secret smile that came to Janna's lips and didn't know whether to laugh or swear at the sudden hot rush of his blood.

"I was referring to exploring the beach," Raven continued, "but I'm open to suggestion." Knowing he shouldn't, unable to stop himself, he bent and kissed Janna slowly, savoring the taste and textures of her mouth. "In fact," he said, unzipping her wind shell and sliding his hand up beneath her sweater, "I've got a few suggestions of my own."

Janna threaded her fingers deeply into Raven's hair. "You know," she said, biting his lower lip with sensual precision, "I ought to call your bluff. Because after this morning, bluff is all it could be!"

"Wanna bet?" he asked, smiling darkly.

Raven knew he should release Janna from the net of his sensuality. That was why he had come to the beach of illusions—to let her go. Yet his free hand was even now caressing her buttocks, kneading the firm flesh as he pressed her body tightly against him.

Janna's breath came in swiftly. Raven was as hard and ready as though they hadn't just spent the morning hours exploring his strength and endurance.

"Yeah," Raven said, smiling oddly when he saw Janna's expression change. He moved his hand up to caress a velvety nipple that hardened beneath his fingers. "It's the damnedest thing," he admitted. "I never had this problem until I met you."

"Neither did I," Janna said, feeling sensual heat rush through her as she arched her body against him in a long, intimate caress.

"So which one of us is going to be sensible about it?" he asked.

"How do you define sensible?"

"Not making love on a public beach," Raven said succinctly.

"Oh." Janna sighed. "Damn."

"Yeah. *Damn.*" With a reluctance that almost undid his good intentions, Raven slid his hand out from beneath Janna's sweater—but not before he saw the ruby nipple rising between his fingers. "Why am I always covering you up when all I want to do is run my tongue over you?" he groaned, easing the sweater back into place on her body.

Janna laughed softly. "Covering me up? Since when?"

"Since the first time I saw that ripe berry peeking

out from beneath a corner of the survival blanket, that's when," he retorted. "All I wanted to do was take you into my mouth and feel you change as my tongue loved you."

Suddenly Janna remembered the moment when Raven had tucked the blanket around her shoulders and she had been devastated, thinking that he was utterly indifferent to her as a woman.

"You wanted me then?" she whispered, hardly able to believe it.

"I wanted you the instant I saw you fighting the storm," he said flatly.

"You should have taken me, Raven. I was yours the first time I heard your voice calling to me over the waves, telling me that I wasn't alone. I was yours before I even knew who you were," she whispered. "I still am yours. I always will be. I love—"

Janna felt the heat and sweetness of Raven's mouth as he kissed her, stilling the torrent of whispered words. It was a long time before he released her, laced his fingers through hers and led her farther down the untouched sands. For an instant Janna closed her eyes, walking blindly, trying to ease the pain of not being allowed to speak her love. The wind combed through her hair, freeing it from restraints, making it a soft cinnamon radiance around her face.

The doubts that faded each time Raven made love to Janna came back to her now with redoubled force. He was an honest man, a compassionate man, a kind man. If he didn't love her, he would try very hard not to hurt her. And one of his kindnesses would be to make certain that she wasn't left to hear her soft declarations of love echo unanswered. That was why he always kissed her words away, sparing her all that he could. He had proven to her that she was an endless fire in his body, but somehow she had left his soul untouched. Passion, not love.

Why can't one person love enough for two?

No answer came to Janna's silent cry, nothing but the wind keening over the unmarked sands.

Raven tried to look at the empty land and the wind-tossed sea but could not glance away from Janna for more than a few moments at a time. He sensed the sadness in her, a darkness that only made her smile more luminous, more achingly beautiful each time she turned toward him. It was her courage that had drawn him to Janna, even before he had seen her beauty and sensuality. He sensed that courage now, a determination to smile that was as great as her sadness. He ached to hold her but knew that in the end it would only make things worse for her, not better. Today he had to open his hands and return his gift from the gods.

"You're walking like a man with a destination," Janna said, holding her voice so tightly that her throat ached.

"Am I?"

"Yes. All broad shoulders and long-striding purpose."

Raven smiled at the image. "I just wanted to get up the beach before the illusions fade."

Janna gave him a sideways, here-we-go-again kind of look.

"A little farther, where the beach curves away to the north," he explained. "That's where they dance, but only on clear days."

There was a three-beat pause before Janna said triumphantly, "Bandersnatches, right? And it's 'wabes' not 'days.'"

"No, it's rose-colored mirages dancing between Eden and Alaska," he countered, stopping suddenly. "See?"

Janna felt the warmth of Raven radiating through her as he fitted her spine against his muscular chest. His powerful arm came over her shoulder as he pointed toward the northern horizon.

"There," he murmured. "See them dance?"

"Oh sure," she said agreeably. "Right next to the pink elephants tripping the light fantastic. They—" Janna's breath came in sharply and the hair on her neck stirred. Her eyes narrowed as she focused on the rose-tinted distance. *"Raven, there's something out there."*

"Yes," he whispered. "Aren't they beautiful? Everything man has ever wanted shimmering and dancing just beyond his reach."

Janna couldn't answer. The eerie, compelling illusions twisted and changed like pale rose flames, whispering to her soundlessly, haunting her. The rational, educated part of her mind calmly told her that the gently seething apparitions were simply a trick of light and atmosphere, like the mirages that had led so many desert explorers to madness and death; but the most primitive part of Janna looked at the illusions and saw pieces of her own soul calling soundlessly to her, telling her that everything she had ever dreamed of beckoned just beyond her fingertips.

The visions were drawn in flames of transparent silver and luminous rose, a world both dreamed and real. It was the sea and a deserted inlet and a single tree that was unique upon the face of the earth. It was a raven's song sung in silence and answered in the beauty of a smile. It was a man and a woman created for this radiant instant that knew no time, created for this beautiful and savage Eden, created each for the other. They glimmered and intertwined between sky and sea, time and timelessness, being and dreaming.

Raven saw Janna's face both haunted and radiant, sadness and ecstasy combined. He wanted to ask her what she was seeing in the enigmatic sky but knew that he had no right. Visions could only be shared, not demanded, a gift from one mind to another, one soul to another. He had taken too much from her already, more than he had any right to take. And he would pay for it in the torment of his memories when he touched again each moment of his days in Eden and thereby measured the immensity of his loss when he lived in Eden no longer.

Raven looked at the heartless, haunting mirages shimmering over the water; and he saw a time years ago, when he had been alone.

"The summer I built the cabin in Totem Inlet," Raven said quietly, "I was restless, lonely, a bird without wings, a fish without fins, nothing fit and nothing was right. I had been alone before, but never lonely." He hesitated, seeing again the summer that had begun so like this one and had ended so differently. "A few days after I finished the cabin I was restless again. I prowled through the forest, trying to wear myself out enough to sleep at night."

For an instant Raven closed his eyes, remembering,

seeing a green Eden that at the time had looked more like hell.

"I found a young doe trapped in a moss-covered deadfall. She was half dead from thirst and terror and pain. When I freed her, I saw that one of her legs was injured. If I let her go, she would die. Yet if I kept her, tamed her, made her dependent on me, then I would be dooming her to a different, even more cruel death when I abandoned her. Because I knew the summer would end, the winter would come and I would go. I knew this, but the doe did not. She only knew each moment as it came."

Janna waited, feeling silence gathering like cold mist around her, chilling her. She sensed that she didn't want to know the end of the story Raven was telling.

And she had no choice but to know it, to understand the man she loved no matter what the cost.

"What did you do?" she whispered, forcing the words past the ache in her throat.

"I carried the doe to the cabin, bound her leg and wove cedar boughs into a fence upwind of the cabin. There was natural food, clean water and no bears to feed on her helplessness." Raven paused, seeing again the fragile, shivering doe who had calmed so quickly beneath his voice and hands. "It would have been very easy to win her trust. She was gentle, intelligent, adaptable as all young things are. She would have learned to run toward my voice, making me smile. She would have been company, and I was…lonely."

Janna started to ask why Raven had been so lonely, but he was talking again.

''I left the doe alone behind the cedar fence. When I checked on her I made sure that she neither saw nor scented me. In time she didn't limp anymore. She even chewed off the shirt I had used to bind her wound. The fence was high enough to restrain an injured doe, but not too high for a healthy one to jump. One day I came to check on her and found nothing there but silence and cedar.''

Wind breathed across Janna's cheeks, cooling the tears that welled in her eyes. Raven saw the silver gleam and smoothed his palm very gently over Janna's hair.

''There was nothing sad in her leaving,'' he said. ''My reward for helping the doe didn't come from winning her trust. My reward came when I saw her last graceful leap as she fled into the forest where she had been born. She never looked back. She never returned to the clearing or the cabin.'' Raven lifted his hand from Janna's hair. ''And that was the way it had to be. To have taken anything more from the doe in her helplessness would have made me less of a man.''

Janna bowed her head as she fought against tears and the realization that in some way Raven thought of her as he had the doe—something wounded, helpless, given into his care only long enough to be rescued, healed and then freed.

Like Angel. She had been another gift to be healed and freed. That was what Raven had meant when he said that he had finally realized Angel's life was more valuable than his chance to win her love. He had gone to her, pulled her out of the trap of her rage and despair, shown her the way to heal herself...and then watched her slip from his hands without a backward look.

At least Angel had finally returned. But did that make it better for Raven, or worse?

"It was Angel, wasn't it?" Janna whispered. "That's why you were restless the summer you built the cabin."

The slight trembling of Janna's voice made Raven wish that he had never brought her to this beach, this instant, tearing her illusions from her and leaving her nothing in their place. Yet illusions could be very cruel. Then they had to be taken away. Janna had to realize that she was free, that she owed nothing to the man who had pulled her from the sea, certainly not the love that she thought she felt.

"I don't feel that way now," Raven said quietly. "Seeing Angel and Hawk together brings me a feeling very close to joy."

"Now. But not then. Not the summer you built the cabin."

The slight flinching of Raven's eyelids told Janna that she was right.

"Angel had just married Hawk," Raven said, his voice rough with restraint. "I loved both of them, but seeing them together sometimes made me feel…" He hesitated.

"Terribly lonely," Janna whispered.

"It was nothing they did deliberately. It was just…" again Raven paused, searching for words to describe the feelings he had never before tried to articulate.

"Seeing them made you wonder if you would ever love and be loved like that," Janna said.

Raven closed his eyes and wondered how Janna saw so easily, so clearly, into his soul. "Yes," he said simply.

"I love you like that, Raven."

"Hush, small warrior," he whispered, brushing the back of his fingers across Janna's cheek.

"Why?" Janna asked, her voice trembling. "Why won't you let me say that I love you?"

Raven breathed Janna's name against her hair as his hands closed around her shoulders with a force that he could barely control. He didn't let her turn toward him. He was afraid that if he saw her eyes he would be lost again, he would close his hands and keep her for himself because he had never felt so alive as he had when he was with her.

"What you feel is gratitude and passion, not love," Raven said, his voice so tightly held that it rasped harshly on his own ears. "You would have felt those things for any man who saved your life and then lacked the self-control and common decency to keep from seducing you while you were so vulnerable."

The bitterness and self-recrimination in Raven's voice shocked Janna. "That's not—" she began.

"No," Raven interrupted roughly. "Listen to me, Janna. You are a beautiful, incredibly sexy woman who married one of the few men around who couldn't appreciate you. I'll never forget our time together in Eden. I'll remember your wit and your laughter and your sensuality until I die."

And the last word I say will be your name.

Raven had just enough control left not to speak that cruel truth aloud. He had come to stand here on the shore of illusions and give back his gift from the gods.

He had come here to release Janna, not to continue her captivity to the mistaken belief that she loved him.

"You owe me nothing," Raven continued, giving Janna no chance to speak. "We met by accident in a place out of time. There were no other people, nothing to remind you of your real life. You gave yourself to me out of gratitude, because I had taken you from the sea and you knew how violently I wanted you. If we had met any other way, you wouldn't have wanted me as a lover."

"That's not true," Janna whispered, trying to turn toward Raven but unable to move for the strength of his hands forcing her to face away from him. "I would have loved you if we'd met in Pike Place Market with a thousand people milling around and nothing more urgent on my mind than dinner. Haven't you been listening to me? I've always loved you, Raven. Always. That won't change—ever, anywhere, under any circumstances!"

"Janna," he said, wanting to believe her, knowing that he could not allow himself to reach for what he wanted so much that he couldn't trust himself anymore. Gratitude faded. Passion faded. Love endured. He knew that he wouldn't be able to let Janna go a few years or a few months from now. Or even a few hours. It had to be now. It had to be before she woke up in his arms and realized the difference between gratitude and love, before she looked at him with compassion and unhappiness. "Once you're back home, you'll think about what happened here. You'll see it differently. It will be like a dream. A joyous dream," he whispered very softly. "Please, God, at least that."

"What can I say to make you believe me?" Janna asked in despair. "Nothing can change how we met. Nothing can change how I feel about you now." She spun toward Raven suddenly, eluding his grasp, not caring that he would see the tears on her face. "Raven," she said, her voice trembling. "Raven, let me love you. Let yourself love me just a little in return. Raven, *please*."

"Don't," he said gently, covering Janna's mouth with his hand. "I already hate myself for making love to you. Don't make it any worse."

Pain twisted through Janna, making her helpless. The realization that Raven regretted making love to her was devastating, taking the world out from beneath her feet, leaving her with nothing to hang on to but herself. Distantly she heard voices on the wind and thought that the rosy illusions were calling to her again, taunting her with the specter of things that would never be.

The voices dissolved into laughter. Angel and Hawk were coming up the beach, following the footprints of the two who had gone before. Angel, the woman Raven had once loved and lost and then finally loved again, but differently. Hawk, the man Angel loved in ways that she hadn't been able to love Raven. Raven had not only accepted that, he celebrated it, loving both Angel and Hawk equally, enjoying the visible evidence of their love for one another. Janna had learned to enjoy it, too. In the past few days she had come to appreciate the intelligence and courage that existed beneath Angel's honey-blond exterior. It was the same for Hawk, a gift for gentleness and laughter unexpected in a man of his hard good looks.

Yet suddenly Janna knew that she couldn't bear seeing Angel and Hawk together, much less take pleasure from their nearly tangible love. Not now. Not when she had just been told that the man she loved regretted ever having touched her.

She closed her eyes for an instant, gathering her courage. She had promised herself a perfect day before she spoke of love and it either was returned or not. She had had the day, she had spoken of love...and she had heard the gate to Eden closing behind her, leaving her alone in a world without love. All that remained was to walk away before she embarrassed Raven any further with her pleas.

"Are there really illusions out here?" Angel asked, coming up behind Raven.

"Delusions, actually," Janna said, her tone desperately normal as she opened her eyes. "There's a difference, you know. Like the difference between gimble and gambol, wabe and wave."

Angel went very still, sensing the pain in Janna even before she saw the evidence of spent tears. She looked at Raven. His face was hard, closed, as though he had been created from stone instead of flesh.

"Raven will explain it to you," Janna continued, looking through Angel. "He's good at inexplicable explanations. If you want to hear a real jaw-dropper, ask him about the difference between gratitude and love. Educational, I can assure you. A regular dissertation on sneezing bandersnatches."

"Janna," Raven said quietly. "You're not making any sense."

"Of course not. I left my brains at the bottom of an inlet." She looked around at the broad beach and the savage perfection of the land. "A pity this is Eden instead of the Ark. Two was a magic number for Noah and getting across water was no problem. But this is Eden and I have a ferry to catch. I'll bet the captain's name is Charon."

Without another word Janna turned and began walking away from the others, going where no tracks marred the glistening surface of the sand.

"Where are you going?" Raven asked.

"Across the river Styx."

"It ran around hell, not Eden."

"Somehow that doesn't surprise me."

"It's three miles to your cabin," Raven called. "Let Hawk take you home."

"It's all right, Raven," Janna said calmly, looking over her shoulder. "I'll walk on the edge of the sea. When the tide turns, it will be like I never was."

Raven closed his eyes, wanting to go to Janna, hold her, comfort her and himself. But it would be a cruelty, not a kindness. He had to be strong enough to be kind.

Janna watched Raven for a long moment before she turned away. She walked swiftly, cleanly, and she didn't look back again.

Raven opened his eyes and watched her until he could stand it no longer. Then he closed his eyes against the agony twisting through his soul.

"Carlson?"

Raven flinched from the soft voice and softer touch on his arm. Deliberately he stepped aside, beyond Angel's reach.

"Aren't you going to go after her?" Hawk asked.

"I never should have touched her." Raven's eyes opened. They were black, wild, almost frightening in their intensity. "I couldn't stop myself. I knew Janna was mine in some primitive, unspeakable way the first time I saw her. I *knew* it."

"So did she," Hawk said. "She loves you, Carlson. It shows in every—"

"Gratitude," Raven interrupted in a harsh tone. "Not love."

"How can you be so sure?" Angel asked.

His sudden laughter was as dark and savage as his eyes. "Angel Eyes," he said gently. "Sweet, beautiful Angel Eyes. It's so simple. I'm not the kind of man a woman loves. Of all people on earth, you should know that."

Angel went pale. "Carlson," she said, throwing her arms around him, "I never meant to hurt you like that. It was my fault, not yours. There's nothing wrong with you!"

"Don't cry for me," Raven said quietly, stroking the burnished gold of Angel's hair. "Even if I could, I wouldn't change what happened in the past. I'm not the other half of your soul, and I never could have been. Hawk is. And," Raven murmured, "you aren't the other half of mine. I know that now."

"But Janna is," Angel said urgently. "She's the other half of you."

"I know," Raven said. "And I know that gratitude isn't love."

"You're wrong about Janna," Hawk said quietly. "I was raised on gratitude, not love. I know what gratitude is and what it isn't. It isn't a woman's eyes following you everywhere, her fingers touching you when there's no need, her voice softening when she says your name, her smile more beautiful for you than for anyone else on earth.''

Raven couldn't bear to hear any more words. He wanted to believe them too much. He no longer trusted himself to listen.

Abruptly he turned away and walked toward his car, letting his tracks mingle with the others, blurring all distinctions as to whom had gone out to the beach of illusions and who had returned. Yet still Hawk's voice followed, carrying clearly on the wind.

''Janna looks at you the way Angel looks at me. The way I look at Angel. The way you look at Janna. Not gratitude, Carlson. *Love!*''

Overhead, gulls wheeled on a gust of wind, keening and crying to one another, and their calls became Janna's name echoing in Raven's mind. The breakers took up the cry, chanting in deeper tones, while the wind's supple voice mourned in counterpoint. He saw Janna wherever he looked, tasted her on his lips, felt her in the heat of his own blood sliding through his veins. She was everywhere, a part of everything; but most of all she was part of his soul and he was crying her name within the silence that only she had ever touched.

Raven drove quickly to the *Black Star*, wanting only to pack up and get as far away from the Queen Charlotte Islands as possible. Once aboard he began stripping his clothes from lockers and drawers, throwing things haphazardly into a duffel bag. He opened the last drawer and froze. Angel's sketchbook lay on top, the sketchbook that Janna had used in Totem Inlet.

Slowly Raven pulled the book out. He had never looked at Janna's sketches. She had never offered to show them to him, saying that after seeing Angel's stained glass creations, anything else would be a disappointment.

The sketches were like Janna herself—direct, often humorous, honest, and with an underlying sensuality of line and shading that made Raven ache with memories. He could hear her rueful laughter in the drawing labeled ''God's Own Washing Machine,'' which showed jeans and shirts slung over any handy railing while rain poured down over them, washing away salt and sand. He could see Janna's honesty in the sketch of a totem labeled simply ''Before.'' She drew the Haida icons without embellishment or softening, accepting without evasion the Haidas' comfortless view of man in relation to the universe.

Page after page turned beneath Raven's careful fingers until there was only one page left. He turned it and felt his scalp tighten in primitive response. At first the sketch looked like the others, but there were aspects of it that teased his mind until realization came. There were shadows that suggested a man's watchful eyes, a seemingly random collection of curves that became a face superimposed on the sea, a mist-wrapped mountain that evoked a man seated, thinking, a very powerful man with black hair and granite strength and eyes that flinched from nothing.

And all of the men were Raven.

Raven's features in infinite variations, his eyes and mouth repeated in forest and mountain, ocean and totem, Raven smiling or intent, asleep or in the grip of passion, calm or at the instant of hottest ecstasy, gentle or fierce—Raven, always Raven. It was as though nothing lived, not even the sea itself, that wasn't animated by Raven's own breath, his own life flowing into everything, becoming part of it.

He looked at the drawing until he could no longer see it, and then he put his face in his hands and wept, knowing that he had finally heard a love song for a raven.

Mist condensed with the falling sun, giving the land a mysterious gloaming that was as haunted as the vanished rose illusions. Janna had stopped a hundred yards from her cabin and turned to look at the long, wandering trail she had left on her walk out of Eden. She didn't know how long she had been standing there watching the ragged black stitches she had left behind in the sand, stitches that were being unraveled by the returning tide. Now there was nothing left but shadowy hollows where spindrift gathered. The next wave would wash away even that, leaving nothing at all.

"If I could, I would paint sky and mountains, sea and forest, and they would all be you."

The soft, deep voice sent shivers over Janna's skin and made her doubt her sanity in the instant before she spun around. Raven was standing within reach, as though he had condensed from the primal night and her own dreams.

"If I could," Raven said, "I would have the wind calling your name in all times and seasons, and the mist-veiled forests would have been created just to match your eyes. But I'm not an artist or a god. I'm only a harsh-voiced raven flying over an empty Eden, crying for what I wanted so much that I was afraid to believe that it was finally mine." His big hands came up, framing Janna's face, trembling as they touched her softness and warmth. "I have no beautiful songs to fill your silences, no worlds to remake in your image, no special way to tell you that you're the other half of my soul."

"Raven—" Janna's voice broke. "I don't need special gifts or songs or anything but you. Just you, Raven. *I love you.*"

The words swept through Raven, transforming him.

He lifted her high in his arms and held her close, telling her with his strength and his gentleness and his whispered words how much he loved her, feeling his love returned with every touch, every breath, her vital warmth enveloping him as he held her.

Beyond them the last of the footprints leading from Eden dissolved into the mist and moon-silvered sea. Neither Janna nor Raven noticed. They had found the only Eden that mattered, and they would hold it forever in their arms.

THE FIVE-MINUTE BRIDE
by Leanne Banks

* * *

A big smile and cheer for all
the sandbox princesses, especially those
who got their start on Pawling Street in Roanoke.
This book is dedicated to my favorite feminine wonder
who makes my life so rich—Alisa Anne Banks.
How did I ever get so lucky
to have such a wonderful daughter?

Dear Reader,

Do you remember playing dress-up as a little girl? Do you remember how you could be anyone you pretended to be? Fond memories of my childhood days spent as a "sandbox princess" inspired the opening to *The Five-Minute Bride*. I loved Emily, the "she-ro" of this book, because she tried so hard to be who she thought she was supposed to be, but she truly came into her own and made her greatest contribution when she started being her own person. And the cool part was, along the way she found a great man and the beginning of a great love!

Being able to write about the transforming power of love between a man and a woman is one of the things I love most about writing for Silhouette Desire. I also enjoy knowing who you, my readers, are, because I secretly believe that my readers are "she-ros" in their own lives. So you deserve the best—a terrific hero who is a fabulous lover within a satisfying, feel-good read—a Silhouette Desire novel.

For a night when only a little romance will do,

Leanne Banks

Prologue

When Emily St. Clair grew up, she wanted to be a cowboy. A loud cowboy with a big black hat, one of those fringed jackets and noisy boots. She wanted a horse named Black Devil, too.

But right now she was only an eight-year-old girl with blond hair, a pink-and-white shorts set and a too-tight ponytail with a pink satin ribbon. Her poodle's name was Teenie.

Her mom always said it was best to be practical. If Emily couldn't be a cowboy today, she supposed she'd just be a princess. She looked down at the box of play clothes on the ground. It was a typical spring day on Cherry Lane. The birds were chirping, the bees were buzzing, and she and her friends had to play at the fence because Maddie was grounded again.

"Can I have the red ones this time?"

Emily nodded and handed her mother's red high heels over the chain-link fence to Maddie Palmer. She tugged at the pink satin bow her mother habitually put in her hair. Emily liked Maddie because she was loud. "What are you in for this time?"

Red-haired Maddie made a face. "I took a grape Popsicle without asking and told Ben he could have half of it if he wouldn't tell Mama. But the little twerp got purple all over his shirt, so he had to tell." She shook her head. "Brothers!"

Emily didn't have a brother or sister, so she just wiggled her shoulders the way she'd seen the older kids do it. Then she turned to ten-year-old Jenna Jean who was sitting on the ground and making whistling sounds with a blade of grass. "Do you want the black shoes or the white ones this time?"

"I'll take the white," she said, and began to untie her tennis shoes.

Emily set the heels down beside Jenna. New to the neighborhood, Emily feared the only reason the older girls let her play was because she had three pairs of high heels to share with friends.

If the shoes didn't impress the kids on Cherry Lane, then the tiara did.

Her mother had a ton of them because she used to win beauty contests, so she'd given Emily one of her crowns. She tugged at her ribbon again and wished her mother wouldn't make her ponytail so tight.

Jenna Jean squinted her eyes at Emily. "How come you always wear a pink ribbon?"

Emily sighed. She'd asked her mother the same

question a zillion times. "My mother likes pink. Are we going to play princesses again?"

Jenna Jean stood and stuck her feet into the high heels. "I don't want to play princesses."

Emily tamped down her disappointment and remembered her mother had said she'd make friends more easily if she played what they wanted to. "Okay. We can pretend we're grown-ups. We can pretend we're married and we're rich and we have to order our servants around all day long."

"Yeah," Maddie said with enthusiasm. "When I grow up, I want to marry Davey Rogers from the Pink Bubblegum Rockers."

"He's too old," Jenna Jean said.

"He is not," Maddie said adamantly. "He's just nineteen."

Jenna Jean rolled her eyes. "Well I don't want to get married."

Emily and Maddie looked at her in shock.

"I don't," she insisted. "Boys are dumb, and my mother's always complaining about my dad's underwear on the bathroom floor. When I grow up, I want to get rich all on my own and live by myself and not have to share my room with anybody."

Everybody knew Jenna Jean had five younger brothers, and they were always getting into Jenna Jean's stuff. "Okay," Emily said, although she wished she had a brother or sister or just *somebody* besides her mom and Teenie.

Since her dad died two years ago, they'd had to move, and her mother made so many rules that sometimes Emily got a headache thinking about all of them. Just yesterday, her mom had told her about the charm classes at the local department store. She sighed and decided to think about that when she took her bath tonight. Sitting in a bathtub made it easier to think about things that bothered her. Even though she wanted to wear the tiara today, she gave it to Jenna Jean. She really wanted the girls to like her. "You could be a rich and famous movie star," she suggested.

"That's cool." Grinning, Jenna Jean stuck the tiara on her head and pulled a fake stole around her shoulders.

"And I'll pretend me and my husband are rich and famous rock stars." Maddie pulled her shirt down to bare one shoulder and made a sneer. She glanced at Emily. "What are you gonna be?"

Squelching her secret, secret fantasy along with her wish to never wear another pink satin ribbon, Emily was practical. "I'm going to be a doctor's wife," she said decisively, and put her nose in the air like she thought a snooty person would. "My mom says if you marry a doctor, you're set for life."

One

Beau lost the coin toss.

Jimmy's face split into a wide grin. "You get to address the little problem over there in the corner."

Beau Ramsey sighed and glanced around the nearly empty bar. Officially off duty, he was beginning to think he should wear a sign announcing that fact to the world. Right now he should be home nursing a beer watching the baseball game he'd taped earlier. "Technically this is a matter for the business owner to handle. You don't need the sheriff."

"She's drunk 'n' disorderly."

Beau glanced over at the little problem in the corner. "Drunk," he agreed. "Not necessarily disorderly."

"Just give her time," Jimmy said knowingly. "She's been knocking back tequilas for two hours. She's either gonna get disorderly or she's gonna fall on her face.'' Jimmy gave a meaningful glance at his watch. ''It's closing time, and Thelma's waiting for me.''

Stifling a groan, Beau took another swallow of his beer and studied the little problem taking up space in The Happy Hour Bar. Pretty and blond, she was dressed in yards of white satin and lace that suspiciously resembled a wedding dress. From her painted nails to her satin pumps, she was a vision of feminine class. Her BMW was parked in the gravel lot. According to Jimmy, the only words she'd uttered had been ''Tequila, please,'' and ''Thank you.''

There was a story here, and Beau was convinced he didn't want to hear it. As a man who'd been surrounded by women his entire life, he could tell this one was in extreme distress. Unfortunately, as the primary lawman in the rural town of Ruxton, North Carolina, he was asked to address some pretty outrageous situations. ''You owe me for this one, Jimmy.''

Jimmy whipped his towel over the counter again. ''Put it on the tab.''

The tab was endless. Beau had been pulling Jimmy out of scrapes since elementary school. He rose from the stool and walked to her side. ''Excuse me, ma'am.''

Her blurred blue gaze rose to his. ''Yes, sir,'' she said in a husky voice.

Beau's lip twisted at the way her sexy tone mixed with the polite words. Her skin was flawless, her cheeks pink, her lips slightly parted. Her white dress drooped over one shoulder, revealing the shadow of her cleavage. Tendrils of blond hair escaped from what he guessed had once been a classic knot.

A dozen questions came to mind, starting with "Why aren't you in the honeymoon suite of a hotel with some lucky man?" and "Who's the poor sap that isn't going to see what's underneath all that lace?"

A shot of pure masculine curiosity thudded through his veins. Deliberately lifting his gaze from her breasts, he cleared his throat. "It's closing time. Do you need to call someone to take you home?"

She wrinkled her brow. "Home?"

"Yes. You've had too much to drink, so you can't drive."

She looked around and swept the skirt of the dress to one side to lean closer to him, then whispered, "Are you suggesting that I'm drunk?"

If he lit a match near her mouth, her breath would probably set the place on fire. For an insane moment he suspected that in a different situation her mouth would set a man on fire. He stifled a curse.

"Yes," he finally said, noting the pink garter just above her knee. "I am."

"Oh, my." She bit her lip, and Beau felt a tinge of sympathy despite his ongoing vow to remain unaffected by women in distress. "Where am I?"

Beau's hopes sank. She was worse than he'd thought. "Ruxton, North Carolina."

She looked at him blankly.

"Where do you live?"

She shook her head vehemently, then clutched her forehead as if the movement had been painful. "I'm not ever going home again. Never, ever. Not in a million—''

Beau lifted his hands. ''Fine, but you've got to stay somewhere tonight.''

''Why can't I get a room here?''

''Because there aren't any rooms here, Miss—''

''Emily,'' she told him, in that soft sexy voice that threatened his neutrality. ''My name is Emily.''

''And your last name?''

She frowned for a long moment. ''I'm not sure.'' She grimaced. ''I've never had this much tequila before. My stomach hurts.''

''That's not the only thing that's gonna hurt,'' he muttered. ''Okay, let's get you out of here.'' He offered his hand.

Emily took it and rose unsteadily. The woman was too trusting, Beau thought with disapproval, but he supposed her judgment was impaired.

''Where you takin' her?'' Jimmy asked as he opened the heavy wooden door.

''I don't know,'' Beau said darkly. ''My sisters' houses are crammed full with kids. It'll either have to be my house or the jail.''

Jimmy shook his head. ''She don't look like the jailbird type.''

Beau just swore as Emily leaned against him, the soft floral scent of her hair rising to his nostrils. He urged her into the quiet night toward his Jeep.

''Today was my wedding day.''

''You don't say.'' Beau glanced at her and felt another sinking sensation. He wasn't surprised. A beautiful married woman. This was not his lucky night.

Emily nodded solemnly. "He was a doctor." Her face tightened. "But he loves somebody else, so I left. My mother will have to be sedated. I'm never going back. Never, ever."

"I had a clue you might have been coming or going to a wedding," he muttered. "Your dress."

Emily jerked to a stop and stared down at her long white dress in horror. "I'm still wearing my wedding dress," she whispered, as if she'd just realized that fact.

Beau shot her a wary glance. "Yeah."

"I can't do this anymore," she said to herself. "I just can't—" She tugged at one of her lace sleeves, then shoved one of the satin shoulders halfway down her arm, exposing the prettiest strapless bra Beau had ever seen. It was so low it revealed the tops of her rose-colored nipples.

The woman was a nut. No doubt about it. But, sweet Peter, the way she was shimmying was distracting as hell. Beau shook his head and cleared his throat. "Miss—"

Making a husky sound of frustration, she reached behind her and started to pull at her zipper. The entire front of the dress fell to her waist and Beau's mouth went stone dry. Her breasts were plump, high, and the baser part of him was praying she would keep wiggling until they escaped the confines of her bra. He felt as if his brain had just plunged into his jeans and all he could do was stare.

The sound of an engine backfiring down the road snapped him out of his fantasy. "What in hell are you doing?"

She continued to squirm, mesmerizing him with her movements. "I'm getting out of this dress, this *wedding* dress," she said.

The woman was most definitely a nut. It went against every bit of testosterone in his body to prevent an attractive women from undressing, but someone had to lend sanity to this situation. Beau put his hands on her arms and tugged the satin dress upward. "You can't take the dress off. You're in a parking lot. A public parking lot."

Adamant, Emily pushed his hands away and her dress back down. "I don't care. I'm not wearing this farce, this lie, this *joke* one minute more."

Beau swore and jerked the dress up again, this time keeping his hands on the satin. "Just keep it on until I get you home."

She shook her head and tugged at the same time he did. "No!" A tearing sound permeated the darkness. She froze. "Oh, no."

Beau saw the stark distress in her wide eyes and felt his gut dip. He'd torn her wedding dress, for Pete's sake. *Oh, no.* She was going to cry. He cringed. He hated it when women cried. "Listen, it'll be okay. You'll—"

She shook her head and gave him a desperate look. Her face went pale. "Excuse me, but I think I'm going to be—"

Then Miss Emily lost her tequila on his boots.

The bride from hell slept late the following morning.

After a quick shower, Beau checked on Miss Emily

and sighed impatiently. Sunday morning was a great morning to sleep in and wander around the house in his underwear. His unexpected visitor, however, had nipped those plans in the bud.

Emily might look like an angel, but his boots knew better. He'd sprayed them with a water hose at Jimmy's, then driven home. It was tough to hold a grudge, however, when the woman expressed her apologies every other minute. After he'd directed her to his bed, the only *real* bed in his house at the moment, he'd crashed on the sofa which was about a foot too short for his long frame.

Beau liked his solitude. He liked messing up his dishes and not having anyone gripe at him. Drinking a beer and smoking a cigar alone in the privacy of his home was one of his top-ten most relaxing things to do. It wasn't that he was a hermit or misogynist. He appreciated women, the sound of their voices, their bodies, the way they walked. Hell, he loved the way they smelled and breathed.

But Beau had learned through hard personal experience that associations with the female gender were best conducted in controlled doses. Convinced that many of his buddies' main problems stemmed from overexposure to estrogen, the only female he allowed around him on a regular, twenty-four hour basis was his black lab, Cookie. Unlike his beloved but bothersome sisters, she was quiet and easy to please.

Sipping his coffee, he scowled at the woman sleeping peacefully. He was irritated because he'd missed his ball game, his boots would never be the same and he had a crick in his neck. All thanks to Miss Emily.

He looked at her critically. Even in sleep with her hair mussed and her makeup smudged, she was pretty.

She was pretty, but she was a pain.

Her body completely still, she surprised him when her big, blue eyes fluttered open and her gaze latched onto his.

"You're not Carl." Emily said the first words that came into her pounding head as she looked at the big frowning stranger in the doorway.

His expression didn't change. "I'm Beau Ramsey. You're in my bed."

Alarm shot through her and she quickly sat up. Her head screamed in protest and her stomach wrenched. "Oh, my, what—where—"

She clutched her forehead and took deep breaths. When she was able to open her eyes, she noticed the white lace around her wrist. She was still wearing her wedding gown. Her stomach sank further as a flood of disorganized memories rushed through her.

Her wedding had been yesterday. Of course she'd left midway through the ceremony. The shocked faces of her fiancé, mother, bridesmaids, and all three hundred and fifty-four wedding guests crowded her mind.

Along with the imposing presence of the unhappy man in the doorway.

He didn't look at all like Carl. Carl was tall but thin, with a fair complexion and prematurely receding hairline which she'd insisted she never minded. Carl was elegant and refined.

On the other hand, this man was uncivilized looking. Everything about him was dark, from his full head of black hair to his dark eyebrows and brown eyes to his forbidding scowl. His casual shirt was stretched across broad shoulders and failed to conceal well-developed biceps. Her gaze dropped to his jeans and she blinked at the way the denim molded his hips and thighs with heart-stopping accuracy.

The physical package was threatening enough, but the way he stood watching her, with casual, masculine ease and more confidence than any human should possess shredded her already tattered nerve endings.

Gutless wonder that she was, Emily saw the vast potential for panic in this situation. If she wasn't afraid that it would split her head in two, she might scream, but she suspected she would need every bit of brainpower she could muster with this man.

She swallowed. "Please pardon me. I'm not at my best this morning, and there are a few gaps in my—uh—short-term memory."

He nodded. "You were knockin' back tequila last night at the Happy Hour Bar until you were drunk on your a—"

He must have seen her eyes widen in alarm. Clearing his throat, he altered his tone. "Until you became incapacitated. Since I'm the sheriff of Ruxton, North Carolina, I'm often called in for this kind of insanity, even," he added in a tone oozing resentment, "on my nights off."

"Oh," Emily said, and more pictures came to mind. She remembered the rustic bar and her original plan to get a soft drink. Depression had taken over, however, when she realized she was spending her wedding night in a bar. She didn't recall much of her conversation with the sheriff. Unfortunately she did recall getting sick on his boots.

Emily closed her eyes again, this time in embarrassment. "I'm very sorry about your boots. I'll be glad to replace them."

"All starting to come back to you?" Beau prodded.

"Yes," she whispered full of disappointment and shame.

"Then I reckon you've learned an important lesson, Emily," he said, his voice stabbing her consciousness like black coffee.

An important lesson? Just one? How about ten! She couldn't begin to catalog everything she'd learned in the last twenty-four hours. She peeked at him between her fingers. "What important lesson?"

"Tequila's a helluva lot better going down than coming back up."

Emily blinked. Her life was completely devastated and this man was talking about tequila. "How profound," she said, and lowered her hands to look at him. His gaze unsettled her. Behind his easy confidence, there was an intensity about him that made her uncomfortably aware of the fact that she was in his bed.

Emily suspected that when a woman woke up in Beau's bed, she rarely woke up alone. And she'd bet her mother's diamond tiara that whoever he chose to take to his bed never woke wearing a stitch of clothing. If he didn't remove her clothes with his hands, he could probably burn them off with his hot gaze.

Her stomach gave a jolt and she decided it might

be best if she got out of bed. Clearing her throat, she pushed off the covers and slid her feet to the floor. Her head pounded and her stomach twisted with nausea. She lifted her hand to her forehead.

Beau stepped toward her. "You gonna be sick?"

She shook her head and winced at the motion. "No. I just—" She took a deep breath and smelled the shower-clean scent of him. She kept her gaze averted, and frowned when she saw the rip in her dress. "When did that happen?"

"What?"

She pulled at the torn seam. "This? I don't remember—" She broke off and made a frustrated sound.

"You really don't remember how it happened?" he prompted.

Her mind drew a blank. She looked up at him and shook her head. "No."

He nodded. "Okay."

Emily waited for him to explain, but he remained silent. "Are you going to tell me?"

He gave her a considering glance and shook his head. "Nah," he said, and turned to leave the room.

Surprised, she stumbled after him, wondering how his easy stride ate up so much space. Must be his long legs. "But you know...when it happened."

"Yeah. Do you want some coffee before I take you to get your car?"

She stepped in front of him. "I'd like to know how this dress was torn."

His gaze swept over her breasts, then back up to her eyes. "No, you don't."

Irritated and more than a little rattled, she thought

of all the times she'd been told what she wanted and what she didn't want. Emily stiffened her spine. "Yes, I do."

He gave her a long assessing glance, then shrugged. "You tried to strip in the Happy Hour Bar parking lot last night and I *prevented* you."

Emily gaped at him. "That's impossible. I don't believe you. You tore my dress!"

"You were pushing it down. I was pulling it up."

"You're crazy."

He lifted a dark eyebrow as if he was certain *she* was the one with one sandwich short of a picnic. "You said, 'I'm not wearing this farce, this lie, this joke one minute more.'" His gaze dropped to her breasts. "And your strapless bra has two little white roses right in the middle."

Emily blinked, his words echoing through her mind. They sounded familiar. *Farce, joke, lie.* Her stomach rolled. "I didn't *really* try to undress in a public parking lot, did I?" she whispered.

"Yeah, you did. And next time you decide to strip, Emily, don't expect me to stop you."

A knock sounded at the door. "Oh, Beau," a singsong feminine voice called. "Jimmy's wife called Valene and she called Rosemary, so we—"

Beau swore and looked at the ceiling as if he needed help. "Just a minute. Just a minute," he called, then turned to Emily. "It's my sisters. If you want to get out alive, you better hide in the bathroom."

"Bathroom?" Emily echoed.

"At the end of the hall."

"Oh, Beau," the singsong feminine voice called again.

Beau swore again. "Better get the lead out, Emily, the bridal party's almost here. Hell, this day's gotta get better. It can't get worse." He strode toward the kitchen.

"Down the hall," he told Emily, and braced himself for the invasion. Hearing the click of the bathroom door, he jerked open the side door to his house and calmly greeted his sisters. "Good morning. This is not an approved time for visiting your brother."

Rosemary looked hurt. Valene widened her eyes as if she hadn't a clue about his comment. Caroline just smiled and shoved through the doorway. "Oh, you!" she said and jabbed him in the ribs with her elbow. "We usually leave you alone in the mornings in case you've got a visitor, but this one's different. She was wearing a wedding dress, and everybody knows no woman in a wedding dress has gotten within five miles of you."

Beau watched his three wily sisters work their way into his den. Rosemary straightened a picture. Valene plumped a pillow. Caroline plopped down in his favorite chair.

He squinted his eyes to keep them from twitching. "It was part of the job. The woman was incapacitated."

Valene nodded. "Jimmy said she was a pretty thing."

"I heard she was drinking straight whiskey," Rosemary added.

Beau restrained the urge to correct her. "She was just passing through."

Caroline sat up. "She can't be gone. Her BMW is still in Jimmy's parking lot."

"She's just passing through," he said firmly.

The sound of running water coming from the bathroom may as well have been a stage whisper. In unison his sisters perked up.

"She's in the bathroom," Rosemary said triumphantly.

Beau ground his teeth together and watched Valene adjust a lamp shade. He just hoped his sister didn't go fishing in the drawer on the end table where she'd find where he kept his cigars. Best to get Emily out in the open. "Come on out, Emily," he called, then added dryly, "My sisters are dying to meet you."

He heard the doorknob rattle and her footsteps on his oak hallway. Hearing his sisters' gasps, he glanced up and felt a punch in his gut. She'd washed her face and released her shoulder-length golden blond hair from its knot. The only evidence of last night's excess was her pale complexion. Her blue eyes looked huge, her rose mouth was parted slightly. Her hand clutched the tiara veil. Dressed in the elaborate white gown, she looked like a—

"She looks like a princess," Rosemary whispered.

Emily's lips tilted into a wry smile and she shook her head. "I think I'm ready to hang up my crown."

Caroline tossed Beau an inquiring look. "Where'd she sleep last night?"

The question put color in Emily's cheeks. Beau rolled his eyes. "She got the bed. I got the sofa."

Valene stepped closer. "The gown. It's Dior, isn't it?"

"Yes," Emily said, and her mouth tightened in a firm line. "Do you know someone who could use it? It has a tear, though…"

Valene lifted her hands to her cheeks in amazement. "But it's your wedding dress. A Dior," she repeated.

"Was my wedding dress," Emily corrected. "I won't be needing it after I get to the suitcase in my car."

That announcement left his sisters speechless for a moment. He could sense their combined curiosity swell. Beau saw the flicker come and go in Emily's eyes, anger and womanly determination, and he felt an alarm go off inside him. He had an instinct for identifying potential problems. It served him well in his capacity as sheriff. And as a man. He'd seen that expression before, the look of a lady pushed too far, the expression of a good woman ready to go *bad*. Give well-bred, soft-spoken, classy Emily a little time and she would wreak havoc. Underneath that white lace, she was dangerous. He would just as soon she do her wreaking somewhere other than Ruxton.

Caroline stood, continuing to give Emily an assessing gaze. "We'll take you to your car. Beau says you're just passing through, but Ruxton's a friendly place if you think you'd like to stay awhile."

Emily lifted her hand to her forehead. "I hadn't really decided what I was…" She grimaced. "Is there a hotel?"

"No," Beau said, quickly, firmly.

Rosemary shot him a dirty look. "You could stay with one of us until you find a place to rent."

Beau bit back an oath. He'd seen his sisters do this before. Take in a stranger as if she was a lost puppy. The action was partly motivated out of the goodness of their hearts and partly motivated out of sheer nosiness. "Emily may not find Ruxton's atmosphere to her liking."

"Why not?" Valene asked.

"I don't think she's the kind of woman who'd be happy living in a place where the primary entertainment on Saturday nights is a tractor-pull race."

"You don't know about her background, do you?"

"I can guess," he told Rosemary. "She probably went to a private liberal arts college and majored in something like English."

His sisters looked at Emily expectantly.

"Fine art," Emily corrected. "I have a master's degree in fine art."

Beau nodded. "And are you employed?"

Emily cleared her throat. "I've primarily been involved with charity work for the last six months."

Beau's lips twisted in satisfaction.

"There's no need to be nasty," Caroline said. "Why don't we ask Emily what she wants to do?"

All eyes turned to Emily.

She blinked as if she'd never been asked her preference. Then her face cleared, and she smiled so brightly Beau would have sworn he didn't need any lights in his room. "I want to get out of this dress, and I want to stay."

Two

Emily St. Clair was wreaking havoc by the following week.

"It hurts me," Jimmy said to Beau. "But I'm not sure I'm gonna be able to keep her."

"What's the problem?" Beau asked, glancing at Emily as she worked the other end of the bar. "She can't remember the beer orders?"

Jimmy shook his head. "No. She's smart enough. It's the customers and, uh—" he lowered his voice "—Nadine. I had Emily waiting tables, but she kept getting offers."

"Kept getting hit on," Beau clarified as he sipped his beer. He wasn't surprised. If he didn't have that itchy instinct warning him away from her, he might be making a few indecent proposals himself.

"No. She kept getting marriage proposals."

Beau choked. "Are you joking?"

"No. These guys wanna take her home to mother and then to bed or vice versa. Anyway, I put her behind the bar to kinda, you know, protect her a little." Jimmy sighed. "The damn bar's packed now. And Nadine's pissed because her tips have dropped down to nothing."

Beau looked at the crowd around the other end of the bar and nodded. "Looks like you've got a problem."

"Well, how you gonna help me?" Jimmy whined.

"I'm not. She's not doing anything illegal." *Technically,* he added to himself. Her smile and husky voice should be on the books at least as a misdemeanor. And her body would be a felony.

"Aw, come on. This is your fault," Jimmy said.

"My fault," Beau echoed in disbelief, still watching Emily. "This should be good. Somebody needs to tell Hank to wipe the drool off his chin."

"Hank's the worst of the bunch," Jimmy agreed. "But this is all your fault. It's those sisters of yours. They talked to Thelma and persuaded her to influence me to hire Emily."

Beau gave a rough chuckle. "And you're afraid Thelma will stop *influencing* you if you fire Emily. You must have liked the way she used her influence."

Jimmy scowled. "Stop it, Beau. It's not a joking matter when a wife withholds her—" he cleared his throat "—affection. It can be downright painful."

Beau smirked. "You can handle it."

Jimmy sighed and hunkered closer to Beau. "What I need is for someone to take Emily off the market.

Then these dogs would go back to buying beer and leave her alone.''

His bachelor survival instinct rose inside him higher than a killer wave. Beau immediately shook his head. "No way. Get another sucker. Besides, nobody would believe I'd let a woman get her hooks in me.''

"But you—''

At that moment Hank dropped to his knees in front of Emily and took her hands in his. Emily looked down at him in bemusement as the crowd roared with laughter.

Beau watched Hank's mouth form those timeless suicidal words, "Marry me.''

"This is pathetic,'' Beau muttered, and noticed that most everyone grew silent in order to hear what Emily would say.

She disengaged her hands and backed away. "No thank you,'' she said quietly, but firmly. "I won't marry you.'' Frustration tugged at her face and she raised her voice. "I'm not getting married. Do you hear me? I'm not getting married. Ever.''

A long silence followed.

Hank's disappointment showed, then another idea must have occurred to him. "Does that mean you'll consider living in sin?''

During his late-night driving patrol, Beau rounded the turn, and the beam from his headlights skimmed over the vehicle pulled off the road. He slowed. Pine Mountain Lake was off-limits after sundown. It took only a second look for him to ID the car—the only BMW in town.

Beau pulled to a stop and sighed. What was Emily doing here? He checked his watch and got out of his car. It was almost midnight.

She stood a few feet from the moonlit water, her hair catching the reflection of the moon. An ethereal sight, she stared down at something in her hand. She looked lonely. The notion made him uncomfortable, though he wasn't sure why. He cleared his throat. "Emily," he said, keeping his voice low so he wouldn't startle her.

"Hello, Sheriff Ramsey," she said without turning her head.

He came to a stop beside her. "How did you know it was me?"

"The squad car."

She was looking at her engagement ring, Beau noted. "Did you see the No Trespassing After Dark sign?"

"Yes," she said, closing her fingers around the ring and shaking it as if it were dice.

"Then you know you're not supposed to be here."

Her face went solemn for a moment, then seemed to clear. She turned to him. "I guess that means I'm breaking the law. What are you going to do about it?" she asked with an odd mix of politeness and defiance, then strolled closer to the water.

Beau stifled a sigh and followed. He could opt for a hard-nosed approach, but he knew what kind of effect his sisters could have on a person. "Are my sisters driving you nuts yet?"

"Not really," she said. "But sometimes it's difficult to think with people around, even if they're kind. And your sisters are very kind." She glanced at him. "I like it here at night. You should change the law."

Beau bit back a wry grin. "You've got me confused with the town council. I don't make the rules. I just try to keep the peace."

"I bet you could get them to change it."

He glanced at her curiously. She was a strange bird. "Why would I want to do that?"

"Because it's nice here at night. Quiet and peaceful. You can almost hear yourself think."

"The teenagers used to go parking here. The parents got bent out of shape."

"Where do they go now?"

"Dirt road behind the Massenberg farm."

She nodded, but didn't say anything.

Beau studied her. Again she reminded him of a woman who had been pushed just a little too far. Thank God, she didn't look like she was going to cry, but the anger and apathy glinting in her eyes made him uneasy. Through personal experience, he'd learned anger and apathy could be a damn dangerous combination.

"What's on your mind, Emily?" he asked, struggling with his oath to stay away from damsels in distress.

She sighed and shook the ring in her hand again. "I'm trying to decide what to do with this ring. Since I technically broke the engagement, I suppose proper etiquette would indicate that I should return it."

Proper etiquette had been the guiding force in her life since she could remember.

He shoved his hands in his pockets. "Do you think you earned it?"

She looked at him. "The ring? Earned the ring?" Emily frowned as she considered that. She wondered why it was easier to talk in the dark sometimes. "Do you mean sexually?" she asked.

He stepped closer, and his warmth rippled against her like a touch. She shivered, denying the sensation. She felt his intent gaze on her, but it was easier to pretend his dark eyes weren't quite so penetrating under the cover of night.

"It doesn't have to be sexually. You probably shelled out the bucks for the wedding."

Emily felt a familiar sinking sensation in her stomach. "My mother and stepfather did." She had tried to call her mother several days ago to explain, but according to the housekeeper, her mother was *indisposed*.

"Bet you had a good reason for calling it off."

"I didn't really call it off," she said, recalling the way her mouth had refused to promise her undying love to a man who didn't love her.

Beau didn't say anything, and because he didn't prod she felt free to tell him.

Emily opened her hand and looked at the one-carat diamond solitaire. "You know that part of the ceremony where the minister says, 'Do you take this man to be your lawfully wedded husband?' That's when you're supposed to say 'I do.'"

"I guess," he muttered as if he was strictly luke-warm on the subject of marital vows.

"I said, 'I don't believe I will. Thank you very much.'"

He paused, then let out a rough chuckle. "Is that when your mother fainted?"

Emily tried to recall. "No. The minister asked me to repeat myself, so I did. I told Carl to make sure he returned all the gifts, then I left. I think her head hit the pew in front of her when I stepped down from the platform."

He continued to chuckle.

"It wasn't funny," she told him stiffly, but the im-age of her slack-jawed never-to-be husband had her swallowing her own laughter. "I did give Carl my bouquet. I thought it was appropriate since he—" She broke off when Beau snorted.

"He was probably hoping for more than flowers."

Emily felt the familiar burn of anger run through her. When she'd first learned Carl was in love with another woman, she'd felt hurt, betrayed and angry. "He'd gotten that the week before with his girlfriend in South America."

She took a deep breath, hoping the good sheriff wouldn't give her some platitude about how it was better to find out before the wedding than after. It might be true, but she still wasn't in the mood to hear it. She glanced down at the ring, tossed it slightly above her hand, then caught it. "So now I need to decide what to do with the ring. I could return it."

"Nah. I'd say you've earned it."

Emily felt her heart lighten. She tossed the ring up again. "I could have it remounted into a necklace."

"Be careful how far you throw that. It's dark out here."

"I could give it away," she continued, tossing it higher as if she hadn't heard him.

"Emily—"

"I could throw it in the lake." The appalling notion delighted her. She tossed the ring still higher. "Imagine that. Sensible Emily St. Clair throwing her engagement ring into the—"

Beau's hand stretched in front of her and he caught the ring. "Did you fall into the tequila again? Let me smell your breath."

"Give me the ring," she said, extending her hand.

"Not until you prove you're sane."

Anger licked through her. "Is it part of your job description to determine sanity?"

"In this county?" he asked. "Yes."

"I'm perfectly sober," she told him and stretched on tiptoe so he could smell her. "I told you. Wintergreen," she murmured, describing the flavor of the mint she'd eaten.

He slid his hand around her back to steady her, and her heart started to pound against her rib cage. She was struck again by his size, his broad shoulders that looked as if he could carry whatever was thrown at him. The combination of his aftershave and elusive masculine scent wrapped around her. She instinctively inhaled deeply and felt a disconcerting surge of dizziness.

"Exhale," he muttered, dipping his head.

She breathed in again. "What?"

"Breathe out."

Feeling confused and ridiculous, she pursed her lips and blew in his face. She stared at his mouth, inches from hers, for a long moment. *Did it feel as hard as it looked?* She shook her head. "I told you," she said breathlessly. "Wintergreen. Now give me the ring."

He paused and studied her, his hand still wrapped around her. "What are you going to do with it?"

She wiggled slightly, but she might as well have been trying to move a boulder. "I'm considering my options."

"I'm not letting you throw it into the lake."

"I wasn't aware there was a law preventing me from throwing my ring in the lake," she told him, wishing he weren't so close, wishing she was having an easier time breathing.

"There is tonight," he said.

Emily reached for his hand, but he ducked it behind his back. "I don't make a habit of discussing a person's size, but you should know that your body could intimidate a smaller person."

His dark gaze caught hers and his lips tilted slightly. "Is that what you're feeling, Emily? Intimidated?"

Frustrated. Annoyed. Frustratingly, annoyingly attracted. *Where had that thought come from?*

"Give me my ring. I can throw it in the *sewer* if that's what I want to do." She widened her eyes at the shocking idea. She almost couldn't believe she'd thought of it. *"The sewer,"* she whispered. "That's even better than the lake."

Beau stared at her and swore under his breath. "Lady, you are not playing with a full deck."

"No one has ever called me crazy," Emily told him solemnly. "I've been described as sensible and dependable. I've always saved for a rainy day, invested in a conservative mutual fund, voted Republican and was engaged to a doctor. I've never gotten a speeding ticket, never gone parking at a lake or behind anybody's farm, never been drunk until last week."

She pursed her lips, silent for a moment. She looked as if she were considering the direction her life had taken. A wildness glinted in her eyes. "Give me the ring."

Beau swore again. No skin off his back, he tried to tell himself. He should just let the crazy lady toss her ring into the lake, but he knew she would regret it later. Lowering his head so that she was forced to look into his eyes, he quickly stuffed the ring in his pocket and took her shoulders in his hands. "What is it gonna take to get your attention?"

Her eyes met his, dropped to his mouth, then returned to lock with his. He watched her lips part slightly and felt a jolt in his gut.

"I, uh—" she said in a husky voice and swallowed "—think you've got my attention," she finished in a whisper.

Her eyelids fluttered and he breathed in her soft, floral scent. "Then you know you can't throw a diamond ring in the lake," he said, sticking to the original issue, though a rush of sexual curiosity was flooding his veins.

"I can't?" she echoed.

"You can't," he said, fighting a compelling urge to kiss her. "Hock it and buy something you want."

"Like what?"

He shrugged, still distracted by her mouth. "I don't know. Women always want things." He was *not* going to kiss her.

"Hmmm," she said.

The sound she made affected him like an intimate caress. Beau bit back a groan and cleared his throat. "A shopping spree, some kind of trinket, a trip."

Beau watched in disbelief as she lifted her face closer to his. Inch by incredible inch, Emily closed the distance between them and her lips meshed with his.

It was the barest brushing of lips, yet he would have sworn a spark of static electricity flickered between them. Wide-eyed, Emily immediately backed away. She looked as surprised at her overture as Beau was.

Irritated with his exaggerated arousal, Beau dropped his hands from her shoulders. "Why in hell did you do that?"

"I'm sorry," she said quickly. "It was incredibly forward, wasn't it? I've never done it before, never really initiated kissing a man, that is. But you were so close and I kept staring at your mouth. I wondered if it was—" She broke off, clearly struggling for composure.

"You wondered what?"

She folded her hands. "I wondered if your mouth was hard. Or not." Her gaze slid self-consciously from his. "Again, I apologize. Could I please have my ring? I'd like to go home now."

Beau switched gears again, trying to keep up with her. He would think about that kiss later, about how warm and soft her mouth had felt, about how he'd wanted to taste her, about how he'd wanted to feel her body pressed against his. He pulled the ring from his pocket and narrowed his eyes. "Are you going to throw it in the lake?"

She hesitated. "Not tonight."

He shook his head and gave it to her. "If you get the urge to toss that ring, call me first. Okay?"

She closed her hand around the ring and began backing away. "I'll certainly give that some thought. Good night, Sheriff."

Then Beau watched as she practically ran to her car. Now that was one weird cookie, he thought.

So why were his lips still burning?

Emily closed the guest bedroom door behind her and took a long careful breath.

She was going insane.

Glancing down at the ring in her hand, she still wished she'd thrown it into the lake. She supposed flushing it down the toilet would accomplish the same task, but her creative nature liked the lake idea better. She liked the image of sending Carl for a long walk on a short pier.

It wasn't that she'd been desperately in love with Carl, but she had made plans. She'd set her mind and will to the life they would share together. If her heart hadn't exactly followed, well, she hadn't focused on that.

She thought now as she stared at the ring, perhaps she should have.

Emily was beginning to think she might need to start listening to her heart and not just her head. It was a different approach for her, and she wasn't exactly sure *how* to do it.

She suspected kissing the sheriff just because she was fascinated by his mouth wasn't a great first step. Groaning in embarrassment, she covered her eyes. It was obvious Beau Ramsey not only didn't approve of her, he didn't like her. He thought she was a frivolous mental lightweight. Which wasn't true! she thought in frustration.

Memories of the past ten years of her life rolled through her head. Almost every decision she'd made, from her clothes, to her education, to her fiancé, had been made because it was expected of her.

She was expected to be sensible and accommodating. She was the one everyone depended on to just go along with what was best.

Impatience flashed through her. The feeling was rising inside her more and more frequently. She'd had enough of doing what everyone else thought she should do. She'd done it so much she wasn't completely sure what she herself wanted anymore.

Enough.

It was time to cut Emily loose and find out what Emily really wanted in life. Ruxton was the perfect place. Nobody knew her, so she didn't have to be totally sensible. She could even go a little wild.

Three

"Beau's not all bad," Rosemary said, as she gave her four-year-old daughter a graham cracker and quick kiss. "He'd make a wonderful father and a nice husband."

Caroline sipped her coffee and rolled her eyes at her sister's remark. "Are you confused? Beau would make a nice husband if he wanted to get married, Rosemary."

"You're being too hard on him. He just hasn't found the right woman, yet."

"He prefers floozies," Caroline said. "That Donna woman he's seeing now has been around the block more than once."

"Donna?" Emily prompted when she could get a word in edgewise. Beau's three sisters got together for coffee at least once a week, and they had insisted she join them. She hadn't expected them to be so free with their discussion about Beau, but she was curious about him. Too curious, she thought, recalling the way she'd kissed him last night. She gave herself a hard shake.

Knowledge was power, she told herself. The more she knew about Beau, the less curious she would be. When no one responded to her, she repeated herself. "Donna?"

Valene nodded. "Donna is his current…" Her face creased as she searched for the appropriate word.

"Lady friend," Rosemary offered uncertainly, as she sent her daughter into the next room to play.

Caroline snorted. "Try occasional bedmate."

Valene frowned at her sister. "There are children within hearing distance."

"Excuse me. How would you describe her?"

"I'm not sure I would call her a true lady. Their relationship is difficult to categorize."

Caroline turned to Emily. "Donna and Beau don't have a relationship. They have an arrangement. A no-commitment, no-strings arrangement."

"So, they're lovers," Emily concluded, and felt her curiosity grow. She'd never been anyone's *lover*. She didn't think any man had ever felt that passionate about her, and she'd never felt that kind of passion for any man. Even for the man she had planned to marry. Emily suppressed a wince at that thought.

All three sisters looked at her in shock.

Valene shook her head. "I'm not sure Beau uses the *L* word."

"Or the *M* word," Caroline added.

"Love and marriage?" Emily asked, and watched

Caroline nod. "It sounds as if he may have a limited vocabulary."

Valene laughed. "I think I like that assessment best," she said, then refilled Emily's coffee cup. "The truth is that several years ago Beau was head over heels with a debutante who lived in the next county. She played with him and led him on, then married a lawyer from Raleigh. Soon after that, Beau left Ruxton for a long time."

Rosemary sighed. "He's never been the same. I think, deep down, he's lonely."

Emily wondered about that. Beau seemed like a completely self-contained man, under control. He was the kind who called the shots. "It's hard for me to imagine him falling that hard for a woman."

Caroline nodded. "It was a long time ago. The way he protects his bachelorhood now you'd think he was guarding Fort Knox. But he still has a man's normal drive."

"Caroline," Valene said, "it's not appropriate to discuss Beau's drive."

"I'm only explaining for Emily," she retorted. "It's a sad waste of masculinity. Beau is all man. Yes, and women seem to sense it. They're always throwing themselves at him and making fools of themselves."

Emily's stomach sank. "Throwing themselves at him," she repeated.

"Bringing him meals," Rosemary said.

"Offering to clean his house," Valene offered.

Emily didn't know whether to feel relieved or not. At least she hadn't cooked for him or offered to clean his house.

"Of course, there are others who try a more physical approach." Caroline lowered her voice. "You know how some women rub up against men like cats in heat. I know of one who was even bold enough to kiss him."

Emily nearly scalded her tongue with her coffee. She winced.

"Caroline," Valene said in a warning voice, then turned to Emily with a gentle smile. "Don't worry. He stays away from the good women. You won't have a bit of trouble with him."

From the screen door of her rented home, Emily saw the mattress first, then the man's boots. "Tom?" she said, expecting Rosemary's husband.

"No," the distinctive baritone voice behind the mattress said.

Emily grimaced. "Sheriff Ramsey," she managed to say, feeling a strange shimmy inside her. "How kind of you. Rosemary told me she would send Tom with the bed."

"He was busy. You gonna hold that door open?"

"Of course." Emily opened the door and moved to the side.

"Which room?"

"Upstairs at the end of the hall."

He grunted. "Figures."

"I can help—"

"Please don't."

Emily watched him haul the mattress upstairs, and despite his sour attitude, she couldn't help noticing what a nice rear end the good sheriff had. She blinked at her observation and shook her head. The last time she'd gotten fixated on part of Beau Ramsey's anatomy, she'd kissed him. What was she going to do this time? Pat him or pinch him? Emily bit back a groan.

He brought up the box spring and frame, and she followed with the headboard. It took just a few minutes to put it all together. Emily stared at the bed and felt a rush of excitement.

"You look like you've got plans for this bed," Beau said dryly.

"I do," she said brightly as she reached for the shopping bag of new linens. "I bought two sets of sheets and a comforter. It's hard to believe, but this will be the first time I've lived alone," she confessed.

He raised his eyebrows. "Is that so?"

She wondered why she felt uneasy under his intense gaze. Other men had looked at her before, and it hadn't affected her at all. She tore the plastic wrap off one set of linens and filled the silence. "Yes, my mother was a little overprotective. She was always afraid some hoodlum on a motorcycle would seduce me away from what she called 'a better life.'" Emily laughed. "Now that I've lived the better life, I'm wondering…"

Beau narrowed his eyes slightly. "You're thinking about finding a hoodlum on a motorcycle to seduce you."

She looked at him in surprise. "No. Actually I was wondering what it would be like to *be* a hoodlum on a motorcycle."

Beau pictured Emily decked out in leather on a Harley-Davidson, her blond hair flying, her soft smile slipping into a bad-girl grin, and felt a jolt to his system. Before everything was said and done, he suspected he was going to have to lock this woman up. He cleared his throat. "Let me help you get these on the bed."

"It's not necessary" she said, tossing the bottom sheet over the bed. "You've already done enough."

"No big deal." He helped make the bed in sheets with tiny pink rosebuds. He chuckled to himself. Emily might say motorcycles, but she was still a flowers and lace kind of woman. Beau had learned a long time ago. It was no use fighting who you were, and though it wasn't his nature, he felt compelled to remind her of that fact. "Emily, sometimes a little freedom affects people like tequila, makes them do things they wouldn't normally do, things they might regret later."

She smoothed her hands over the sheets and glanced up at him. "What do you mean?"

He was distracted by the way her hands stroked the crisp cotton. The movement was sensual, and it made him wonder how her small feminine hands would feel on his bare skin, on his chest and abdomen, and lower. He frowned at the thought and looked away. "I mean, you've got to be who you are. Take for example these sheets. Roses. Now why doesn't that surprise me? You look like a roses, diamonds and champagne kind of woman."

Emily stopped and stood. "The sheets I choose to buy have nothing to do with the kind of person I am. I don't like champagne very much, and I haven't had much luck with diamonds, so in my case, appearances must be deceiving.''

She had that hint of a wild look in her eyes again. Beau felt a lick of uneasiness. ''You didn't throw away that diamond ring, did you?''

''No. I took your suggestion and pawned it. As a matter of fact, I'm using part of the money to rent this house.''

''Great,'' he said, wondering if he should have told her to toss it. Then maybe she would have left Ruxton behind. ''You've decided to stay awhile. You're ready to stay in a town where we get excited about the tractor-pull race on Saturday night?'' he asked, reminding her that she might be happier elsewhere.

''Where will it be held?''

He chuckled and shook his head. ''I don't think it's your kind of entertainment.''

She lifted her chin, tempted to show Mr. Know-it-all the other sheets in the bag, which were *not* covered with roses. ''Do you always jump to rash conclusions about newcomers?''

''Rash?'' he drawled. ''Considering your intoxicated state and your dress the first time we met, I think I've been reasonable.''

She felt a pinch of self-consciousness and wished she wasn't blushing. ''I would like to believe you could get past that.''

He nodded. ''A week later I watched a man drop to his knees to propose marriage to you in the bar.''

Emily frowned, feeling her cheeks blaze. ''I didn't encourage him.''

''Soon after that I watched you nearly throw a diamond in the lake.'' He said it as if he still couldn't believe it.

''And now I suppose you're going to bring up the fact that I kissed you,'' she said heatedly, to get it out of the way. ''I apologized. I told you—''

He shook his head slowly and looked deliberately at her mouth. ''I wasn't going to bring that up.'' His voice was low, and if she didn't know better, she might think Beau hadn't minded her kissing him nearly as much as she'd first supposed.

Turning away from that insanity, she gave a heavy sigh. ''I need a new start. A clean slate with new people and no expectations. You're never going to understand this, but I feel as if I've been living my whole life to meet other people's expectations. Somewhere in all that, I got lost. And I don't want to be lost anymore.''

A long silence followed, a silence when she wondered why she'd felt compelled to explain herself to Beau who obviously didn't approve of her.

''What makes you think I wouldn't understand?''

''Oh,'' she said in frustration, picking up a pillow to fluff it. ''You were probably born with enough self-assurance for three people. You know who you are, and if someone doesn't like it, you couldn't care less. You don't have the plague of being a people pleaser.''

''I was just plagued by three interfering, busybody sisters,'' he said in his distinctive, wry voice.

Emily bit her lip to keep from smiling and met his gaze. From her own experience, she'd learned that although Beau's sisters were as kind as the day was long, they could *hover*. "It must have been challenging in high school," she murmured.

"It's challenging *now*. They show up at my house at the crack of dawn, Rosemary straightens everything up so I can't find anything and Valene confiscates my—" He broke off abruptly as if he changed his mind about revealing more.

It wasn't polite to pry, she thought, and prompted him anyway. "She confiscates what?"

He met her gaze and reluctantly muttered, "My cigars."

"Cigars," she echoed. "I didn't know anyone besides Rodney Dangerfield smoked them anymore."

"Don't get started on the health risks," he growled.

"Oh, I wasn't," she said, sinking down on the bed. "I've always been a little curious about cigars."

"You want to smoke a cigar?" he asked in disbelief.

Emily felt her cheeks heat again. "Not really smoke," she murmured, recalling the sensual image she'd once seen in a movie that had stirred her curiosity.

He stepped closer, his large frame pushing into her personal space. Her gaze fell helplessly down from his belt buckle. His jeans might as well have been custom made, the way they skimmed over his muscular thighs and cupped his masculinity.

"Then what?" he asked.

Dropping her gaze to his boots, Emily shifted on the bed and took a careful breath. "It's silly. Nothing really."

"If it's nothing, then why not tell me?" His husky drawl taunted her.

Rattled, she responded to the challenge. "I always thought it might be fun to—" She stopped mid-sentence, changing her mind.

"Fun to do what?" he prompted as he sat down beside her, using the mild tone he probably used to interrogate suspects.

No way out, she thought, reluctantly meeting his gaze. She finished in a low voice. "Fun to light a man's cigar."

His dark eyes flickered dangerously, but he didn't move closer. "You mean in a restaurant or a bar?"

"Not really," she said, curious about that flicker in his eyes, curious about the sensation in the pit of her stomach. "I mean in bed."

His nostrils flared as he sucked in a deep breath. He leaned over her. "Emily, since you haven't been on your own, I'm gonna give you a little warning. You might not want to tell a man you're curious about lighting his cigar in bed, or he'll expect you to do more than strike a match."

Her chest tightened, and she breathed in his scent. His dark eyes fascinated her. She swallowed. "I haven't told anyone about the cigar thing," she told him. "Besides you're the sheriff and you think I've got as much substance as cotton candy, so you don't really count."

"I don't count," he repeated.

Her stomach flipped again. "You're not attracted to me."

He just stared at her.

"You don't approve of me," she babbled to fill the silence. "You're the sheriff. I can trust you."

"Oh, Emily." Beau swore under his breath and rubbed his face. "I'm sworn to uphold the law, but I'm no priest." He waited a beat, and his gaze swept over her. "Your body's fair game."

Emily gulped. "Bu-but—but you think I'm a piece of fluff."

He shook his head. "I never said you were a piece of fluff."

"But you think it," she insisted.

"I think," he told her, "you are a woman on the verge of causing a lot of trouble. I'm torn between locking you up or locking up the entire male population of Ruxton. Here's a newsflash, princess, I'm a member of the male population."

"Is this your way of saying you're somewhat attracted to me?"

"It's my way of saying I saw you half-naked that first night, and I haven't forgotten the color of your nipples and the fact that your breasts are larger than they look hiding under your clothes. It's my way of saying I liked what I saw and wouldn't mind seeing you that way again." He leaned closer, but lowered his voice. "It's my way of saying *I count.*"

She felt a blast of hot, purely sexual curiosity mixed with a tingle of apprehension, and she didn't have a clue what to do with either feeling. The tension between them was as tight as a steel spring.

"Do you understand what I'm saying?" he asked as he lifted his finger to her chin, then grazed it upward over her mouth.

She could have pulled back, but something inside her wouldn't allow it. Instead, she instinctively parted her lips and he slipped his finger inside her mouth. A sensual invasion. Her heart pounded against her rib cage.

As her gaze locked with his, she flicked her tongue over his skin and tasted him.

He went very still. "You're not listening, Emily. I said I count."

The warning in his eyes, more than his voice, got through to her. She gradually backed away, then looked away from him. "I understand," she managed finally. "You count."

She heard the ragged release of his breath. "Don't forget it," he muttered and stood.

Too restless to remain seated, she stood, too, and tripped over the bag of the other sheets. They slid out of the bag across the floor. Emily winced.

Beau reached down and picked up the sheets from the floor.

Emily felt as if he were looking at her lingerie. She didn't need to see his face to hear the question in his mind. "Just another set of sheets," she said, and pulled them from his hands.

He chuckled, but the sound was strained. "Right. Just another set of sheets." He walked away, and she heard him swear before he muttered, "Black satin."

In the darkness of his den, in his favorite over-stuffed chair, Beau inhaled the fine cigar and waited for the familiar mellow sense of satisfaction. With his black lab lying quietly at his feet, he waited. And waited.

Irritation nicked at him. He set the cigar in the ashtray and brooded. He'd taken a woman out for the evening. Donna Grant had given him all the right signals that she would be willing for him to stay with her until morning. He and Donna had an arrangement. She didn't try to pin him down, he didn't make promises he wouldn't keep, and they got along because they could bring each other satisfaction without a lot of extra baggage.

Beau could have been in Donna's bed at this very minute, but his mind was filled with the image of another woman and another bed. A woman with silky blond hair, a quick, honest smile and blue eyes that changed like the weather. It was easy for him to visualize her wrapped in nothing but a black satin sheet. Easy for him to imagine the creamy softness of her throat, the upper curve of her breasts and the pebbled hardness of her small rosy nipples.

His body swelled in response. Still irritated, Beau picked up the cigar and drew on it again. He narrowed his eyes. She was curious about him. He'd seen the sexual curiosity in her gaze, the drive to explore his desire and her own. She had an innocent look to her. For a crazy moment, he wondered if she was a virgin.

He shook off that notion. Women, no, make that girls, shed their virginity at a younger age nowadays. She was just inexperienced. With her wedding fiasco still fresh in her mind, she was also vulnerable. She was probably convinced she wasn't the marrying kind, and under the right conditions, could be coaxed into an affair to soothe her wounded feminine ego.

Beau flicked his ashes into the ashtray and considered the situation from a different angle. If he was a nice guy, he would leave her alone. He would give her a wide berth and let someone else console Emily. If he followed his instincts, he would stay the hell away from her. She was like a champagne bottle that had been shaken up. When her cork popped, all hell was going to break loose.

The image of her wrapped in a black satin sheet, however, was like an intimate stroke that teased and promised satisfaction. And Beau was suffering from a gnawing sense of dissatisfaction. He wondered how she would taste. He wondered how her eyes would change when he touched her. He wondered what husky words of need she would whisper.

He wondered a helluva lot about Miss Emily. If he was a nice guy, though, he would leave her alone. Beau had never considered himself a nice guy. He was a wolf. There was still the matter of his instincts, however. He rarely strayed from the practice of following his instincts, because on the few occasions he had, he'd gotten burned. Unfortunately, with the image of Emily singeing his mind, he was already burning up and he hadn't done a thing.

Emily didn't make it to the tractor pull, but she did take in the Ruxton Flea Market on Saturday morning. Held in the parking lot of the big Methodist church on Main Street, the flea market exhibited a carnival atmosphere. Aside from a myriad of vendors, a group of musicians played bluegrass, a woman gave Tarot card readings and another woman, dressed as a clown, twisted balloons into animals and crazy hats.

She was surprised to see Beau strolling among the vendors. He nodded slowly upon seeing her and moved toward her. She watched his face and would have sworn she'd seen something primitive and predatory flash across his features, but then he gave her that cocky half grin. "Missed you at the festivities last night," he said.

"I'm sure you did," she said, full of skepticism. "I wouldn't have thought this would be your choice of venue for a Saturday morning."

He walked alongside her. "We had a little problem with homemade liquor last month."

"Oh," Emily said, and lowered her voice. "Moonshine. Did you have to make a raid?"

"I confiscated it," he said with a too-straight face.

Emily studied him carefully. "Did you taste any of it?"

"Only to validate the fact that it hadn't been approved by the ABC. We don't have a lab available for small cases."

She laughed despite herself. "How much did you drink for this validation?"

"Not much," he admitted. "I needed a fire extinguisher after one gulp."

She stepped up to the pretzel vendor. "Would you like one?" she asked Beau.

He looked surprised. "Yeah."

She handed him the warm, salty pretzel and took a bite of her own. "I'm still surprised you didn't find someone else for this detail. Shopping,'' she said with a smile.

''My part-time deputy's on vacation. It's not so bad. Pretty blondes buy me pretzels. Changed your sheets yet?'' he asked slyly.

She willed her cheeks not to heat. ''I usually change them once a week. I've never slept on satin, so it'll be a new experience.'' *Give it back to him,* she told herself. ''Have you?''

He gave her a double take. ''Have I what?''

''Ever slept on satin sheets?'' she asked, and watched a fleeting uneasiness cross the sheriff's face. Something about that expression gave her a strange sense of power.

He paused, his uneasiness short-lived. ''No,'' he said, taunting her with his devil dark eyes. ''Care to give me a new experience?'' His voice was as slick as her satin sheets.

Emily felt herself getting in over her head. She took a quick breath. ''I—uh—'' She glanced around wildly. ''Ever had a balloon hat before?''

''No, but—''

Emily gave the clown the high sign before Beau could finish, and within a minute, she placed the balloon Indian hat in his hand with a smile. ''There. Now you can't say I've never given you a new experience.''

Beau looked at the balloon. ''You're not as fluffy as I thought.''

Emily gave a low laugh. ''You're not quite as fast as I thought.''

His eyes instantly proved her a liar, moving over

her body at Mach speed. "I was a rodeo rider, princess. You'd be surprised what I can do in eight seconds."

A rodeo rider? A cowboy? She was so surprised that she didn't immediately respond. The moment passed, and a child's wail cut through the happy sounds of the crowd.

Beau glanced away from her and moved toward the wailing. Emily instinctively followed behind him. At the end of the row of vendors stood a little girl, crying at the top of her lungs. Tears stained her cheeks, and the look of fear on her face grabbed at Emily's heart.

Emily watched Beau kneel down in front of her and speak quietly. The child's eyes rounded with even more fear until he offered the balloon hat. The moppet eyed him suspiciously, but clenched the balloon in her hand. "I can't find my mama."

"Well, we should be able to fix that. Can you tell me your name?"

"Hil'ry." She backed away slightly.

Beau nodded. "And your mother's name."

Hilary frowned at him. "Regina," she whispered.

"And your last name?" Beau prompted.

"I don't want you. I want my mama." She began to cry again.

The sound tore at Emily. She didn't want to intrude, but didn't think she would hurt the situation any. Stepping closer to the little girl, she pulled a generous piece off her pretzel. "Would you like a bite of my pretzel until your mother gets here?"

Hilary scrutinized Emily and the pretzel, then

sniffed and wiped her nose with the back of her hand. "Yes, ma'am. Thank you."

Within a couple of minutes, Hilary scarfed down the rest of Emily's pretzel and had taken residence in her lap. The experience bemused Emily because she'd never considered herself particularly adept with children, even when she'd been one. The slight weight of Hilary in her lap, the sunshine scent of her hair and the simplicity of a shared treat tugged at her. There was an indescribable pleasure having a child befriend you even if it was by way of a bribe.

"See if you can get her last name out of her," Beau muttered, as he brought another pretzel.

Emily nodded. "Hilary's a nice name. What's your last name?"

"Bell," she said around a bite of pretzel. She tossed Beau another scowling glance.

Emily laughed. "Is this your first experience with a female who refused to be charmed?"

He shot her an aren't-we-clever look and bent next to Emily's ear. The sensation gave her such a rush she almost didn't hear him. "Get her to talk about her mother. I've asked around and nobody here knows who she is."

"Hilary, where did you last see your mother?"

"She was playing bingo in the church, and I wanted to look at the clown, so I went to the window and watched. And then I kinda went out the door. For just a minute!" she insisted desperately, her face crumpling. "I went back and she was gone."

Emily gave her a comforting squeeze. "I bet that felt scary."

"Yeah," Hilary said in a quavery voice so quiet Emily almost couldn't hear it. "Can you make that man go away?"

"Why? He's the sheriff. He's here to help you."

Hilary looked unconvinced. "Does he hit? My daddy's big like him, and he hits."

It was a hot, summer day, but Emily felt as if someone had just injected ice water in her veins. She took a deep breath and searched for her composure; at the same time her gaze met Beau's. "No, sweetheart. The sheriff doesn't hit."

She watched something happen in Beau Ramsey's eyes—anger, rare, righteous anger; and compassion, strong and powerful. And that combination rocked her world.

Four

Beau's tension surrounded him like a force field. Within minutes he'd located Regina Bell and had a quiet talk with her while Emily entertained Hilary. Regina had been frantically searching for Hilary inside the church. Regina and Hilary left with Emily promising to visit her new little friend again soon.

The swap meet began to disassemble—a morning crowd of people who obviously had other things to do in the afternoon. From a few feet away, Emily sensed the strength of Beau's disquiet as she watched him making some notes as he sat in the squad car. Her ability to feel his feelings disturbed her. While she often read other people's emotions accurately, she also could usually distance herself. This time she couldn't, and she wasn't sure why.

She took a couple of steps closer to Beau and crossed her arms over her chest. *What to say,* she wondered, yet knew she had to say something. "No white lightning today," she murmured.

He glanced at her, the anger and compassion still glowing from his eyes. "White lightning's a helluva lot easier to deal with."

"She wouldn't press charges?"

"No." He rose from the car as if he couldn't bear to sit any longer. "She said he's not living with them anymore. She just wants to put it in the past."

"And you're concerned it won't stay in the past," Emily continued.

He narrowed his eyes. "She's serving him with divorce papers, and he's got a nasty temper."

Emily felt a chill. "The story's all too common, isn't it?"

He slammed his car door. "Not in Ruxton, dammit. Not in my town."

His anger washed over her, surprising her into momentary silence. "What did you do?" she asked when she found her voice.

"I told her to call me if she changed her mind or if her ex comes calling." He shook his head. "She won't."

It made no sense to her, but she wanted him to feel better. "You did what you could."

"It's not enough."

Her immediate thought was bold, and she almost didn't say it, but she decided to go with her heart and not her head for a change. "Do I hear the beginning of a superhero complex?"

He swiveled to stare at her.

Her courage bolstered by his response, she walked

closer. "Do you have secret powers to make sure Ruxton is a perfect place?"

"What's your point?"

"My point is that you might have a lot of influence, but you're dealing with humans. And humans aren't perfect. It's great that you care so much, but you'll never make Ruxton perfect."

"I didn't say perfect," he told her.

"The domestic disputes get to you, though, don't they?"

He shrugged. "A little." He sighed. "Okay, a lot. When they won't press charges, my hands are tied."

"But you leave the door open?"

"Yeah," he muttered.

"And you still care?"

"Yeah."

"Then I'd say the community of Ruxton is very lucky to have you." She smiled. "Even if you don't wear a superhero uniform under your clothes."

He shot her a disgruntled look, but she felt his mood rise, and strangely enough, she was pleased.

His gaze trapped hers. "Trying to cheer up the sheriff?"

Her cheeks heated. She should have known he would catch her. "Would a pretzel help?"

He flicked his gaze down her body again, making her wonder if he indeed did have superpowers from the heat he generated inside her. "Black satin sheets would help," he said, in a low silky voice.

Her breath stopped somewhere between her throat and her chest. "Your bed is larger than mine," she managed to say, remembering the fateful morning she'd awakened in his big bed. "So my sheets wouldn't fit your bed."

He moved closer to her, his gaze still holding her tight with nerves and anticipation. "You don't have to make the bed with them, Emily. You can just wear them." He paused a half beat. "For a while."

Taking a step backward, she gulped. "Black satin would be too hot for summer."

He matched her step with a cocky, coaxing grin and moved closer again. "You wouldn't have to wear it very long," he promised, then put his index finger over her lips when she opened her mouth. "You've got some very nice excuses, Miss Emily. I've got an answer for all of them."

He would, she thought, and knew he was waiting to bait her while she tried another polite way to wriggle out of this dilemma. She hated the idea of letting him win this little battle of wit and seduction. A series of platitudes about pride and the uselessness of one-upmanship ran through her mind.

Emily paused. *Screw the platitudes.*

"You might have some of the answers," she told him in a voice she tried to make just as silky as his. "But you don't have all of them. Try this one on for size, Sheriff Ramsey." She hitched her chin and met his gaze boldly. "No."

She grinned, immensely pleased with herself. She'd just faced down the sexiest man she'd ever met, and she hadn't even stuttered. "But if you change your mind about the pretzel, let me know. Bye, now."

Then Emily broke another one of the rules for etiquette and left before Beau had a chance to respond.

* * *

Beau flipped on the lights in his office, set his cup of fast-food coffee on the corner of his desk and greeted the computer by the obscenity he'd named it. Then he grabbed the sheaf of papers from the fax machine.

Reading the top sheet, he grabbed the coffee maker's glass pot, gave it a quick rinse in the bathroom sink and filled it with water, then added a new filter and coffee, and poured the water.

It was Monday morning. There was a boatload of paperwork from the state and county, and if he was going to separate the wheat from the chaff, he needed his caffeine system running smoothly.

There were a few things Beau didn't like about being the chief lawman of the township of Ruxton. The first was the paperwork. It amazed him how the tentacles of bureaucracy could find their way all the way to such a small town.

The second was that damn computer.

Due to his extensive futile experience with the machine, when he said computer, the word *damn* was always attached. The county had sent it to him several months ago, so he'd glanced through the instruction booklets and given it a whirl. It was the most frustrating three days of his life. He'd been thrown from wild bulls more amenable than the blasted machine.

The damn computer, Beau concluded, was a female. She did, however, come with one handy feature. An On-Off switch. Beau derived a great deal of pleasure in turning her off. But that was the only thing he really knew to do with her.

For the next thirty minutes, he filtered through the

paperwork, making a small pile for the useful information, another pile for his part-time help to file and ditching the rest.

He was pouring his third cup of coffee when he heard someone step into the outer office. Poking his head through the door, he did a double take when he saw Emily St. Clair meet his gaze. She'd practically run away from him on Saturday. At the moment she looked as if she was struggling unsuccessfully for nonchalance.

"Emily," he said with a nod, and allowed his gaze to drift over her. Her hair was pulled back in a ponytail low on the nape of her neck, and she wore a conservative skirt and white blouse combination. It was both a blessing and a crime, he thought, how her clothes concealed the curves of her body.

"I'm here to set up your computer," she told him.

That stopped his perusal. He glanced back at her face. "My computer?"

"Yes. I've been hired as a temp to get your computer running."

"You?" he said, incredulous. "But you've got a degree in fine art."

The slightest spark of impatience flashed through her eyes before her mouth tilted in amusement. "Yes, but my minor was in computer science. Where's your hardware?"

When he recovered from his shock, Beau almost told her exactly where his personal hardware was, but he bit his tongue, torn between disgust and wry humor. He'd clearly underestimated Emily. In more ways than one, he thought, recalling the satin sheets.

"C'mon back," he muttered, and turned around. "She's in the corner of my office."

"She?" Emily echoed.

"Yeah." Beau chuckled under his breath. "I've got a couple of names for her. The latest is PMS."

Emily met his gaze as he glanced over his shoulder, then shook her head. "I would have expected something more original from you. Men are forever using PMS as an explanation for why they don't understand women."

"We like having a label for it, but everyone in this office has taken a whack at her," he explained, and handed Emily the instruction books.

She glanced at them, then blew the dust off the top one. She lifted her eyebrows in mock sympathy. "Your Achilles' heel?"

"You're enjoying this," he said.

Her eyelashes fluttered downward. "Just a little. It's nice to know that even Ruxton's superhero has a weakness."

When Beau looked at Emily, he was entirely too aware of his weakness, but he kept that information to himself. She made him aware of needs long denied. Needs more than physical. "How long are you supposed to be here?"

"As long as it takes to get you operational, then train everyone who works with the computer."

Beau hid his grin. "That long, huh?"

Frowning, she took a seat in front of the computer. "Shouldn't be more than a week."

Beau thought of his part-time help, old Mrs. Bing, who was even less inclined toward computer matters than he. Then there was his deputy. He coughed. "I'll let you get to work."

By lunchtime, Emily was eyeing the weapons in the office. She'd never seen such a mess in her life. Missing files, files in the wrong places: the computer needed therapy. Beau mentioned something about lunch, but she thanked him and shook her head. She was determined to make progress.

Sometime in the afternoon a sandwich appeared beside her. She absently ate it. Later, she'd rolled up her sleeves and discarded her shoes. Her biggest distraction was Beau. She would have worked far more effectively if she hadn't been so aware of him. When he talked on the phone, his low voice seemed to stroke her skin, and his scent seeped into her pores. When he walked in or out of the small room, she had to force herself not to watch the way he moved—a purely masculine stride that was just this side of cocky, but over-the-edge sexy.

Every now and then she felt his gaze on her. The knowledge made her feel hot and achy. Her heart tripped over itself, and she shifted in her seat.

With one glance, he upset her equilibrium.

She hated it.

And liked it.

At the moment she had a reprieve from Beau since he was out of the office. Taking a deep breath, she leaned back in her chair and closed her eyes. Her wrist ached a little from her nonstop disagreement with the computer. She absently rubbed it.

She caught his scent and heard his boots scrape on the floor before she saw him.

"Falling asleep on the job already?" he asked, then glanced at the clock on his desk. "It's past quitting time."

"I know," she murmured, sitting up and turning off the computer. "I had just hoped to get further today."

He nodded and pulled up a chair beside her. "You were rubbing your wrist when I came in."

Emily lifted her right hand. "It's nothing, really. Just overworked it a little today. I—"

He took her wrist in his big hand and gently massaged. The action stole her words and jammed her mind for a full minute. His hand was big and tanned against her smaller fair wrist. The sight of his fingers on her was sensually evocative.

A protest formed in her throat, but his gentleness killed it. She wouldn't have expected him to be so gentle. His callused thumb massaged a sore joint, and she felt her muscles relax. Even her neck muscles loosened. She sighed.

"Carpal tunnel?" he asked in a low voice.

She shook her head. "No. I just overwork it every now and then."

He stretched her fingers and rested her hand on his knee while he rubbed her palm. She bit back a moan and took a deep breath. "I wouldn't have thought giving a hand massage would be one of your talents."

Tossing her a wicked glance, he lightly skimmed his index finger along the inside of her fingers. The move was provocative. ''I have several talents you've never seen me exhibit.''

Emily's heart bumped inside her chest. She wondered why she felt as if he was doing something intimate, something sexual to her, when he was merely rubbing her hand. But the strength and warmth of his knee on the underside of her hand, and his fingers alternately massaging and caressing her palm made her conscious of him all over her body. He lightly traced the length of her fingers, and she was amazed to feel warmth suffuse her skin. Her stomach tightened and her breasts ached.

He twined his fingers through hers. ''You've got pretty hands.''

Emily stared at their joined hands and felt her stomach dip. She'd never thought of her hands as pretty. ''Yours are big,'' she said quietly, wondering how those big, gentle hands would feel all over her body. Wondering, but knowing she wouldn't find out.

Then he shocked her again by lifting her hand to his mouth. His lips were just as she'd remembered, firm but tender.

''Soft,'' he said, and when she was sure he couldn't surprise her again, he flicked his tongue over her skin. ''And sweet.''

Emily shuddered. *Where was her mind?* Sanity came screaming to her rescue, and she pulled her limp hand from his. If a hand could protest, hers would have. It was almost as if he'd made love to her fingers and they couldn't seem to function. She cleared her throat. ''Uh, thank you. It's uh—much better. You're very good,'' she managed.

Beau gave a ghost of a grin. "My pleasure."

Emily stood and turned away from him, discreetly fanning herself. She searched wildly for a change of subject. "You mentioned something about being on the rodeo circuit for a while. Do you miss it?"

She felt him stand behind her. "I was on the circuit for seven years and came back to Ruxton after the mayor tracked me down and told me I'd been appointed sheriff. I'd won a few titles, busted everything that could be busted twice, and was tired of traveling."

She stepped slightly away, but turned to face him. "Do you ever miss it?"

"Not much," he muttered. "It wasn't glamorous."

"You rode horses or cows?"

"Mostly horses. I gave up on the bulls," he said, his dark eyes amused, yet somehow sexy. "I never rode any Jersey dairy cattle."

Emily remembered her frequently denied requests for horseback riding lessons. "I always wanted to ride," she murmured, then shook her head when she realized she'd said it aloud.

"What did you say?"

She felt self-conscious. "Nothing really. I—"

"Did you say you wanted to ride?"

"It was a long time ago."

"Just answer the question, Emily," he said, and she noticed he was suddenly entirely too close.

She took a deep breath and made herself meet his gaze. "Okay, yes I wanted to learn."

His lips tilted in that kill-the-ladies-and-make-them-love-it grin. "Oh, Emily, it'll be my pleasure to teach you to ride."

"He's big," Emily said as she gazed warily at Beau's horse, Blue.

He heard the tentative note in her voice. "He's a gelding."

She glanced at him, then back to Blue. "So?"

He chuckled. "So his temperament is nice and easy." He tightened the straps of the saddle and added. "Plus he's older. He doesn't mind taking his time."

Blue pawed the ground, and Emily backed away. "Are you sure about that?"

"Yeah." He rose and looked at her. "Why?"

"Well, just because he's old doesn't mean he's good-natured. I've met quite a few cranky older people." As if she didn't want to offend, she rushed to clarify. "Not that they don't have reason for being cranky. I've met some who have arthritis and others with digestion difficulties. Others are cranky because their children don't visit often enough."

She was so earnest, Beau thought. He nodded soberly, chewing the inside of his cheek to keep from laughing so hard he would burst a rib. "Blue only gets rheumatism on bitter cold winter mornings. His digestion system works just fine. Before he was a gelding he sired about twenty foals, and he's delighted they never come to visit."

"Really?" Still pensive, she looked at Blue again.

Beau realized he'd pushed her to do this. It was completely out of character for him. More than one woman had tried to wrangle riding lessons from him, and he'd become quite adept at dodging the rope. Emily, he knew, wasn't trying to rope him. *She* was trying to dodge *him,* and he knew why. He unsettled her. He was impossible for her to ignore. He made her aware of herself, of her sexuality.

He made her sweat.

Beau hid a grin. He liked making Emily sweat.

He should, however, show a little compassion if she was terrified of horses. "Listen, if you don't want to ride, you don't have to."

Emily swallowed and looked as if she were reaching deep for her fortitude. She shook her head. "No. I want to ride," she told him, as if she were reminding herself. "This is the perfect time for me to do all the things I've wanted to do, but haven't."

Beau could have recommended some other activities to try first, but he thought he was going to have to ease her into those. Ease her out of her clothes and into bed. The thought made his body tighten, but he brushed it aside. He'd promised a riding lesson to the lady, and she was going to get it.

"Good," he said. "Let me help you get a leg up. Left foot in the stirrup. You always mount from the left."

Whispering something under her breath, she did as he instructed. Beau allowed her to brace her hand on his shoulder as she swung her shapely rear end into the air. Beau watched the denim stretch taut over her bottom. He could almost imagine what that sweet derriere would look like nude—fair skin, tight muscle, and the kind of curve that could make him moan. He bit his cheek again, but this time he was holding back that moan, not laughter.

On horseback, Emily followed Beau and his mount back to the barn. It was a warm, humid afternoon, but the summer breeze brought blessed relief. She'd enjoyed the ride around Beau's property, and she was delighted with the fact that she hadn't embarrassed herself by falling off the horse. "I still think I could ride a little longer," she told Beau as he dismounted, then removed the saddle and bridle and released his horse into the pasture.

Emily pulled back on the reins slightly and smiled when Blue stopped. "It's almost like brakes," she murmured.

Beau squinted up at her. "With the right horse, it is," he said, and waved her down. "We've been out a couple of hours. You'll be surprised at all the muscles you used. I don't want you too sore."

"Oh, I won't get sore." She carefully swung her right foot over and slid down the side of the horse.

Beau slowed her swift descent with his hands on her waist. She was surprised at how heavy her feet felt when they touched the ground. Her knees felt as if they'd been pried open, and her muscles were completely uncooperative.

Disconcerted, she stared down at her legs and turned toward him. "They feel like lead jelly."

He winced. "That means you'll be sore tomorrow. I shouldn't have kept you out this long the first time."

She looked up at him. "But I loved it."

His gaze meshed with hers and gentled. "I'm glad."

Emily took a careful breath at the glitter in his dark eyes and smelled the earthy scent of horse, hay and man. His body was close, his large hands encircling her waist. His attention was focused on her, making her feel surrounded by him. He jangled her nerve endings and kicked her stable sensibility straight into the pasture.

Emily had always considered herself a quiet person, inside and out. Being close to Beau, however, made her insides feel as noisy as the percussion section in a high school band.

Struggling with a myriad of sensations, she fell back on her upbringing. "Thank you very much for the lesson," she said.

"You're welcome very much." He lifted one of his hands to cup her jaw. "Your skin's a little pink. Sunburn?"

Emily swallowed the knot of tension in her throat. "It shouldn't be, this late in the day."

"Your skin's so fair I bet you burn like crazy in the summertime." Holding her gaze, he rubbed his thumb under her chin.

His touch made her feel languid and disinterested in moving. "I don't usually stay out in the sun very long in the summertime."

"Your skin is so soft here. Makes me wonder what it feels like other places," he muttered, and moved his index finger down her throat.

Her heart jolted, and her stomach twisted with a

painfully sweet combination of apprehension and anticipation.

Still watching her, he slid his finger down her chest, beneath the open collar of her white cotton shirt, over the upper swell of her breast.

Her breath stopped, and though she knew he would allow her to step away, all she could do was stare into his dark, sensual eyes and wait.

Five

If Emily didn't know better, she would think Beau's eyes were making love to her. But she knew better, a small voice inside her whispered. She knew better.

When he slid his finger over her nipple, however, she didn't know anything. Feeling an overwhelming surge of arousal, she closed her eyes and took a deep breath. "Oh." Her moan escaped her throat.

"Soft and hard," Beau murmured. "Your breast is soft, but the tip is hard." He continued to caress her with just his fingertip.

She should tell him to stop, but she wanted more. He rolled her nipple between his thumb and forefinger. "Touching you isn't enough," he told her and she felt his breath on her face as he lowered his head.

"Touching you makes me want to taste you." His mouth captured hers and his tongue tangled with hers, tasting and taunting.

Emily felt as if her blood were gasoline and Beau had lit a match and tossed it inside her. She leaned into his hand, pressed her mouth into his and kissed him back.

Beau caught her nonverbal signal and immediately returned it by tugging her shirt open and closing his hand around her breast.

Emily moaned into his mouth and got drunk on his flavor. He tasted warm and seductive. Passionate for *her*. The thought made her weak.

Distantly she felt her shirt slide off one shoulder. It seemed only a second passed and his mouth was closing around her nipple. The sensation was incredible. "Oh, my." He kept on as if he couldn't get enough of her, flicking his tongue, cupping it around the sensitive beaded tip. Emily felt a sharp tug deep in her nether region. Her knees dipped and he caught her against him, reluctantly moving his mouth from her breast.

His heart pounding against hers, he gazed at her with turbulent dark eyes. "I've wanted to do that since the first night I saw you."

One of his hands slid down to her rear end and brought her intimately against him. He was hard and full. She could feel the power of his desire flowing from every pore of his body, moving her, melting her.

He rocked his hardness into the notch of her thighs. With shocking speed, she felt herself grow wet and swollen.

"There's more I want to do with you, Emily," he said low and deep. "A lot more."

Dipping his head, he kissed her again, his tongue

sliding in and out of her mouth in an erotic motion that simulated what he clearly wanted to do to her with his whole body.

Emily wanted him. She wanted his mouth and his hands on her. She wanted him deep inside her where no man had ever been. She wanted so much she trembled with it. She wanted everything she'd never had before.

The horse behind her snorted and pawed the ground.

Emily distantly noticed the sound.

The horse made another movement, distracting her, and she blinked. The early-evening sunlight was still bright. Her mouth stilled against Beau's. In gradual but swift degrees, Emily realized that given another sixty seconds or so, she would have been in the dirt, tearing off his clothes.

They were both breathing as if they'd run a race. His gaze burned a hole clear to her soul. Somehow he *knew* what was going on inside her.

"I don't know what to say," she whispered.

"We could go inside," he told her.

Emily swallowed hard over the knot of desire in her throat and shook her head. "I—I—I'm not ready."

"For sex," he said.

Agreeing, though her body still called her a liar, she moved her head in a circle. "Right. And you. I'm not ready—for you."

Beau lifted his hand to stroke her hair from her forehead. "It would be good, Emily. Very easy."

Emily gave an involuntary shudder. "Yes, but I

was almost getting married three weeks ago." It boggled her mind to recall it.

"Almost," he said pointedly. "I'm not asking for anything permanent. Not marriage," he said. "But we could be good together."

So why not, Emily? She stared at him. Part of her wanted to go inside and let Beau Ramsey make love to her, to make love to him. Part of her wanted to go too far, too fast and do too much. But more than her sensible side was resisting; her heart wasn't ready, either.

Exasperated with her conflicting feelings, she lowered her head and backed away. "I—can't."

"Emily, this is Jenna."

"And Maddie."

The voices of her two longtime friends on the telephone immediately lifted Emily out of her doldrums. Before she picked up the phone, she'd been brooding over Beau Ramsey. She didn't know whether to pat herself on the back for stopping things before they went too far, or kick herself for not giving in to her passions. It didn't help that her posterior was sore from the ride.

"Hi," she said, smiling into the phone. "Both of you at once. Is this a conference call?"

"In a manner of speaking," Jenna said.

"I'm at Jenna's place. I'm talking on the extension," Maddie said. "But what I want to know is why in Hades you're living in a place like Ruxton?"

Emily heard Jenna's sigh. "Maddie, I thought we

agreed we were going to handle this delicately, but since you've asked. Why Ruxton, Em?''

A long silence followed while Emily tried to formulate her answer.

"Emily," Jenna prodded.

"It wasn't exactly planned," Emily said, winding the phone cord around her fingers. She would never confess the truth to anyone but these her closest friends, and she was reluctant to tell them. "I had to use the bathroom and I was thirsty, so I thought Ruxton was as good a place as any to stop."

"But you didn't just stop," Maddie said. "You're *living* there, aren't you?"

Emily glanced around her small kitchen and gave a small laugh. "I guess I am. I'm definitely not coming back to Roanoke."

Jenna cleared her throat. "You mean not right away," she said in her attorney's voice.

"I mean not in this lifetime," Emily said, though she knew her response wasn't the least bit rational.

Another long silence followed.

"I told you, Jenna Jean," Maddie said.

"Jenna," Jenna Jean automatically corrected. She'd been trying to dump what she considered the juvenile addition of her middle name for ten years.

"She's gone straight over the edge."

"She has not. She's just a little rattled," Jenna retorted.

"Off the deep end," Maddie corrected.

"She is not. She's just—"

"Recovering from walking out on her wedding," Emily interjected.

"The wedding of the century," Maddie piped in with an awed tone, making Emily wince. "You've never looked more gorgeous than when you gave your bouquet to Carl."

Emily gave a wry smile. "Thank you. I think."

"We're concerned about you," Jenna said in a quiet voice. "This is out of character for you."

Emily sighed and felt her heart expand at the true care in her friend's voice. "I know it is. When I found out about Carl—"

"And his girlfriend in South America," Maddie added. "I would have kicked him where it counted. You should have taken one of those metal candelabras and bonked him on the head with it."

"Assault," Jenna muttered. "But I must confess I thought you should have set his tux pants on fire."

Emily laughed. "I didn't know what to do, but I couldn't marry him. And I knew it was going to *kill* my mother." Emily began to pace. "I think the wedding was more important to her than it was to me."

"The wedding of the century," Maddie repeated, making Emily's stomach twist in distress again.

"Have you talked to your mother?" Jenna asked.

Emily struggled with guilt and relief. "Her housekeeper, Marie, is her liaison. My mother is *indisposed,* but Marie has had a list of questions each time I called."

"I heard she's gone to one of those exclusive spas," Maddie, who had a good ear for gossip, told her.

"Emily, are you working? Have you met some friends?" Jenna asked.

"Are there any men under the age of eighty?" Maddie asked.

Emily smiled to herself. "Yes, yes and yes." Strange how talking to her longtime friends made her feel stronger. "I'm assessing my life, thinking about what I want instead of what everyone else might want. It'll be easier for me to be different if I'm not in Roanoke."

"Good," Maddie immediately said. "And you're well rid of that prig, Carl Yancey. I always thought he would be rotten in bed, anyway."

Emily sucked in a quick breath and waited for someone to politely fill the silence. No one did. "I wouldn't know," she finally said.

"Oh," Jenna murmured and hesitated a second. "Em, you're not involved with a man already, are you?"

Emily started to move around the kitchen. It gave her the illusion of being a moving target, and Jenna was definitely on the hunt. Jenna Jean Anderson was one of the most disturbingly intuitive people Emily had ever met. "Not really," she hedged. "How's everything at the D.A.'s office?"

"Fine. When you say not really, does that mean you've met someone who appeals to you?"

Emily felt her stomach tense. She really didn't want to discuss this. "I'm not going to do anything about it. I might be doing *some* things I've never done before, but I'm not ready to—"

"Hit the sack," Maddie finished for her and gave a big sigh. "It might be the best thing in the world for you."

"Maddie," Jenna said in an iron tone that intimidated just about everyone. Except Maddie. "We wouldn't be very good friends if we encouraged Emily to do something reckless."

"Okay, okay," Maddie said. "If you decide to hit the sack with this guy, make sure you use contraception," she added, completely missing Jenna's point.

Jenna groaned. "Emily, we care about you. If you need us for anything, anything at all, call. Okay?"

"Thanks, Jen."

"I've got to go," her friend said. "Be careful."

Before Emily could say a word, Maddie piped in. "Here's your chance, Emily. Let her rip. G'night."

Emily said goodbye and hung up, thinking about the divergent advice offered by her two best friends. *Be careful. Let her rip.* It was difficult combining the two.

The next morning Emily walked into the sheriff's office, struggling to shove her edginess way below her outer surface where it wouldn't be seen. She'd always been told to think of Grace Kelly's serene beauty during her times of turmoil. The nervous habits of her youth had been drilled out of her long ago in finishing school. But those same habits, such as biting her lip and fidgeting with her hands, were popping up like pesky, persistent weeds this morning. It didn't help that she knew she wasn't walking normally. Her legs felt stiff and uncooperative from her ride yesterday.

Beau glanced up from drinking his cup of coffee and stopped her with a gaze that slid all the way up and down her body. His gaze lingered at the tops of her thighs, making her struggle with the instinct to rub her legs together to cure the restlessness he caused inside her. Then his dark eyes met hers. "Sore this morning?" he asked in a low, deep voice that made her think of a different, more intimate ride with Beau. His expression said "You could have been with me, sweetheart, and I would have made sure you liked it."

She bit the inside of her upper lip, then realized what she was doing and gritted her teeth together. "A little," she admitted and moved toward the computer. "Thank you for asking. I don't want to interrupt your routine, so I'll go ahead and get to work."

As if he could sense her uneasiness, he grinned slightly and said in a silky tone. "No interruption at all."

She sat down, booted up the computer, narrowed her eyes in deliberation at the screen and told herself to ignore the buzzing sensation inside her. For the next hour and a half, she got a headache trying to get past the Error messages. She repeated commands and backtracked. Despite the fact that her concentration was in the toilet, Emily finally got the programming straightened out. She immediately began sketching out user-friendly instructions for Beau and his office. By the end of the day, she'd obtained a template and mapped out a plan.

"I think this calls for champagne," she murmured to herself, and she leaned back in her chair.

"Good news?" Beau asked.

"Oh, yes," Emily said, the phone ringing at the same moment.

He lifted his hand and picked up the receiver. "Just a minute," he said, and listened to the caller.

Emily watched his face darken and wondered at the cause until he scratched something on a piece of paper and muttered, "Regina Bell".

Emily felt her blood run cold. He asked a few terse questions, then finished his call and headed for the door. Emily stood. "It's Regina. What happened?"

His eyes were as cold and hard as steel. "Her estranged husband decided to pay a call this morning. Her neighbor just took her to the emergency room."

Emily immediately thought of Regina's daughter, the little girl she'd held in her lap. Her heart twisted. "What about Hilary?"

"I think she's in the waiting room."

Emily grabbed her purse. "She's probably scared to death! I'll follow you there."

A flicker of surprise and respect flashed through Beau's eyes before he nodded and shrugged. "Okay."

Emily pulled the slice-and-bake cookies from the oven and smiled at the sight of Hilary tottering in a pair of Emily's high heels. Dressed in a sapphire blue sequined cocktail dress Emily had planned to wear on her honeymoon, the little girl adjusted the tiara on her head. It had required a swift in-depth review of her early childhood, but Emily had been able to successfully distract the child.

"When did you get this crown?" Hilary asked.

Emily smiled. "It's called a tiara, but we can call it a crown. My mother is very beautiful. She is so beautiful that when she was younger she used to win beauty contests, and they gave her tiaras."

Hilary studied Emily. "You're pretty, too. Did you win a contest and get a crown?"

Emily laughed and shook her head. With a spatula, she removed the warm cookies from the sheet. "My mother gave me that crown to play with when I was a little girl. I didn't win any contests. Although she tried her best," she muttered to herself, shuddering at the memory of being primped and coached for hours.

"Why didn't you win?"

Glancing at the child, Emily took the plate of cookies in one hand and Hilary's hand in the other and led her into the front living room. "Why didn't I win?" she repeated, sitting on the sofa. "Three very good reasons."

Outside the screen door, despite the sadness of the Bells' situation, Beau felt the slightest jab of amusement. He cocked his mouth into a half grin at the exchange between the two females. He might have expected Emily to be too fussy about her clothes to let a little girl trot around in them. But he would have underestimated her. Again.

Pausing, he decided to watch the two for just a couple more moments. Besides he was curious to learn why Emily hadn't won any contests.

"Two of the reasons," Emily told Hilary as she lifted her hair, "are my ears. I got my father's ears."

Hilary was silent for a moment as she munched her

cookie. "I like your ears. They remind me a little bit of Dumbo, the Baby Elephant."

Emily let out a throaty laugh, and Beau felt the sexy purr deep in his gut.

"Why, thank you," she said. "No one has ever said that to me before. The third reason I didn't win was because I also inherited my father's musical talent."

"Musical?" Hilary echoed, confusion evident in her voice.

"He was very good at listening to music, but he wasn't good at making it."

Beau chuckled again and tapped on the door. "Emily, it's Beau."

She moved quickly, and he sensed an immediate change in her easy demeanor as she opened the door. Her eyebrows drew together in concern. "How is Regina?" she whispered.

The heaviness of the day hit him again. "She's going to be okay. Two cracked ribs and some bad bruises, but she signed a warrant for her husband's arrest," he told her in a low voice as he stepped into the room. "She remembered you offered to keep Hilary for the night, but she asked me to make sure it was okay. They're keeping her overnight at the hospital. She'll pick up her daughter tomorrow."

"Of course," Emily said, and looked at Hilary. "The sheriff says your mommy is going to be okay and will be leaving the hospital tomorrow. Would you mind staying with me tonight?"

Staring at Beau, Hilary bit her lip. "Okay."

Seeing the fear in the little girl's eyes, Beau knelt

down next to the couch. "Any chance I can have one of those cookies?"

Tentatively she lifted one from the plate and offered it to him as if he were a wild animal not to be trusted.

"Thank you," he said in the gentlest voice he could muster, and silently damned Hilary's father to hell for distorting her view of men. The child wore no visible bruises, but it would take a long time to heal the inner scars.

"I think it's getting close to bedtime," Emily said and gathered the little girl in her arms. "I'll be back in a minute. Help yourself to the cookies," she told him.

"I don't have a nightie," Hilary told her.

"I'll let you use one of mine," Emily told her, as she carried her toward the steps.

"I don't have a bed."

"You can use mine."

"I don't got a toothbrush," Hilary's voice carried back to him.

"I have an extra one," Emily reassured her.

Almost thirty minutes later Emily returned to the living room and sank down on the sofa. "I wonder who taught that child the game of twenty questions."

Beau studied her, liking her disheveled appearance. With her hair mussed and blouse pulled loose from her skirt, she looked more touchable. Even at this moment his fingers itched to feel the satin smoothness of her skin. He would have liked to pull her into his lap and play with her hair. "You could have sung her to sleep."

Emily shot him a dark look. "I didn't want to give her nightmares."

"Your father's musical talent?"

"Tone deaf," she told him. "I sing in the shower, for my ears only."

"Speaking of your ears," he began.

Her blue eyes accused him. "You were listening."

"I didn't want to interrupt," he said, and leaned closer.

She looked at him suspiciously. "What are you doing?"

Giving in to the urge to lift her hair, Beau grinned. Emily's ears weren't large, but they did stick out. "I never would have compared them to Dumbo's."

She swatted at his hand. "Stop! I don't make a habit of showing my ears to the general public." She laughed despite herself. "I'd rather reveal my bra size."

Beau felt her throaty laugh again, this time in his groin. "I already know your bra size."

"I think you already know too much."

"There's where you're wrong, Emily. I want to know more," he told her. "A whole lot more."

Six

Emily stared into Beau's dark eyes and felt herself melt: her heart, her mind, her resolve. How did he do that so easily, she wondered. She took a careful breath and tried to make her brain work.

Though she suspected Beau wasn't all that interested in her statistics, she couldn't think of anything else to say to break the tension between them. "I'm twenty-five, an only child," she managed in a voice that sounded husky to her own ears. "You probably heard my mother was a beauty queen. My father died in an automobile accident when I was six."

Beau blinked and backed slightly away. "My father died when I was eight. Accident on a tractor."

She identified with the quick grief that flashed through Beau's eyes. Even after all these years, she still felt the loss of her father. "That must have been difficult for you. Only son with three sisters and mother.''

''It was no picnic,'' he admitted. ''How was it for you?''

Emily smiled sadly. ''He made my mother and me laugh. She could have married any number of men, but he made her laugh. She always said my father was magic. He could find the humor in the blackest situation. When he died,'' she said, remembering those early, sad days, ''my mother stopped laughing. I think it must have frightened her, so she became very protective and controlling.''

Beau nodded thoughtfully. ''And what about you? Do you miss him?''

''I was so young,'' she said, seeing mental pictures of her father. ''I should be over it. Most of the time I don't brood over him. But there's this feeling of loss. It's not overwhelming,'' she told him quickly, ''but it never goes away. It's like a hole and no one else will be able to fill it up.''

Beau narrowed his eyes in disbelief at Emily. She'd said all the things he'd repeated to himself time and time again. He'd talked to others who had lost parents, but he'd never felt such a connection with them. It was almost as if she'd touched a sore spot inside him. And soothed it.

''Why are you staring at me?'' she whispered.

He laughed to shake off the uneasy rumbling inside him. ''Because you keep surprising me.''

She lifted her hand toward his, then hesitated, meeting his gaze. Instinct, swift and sure, had him closing his hand around hers.

"Tell me about your father," she said.

A flood of memories rushed through him. "He was a farmer. His first love was the land, but he could ride like the wind."

"And he taught you?"

"Yeah, he taught me to ride, but he taught me other things, too. How to shoot. How to block a punch. He taught me to thank my mom when she fussed over my scratches and scrapes and put on Band-Aids. He helped me catch my first fish. He told me a real man says he's sorry when he's wrong, and if someone needs help to give it, because you might be the one needing help someday."

"He sounds like he must have been great."

"Yes. He just left too soon."

Emily closed her eyes. "I know what you mean. I feel lucky—" she shrugged "—blessed, that I knew my father as long as I did. But another part of me can't help wishing I could have had him just a little longer. There's so much I would have loved to talk with him about."

Beau looked at Emily again and felt a curious lump in his throat. She was doing it again. Saying what he'd thought, what he'd kept to himself. "A few times, when I got myself into some messes, it was easy for me to imagine what he would say."

She opened her eyes and smiled. "What?"

"Boy, you must have left your head in bed this morning!"

She laughed softly, then was quiet and thoughtful for a moment. "You'll think I'm crazy if I tell you this."

Beau looked at her curiously. "What?"

She shook her head and tried to pull her hand from his. "No. You'll think I'm nuts."

Beau held on to her hand. "What? Tell me." When she just looked at him sheepishly, he lowered his face closer to hers. "I already *know* you're a little crazy, Emily. What do you have to lose?"

She rolled her eyes. "Gee thanks, Beau." She took a deep breath. "Okay. Sometimes, when I'm all alone and I'm having a tough time, I talk to him."

Stunned, Beau just stared at her silently.

"I told you you'd think I was crazy! He doesn't really answer back," she quickly assured Beau. "I'm sure it won't make a bit of sense to you, but it makes me feel better, especially if I've been upset." She glanced at Beau again. "I wish you would quit looking at me like I belong in the loony bin."

Beau tugged her closer. "You misunderstand," he told her. "If you're crazy, then I am, too. I've talked to my father since he's been gone, too."

Her blue eyes met his. "Does he talk back?"

Beau shook his head. "No, but if he did, I know what he would tell me to do right now."

"What?"

"He'd say 'shut up and kiss the girl.' And, Emily, the older I get, the more I appreciate his advice." Beau took her mouth and was struck by the power and sweetness of her. Pulling her onto his lap, he felt so hungry for her that he wanted to eat her alive.

Instead, he made love to her mouth. A primitive instinct to claim urged him to thrust inside her, but Beau focused on the texture of her lips, the taste of her tongue. He coaxed the inhibitions from her and drew out her response.

She wiggled in his lap and he fought back a groan. Beau was hard and wanting. His arousal more than physical, he'd never experienced such an overwhelming need for a woman. It was all over him, his skin, his blood, his heart and lungs, his loins. He needed *Emily*. It was as if his body was calling out for her.

Driven to possess, he opened her mouth with his tongue and claimed her with carnal, sexual kisses while he slid one hand over her breast and the other beneath her skirt. She was caught up in the same sensual whirlwind he was. He knew it by the way she sucked his tongue into her mouth, rubbed her thighs against his hand, and undulated her bottom against his hardness.

He could feel it in the distended peak of her breast against his palm. He could hear it in her breath: soft gasps that urged him onward. He slipped his fingers beneath her silk panties and found her wet and hot.

"Oh, Emily, you feel so good," he muttered against her mouth. He stroked her silken secrets and eased his finger inside her at the same time he plunged his tongue into her mouth. In and out he stroked, simulating the intimacy he craved with her.

She shuddered and a soft whimper escaped her parted lips. She was clinging to him as if she couldn't let go. His chest swelled at the deep-down knowledge.

"Pull me closer, sweet lady," he whispered. "Let me inside." He'd never admitted he was lonely, even to himself, but he had been. And Emily could take his "lonely" away. "Let me inside," he repeated, still stroking her intimately.

Emily shuddered again. Her eyelids drooped, as heavy as the arousal pulsing between them. She dipped her head. "Beau. I—" She gasped and tightened her fingers on his shoulders.

He could tell when reality hit her. Her eyes widened and her soft thighs went rigid against his arm. She swallowed audibly and shook her head.

Though it cost him, he had to respond to her withdrawal. He moved his hand from her sweetness and lifted her chin so she would meet his gaze. "You want me," he said. He wanted to hear the words.

She clenched her eyes shut. "I—shouldn't. I—"

A primitive need to possess roared through him. "You want to be with me. Admit it," he demanded.

"I shouldn't," she wailed. "I was going to marry another man just weeks ago. I *can't* want to be with another man so soon. I *can't.*"

The shame in her voice was a balm to his frustrated need. She was nearly crying. He pulled her against him, cuddling her head against his chest. "You didn't really want him, Emily. Not like you want me."

"Oh, Beau," she said, clinging to him. "I can't want you right now. I just can't."

Minutes later Beau left, and Emily was left with a burning ache, a terrible emptiness. She instinctively put her hand to her chest where she felt tight, yet hollow. The hurt was so strong it was physical.

Taking a deep breath, she walked upstairs to check on Hilary as she slept. She watched the little girl for a few moments, then returned to her small kitchen and began to pace. If someone had told her last week that she could want a man this much, she would have told them they were crazy. It was insane to feel this much desire. Unreasonable. Illogical. Completely irrational.

Yet she did.

Emily shook her head. "There he goes," she muttered darkly. "Shifting my platelets again."

She sighed, feeling betrayed by her own body. The tips of her breasts were still hard. Deep down where he'd touched her, she was still wet and swollen. When Beau had left he'd looked too calm, too sure, for her peace of mind. He looked like a man who understood the inevitable and also understood that it was only a matter of time before Emily accepted the inevitable, too.

Be careful.

Let her rip.

Emily felt the tug and pull of her friends' words. They echoed the opposing instincts at war inside her. She wasn't the same woman she'd been when she'd blown into town three weeks ago. She wasn't as reserved. She was more impatient, more restless, less careful. The knowledge disturbed her.

At the same time she took the man's order for another pitcher of beer, Emily felt a buzzing sensation at the back of her neck. She glanced toward the door and saw Beau enter the room. Her heart jumped and her mind scowled. His gaze met hers, and she tentatively lifted her hand to wave at him.

He nodded and walked toward her. Then a woman stepped in his path and hooked her arm through his. Beau glanced at Emily again, shrugging as he allowed himself to be led to the woman's table.

Holding an empty beer pitcher, Emily stood staring at them for a full minute. There was an easiness between them, she thought, a *physical* easiness. As if they were friends. Another image flashed through her mind. As if they were more than friends. The notion sliced through her like a sharp knife, surprising her with the quick stab of pain.

"Hey, sweet cakes! Where's my beer?"

The voice snapped her out of her daze. "Just a minute, please," she said, and she returned to the bar.

Since she'd started her temporary position for the county, Emily didn't work every night at the Happy Hour Bar. She had just started getting the hang of deflecting marriage proposals, so she hated the idea of completely giving it up. If she was going to run into Beau and his lady friend at the bar, however, she didn't know if she would have the stomach for it.

There was no rational reason for her to feel jealous, she told herself. She and Beau had certainly never made any promises to each other. They hadn't even gone out on a date. If she had felt closer to him last night than she'd ever felt to another human being, then that was her problem. He clearly didn't share the same perspective. She wouldn't give it another thought, she told herself.

Her gaze returning to Beau and *that woman,* Emily automatically filled a pitcher. She wondered if it was Donna.

Emily bit back a groan. Okay, she felt curious and jealous, she admitted. If there was one thing her mother had given her, however, it was the training to conceal everything from a pimple, to under-eye circles, to every disturbing emotion known to womankind.

Emily smiled.

From across the bar, Beau heard Donna continue her mostly one-sided conversation. He nodded every ten seconds or so, but he'd lost the thread of the conversation minutes ago. His attention was focused on the blond waitress bestowing a dazzling smile on every guy within ten feet of her.

Beau frowned.

"You want to come back to my place?" Donna murmured in an inviting voice next to his ear.

The suggestion should have been a turn-on. He waited to feel the slow, easy pump of arousal and excitement. Donna was attractive and intelligent. Any man in his right mind would take her up on what she was offering. *Any man in his right mind...* He waited for just a flicker of interest and was alarmed when he felt none. He would have to think about that later.

Beau cleared his throat and tapped his empty glass. "I think I need a refill. Let me get one for you, too," he offered, then took their glasses and made his way to the counter. By way of Emily.

"How did the training go today?" he asked, and noticed that her smile slipped a little. "I wasn't in the office much and I wondered how Mrs. Bing would handle the computer."

"Very well. I have all the basic instructions printed

out for quick referral, and I found a template for the word-processing program. It went so well,'' she continued, setting a pitcher of beer down and giving another customer her dazzling smile, ''that I'm going to let her train you and your deputy.''

That announcement jolted Beau. He raised his eyebrows. ''I thought you were supposed to train everyone.''

''Well, I was, but Mrs. Bing caught on so well it seemed a waste for me to stay on.''

Amazed at the disappointment that shot through him, he followed her to the counter. ''So you're not coming back?''

She shrugged. ''I guess that depends on the county. I think I'm a cyber fireman. They're putting me wherever they're having problems, then as soon as I solve those problems, they move me to the next one.'' She glanced at the glasses in his hands. ''Would you like me to refill those for you?''

''Uh, yeah.''

Emily returned the filled glasses to him with a smile. ''There you go.''

''Thanks,'' he said, studying her facial expression. Something wasn't quite right. ''You look busy tonight.''

Her eyes flashed something dark and secret. The emotion came and went so quickly it was as if someone had pulled apart the curtains in her bedroom, then jerked them back together. ''*You* look pretty busy yourself tonight,'' she said, then whirled on to the next customer.

Beau hesitated, narrowing his gaze at her. If he

didn't know better, he'd say Emily was a little green about Donna. But Emily had turned him down. Twice now. He shook his head and dismissed the possibility. A woman ready, willing, and able to take care of his physical needs was waiting for him. And he was gaping after the one who kept saying no. He was not in his right mind. Beau headed toward the woman who was ready to say yes.

Frustrated, confused and unwilling to go home after work, Emily went to the lake again. She cut her engine, got out of her BMW and walked toward the water. It was a muggy night; the air was thick with heat and humidity, making most humans feel damp and uncomfortable. Emily was no exception.

She lifted her hair from her neck and continued to look at the lake as if it could offer her answers. She thought about all the things she'd always wanted to do but hadn't. Her mother had, at least temporarily, cut Emily out of her life. It was crazy, but the action both freed and hurt Emily. Now her choices were her own. She was responsible for what she did and didn't do. If there was a niggling thought that she couldn't run away forever, then Emily could temporarily brush it aside.

If she wanted to serve beer in a bar, she could. If she wanted to baby-sit a little girl named Hilary, she could. If she wanted to make love with a bad-boy sheriff... She hesitated and swore under her breath, glaring at the water again.

An idea came to mind. If she wanted to break the law by going to the lake at night, she could. If she wanted to wade at the edge of the lake on a hot summer night...

She could.

Beau wasn't sure if it was instinct or insanity that led him to the lake. Technically, he wasn't on duty, so he didn't need to cruise the area. When he saw Emily's BMW, however, the excitement he'd sought in vain earlier that evening hit him full-force.

He scowled at himself. He should either drive past or call the deputy to arrest her. Instead, he brought his truck to a stop and got out. Slamming the car door because it made him feel better, he took a deep breath and walked toward the lake.

The splashing sound stopped him mid-step. He quickly scanned the surface of the lake and saw Emily's head bobbing on the surface. He paused to listen more closely and heard her laughing. Shaking his head, he continued down the slight hill.

He stopped again when he came across the little pile of her clothes. Her lace bra and panties lay on top. His internal temperature rose, and Beau tugged at his shirt collar. What was he going to do with this woman? He heard her blowing bubbles. She obviously didn't realize she had an audience.

"How's the water, Emily?"

The blowing noises ceased, and Beau heard a strangled, choking sound. "You okay?"

When she didn't say anything, he became concerned. "Emily, answer me. Do I need to come after you and—"

"No!" she yelled, and swam closer so he could see her.

"Are you having a good time?" he asked mildly.

Brief silence met his question. She frowned at him. "I was."

He swallowed a chuckle at her prissy use of the past tense. Her hair was slicked back from her face, and her shoulders gleamed in the moonlight. She looked like a water goddess—a peeved water goddess. "Do you remember that you're not supposed to trespass after dark at the lake?"

"I'm not really trespassing," she told him in the finishing-school voice she reserved for sticky situations.

"Oh really," he said. "Then tell me what you are doing?"

"I'm performing an important service to the community," she told him. "I'm making sure it's safe to swim in the lake."

"And have you?"

"Oh yes," she said, her first smile breaking through, the same dazzling smile she'd thrown at umpteen men back at the bar. "It's as safe as can be."

"Then your job is done," Beau said, catching her with her own net. "You can come out now."

Her smile fell. "I—I haven't had a chance to check—"

"Emily, if my deputy decides to patrol the lake tonight, which he always does, he will arrest you for trespassing and take you in buck-naked." He leaned over and picked up her panties. "I don't know how much tequila you got into tonight, but—"

"I haven't had a drop of tequila since the first night I was in town!" she told him.

"Then why are you acting like you have?"

"This was just one of those little harmless things I've never done but wanted to do. It would have been fine if you hadn't stopped by."

"Harmless," he echoed. "Harmless like tossing your ring into the lake—"

"I didn't do that," she retorted.

"And sleeping on black satin sheets," he continued, watching her shift in the water. "Driving a motorcycle, riding a horse, lighting a man's cigar in bed and—"

"The least you can do is turn around while I get out," she said, frustration oozing from her voice.

Beau thought of how many nights the image of Emily, naked and wanting him, had made him sweat with unfulfilled need. He remembered how she took him to the edge with her kisses, then pulled back. He thought of how she'd seduced his attention so that he couldn't muster the least bit of interest in other women. Any compassion or sense of decency he might have had dissolved.

"No," he simply said.

She gasped. "Beau—"

He shook his head and picked up her bra. "It seems to me, Emily, that you haven't had enough excitement in your life, so you're determined to make up for it now. I consider it my duty to help you."

"Help me," she repeated, her voice full of skepticism.

"Yes. With your upbringing, I'll bet you missed out on a little game we played when we were growing up."

She frowned. "Little game."

"Yeah. It's called Take the Dare. I dare you to walk out of the lake." He lifted her bra to his face and inhaled the faint scent of her perfume. "Come to me, Emily."

Seven

Emily sank beneath the water's surface. The one time she decides to go skinny-dipping, the sheriff catches her. Maybe she should just drown herself, she thought darkly. Instead, she emerged and sucked in a breath of air. His voice was entirely too inviting. She couldn't make out much more than the outline of his body, but she could easily imagine the dare in his dark eyes. She could easily imagine her entire bare body turning pink beneath his gaze.

"Come to me," Beau repeated in a seductive tone that made her glad she wasn't standing, because her knees wouldn't have supported her. Dracula had probably used the same words when he lured his victims.

Shivering both from the cool temperature of the water and her apprehension, she realized she wouldn't be able to outlast Beau. She closed her eyes briefly and made a quick promise to herself that it would all

be over in a couple of minutes. She would walk out
of the water, pull on her clothes as quickly as possible
and go to her car.

Taking a deep breath, Emily walked toward Beau
with as much dignity as she could muster. She refused
to look at his face, keeping her eyes focused on the
ground for her clothes. A terrible panic invaded her
when she didn't spot them and she was forced to meet
Beau's gaze.

He swore.

She saw her clothes in his hands. "I need my
clothes."

He swore again.

Her panic spiked. "I need my clothes, Beau!"

As if to shake himself from a daze, he gave a quick
jerk of his head. "Yeah, you do. Come here."

"I don't think so," she told him, through chattering
teeth.

"Come here," he said in a tone that allowed no
disagreement. "I'll help you get dressed."

She simply stared at him as he stepped closer to
her, slung some of her clothes over his shoulder, and
pulled out her bra.

"Come on. Put your arms through. You're freezing."

Emily did as he said, still astounded that he was
dressing her. The backs of his fingers burned as he
brushed them under her breasts to fasten the front of
her bra. He could have fondled her breasts and caressed her nipples. The almost-touch of his hands sent
her temperature soaring.

He bent slightly and held out her panties for her to

step into. He could have stroked her thighs and slipped his fingers between her legs where she was moist. Her thighs trembled, her heart tripped at the strange intimacy of his actions. There was something tenderly erotic about his attitude. She could feel his gaze on her. She could sense his need. It made her defenses as substantial as a house of cards.

"Why are you doing this?" she asked in a voice that sounded thin and wispy to her own ears as he buttoned her blouse.

"You were cold. You were naked," he muttered. "You needed to be dressed."

"But—"

Beau shook his head and held out her jeans. "Don't ask too many questions, Emily. You might not like the answers."

She braced herself on his shoulders, but after she pulled up her jeans, her fingers wouldn't cooperate when she tried to fasten them. He finished the job for her, and she was stunned at what she saw. "Look at your hands," she whispered. "They're shaking. Why?"

He inhaled quickly and backed away. "You really have no idea how beautiful you are, do you? You have no idea what the sight of your naked body can do to a man. No idea," he said, giving a forced, rough chuckle. "Get in your car, Emily. I'll follow you home."

His self-denial confused her. "But—"

He swore. "*Now*, Emily—"

Grabbing her shoes from the ground, she shrugged and walked to her car, her mind awhirl at what Beau

had just done for her, to her. Automatically she drove
to her house, her mind stuck back at the lake with a
sense of wonder. Why would a man do that? Touch
her and yet not touch her?

When she pulled into her driveway and got out of
her car, she struggled with a sense of inevitability.
She saw him park at her curb and stand beside his
truck. Her hair still damp, she walked toward Beau.
A faint inner voice reminded her that she'd only met
him a few weeks before. She didn't know him well.
A stronger voice told her she knew what she needed
to know about him.

His tension twisted around him like an over-
stretched rubber band. His eyes were narrowed as if
he were angry at her, but she suspected his anger was
directed at himself. Her stomach twisted with a mixed
sense of destiny and apprehension. It was as if fate
had brought her to this very place on this very night.
With this very man.

"Go on in," he told her. "I'll leave after you lock
up."

He was so accustomed to having his orders followed, she thought. She would have smiled if she
hadn't felt so nervous. "No," she said.

He blinked. "Go on in, Emily," he said, his tone
less gentle.

"No," she repeated. "I'm still cold."

He stared at her for a long moment and didn't
move.

So she did. Stumbling forward, she flattened herself
against his body and stretched her arms around him.

His posture rigid, Beau swore. "What are you doing?"

"Trying to get warm." *Trying to get close.*

He shuddered. "Emily, I've seen you. I can't go partway with you anymore."

Her heart was pounding so hard she wondered if it might burst. "Then don't," she said. "Take me all the way."

He went completely still. "What are you saying?"

She looked into his wary face. "I need to be close to you," she whispered. "As close as we can get."

An oath spilled from his mouth a breath before he closed his arms around her and kissed her. It was a claiming kiss that went on and on until Emily's head began to spin. Her knees dipped, and she stiffened them. She felt his hunger mirrored deep inside her.

"Let's go in," he muttered, then urged her toward the front door. She tried to put the key in the lock, but couldn't do more than jangle the key ring. He took over the job and had them inside within seconds, her back against the foyer wall, his mouth, hungry and demanding, on hers again. He discarded the clothes he'd so carefully put on her at the lake, and within moments she was naked.

Emily was hot inside, but her nerves made her feel cold on the outside. She wanted closer, and his shirt was in the way. Tugging at his buttons, she pushed it aside and slid her hands over his bare skin.

Closing his palm over her breast, he groaned. "Let's go upstairs, sweetheart," he murmured, then nipped at her earlobe.

Emily swallowed at the heady sense of anticipation

invading her body. Why did this feel so right? she wondered. "The sheets aren't satin."

He gave a muffled chuckle. "I won't be noticing the sheets." Then he swung her up into his arms and climbed the stairs to her bedroom. He took her mouth again and allowed her body to slowly slide down his until her toes touched the floor. She felt his hardness pressing insistently against the front of his jeans.

He opened his mouth and teased her with an almost-kiss, his lips against hers, then pulled away just when she started to respond. "Reach into my left pocket," he told her.

She slid her hand down and pulled out the plastic packet. She felt a rush of both chagrin and relief. Thank goodness *he'd* prepared. He plucked the packet from her fingers and tossed it on the bed. For a split second she thought about telling him this was her first time, but he kissed her again and put her hand on his belt, and her mind went blank.

Fumbling with his belt, she loosened it, then edged his zipper down, the hissing sound echoing inside her like a flame. She'd have thought she would feel awkward, but he made her feel as if it was the most natural thing in the world for her to be undressing a man.

He kicked off his shoes and pushed down his denims and briefs. Her heart jumped into her throat at the sight of him naked and fully aroused. His shoulders looked impossibly broad, his chest well muscled and defined, with a sprinkling of hair. His masculinity jutted proudly between his thighs. Meeting her gaze, he walked her backward toward the bed until the backs of her legs bumped the edge of the mattress. The sensual look in his eyes took her breath.

He brushed her hair back and gave a half grin. Catching her breath, she wondered how he managed to look both amused and aroused at the same time.

"I like your ears."

Groaning, Emily ducked her head into his chest, his soft hair tickling her warm cheeks. "Oh, did you *have* to mention them?"

"Yeah. They remind me that you're human. Everything else," he murmured, sliding his hands down the outer edge of her breasts to her waist and hips, "is perfect."

She shook her head. "Not perfect. Not perfect at all."

"Yeah it is. Dressed, you're pretty as a picture. Undressed," he said with a sigh, "you're perfect. Quit arguing with me," he said when she opened her mouth to do just that. "Kiss me instead."

The dare in his voice tickled something inside her, and she pressed her open mouth against his throat and licked him.

He swore. "Your mouth is incredible. I've had dreams when all I did was kiss you."

"Really?" She was surprised, secretly delighted.

"Really," he told her in a deep voice, and lifted his hands to her breasts. "And I've spent an inordinate amount of time thinking about your nipples." He plucked her beaded tips until she felt a pull deep down between her thighs. Lowering his head, he sucked her into his mouth, laving her with his tongue.

Emily clung to his shoulders and bit back a moan.

She felt like a whirlpool of sensation, spinning, sinking.

He slid one of his hands down between her legs and found her where she was moist and sensitive. "Oh, Beau."

"You're wet," he said, and fondled her with breathtaking persistence. "There's so much I want to do with you, but I don't think I'm gonna be able to wait long tonight. I feel like I've been waiting half a lifetime already."

His need for her accelerated her own. He slipped one finger inside her, making her gasp. "Touch me," he told her in a husky voice.

Eager to arouse him as he'd aroused her, she wrapped her hand around him. He slid gently within her hand and stroked her intimately at the same time. It was erotic to see him so turned on, to know she was doing it to him. Her arousal spiked. Edgy, excited, she rubbed her thumb back and forth over the honeyed tip of his masculinity.

Beau closed his eyes and began to swear. "Emily, I want to be inside you."

"Yes," she whispered. She wanted that, too. She wanted him, all of him.

Gently nudging her backward, he followed her down on the bed. His body covered hers, his mouth took her lips, his arms were braced on either side of her, and she felt deliciously surrounded by him.

Pushing her legs apart, he caressed her until she couldn't stay still beneath his fingers. His tongue teased and taunted, sucking hers into his mouth as if he couldn't get enough of her. He touched her as if everything about her delighted him.

She was hot, reaching for him, reaching for something inside her. She stared into his dark, sexy eyes. "Beau—"

"What, sweetheart?" he muttered, nuzzling her neck.

"I need—" She wriggled beneath him, still reaching.

"You need what?"

"Oh." She arched against him. "You."

Beau groaned, and she felt him shift. Pushing her thighs farther apart, he held her with his gaze and thrust inside her.

Emily felt a burning sensation inside her. She watched Beau's eyes widen at the same time hers did. He started to pull back, and she instinctively tightened her thighs around him.

His nostrils flared. "You—you—"

She took a careful breath and licked her suddenly dry lips. "I meant to tell you, but I forgot."

Still poised just inside her, he studied her. "Forgot?" he asked in a voice he clearly struggled to keep neutral.

"I haven't done this before," she admitted.

His nostrils flared again. "You're a virgin."

Her body accommodated him and she wiggled experimentally. "Was. You feel big."

He swore, then chuckled roughly. "You feel incredible. Incredible." He lifted his hand to her cheek and looked at her with a sense of wonder. "Why didn't you tell me?"

He was inside her, but she wanted more. She was still reaching. "You, uh, distracted me."

He shook his head. "Oh, Emily," he murmured, then slid the rest of the way inside her.

She undulated beneath him, revelling in the full sensation. "You still feel very big."

His mouth tilted into a sexy grin. "Is that bad?"

Restless, she shook her head and arched into him. "Beau?"

"Yeah." He kissed her, distracting her again for a moment.

"Take me all the way," she whispered.

In an instant his eyes changed, his body tensed. "Hold on." Then he took her with fluid, sensual thrusts, pumping inside her. With each long stroke, he rubbed a sensitive spot deep inside her, making her tighten and cling to him.

"You're so good, Emily. Let it go," he urged her.

Again and again, he pumped until she jerked, the tension inside her bursting like stars. She thought it was all over, but he kept on and she burst again, whimpering his name.

Writhing, she flexed around him, staring into his eyes as he went over the top. Holding her tight, he cradled her as if, for that single glorious moment, she was his world. And Emily knew she would never be the same.

Beau pulled the covers loose and dragged them over their cooling bodies. He took a careful breath and looked at the woman who, for the last three weeks, had disturbed his waking and sleeping hours.

She looked dazed and thoroughly loved, her mouth swollen from his kisses. He was stunned to see faint marks on her fair skin.

Pushing his hair back from his damp forehead, he struggled to get perspective. His emotions were all over the place. At the same time he felt protective of Emily, he was scared spitless of her. The woman had turned him upside down. Rather than defusing his hunger for her, making love had only made him want her more.

She lifted her fingers to his mouth and looked at him with a searching gaze. "How many hundreds of women line up outside your door to ask you to make love to them?"

Her question was so ridiculous and flattering that it temporarily pushed back his uneasiness. "None," Beau said, shaking his head. "This was your first time, Emily. Why me?"

Her eyelashes fluttered down, shielding her expression from him. She shifted as if she wasn't totally sure of herself. "I'm not sure how to explain it, but I've never felt as close to anyone as I have you. I felt a connection. It doesn't really make sense, but it felt right." She gave a hard sigh. "It seemed right to be with you."

She glanced up at him quickly, then away again. "I thought you felt the same way. Maybe I was wrong. Maybe it was just me and—"

He pressed his mouth over hers to silence her doubts. Despite his own confusion, Beau couldn't let her think he didn't feel the same *connection*. "I did. It was different for me, too."

Of its own volition, his body began to respond to her again. His skin still burned, he was hard, primed to take her yet again. And he'd just taken her.

He could spend the night touching her, sipping kisses from her lips, sliding between her thighs, making her sigh and moan. He could, he thought, spend more than a night. The thought disturbed him. The feelings deep inside him disturbed him even more.

The sight of her bare body aroused him, but it was the way she responded to him, the way she so obviously wanted him. It was her personality, her trust, that urged him to get inside her. To stay.

Frowning thoughtfully, Beau decided he should go. He needed to get a grip. Besides, there were other considerations. He pulled her closer and kissed the top of her head, surprised at the force of his desire to stay. He'd never wanted to stay all night with a woman before.

"I can't stay," he told her while she snuggled against him. "The bad thing about being sheriff is everyone knows my truck. If my truck is here in the morning, everyone will know I've stayed all night."

Emily stilled and was silent for a long moment. She pulled away, and Beau felt the gap more than physically.

Brushing her hair from her face, she didn't meet his gaze. "I hadn't thought of that. It must be difficult for you."

He resisted the urge to pull her back into his arms. Barely. "It can be."

She paused, clutching the sheet as if she wanted to

wrap it around her. Then she moved to rise from the bed.

Beau felt an inexplicable sting of regret. He stopped her, wrapping his fingers around her wrist. "Emily—" he began.

"I just need to get my robe so I can walk you to the door," she said, tugging ineffectually. Her blue gaze finally met his. "You said you need to go."

In her eyes, he saw no censure, no accusation. But she couldn't hide the vulnerability. Biting back an oath, he released her and rose from the bed, too.

She practically flew to the closet and wrapped her robe around her as he pulled on his jeans and shirt. He shoved his feet into his shoes, all the while hating the silent tension building between them.

They walked down the stairs, and it would have been the most natural thing in the world for him to take her hand, but something stopped him. When they reached the foyer, he looked at her. "I'll call you to—"

"You don't have to," she blurted out, rendering him speechless.

Eight

Beau stared at her.

Unable to dodge him, Emily met his don't-try-to-fool-me gaze. Her heart twisted, but she tried for a casual shrug. She'd just been through the most powerful, moving experience of her life, and she felt as if she was holding herself together by a thread.

"No. Really," she insisted, trying to sound rational when she felt anything but. "I understand that just because we made love doesn't necessarily change our relationship. You're very committed to not being committed to a woman, and I don't expect you to act differently with me." Feeling her cheeks heat, she couldn't bring herself to use the word *arrangement,* but she forged on. "I don't want you to think that since I'm not experienced I expect something you don't want to give."

He let her statement hang between them for a long

moment. "You don't think anything's changed between us after making love?" he asked in that silk and stone voice.

"I didn't say that. I said I didn't expect you—"

He shook his head. "I heard you. Now you hear me. I'll call you tomorrow." He bent down to kiss her firmly on the lips, then backed away. "Everything between us is changed. *Everything*."

From the expression on his face, Emily wasn't sure that was good or bad.

By morning Emily was searching for her inner calm. The problem, she'd determined, was that she didn't have any instructions on how to deal with Beau. No etiquette books offered practical tips for this situation. Advice to the lovelorn might provide something, but Emily wasn't exactly *lorn*. Loony perhaps, but not lorn.

She didn't regret making love with him. How could she regret such a beautiful, powerful experience? How could she regret the moments that had brought her a feeling of such connection to another human being? She couldn't, but she wasn't exactly sure where things between Beau and her would go now.

Heaven knows, he didn't want commitment, and she wasn't ready. After all, she'd been walking down the aisle to marry another man just one month ago. Emily cringed at the thought. She needed the perspective time would bring. Every day made her see things a little differently. The last few days she'd felt a fleeting inclination to pay a quick visit to Roanoke. Perhaps that would give her a sense of resolution, she thought, but dismissed the possibility when it filled her heart with dread.

None of her thoughts diminished the disconcerting vulnerability she felt this morning. She felt stripped naked. The fact that she was scheduled to join Beau's sisters and their families for Sunday dinner today at Rosemary's was almost enough to give her a case of the hives.

She considered begging off, but pride wouldn't allow it. Taking some solace in the fact that Beau rarely joined his sisters for Sunday dinner, she pulled herself together and went. Helping Rosemary with last-minute preparations for dinner distracted her until Beau walked in just as everyone sat down at the table.

She looked at him, and her feeling of vulnerability shot to the surface. He sat directly across from her. Giving him a forced, light greeting, she bowed her head for the blessing and felt his gaze on her. Too conscious of his attention, she pushed her food around her plate and made conversation with Caroline's husband. It irritated her how difficult she found it to carry on a simple conversation just because Beau was in the same room.

He was just a man, she told herself.

Just a man who had touched her heart and taken her body. A man who had made her loneliness go away.

Emily swore under her breath. She didn't want Beau to matter that much to her. She didn't want to care about him. She concentrated harder.

"Want some salt?" Beau offered the shaker.

"Thank you." Emily automatically accepted it,

holding her breath when he stroked her fingers before he released the shaker.

"You haven't eaten much," he said.

She swallowed. "I'm not very fast."

His gaze darkened and swept down to her mouth. "That's okay. Slow is better."

Her heart raced and she prayed her cheeks weren't as red as the homegrown tomatoes in her salad. When he said *slow*, he wasn't talking about eating dinner. A shudder of awareness ran through her.

She deliberately turned her attention to Rosemary and Valene's discussion about their favorite cousin's upcoming wedding.

"Her fiancé's going to be shipped out on a nuclear submarine, and they want to tie the knot before he leaves."

"They only have a week," Valene added. "I feel so sorry for Annie. She won't have time to get a special dress or anything."

"She's such a little thing, like Emily. It's hard for her to buy off the rack," Caroline explained.

A thought struck Emily. "Do you think she could wear my wedding dress?"

Rosemary gasped. "Don't you want to save it?"

Emily shrugged. "For what?"

Rosemary looked uncomfortable. "Well, if you decide to get married again."

Everything within Emily rebelled at the idea. "No," she said and hoped that would be enough.

When she saw the expectant expressions of Beau's three sisters, though, she could tell it wouldn't be enough. "I think weddings are wonderful," she told them, *"for other people."*

"The first time we met, you mentioned something about not wanting to get married again, but that was an emotional moment, and you'd had a rough night before—"

"It wasn't," Emily said to Rosemary as gently as possible, "the tequila talking. I think it's marvelous for other people to get married. But I don't know when I'll be interested in getting married." Not daring to look at him even once, she wondered if she was saying that as much for Beau as for herself. She wondered if she was trying to prove something to him.

Bridging the silence, Valene cleared her throat. "It's very generous of you to offer your beautiful dress for Annie when you haven't even met her. That says a lot about what a kind person you are."

Emily felt her cheeks heat. "It's nothing. Really, I—"

"Stop trying to deny it," Caroline said. "We'll call Annie after lunch and she can see about alterations. I'm sure she'll be delighted."

"I'm headed out that direction later today if you'd like me to take it," Beau offered.

Tom snickered. "That's about as close as you'll get to a wedding dress. Sounds like you and Emily have the same attitude."

"Sounds like it," Beau said in a mild voice.

Feeling like a fraud, Emily met Beau's amused gaze. She supposed now wasn't the best time to tell everyone she'd considered burning her wedding gown so she wouldn't have to look at it anymore. Now also wasn't the time to mention that she and Beau shared more than an attitude. They'd shared her bed, their bodies, and at least part of their hearts.

She felt his feet stretch to either side of hers, lightly trapping her, as if he were determined to remind her of their intimacy. Did he really think she needed to be reminded?

She forced down a few more bites, and dinner was almost over when Valene addressed her again. "Emily, I recall your mentioning that you were involved in charity work in Roanoke, and I was wondering if you would join the Friends of the Library. We're meeting Tuesday night to brainstorm a fund-raiser."

Emily regretfully shook her head. "I'm sorry I can't on Tuesday night. I'm keeping Regina Bell's daughter, Hilary, two nights this week."

Rosemary made a tsking sound. "How is Regina? That situation is such a shame."

"Regina's still bruised, but she's much better. I think she's trying to decide whether to stay in Ruxton or go back to Kentucky where her family lives. Her husband—" she continued, then broke off as she glanced at Beau.

"Is in custody," Beau said flatly and didn't elaborate.

Valene sighed. "I don't want you to back out of sitting for Hilary, but we could use your help. We thought about holding an auction, but we can't get donations from any of the businesses."

"Then hold a service auction," she suggested, recalling a successful event she'd coordinated last year.

"Service auction?"

"People donate services and you auction them off. You can combine it with a picnic to increase the turn-out."

Valene looked confused. "What kind of services?"

"Anything. I'll start by donating two hours of computer consultation time. Someone with a truck can donate a couple of hours for light hauling. Teenagers can donate mowing lawns or baby-sitting. People can donate dinners. The way you get started is by asking someone visible and well-respected to donate something. Then you tell everyone else what they donated so it gently pressures them to participate, too."

"I wonder what visible person we should ask," Valene said.

"That's easy," Caroline said. "He's sitting at our table."

"Beau," Valene said with a smile.

Emily could practically feel his groan.

He set down his fork. "Offhand, I can't think of any services I can provide," Beau said.

"I'm sure most of the single female population would disagree," Caroline said dryly.

"Be serious, Caroline. What do you think Beau could do, Emily?"

Emily wished she could hold her glass of iced tea to her face. She sipped it instead.

Beau sat back in his chair and looked at her with an intimate glint in his eyes as if he knew everything that was going on inside her, as if he could see the blatant sexual images that raced through her head.

"Yeah, Emily," Beau said, his voice full of double

meaning. "Since you're the experienced one, what do you think I could do for the auction?"

Choking on her tea, she gave Caroline's husband a weak smile when he gently thumped her on the back. "Horseback riding lessons," she managed to say.

"Perfect!" Valene cooed, clapping her hands. "Beau hasn't given a riding lesson since his rodeo days." She beamed at Emily. "You're brilliant. Isn't she brilliant?"

Emily was stuck on Valene's other statement. *Beau hasn't given a riding lesson since his rodeo days.* He'd made an exception for her. Why? she wondered, searching his inscrutable gaze for answers and finding none.

Brilliant? Try clueless.

Forty-five minutes later, Beau was ringing Emily's doorbell. She opened the door. Just looking at her made him feel like he'd been punched.

"You said you would call."

He shrugged. "Call, visit. Same thing." He walked through the doorway and without pausing, pulled her to him.

"No, it's not," she corrected. "A call involves the telephone and distance."

"I wanted something more personal." Then because he'd waited entirely too long, he kissed her long and well. When he drew away, he was wanting her again. "Why wouldn't you look at me at dinner?"

"I didn't think you wanted anyone to know—" she took a deep breath "—about last night. About us.

Your sisters are perceptive. I was afraid I'd give it away.''

His gut twisted at the vulnerable expression on her face, and he lifted his hand to her cheek. "I don't want to share you. I want this to be just between you and me.''

She gave a tentative smile. "That won't be easy.''

"Yeah, I know," he muttered and shut the door. He linked his fingers through hers and tugged her toward the sofa to sit. Lord, he hoped the intensity of his desire for her lessened. "I could barely keep my hands off you today at Rosemary's.''

"I'm at a loss," she told him, her eyes wide with dismay. "I feel like I've gotten on a wild ride at the amusement park and I don't know where it's headed or when it will stop." She pulled away from him and rose from the sofa as if she couldn't keep still.

When he started to get up, she put up her hands. "No. Please stay where you are. I have a hard time thinking clearly when you get close and I want to get this said." She swept her hand through her hair. "I don't know if I can explain this, but I feel close to you, closer than I've felt to anyone else. And I felt that way before last night. I—" She stalled, looking at the ceiling for help. "That's why I wanted— No, *needed* to be with you." Her eyes crinkled in confusion. "But it doesn't make any sense. We haven't even been on a date.''

He rose then. "We can change that.''

Her gaze searched his. "Are you sure you want to?''

"Emily, come here.''

She hesitated, regarding him warily, but she moved closer.

Taking her hand again, he was uncomfortable with the strength of his feelings. "I'm not making any promises and you aren't, either, but I'd be lying if I said I could get enough of you. I can't." Something inside him resisted expounding further, but her honesty demanded his. "It's more than sex, although I want you right now. I wanted you at Rosemary's. I wanted you as soon as we'd made love last night."

She blinked in amazement, her eyes flickering with fear. "I don't know about this, Beau. I don't know if I'm ready for you. It was just a month ago that I was ready to marry another man."

He'd spent the entire night thinking about the exact same thing. He gave a dry, humorless chuckle. "Do you have a choice?"

Her expression changed. She glanced away, then back at him. "I guess not." She dipped her head and took a deep breath. "So what's next?"

"How about dinner at my house?"

Her lips twitched and she slowly nodded. "Okay, Sheriff. I look forward to seeing how well you cook."

He laughed again, this time with humor, and pulled her back into the circle of his arms. "Yeah, you definitely make me cook." He kissed her lips and felt a tightness in his chest when she slipped her fingers through his hair.

"Monday okay?" he asked her. Why did she feel like sunshine in his arms?

She licked her lips, her eyes slightly dazed. "For what?"

"Dinner."

"Yes."

He slid his hands down to her bottom and nestled himself between her thighs. Why did everything about her mesh with him? He should learn the answers to these questions. He should settle his curiosity, so she wouldn't have such power over him. He would, he decided, and he would enjoy every minute with her. "What are you doing Wednesday?"

"Nothing."

"Friday?" he asked, nuzzling her neck.

"Nothing. Why?"

"Consider yourself booked," he told her, wanting closer. It was strange, but he felt the need to seal their agreement, to know her intimately again. This time, he would do better. He would pay attention and not lose control. "Are you going to let me make love to you now?"

She hesitated, and he felt the echo of her brief silence deep inside him. He read her easily. "What is it?"

She looked away, embarrassed.

"Emily, what is it?"

"Do you have to be in such a rush to leave afterward this time?" she asked, meeting his gaze. "It was hard being close and having you leave so quickly."

Beau's chest tightened again. It was just as she'd told him. She needed him as close as he could get. Other women had wanted his body, perhaps a material commitment from him, but none had been interested in his heart. If Beau didn't know better, he would say something inside him had just yelled "Timber!"

When he'd gone home last night, he'd felt full, yet empty, filled with an urgency to get back to Emily. "I'm in no rush to leave you," he told her. "No rush at all." In the back of his mind, though, there was something about her that conjured up uncertainty. He couldn't put his finger on it, but mixed in with his desire and need, there was a voice that told him not to count on her forever.

Beau brought in the steaks and watched Emily meandering around his den, studying his pictures. Her hands folded behind her, she leaned forward to study the charcoal sketch of him during his rodeo days. He waited for her to adjust the frame. But she didn't. She just kept looking.

Interesting, he thought. "Steaks are ready," he said.

She glanced up and smiled. "They look great. Everything looks great," she said gesturing toward the table. "What can I do to help?"

"Already done," he told her, pulling the potatoes and rolls from the oven and tossing them on the table. "C'mon over and let me feed you."

"I'm surprised you prepared the meal." She sat down and smiled.

"You were expecting?"

"Takeout," she confessed.

He scowled. "That's for sissies."

She laughed. "And broiling is for real men."

"You're a perceptive woman."

"You're just hoping I'll do the dishes."

He chuckled, surprised at how much he enjoyed her presence in his home. Beau truly enjoyed his privacy. She was the exception that proved the rule, he decided. "You're a perceptive woman."

He poured the wine. "Have any of my sisters called you today?"

Emily shook her head. "No. Why?"

"I got calls from each of them asking why I'd stayed so late at your house last night. They wanted to know if I was *seeing* you."

"Oops. What did you say?" She lifted a bite of steak to her lips.

He could have gotten distracted just watching her eat. He shook his head. But he wouldn't. "I told them I didn't have any problems with my vision, I could see just about everyone." He rolled his eyes. "It worked with Rosemary and Valene."

"But not with Caroline."

"Yeah. I told her you'd just baked some cookies and I raided your cookie jar." He smiled. "It was true, in a manner of speaking."

She blushed, lifting her napkin to cover her face for a second, then dropped it. "You wonder why they drive you crazy, but you bring it on yourself."

With a deadpan gaze, he said, "My mother always told me I was a perfect brother."

"But what do your sisters say?"

He paused. "They think I could use some work. Speaking of which, what do you think of my house?" He dug into his own meal.

She sipped her wine. "It's nice. The pictures and

furniture, they say a lot about your personality and interests.''

This was a test. He shouldn't do it, he told himself. It was a sure way to kill the attraction, but curiosity won. "What would you change about my house?"

A blank look crossed her face. She looked around. "Are you unhappy with it?"

"Not really."

She looked puzzled. "Do you want something different? To change the colors or something?"

He tilted his head, looking at her thoughtfully. "No."

She shrugged. "It's your house. If you're happy with it, then it's not necessary to change anything."

Oops. Beau felt a sinking sensation in his gut.

Nine

Emily passed the test.

Beau took a gulp of his wine. He'd expected the more typical feminine inclination to perform makeovers. Women seemed obsessed with fixing things, changing things just for the sake of changing them. Much to his chagrin, he'd learned that the women in his life often wanted to fix him.

He eyed her speculatively. "There must be something you would change, some suggestion you would make."

She met his gaze, looking slightly confused. "No," she said drawing out the word. "When I was growing up, my mother always wanted my room one way, and I wanted it another. I think it's important for people to have their own space and make it the way they like it. It's probably one of the reasons I'm enjoying my house right now."

He nodded slowly, watching her eat again. He should have known she would have a different perspective. "So you're discovering what you like for the first time."

"It's fun, but it might be easier if I had an interesting previous occupation like the rodeo."

"You don't need a previous occupation. All you need to do is figure out what you like." Her point of view raised more questions in his mind. "If you think everyone should have their own space, then how do you blend things when people live together?"

She gave a wry smile. "I guess that's one more advantage to not getting married. I don't have to blend."

A nonanswer, Beau thought, and mulled it over during the rest of the meal. If she'd been another woman, digging beneath the surface wouldn't have been necessary. She appealed to him, he wanted her, she wanted him. That should have been enough, but for some reason, it wasn't.

After dinner they cleaned the dishes together and took a walk to the barn. "The first night I was here," she told him, "I didn't even know you had a barn and horses. I barely noticed when I left the next morning."

"You weren't in the best condition then."

She laughed lightly. "No, but I can see why you would love this. You have your space, your privacy and a couple of horses."

He leaned against a stall and watched her roam around the barn. She was dressed in a butter yellow shirtwaist dress that showed her curves; and the way she moved restlessly about reminded him of a butterfly. She held a sugar cube in her hand to give to Blue, but she was tentative.

"That sugar's gonna melt in your hand if you don't go ahead and give it to Blue," he told her.

"Okay," she said and walked closer. "And you're sure he won't bite."

"I'm sure." Standing close to her, he put his hand under hers. "Hold your palm out flat. Watch him. He'll take it with his lips."

She did as he instructed and slowly lifted her hand toward the horse. She let out a muffled squeak when Blue took the cube.

Beau chuckled. "Did he steal a kiss?"

Shaking her hand, she smiled sheepishly at him. "I don't know. If he did, he must take after his owner."

Beau pulled her into his arms and drew in the soft clean scent of her light hair. "Butterfly. Flutterby."

She looked up at him curiously. "Butterfly, flutterby?"

He brushed his hand through her hair. "In that yellow dress with your light hair and the way you were flitting around, you reminded me of a butterfly. My father used to switch the syllables around."

The years rolled back to a special moment Beau remembered. "I liked catching butterflies when I was a kid. It was a major disappointment when I'd trap them in a glass jar and they would die. My father told me flutterbys were fun to chase, fun to catch and hold for a while. But you had to let 'em go."

His gaze met hers, and it finally struck him. The

niggling doubt in the back of his mind about Emily had its roots in a memory of his father.

Emily seemed to sense his tension. "What would your father have thought of me?"

"He would have thought you were pretty and sweet. Special," Beau said.

"But he also might have thought I was a flutterby." She lifted her eyebrows. "Yes?"

The woman was a little too perceptive. He sighed. "Maybe," he admitted reluctantly.

She cocked her head to one side. "You know, it's interesting to think about what your father would have thought of me, but I must confess I'm wondering what you think, Beau. Do you think I'm a flutterby?"

Beau was a straight shooter, but he would just as soon not answer her question. He lightly chucked her chin with his knuckles. "Too soon to know. It takes a while to determine the species."

"You don't trust me."

Her words were stark and blunt, unexpected. He frowned and shook his head. "I didn't say—"

"It's okay," she said, rubbing her cheek against his knuckles as if she were trying to soothe him and herself. Her eyes were vulnerable. "With the mistakes I've made lately, I'm not too sure I trust myself."

Beau's observation stabbed at Emily like a splinter. It made her wonder about herself. It forced her to reevaluate her impulsive decision to make a temporary home in Ruxton. She began to ask herself questions, and she didn't have answers for all of them.

What was she doing here? Aside from the calamity of her near-marriage, why didn't she have any desire to return to Roanoke? The only thing that nagged at her was the idea that she needed to settle unfinished business.

Her doubts troubled her. Although she understood Beau's reservation about her, she still felt frustrated by it because it stood between them. It was impossible to explain, futile to understand, but every emotional instinct she possessed pushed her closer to him. It was as if she was a river and he was the sea. Her heart allowed no choice. She had to go. In the back of her mind, though, she wondered where all this would lead.

"Where?" she muttered to herself as she joined Caroline for a stroll at the flea market. No sign of Beau today. His deputy was on duty while Beau took care of a crisis with some juvenile offenders.

"Where what?" Caroline said, gazing at Emily with dark eyes that resembled Beau's.

Emily bit her tongue. She hadn't realized she'd spoken aloud. "I wonder where Valene will set up the auction."

"Probably over by the weeping willow," Caroline said, pointing to a lush grassy patch in front of the tree. "Everyone's psyched about this services auction. I think the turnout will be great."

"I hope so," Emily said, picking up a tomato at the vegetable stand.

"I wonder if Beau will bring Donna." Caroline lowered her voice. "Nadine said she saw Donna corral him at the bar last night. She said Donna was all over him.''

Emily felt an ugly twist in her stomach. Beau hadn't visited her last night because she'd taken care of Hilary. He'd asked her to join him for the auction. It would be their first public appearance, but this morning he'd warned her the juvenile case might make him late. Emily's own doubts about their relationship roared to the surface. It required a major effort for her to make a noncommittal sound.

''Valene and I were talking about it the other day. We wish Beau would get involved with someone different. A woman who is decent and kind, who understands the importance of family and commitment.''

Emily smiled weakly and mumbled again.

Caroline stepped closer to her. ''Someone like you.''

Alarm shot through her, and her thumb pierced the tomato skin. Emily paid for the bruised tomato and four almost ripe ones, then put them in her basket. ''I think Beau prefers to make up his own mind.''

''But you think he's attractive, don't you?''

''Well, of course, but—''

''There you go!'' Caroline said in triumph.

''But I'm not inclined toward making any commitments right now,'' Emily quickly said.

''You will later,'' Caroline assured her. ''And surely you can see that underneath his superior attitude, he's a wonderful man.''

''I—uh—yes.''

"There you go," Caroline said again. "You know what I like about you, Emily? You're such an honest, moral person without seeming like a goody-goody."

Emily wondered if this was when she should tell Caroline that just the other night she had nearly been begging Beau to take her on the hood of his car. "I'm glad you like me, but I'm not perfect by any means."

Caroline looked at her sideways and laughed. "Oh, you! Stop teasing me. What's the worse thing you've done? Go five miles over the speed limit?" Caroline shook her head. "If I've ever met someone as pure as the driven snow, Emily, it's you."

Emily sighed as Caroline walked ahead. "Slush," she muttered. "Pure as the driven slush."

Later that afternoon at the auction, Emily set her picnic basket on a blanket and watched the auctioneer fast-talk the bidders. As Beau had predicted, he was late. Glancing at her watch, she glumly began to wonder if he would show at all.

"Are you the new girl in town?" a woman's voice asked.

Emily glanced up and instantly recognized Beau's former lover. Her throat tensed, but she managed a smile. "Yes, I'm very new to Ruxton. And you?"

"Donna Grant," the woman said. "I'm a sales rep and I've lived here for a while. I'm hoping to be moved to a bigger territory soon." She smiled slightly. "They call you the five-minute bride. What's your real name?"

That pinched. *Who* called her the five-minute bride? "Emily St. Clair. It's a pleasure to meet you," she automatically said, thanking her lucky stars for being force-fed how to give polite responses at finishing school. She changed the subject away from herself. "The auction's a lot of fun, isn't it?"

Donna brushed a blade of grass from her jeans. "I guess so if you're into that sort of thing. I thought I might find Beau here. I asked around and people kept mentioning you. Was he supposed to meet you?"

How *direct,* Emily thought. "Yes, but he had some pressing work to do."

Donna looked at her with an evaluating gaze. "I'm not going to beat around the bush. Beau and I've been involved, and I'd like to keep it that way."

Emily wondered how in tarnation she was supposed to respond. She took a careful breath. "I'm not sure I can help you with that."

"So he's started seeing you," she said, her voice hinting at all kinds of conclusions. "You and he have an arrangement."

Her stomach clenched. "I—I—don't think I would call it an arrangement. We haven't known each other very long," Emily managed to say, then stood. "Oh, look. They're starting the bidding on the window-cleaning service. I wanted to try for that one. Please excuse me," she said in a rush. "It was nice meeting you."

Emily escaped the other woman's presence, but she couldn't avoid the word *arrangement* as it echoed inside her mind over and over again. She won the bid for the window cleaners and confirmed her purchase at the registration table. Her head began to throb with tension and she strongly considered leaving, but Beau came up behind her.

"Shopping again?" he teased, putting his arm around her waist.

She managed a smile. "I like the idea of someone else doing my second-story windows."

"Thought you wanted to try all the things you've never tried before," he murmured close to her ear.

A pleasurable shudder ran through her. "Try the things I've always *wanted* to try," she corrected.

"Where do I fit in all of that?"

"You can be trying," she told him, and laughed at his scowl. She met his gaze and lowered her voice. "There are more things I'd like to try with you."

Squeezing her waist, he looked at her with sensual promise in his dark eyes. "Then you will."

His expression was so intense it made her feel hot and restless. She looked away and took a quick breath. "How did your juvenile case turn out?"

Beau shook his head. "The kid's in a tough situation, but this is the second car he's hot-wired and stolen. When I talked to the D.A., I made noises about wanting stronger efforts for rehabilitation so this boy doesn't become an adult offender. Juvenile cases always require an incredible amount of time and paperwork." He brushed his hand through his hair in exasperation. "I've had enough of it today. When's your computer-service offer coming up for bid?"

Emily cocked her head and listened to the auctioneer. "I think they're announcing it now. Did I tell you I received three phone calls from small local busi-

nesses asking me to consult on a part-time basis?"
She felt a rush of excitement. "Right now it's mostly
moonlighting, but it could grow. Who would have
ever thought Emily could become an entrepreneur?"

"An underestimated woman," Beau said wryly,
"can be very dangerous. And, darlin', you have been
grossly underestimated."

"By whom?"

"By just about everyone, including you." The bidding began, and he narrowed his gaze. "Why the hell
is Hank bidding? He wouldn't know what to do with
a computer if it bit him," he muttered.

"All the more reason for him to become educated."

Beau looked down his nose at Emily. "By
whom?"

She smiled. "By *me* if he wins the bid."

Beau frowned.

Emily watched the bidding rise to fifty dollars and
tried unsuccessfully not to think about her earlier conversation with Donna. *You have an arrangement.* She
didn't like the way that statement felt. It sounded controlled and businesslike, when she felt emotional and
out of control. It didn't sit right with her, but she
wondered if it was the truth, at least for Beau.

"Going, going—"

Beau lifted his hand and shouted, "Fifty-five!"

She blinked and watched in amazement as Hank
and Beau drove the bidding higher. When they hit
seventy-five dollars, she tugged on Beau's sleeve.

"Why are you bidding on this when you can get it free?"

He chuckled. "I'm glad you're offering your services *free* for me, but I don't trust Hank's motives."

She opened her mouth to correct him, but he called out another bid. The county would pay for her services to Beau's office. It took her a moment to understand what he'd said about Hank. She couldn't believe this was some sort of macho competitive game over her! When the light dawned, she stifled a groan. "This is insanity," she said, and walked away.

"Emily," he called after her. "Emily," he said again, but she just kept on walking.

Not more than a minute later, Beau was jogging to catch up with her. "Hold on. Why'd you leave?"

"I'm confused. First you act like you think I'm about as substantial as cotton candy, then you give me the rush. You indicate you don't want everyone to know we're involved. You're not interested in commitment. Then you get into a bidding war with Hank over two hours of computer time with me."

He shrugged. "Things change."

His response failed to satisfy her. "Maybe," she thought, and continued walking.

Beau put out his arm to stop her. "What's with you tonight?"

Emily tensed. She didn't want to explain herself. She wasn't certain she understood everything herself. "I don't know," she said. "I've just been thinking a lot this afternoon."

"About what?" he demanded.

"About a lot of things," she said, then changed the subject. "Are you hungry? I think I'd like to eat. I've set up a blanket there," she told him, pointing toward the picnic area.

He hesitated, then nodded. "Okay. We can talk later."

Emily wasn't looking forward to it.

As the evening progressed, Beau noticed Emily seemed more withdrawn than usual. Even when his sisters came by to rib him, Emily was polite, but quiet. By the time they left the auction, he was compelled to learn what was bothering her. He didn't completely understand his drive. In normal circumstances, he wouldn't want to know too much about why a woman wasn't talking, because it usually meant she wanted something from him that he couldn't give.

He brought his truck to a stop outside his house and watched her. She was a crazy combination of women in one, he thought. Pretty, but proper on the outside, polite, impertinent, playful on the inside. As a lover, she was a damn fast learner. Her unguarded expressiveness kept him wanting more.

Even now he wanted to be touching her, but tonight she seemed remote. "What brought on all this thinking?"

She slid a sideways gaze at him. "You say that as if thinking is a bad thing."

"No," he said, carefully considering his next response. "Thinking is good as long as you don't get off on the wrong track. But you didn't really answer my question. What brought it on?''

She rolled down her window. ''I met Donna Grant tonight.''

Beau rubbed his chin and sighed. This could get messy. ''Donna and I were—'' He paused, trying to find the right description for a relationship that had involved his body, but never his heart. ''We had an arrangement.''

''I know. Your sisters told me. Donna told me.'' She paused. ''When people get involved, unfortunately there is sometimes a difference in the intensity of their emotions.''

''What are you saying?''

''Donna wants to continue your arrangement.''

Beau frowned. ''I've been over this with her. I don't know why she dragged you into it.''

''It was a brief conversation. She was curious.''

Impatience licked through him. ''About what?''

''You and me,'' Emily said, still looking out the window. ''She wanted to know if you and I had an arrangement.''

''What did you say?''

''I said I wouldn't choose that term. It sounds cold to me.'' She finally turned to look at him. ''I wondered what term you would choose.''

Irritated with Donna's interference, Beau swore under his breath. ''It's not the same as it was with her.''

''That's good to know,'' she said politely, and he could see she was struggling with it. ''Just out of curiosity, how would you describe us?''

Crazy. Intimate. Unexpected friends. Unplanned lovers. All those descriptions made him uncomfortable. He went for something more rational. "I would say we have an understanding."

She nodded, but he wanted to close the distance he saw in her eyes immediately.

"What do you think?"

"It doesn't reveal anything about your feelings," she told him as she opened her door. "It's noncommittal, which is consistent. I think it sounds sleazy," she finished saying, in a crisp, prissy voice.

And Beau knew by the way she slammed her door when she got out of his truck that he'd really blown it this time.

Ten

"Well, hell!"

Emily felt Beau overtake her quick stride. She stiffly came to a stop. She felt stiff and tense. She felt confused.

"How should I explain our relationship?" he demanded. "You want me to say we're lovers?"

She blinked, taken aback. "I—"

"I could tell people to mind their own damn business," he offered.

"Well, you—"

"Or do you want me to tell them how I really *feel*?" He said the 'F' word with true masculine distaste. "That I want to lock you up in my house and make love to you until we physically can't lift a finger. That I want to punch Hank for looking at you twice. That you've affected me like no other woman has, and I'd like you to stay around a lot longer than

I think you're going to. As much as you say you're staying in Ruxton, I know you're going back to Roanoke."

Emily simply stared at him. His words rattled inside her head like pinballs in a machine, bouncing off emotionally loaded areas inside her. Her knees felt weak. She hadn't realized that the intensity of his feelings mirrored her own. "Give me a minute," she said.

Beau stepped closer, his eyes darkly passionate. "Sometimes I feel like I don't have a minute. Sometimes I'm sure I'm going to turn around and in a flash you'll be gone. My saner half tells me to pull back. Then some other part I didn't even know existed keeps pushing me closer to you. You wanna tell me how the hell to explain that to the folks in town?"

Distress crowded her throat. She identified with much of what he was saying. She wished she knew herself better. A sound of frustration escaped her mouth. "For a twenty-five year old, I feel like I should have a much better grasp on who I am and what I want. But I don't. I'm so afraid of making another mess of my life. I don't want to mess up yours, either. You don't trust me, and maybe you shouldn't. I told you I'm not sure I trust myself right now."

She grabbed her courage in her hand and continued, searching his eyes. "But, Beau, I've never met anyone like you, and I just don't want to find myself missing you someday. Ready or not, I don't want to ever miss you."

He looked away and swore. "The timing sucks."

Her heart contracted. "So what do we do?"

He looked back at her, and she watched something shift in his eyes. From doubt and caution to passionate abandon, it was like watching a rider let out the reins on his horse.

Emily felt a wave of anticipation rush through her, and her own doubts seemed to take flight.

"I think it's time we stop *counting* the minutes and start living them," he told her in a deep voice that sent a shudder through her. "You game?"

It was a risky venture, she knew, and she wouldn't be able to protect her heart. All or nothing. It frightened her, but that same need pounded through her. "Yes," she whispered.

He swung her up in his arms and headed for the house.

Emily struggled for a breath. "What are you doing?"

"We made a deal. No use in wasting time," he told her, and pushed open his front door.

"Guess not," she murmured, certain she'd left half her mind in his driveway.

Beau strode through his den, past his black Lab Cookie, to his bedroom. Setting her down next to his nightstand, he wrapped his hand around the nape of her neck and took her mouth in a hungry kiss.

The room began to swim, and she clung to his shoulders. When she was certain she was going to melt into one of the cracks in his hardwood floor, he pulled away. She had to lock her knees to keep from pitching toward him.

If she'd been unsure of his plans before, she knew

without a doubt what he intended when he pulled a handful of condoms out of the drawer, tore one open and put it on top of the nightstand.

"I have got to have you," he said.

His intensity almost made her nervous. He didn't wear a gentle look on his face or an easy expression in his eyes. Undiluted need. It gave her a rush. When had she been needed like this? A strange sense of power rushed through her.

"Then take me," she said, leaning into him and lifting her mouth to his. "And let me take you."

Tumbling backward on the bed, Beau pulled her with him, catching her against him. He slid his hands beneath her skirt and skimmed them up her thighs to her bottom to rock her pelvis against his. "You have on too many clothes."

His heat cranked up her body temperature, his need spurred her own. "No more than you," she managed to say.

He slipped one of his hands up her blouse and released a few of the buttons to cup one of her lace-covered breasts. He smiled. "I'm not wearing a bra."

Emily's mouth went dry when his thumb flicked across her nipple. She couldn't muster a grin. "I'm not wearing socks."

"Oh, Emily," he groaned, and undid the catch of her bra.

She tugged his shirt free and ran her hands over the hard planes of his chest and abdomen. He sucked in his belly when her fingers trailed just beneath his waistband. He arched his hips against her, and she felt the thrust of his hard masculinity beneath his jeans.

The knowledge of his arousal turned her on even more. She slid her fingertips over his nipples, caught between her desire to go wild with his body or to wait for him.

He put his hand over hers and let her continue stroking him. "What is it?"

"You make me want to do all kinds of things to your body, Beau." She lightly squeezed his nipples and rolled her lower body against his.

He closed his eyes for a second and swore. "What kinds of things?"

"I want to lick—" she began, taking a breath. "You."

He groaned again. "Where?"

Emily looked at his body and felt shamelessly hungry. His chest was a work of art, beautifully carved pectorals with a dusting of hair that arrowed down to his flat belly. He was so strong, and his inner and outer strength was incredibly sexy to her. "Everywhere," she admitted.

"Oh, Lord, what are you waiting for?"

"To see if it's okay with you."

He rolled his head from side to side. "Are you gonna make me beg?"

Emily smiled. "Could I?"

He glanced at her through slitted eyes looking like a hungry lion. "Show a little mercy, devil woman. Payback's hell."

Leaning forward, she skimmed her tongue over his

throat and slid her hands down to unfasten his waistband. "I like this perspective," she murmured.

"You like being on top," he said in a wry, but husky voice.

Scooting back slightly, she eased his zipper down. "Well, I've never really—"

He brushed aside her bra. "You've never done a lot of things."

"I'm trying to amend that," she said, feeling both determined and hot. She lowered her head to his chest and licked his nipples the same way he'd licked her. He arched beneath her, and she was awed again at the power and strength of his body.

Rubbing openmouthed kisses over his chest and upper abdomen, she slid her hand inside his loosened jeans and touched him.

He jerked.

"Do you want me to stop?"

"No, no, no." He rolled her nipples between his thumb and forefinger.

The mesmerizing little caress distracted her, made her restless. She rubbed her hair back and forth against his belly, and felt him stiffen as if he were struggling to control himself.

Inhaling deeply, Emily felt the need to be closer to him grow wider and deeper inside her. It seemed to stretch her and take up every available corner. In her heart. In her mind. In her body. She wondered why she loved the way he smelled, why the texture of his skin fascinated her, why she wanted to taste him so badly. She wondered why she wanted to be what he needed in a woman whatever that was. So many depended on him, but she wanted to be someone he could depend on.

Close enough, intimate enough, just didn't seem to exist. Her desire to pleasure him was endless. She stroked his hardened masculinity again and met his gaze. His eyes were nearly black with arousal, his nostrils flared.

"Come here, sweetheart. I want to kiss you."

Her heart pounded against her rib cage. In all her life, she'd never really been anyone's sweetheart. Not like this. Taking a quick breath, she shook her head. "Not yet," she told him and rode the wave of her instincts. "I might not do this right," she whispered, pushing aside a sliver of uncertainty, as she took him into her mouth.

He was satin and steel against her lips, and she tasted him again and again. She rolled her tongue over the tip of his arousal and was surprised that pleasuring him was such a turn-on. His shudder vibrated inside her. Swollen with wanting him, she continued until he slipped his fingers through her hair and urged her head up.

"I'm on the edge," he said roughly.

"That's okay," she told him and tried to lower her mouth again.

"No. Oh, help me." He sucked in a deep breath of air. "Not this way, not this time," he murmured as much to himself as to her and dragged her up his body. "What am I going to do with you, Emily?"

The hopeless note in his voice wrenched at her. "Let me make love to you this time. Let me."

"But—"

"Let me," she repeated and kissed him. A second passed and he lost it, taking her mouth as if he couldn't get enough of her. Distantly, she felt him pull her skirt up and push her panties down. His fingers searched and found her wet with wanting. He made the ache worse by caressing her, sliding his finger just inside her.

She strained against him, her breaths matching his. With trembling fingers she reached for the protection on the nightstand and fumbled as she put it on him. Her mind a haze of arousal, she shook her head. "I need to take off this skirt."

Beau shook his head and wrapped his hands around her waist, drawing her above him. "Just sit," he told her, rubbing his masculinity at her entrance.

Swallowing hard, she vacillated. They were both still partly clothed, but the urgency between them was overwhelming. Trapped in his gaze, she eased, inch by inch down on him until he filled her.

He closed his eyes for a moment, relishing the intimate moment, then opened them. Emily felt his gaze of approval on her as he released one of her wrists and slipped his fingers between them. She had never felt so voluptuous in her life. She had never known she could.

He fondled her sensitive femininity, making her undulate.

"Oh, yes," he said. "Grab my shoulders, Emily."

She leaned forward needed something to brace herself on.

"Ride me," he told her, moving inside her at a slow, mind-bending rhythm.

Emily followed her heart again. He led. She followed. Then she led, and he followed. In the end he took her mind, body and soul, but Emily saw the reality on his face, and it rocked her foundations. She had taken him, too.

For a few minutes they dozed together. Beau felt her wiggle and tightened his arms.

"I need to visit your bathroom," she murmured.

He allowed her to go, opening his eyes enough to catch sight of her beautiful backside as she slipped out of bed. Lifting his hand to his forehead, he covered his eyes and wondered how he'd gotten into this. He'd never been one to cling to anyone. After living in a houseful of women, being alone and having his privacy had seemed like a gift. Now it was as if Emily had walked into his life and shown him this huge empty hole in his life that only she could fill.

Beau found that notion enormously disturbing because his instincts warned him that she wouldn't stay. Even if he asked her to stay.

She breezed back into the bedroom, interrupting his dark thoughts. He chuckled, suspecting she moved so quickly because she was unaccustomed to being watched while she walked around in the nude. Just as she slipped into bed and pulled up the sheet, she stopped, staring into the open bedside drawer.

She turned to him curiously. "What's in this drawer?"

"What?"

"It looks like buckles. Belt buckles."

"Oh, yeah," he said. "Those are some of the buckles I won during my rodeo days. I stuffed them in the drawer till I could figure out what to do with them."

She looked at him in disbelief. "For two years?"

He shrugged.

She pulled one out of the drawer. "You should display them."

Beau got a kick out of her fascination with his awards. "Uh-oh," he said. "I never would have thought you'd be a buckle bunny."

Her eyebrows wrinkled in confusion. "Buckle bunny?"

Leaning closer, he pulled her to him. "A buckle bunny is a woman who chases the rodeo winners."

She cocked her head to one side thoughtfully. "And this woman has a fixation with—" She met his gaze. "Buckles."

Beau bit back his amusement. "You could say that."

She peeked back into his drawer, then looked back at him, her expression rife with speculation. "You have a *lot* of buckles. Big buckles."

Beau roared with laughter and squeezed her against him again.

When he quieted down, he watched her run her fingers over his buckle. "Did you wear a costume and a hat? Do you ever wear the buckles? Did you have boots? What kind of horses did you—"

"Hold on, Miss Curious. I had a couple of fancy shirts I wore, and yeah, I wore a black hat and boots. The horses—"

"A black hat?" she repeated with excitement.

"Yes."

"When I was little, I wanted to be a cowboy with a black hat."

"A cowgirl," he corrected.

She shook her head. "No. On TV, the cowboys always got to do the fun stuff. I never saw any cowgirls wearing black hats."

Beau took in the sight of her for a long moment, angelic blond hair, fair skin and wide blue eyes. Beneath that classy, demure outer covering lay a gambler's heart. Who would have thought it? Who would have known? The man who won her would need that information, Beau thought. The man who hoped to keep her would need to understand the polite exterior and appreciate the untamed, adventurous part of her.

Beau wasn't sure he was the man who would ultimately win her and keep her, but he could give her this little fantasy. Keeping his odd mix of amusement and more intense emotions to himself, he rolled out of bed and pulled on his jeans.

Emily pulled the sheet farther up her chest. "What are you doing?"

"Just a minute," he said. He thumbed through some clothes in his closet until he found one of his old rodeo shirts, and tossed it toward her.

"What's this?"

"Just a minute," he said again, and grabbed his black hat from the shelf in the closet. He threw that on the bed too. Then he found a belt with one of the rodeo buckles hanging from a nail, snatched his boots from the closet floor, and strolled toward her.

She was already inspecting the hat in her hand, then

she glanced up at him doubtfully. "You don't really think I'm going to—"

"First things first." Beau cracked a smile. "Lift your arms."

She kept playing with the hat, but her expression was self-conscious. "This isn't necessary. The cowboy fantasy was a long time ago. Right after the princess fantasy and before the motorcycle fantasy."

"Are you saying you don't *secretly* still want to dress up like a cowboy?"

Her cheeks flamed, and she lifted her chin. "I didn't say that. I just—" She broke off, looked at the hat, then back at him. "This is crazy."

"Lift your arms," he told her.

She hesitated briefly, then dropped the sheet.

Beau looked at her breasts and felt the punch of want in his midsection. He swore. "It's a shame to cover your body, but—" He pulled the shirt up her arms, and they both worked on the buttons.

She looked at him curiously. "This is the second time you've dressed me."

"Yeah." He pulled the belt around her and put it on the tightest loop, but it still almost fell off her hips.

"Is this some kind of unusual fetish?"

Beau laughed. "Are you worried that I secretly played with my sisters' Barbie dolls when I was a kid and I miss changing doll clothes?"

Her lips twitched. "Did you?"

"You've found out my secret. I did get into my sisters' Barbie dolls." He caught sight of her widened eyes. "I liked taking their heads off and hiding them."

Emily rolled her eyes and sighed. "You're terrible."

"That's me. Step into the boots, wild woman."

"I'm not wild," she protested, but put her feet in the boots and stood.

He put the hat on the back of her head because it was a little too big for her, then tightened the cord under her chin.

"This is ridiculous," she muttered.

Beau tugged her toward the full-length mirror on the back of his closet door.

"This is crazy," she grumbled, nearly tripping because the boots were way too big. "I'm not a child. I don't go to sleep every night wishing for a horse named Black Devil anymore, or one of those fringy jackets or—"

She looked at the mirror and stopped. Beau watched her face light up like a Christmas tree and felt the oddest, most painful tugging sensation in his chest. He shoved his hands in his pockets to keep from reaching for her.

Her eyes met his in the mirror and she beamed. "I love the hat."

"You can keep it," he told her. He suspected she'd be taking a helluva lot more from him than his hat when she left.

Aghast, she whirled around to face him. "Oh, no! This is an important memento from your rodeo days."

"Nah. I like the way it looks on you." When she started to protest, he frowned. "You'll hurt my feelings if you don't take it."

She hesitated, then laughed. "Why do I think that's a slight exaggeration?"

"Beats me. I'm just an honest, sensitive, nice guy."

She laughed harder.

Moving closer to her, he ran his gaze down her full length and shook his head. The black shirt sparkled with studs and beads, and the fringe rippled when her breasts bounced. It stopped mid-thigh, revealing her pale, shapely legs. "I tell you one thing. The shirt never looked that good on me."

"I'm sure that's a matter of opinion," she said, her hands on her hips. "Buckle bunnies?" she prompted.

Beau chewed the inside of his lip to keep from chuckling at her curiosity. "I can't remember."

"I'm disappointed," she said with a mock innocent expression on her face.

"Why?"

"I was hoping you'd tell me what buckle bunnies did." She lifted her arms around his neck.

Beau felt his body begin to heat again. He knew what was underneath her shirt. He knew how good she felt beneath him. "The other guys talked sometimes. I might be able to remember some of the things they told me." He pulled his hands from his pockets and wrapped his arms around her. "It might take a little encouragement."

She gave a little smile and lifted on tiptoe to press her lips to his. "How's this?"

"Good for a start." He lifted her high in his arms and one of the boots fell to the floor. She was taking him by inches, he realized. Taking little bits of his mind, body and soul. A slow and easy invasion, as if she could never threaten his life-style or sanity. It felt like heaven, but a part of him wondered when it would turn to hell.

Eleven

"**Y**ou still haven't let me light your cigar," Emily told Beau as she watched him take a discreet puff on her front porch several days later. It intrigued her that he was so selective about when he smoked in front of her. He was getting ready to leave for a meeting, and it was silly, but she would miss him.

"It's self-protection," he said with an intimate half grin that brought to mind all the pleasures they'd shared. "I'm afraid you'll set me on fire."

"Oh, you're so clever." She bit her lip to keep from laughing. He made her feel light and easy, wanted and wanting. She lifted her hand to his arm, then pulled back.

The afternoon sun played over his hard features. He arched an eyebrow. "Why'd you stop?"

"It just feels so natural to touch you, and I have

to keep reminding myself that you might not be a 'toucher.'"

He sifted his fingers though her hair and gently kissed her forehead. "It feels natural for me to touch you, too. So don't stop on my account."

Emily rested her cheek against his chest where his heart beat. Why did it always feel so right to be with him? Why was it that all she had to do to want him more was listen to him talk about everyday matters? And yet, logically, she knew it was too soon.

She closed her eyes against logic for a second. "What kind of turnout do you think you'll get tonight for the Big Buddy program?"

"I'm hoping for twenty men. Then that twenty can do some arm twisting and bring in twenty more."

Emily admired Beau for using his influence to make a difference among the youth of the town. "If you weren't focusing on male volunteers, I would be happy to come."

"I appreciate it, but you would distract them."

She sighed. "You overestimate my—"

The sound of a vehicle coming to a screeching halt in front of Emily's house grabbed their attention.

"Who in hell—" Beau began.

"Who is—"

Emily blinked, then recognized the two occupants of the green convertible. "Maddie! Jenna!" She grabbed Beau's hand and dragged him with her down the steps. "They're my two best friends in the world. Bridesmaids in my wedd—" She made a face. "Well, my almost-wedding."

Red-haired Maddie swung out of the car, heedless of the wild state of her bob, and practically skipped up the walk. "Surprise!" she called.

Jenna tugged ineffectually to get her brown hair back into place and wore a put-upon look. "Hi, Em. I wanted to call, but Maddie insisted."

"No problem. It's great to see you both." She hugged her friends.

"I thought you'd be languishing here in Podunk, North Carolina," Maddie said, lifting her big sunglasses to peer at Emily. "But you look plenty healthy to me."

"I like Ruxton," Emily told her. "Let me introduce you. This is Beau Ramsey. He's the local—"

"He looks a lot like the officer who stopped me on the interstate about an hour ago." Maddie shook her head in disgust. "Amazing how crabby these lawman types get when you're ten miles over the speed limit."

"It was eighteen," Jenna corrected, "but I talked him down to five. You've got a lead foot." She extended her hand toward Beau. "It's nice to meet you, and something makes me think Maddie just stepped in it again. Do you have some relationship with law enforcement?"

"I'm the sheriff."

"Oh." Maddie let out a squeak of dismay.

"How did you know?" he asked.

Jenna shrugged. "Professional instinct. I'm assistant Commonwealth Attorney in Roanoke."

"Why don't we go inside and I'll get us something to drink?" Emily offered.

As if he knew another couple of tornadoes had rolled into his town, Beau shook his head. "You'll have to excuse me. I've got a meeting."

Emily searched his face, but found it unreadable. "Are you sure you can't stay for a few minutes?"

"I've gotta go."

"Just a minute," she said to Maddie and Jenna and walked with Beau to his truck. "Will you come by after the meeting?"

"It'll be late."

Emily frowned. She wondered why he suddenly seemed distant. "Will you call?"

He met her gaze. "You'll be busy with your friends."

She wished his eyes weren't quite so calm and cool. Her chest grew tight with apprehension, and she withdrew, too. "Okay. Thank you for lunch," she managed politely.

"I'll be in touch," he said, then got in his truck. "You might tell your friend she's parked facing the wrong direction. I'd hate to see her get two tickets in one day."

"Thanks," Emily said, but he was already backing out of her driveway. She wondered why the sudden change in his mood. He'd been so warm, and then it was as if he couldn't get away fast enough.

Glancing at her friends on the porch, she shook her head and decided to think about it later. It wasn't often Maddie and Jenna showed up on her doorstep.

Within two hours, Maddie had managed to coax them into going to a honky-tonk in a neighboring town.

"We thought we'd find you depressed and in seclusion," Maddie said once they were seated and had drinks before them. "But you're blooming. What gives?"

Emily smiled. "You'll probably think I'm crazy, but I believe calling off my wedding was the best thing that could have happened to me."

"You do look happy," Jenna said. "Anything to do with the sheriff?"

"Great eye candy," Maddie added, then scrunched up her face. "But did you have to pick a sheriff? They make me nervous."

"If you would obey the laws," Jenna told her, "you wouldn't have a problem."

"I obey them ninety-nine percent of the time and nobody notices. It's the one percent that kills me. I color outside the lines just a little bit and I always get caught. It must be my destiny," she muttered darkly, and took a sip of her beer.

"The original question was directed to you, Emily," Jenna prompted. "How serious are you about the sheriff?"

Very. She swallowed the immediate response and ignored the tight feeling in her midsection. She shouldn't be, couldn't be... "It's too soon to say." She said the appropriate words, but they didn't ring true. Impatient with herself, she gave up fighting the truth. "I'm in love with him."

Maddie's eyes rounded.

Jenna simply nodded. "Rebound?"

"Honest?" Emily asked. "I don't think so. But I'm going through a lot of changes right now, so I'd like some time to be sure."

"What's the sheriff's story?"

"I think he doesn't trust me." It hurt to say it, more than she'd realized.

Maddie looked offended. "Doesn't trust *you?* Your middle name is dependable."

"Was," Emily corrected. "Since I came to Ruxton, I've reassessed things. I've been trying things I always wanted to try, like horseback riding. I worked in a bar, then found a temp computer job with the county. I'm starting to do computer consultations on the side, and it could conceivably build into a self-supporting business. I rented a house, and I like it here. No one knows me, so they don't expect me to be the way I was in Roanoke. For the first time in years, I feel like I can breathe."

"Your mother *can* be stifling," Jenna said.

Out of habit Emily opened her mouth to defend her mother, but she stopped before she spoke. Jenna was right. "Yes, she can."

"Now *she* has been in seclusion," Maddie said. "None of her friends have seen hide nor hair of her."

Emily winced. "I had hoped she would have started to get over it by now."

"I imagine she still feels embarrassed," Jenna said.

"Embarrassed!" Maddie said. "Try totally humiliated. She was counting on this being 'the wedding of the century.' A bunch of people think you must be crushed, because you moved away.''

Emily frowned. ''I'm not sure I care all that much what they're saying at the country club about me, but I really couldn't be less crushed.''

''We can see that,'' Jenna told her.

Emily waited to hear more. ''I hear a *but*.''

''I'm not suggesting that you should give a rip what the country club set thinks. It looks as if you're thriving here.'' Jenna gave a wry smile. ''As much as I'd like you to come back, you're happier than I've seen you in a long time.''

Emily smiled. ''You're not in court, Jenna. I still hear a *but*.''

''I wonder if it might help resolve things for you and your mom if you paid a quick visit. A quick *visible* visit.''

Sighing, Emily pondered her friend's suggestion. ''I hate the idea of people pitying me.''

Maddie shrugged. ''Tell them to suck eggs and die.''

Emily laughed.

Jenna grinned. ''Not a bad idea. But if that doesn't work, you could just tell them the truth.''

Emily considered what Maddie and Jenna had said. The more she thought about it, the more she knew she needed to pay a visit to her mother. ''What time do you think we should leave in the morning?''

Jenna and Maddie spoke at once.

''Eight a.m.''

''Eleven o'clock.''

Maddie looked appalled. "Eight a.m. on a Saturday morning? Are you a sadist?"

"She'll need to get to the country club by lunch-time," Jenna said, then her lips twitched. "I'll drive. You can sleep."

"Well if Emily's gotta face her mother tomorrow, the least we can do is give her a good time tonight."

Well acquainted with Maddie's concept of a good time, Emily shook her head. Visions of tabletop dancing, too much liquor and police raids danced in her head. "That's not necessary," she said. "A good night's sleep will do me a—"

"I want that one," Maddie said, snagging a waiter. She pointed to a tall man standing alone at the bar. She gave the waiter a few dollars. "My friend would like to buy him a beer. Tell him she's blond."

Emily felt her cheeks heat.

"She means well," Jenna said sympathetically.

When the man at the bar walked toward her with a big grin, she moaned. "Maddie did you have to do this?"

"Don't thank me," she mocked, then snagged another waiter. She pressed a couple of bucks into his palm. "My friend would like to buy that man a drink. Tell him she's brunette."

Jenna choked on her drink and gaped at Maddie.

"She means well," Emily whispered.

Jenna narrowed her eyes. "Maybe so, but she's paying for this one."

After Emily dragged herself out of bed the next morning and showered, she immediately called Beau.

''H'lo.''

His rumbly voice made her smile. She could easily imagine waking up to him every day. Her heart squeezed. ''Good morning. This is Emily.''

A long pause followed, and she almost wondered if he'd fallen asleep. ''Beau?''

''Late night last night?''

Emily laughed lightly. ''Maddie. We practically had to drag her out of The Cherry Bomb. She was determined that Jenna and I have a good time. She thinks we don't get out enough and—'' Emily stopped. ''Did I miss you last night? Did you stop by after all?''

''No big deal,'' he said. ''I drove by after the meeting.''

Something about his tone didn't sound right. ''Darn. I wish I'd seen you. Especially now.'' She took a deep breath. ''Jenna and Maddie talked with me, and I think I should make a quick trip back to Roanoke. I'm only planning to stay overnight,'' she emphasized.

When he didn't say anything, she continued. ''I'm not looking forward to it, but I think it's the right thing to do.''

''When are you leaving?'' His voice was expressionless.

She frowned. ''In just a few minutes, but I'll be back tomorrow because I have to work on Monday.''

''You want me to tell your landlord for you?'' Beau asked.

"Why?" she asked, totally confused. "It's just for one night."

He gave a heavy sigh. "It's easy for one night to turn into two," he told her. "I always knew you'd go back. This was just sooner than I expected."

Frustrated, she crammed her feet into her shoes and began to pace around her bedroom. "This is *one* night," she insisted. "I'll be back tomorrow."

"If you say so," he said, his voice full of disbelief.

"I do. Can we see each other when I get back?"

"Sure," he said, without an ounce of commitment.

"Why don't you believe me?"

He paused a long moment, and his silence hurt her. "Butterfly, flutterby," he said quietly.

His words hurt worse. She wished he believed in her half as much as she believed in him. Fighting the stinging sensation in her eyes, she swallowed over her crowded throat. "I guess you'll just have to see."

"Emily," he said. "Take care of yourself."

This was ridiculous, she thought. "Thank you. I will," she said, switching to her controlled polite mode.

"And if you ever light a man's cigar," he told her with a forced chuckle, "use hickory matches."

Anger, hot and intense, raced through her, burning a hole in her polite control, and Emily did something she'd never done before. She hung up on him.

If one more person asked him about Emily, he was going to punch them. He'd joined his sisters for dinner in hopes of avoiding the too-quiet loneliness of his home. His sisters, however, had each privately grilled him about Emily. He felt as if he'd been poked and prodded by far too many people.

Beau had always figured a sore heart could be cured with a good bottle of whiskey or a great meal or another woman, but he was sadly mistaken.

He resented Emily for blowing into town and turning every man on his ear including him. He resented her because he used to enjoy the quiet solitude of his home. He resented her because he hadn't known there'd been an empty place in his life that only she could fill. He resented her for the laughter and light she'd brought him, because now everything seemed dark and sad.

He wished she'd never come to Ruxton. He wished he'd never made love to her. He wished he'd never fallen in love with her.

Feeling a tug on his pants leg, he glanced down to see Hilary Bell looking up at him. His sisters had invited her and her mother for dinner. He patted her on the head. "How ya' doing, sweetheart?"

"I miss Miss Emily," she said with a big sigh.

Beau felt his chest tighten painfully. Lord, the woman had launched a full-scale invasion and they'd all been helpless against it. Beau patted her again. "Me, too, darlin'. Me, too."

As soon as Marie opened the door to her mother and stepfather's expansive home in Hunting Hills, Emily breezed past the housekeeper with a smile. "Is she in the Florida room or in the bedroom with the curtains drawn?''

"Her bedroom, but—''

Emily made a face. "That bad, huh? I'll go up now.''

The housekeeper trotted after her. "I think it might be best if I announce you.''

"Oh, no. It sounds like she could use a little shock treatment.''

Marie frowned. "I don't know...''

But Emily was already up the winding staircase. She walked down the long hallway to her mother's closed bedroom door and heard the hum of Saturday morning television. *This was bad.* Her mother didn't often give in to full-scale melodrama, but it appeared she'd pulled out all the stops this time.

Bracing herself, she tapped on the door.

"Come in, Marie.''

Emily pushed open the door and saw her mother in a rose chiffon negligee and dressing gown reclining on the bed with the remote control, her pocket poodle and a pitcher of Mimosa on the nightstand.

"Good morning, Mother,'' Emily said, and glanced at the television. "I always thought professional wrestling was an oxymoron.''

Adrian St. Clair Bennet's eyes briefly widened in surprise before she regained her composure. Her mother was the queen of composure. "I'm tired of 'Power Rangers.'''

"Then join me for lunch,'' Emily said, marveling again at her mother's natural beauty. She'd often felt gangly and inferior around her mother. It wasn't hard to imagine why.

"Ralph already invited me."

Emily thought of her filthy-rich stepfather with a heart of gold and smiled. "Where is he?"

Her mother gave a wounded look. "Golfing."

Emily nodded and moved closer to sit on the edge of the bed. "You feel abandoned."

"I can't imagine why," she said. "First, my daughter walks out during the middle of her wedding and literally runs away. Then my husband goes golfing."

"Mom, I can't say I'm sorry for stopping the wedding or even for running away. It would have been wrong for me to marry Carl. I can say I'm sorry this has been so embarrassing for you. You don't deserve it."

Her mother lifted her chin and gave Emily a considering glance. "You've changed."

Emily smiled. "I hope so."

"You need a haircut."

Emily bit back her amusement. "Possibly."

"Are you wearing *any* cosmetics at all?"

"Not much makeup today. I was in a rush to see my mom."

Affection stole into her mother's eyes. "Where did you want to go to lunch, dear?"

"The country club," Emily said, surprised her mother would need to ask. "We have reservations in thirty minutes."

Her mother looked doubtful. "Oh, I don't know."

"People think you're languishing in humiliation, and they think I'm *scared* to show my face in public. To quote Maddie, you've been indisposed long enough. It's time to strut your stuff and give the old bags an eyeful."

Her mother's mouth twitched. "I always thought that with some work, some serious work," her mother added as she gracefully rose from the bed, "your friend Maddie would be a force to reckon with."

Emily laughed. "I think she already is."

Thirty minutes later Emily and her mother walked into the Hunting Hills Country Club. The dining room possessed friendly waiters, good food and an understated elegance. Deep green carpet adorned with a rose-colored floral pattern cushioned the feet of the well-heeled members. The dining room chairs were upholstered in rose, and sterling silver clinked against gold-rimmed ivory china on tables decked in white cloths. The most impressive features of the room, however, were the two walls of large-pane windows and the wealth of its occupants.

Emily's mother picked at her hearts of palm salad while Emily finished the last bite of her cantaloupe. Odd, she thought. She couldn't remember a time when her mother had been more ill at ease.

"I think I'm becoming an entrepreneur," Emily said. "I'm a computer consultant."

Adrian smiled. "I'll have to tell Ralph. He'll be so impressed." She dabbed at the corner of her mouth. "I must tell you I don't blame you for walking out on Carl. Even though he was a doctor, he didn't deserve you."

"Thank you," Emily said, and took a sip of water. "I agree."

Adrian chuckled lightly, then sighed. "You remind me of your father more and more, darling. With each passing day."

Emily resisted the urge to make sure her hair was covering her ears. "Is it my ears?"

"I wasn't thinking of your ears. I was thinking of your independence and sense of humor. Oh, how that man could make me laugh, even during a rough moment."

"Do you feel the same way about Ralph?"

Adrian gave a sad smile. "I love Ralph in a different way. He has given me security and peace. Your father gave me laughter and passion."

Emily felt a tug of her own sadness. "I wish I'd known him longer."

"He would be so proud of you."

"And you?" The little girl question was out before she realized it.

Her mother looked surprised. "I've *always* been proud of you."

Emily raised her eyebrows. "Even when I walked out on Carl."

Adrian took a sip of wine. "Well, after a couple of tranquilizers I was very impressed with your courage."

So tactful, Emily thought, and covered her mother's hand. "Thanks, Mom."

Adrian's eyes softened again. "I do worry that your experience with Carl will keep you from—"

"Adrian. Emily." The familiar voice of Millicent Warner scratched across Emily's nerves like fingernails across a chalkboard. Heading straight for their table, Millicent was a terrible gossip, who delighted in repeating bad news to whoever would listen.

"I'm delighted to see you poor things. It's been so long. I've been very worried about you," Millicent said.

Her false sympathy hit Emily like a flat note. Although her instinct was to quietly respond and pray the old biddy left quickly, she stood and gave the gossip a big hug. She smiled for all she was worth. "It's great to see you, Millicent. What a lovely dress. Is that new?" Before Millicent could answer, Emily went on. "It's so sweet of you to be worried, but there's no need. As you can see, my mother is beautiful as ever."

Blinking back her amazement, Millicent braced her hand on the table. "Yes, I can see she's beautiful." She seemed to recover. "But Emily dear, your wedding and Carl." She made a tsking sound. "All your plans. You must be devastated."

Emily beamed. "Oh, no, Millicent. I consider myself damn lucky."

Millicent gasped and gulped and muttered something about meeting her niece. Emily sat down. "Pardon me for swearing."

"Emily," her mother said with a measured glance of approval, "I do believe you've come into your own."

Twelve

A little more than twenty-four hours later, Emily pulled into her driveway. *Her* driveway in Ruxton, North Carolina. She smiled to herself. Her relationship with her mother was better than ever. She liked where she lived. She liked what she was doing. As soon as she caught up with Beau, everything would be right. She still couldn't believe he'd truly thought she wouldn't return.

Grabbing her bag, she walked to her porch and stared in surprise at three florist's arrangements left on a bench. She quickly read the cards and shook her head in wry amusement. The three men Maddie had bought beers for at The Cherry Bomb had sent their regards.

In a rush to reach Beau, she left the flowers on the porch and walked into her house to her phone. She dropped her bag, punched his number and counted the rings. "Pick it up, pick it up, pick it up—"

"Ramsey."

Her heart tightened at the sound of his voice. "Hi. It's Emily. I'm back."

A long silence followed, and she started to get nervous. "Can we get together? Can we—"

"I'm a little busy now. My deputy asked for the evening off, so I need to do a patrol. Maybe later tonight," he said in a distracted tone.

Emily's heart sank to her feet. "Beau, I'm back for good. I'm not fluttering anywhere."

"Good," he said in a noncommittal tone. "If we can't get together tonight, maybe we can try tomorrow. I gotta go. Welcome back," he added, but it sounded like an afterthought.

The disconnecting click vibrated inside her. Emily moved the phone away from her ear and stared at it. She slowly replaced the receiver, but her mind was racing a mile a minute.

What was going on with Beau? Was it merely his persistent belief that she would leave that made him act so distant? Or, she wondered as her stomach tightened with dread, was it something more?

Perhaps he had reconsidered and decided he'd overestimated his feelings for her. Perhaps he'd had enough of her. Her heart clenched at the thought. Perhaps his desire for her had waned. Emily felt a slice of pain cut deep into her soul.

Sinking to her knees on her kitchen tile, she struggled to gain her perspective. Her hands were icy cold with nerves as she reasoned with herself. Beau was human. He was entitled to his own doubts, even if his doubts centered on her. The knowledge grated at her, but she accepted it.

She just wasn't sure what to do about it. Her first instinct was to crawl into a hole and wait. To hurt and hope in private until he could see her for the woman she truly was. Until he was certain of their love.

Everything inside her tightened into a tangled knot of apprehension. She'd spent much of her life waiting and hoping in private, and it hadn't brought her happiness. She'd been fearful and so eager to please that she'd hidden her true self behind a carefully built wall of manners and social courtesy.

Her heart nudged her. Emily was learning that following her heart often led to better places than she'd been. Her hands balled into fists, she asked, "What do I want?"

There was no pause, not the barest hesitation.

She wanted Beau.

Just thinking it and accepting it made everything click into place. Her hands relaxed of their own accord. The tension in her neck eased. Her heart settled into a regular rhythm. When had anything ever felt so right? she wondered, and a powerful resolve set in.

Hours later she finally caught up with Beau at the Happy Hour Bar. More frustrated than anything else, she spotted him talking to Jimmy, the owner. Jimmy was pointing at two men across the room whose voices were getting louder with each passing moment.

Emily walked quickly toward Beau, threading her way through the tables. "Hi," she said. "I really wanted to see you."

Beau looked at her in surprise, then glanced back at Jimmy. "Just a minute," he said to her.

Not the most enthusiastic welcome she'd received, Emily thought, but she could be patient. Even though she'd spent the last few hours on a wild-goose chase trying to find him.

Jimmy looked cross. "Beau, the last time Leroy and T.D. Fitch were in here they did a helluva lot of damage and—"

"Okay, okay." Beau lifted his hand. "I'll go talk to them," he said, and headed toward the two men.

Emily followed Beau. "I can see you're busy, but I hope later we—"

"Welshing on a bet like you always do, Leroy!" The younger of the two men raised his voice.

"I'm not welshing. You're lying. I never called it an official bet. We never shook on it," the tall one said, and got right in the other man's face.

"Who are they?" she asked.

"Fitch brothers," Beau said in disgust. "Can't live together, can't keep from making each other miserable."

"That sounds just like you, slimy as a snake."

"You keep it up and I'm gonna have to teach you a lesson."

Beau sighed. "Okay, boys. That's enough. You're in a public place."

Leroy scowled at Beau. "This is a family matter. It's none of your business."

Emily saw the expression on Beau's face and cringed. If he ever looked at her that way, she would want to hide under the sofa. Apparently Leroy, however, didn't possess a high enough emotional IQ to see he was getting close to a very deep hole.

"It becomes my business when you're disturbing the peace or when one of the business owners calls with a complaint," Beau said in a lethal, low voice.

"Why's Jimmy complaining?" T.D. asked. "We each bought a beer." T.D. looked at his brother and frowned. "*I* bought the beers. Leroy's too damn cheap."

"That does it, T.D., I'm tired of your belly-achin'—"

"You're right, Leroy," Beau said, clearly unwilling to put up with any more foolishness. "That does it. It's time for you to leave."

T.D. tossed Beau an insolent look, but stomped toward the door. "Okay, I'm leavin'. Don't like it here, anyway."

Emily instinctively stepped closer to Beau.

"Me, too," Leroy said. "Right after I—" He swung around and his quick movement alarmed Emily. She stumbled forward.

He rammed his fist toward Beau and missed. She saw it coming, but couldn't move. He whacked Emily in the eye. Stunned, she stopped breathing. The first rush of pain hit her hard, and two seconds later, she fell to the floor. Her entire head throbbed violently, and she immediately covered her eye.

On the fringes of her consciousness, she heard a lot of swearing and some tussling. She would have sworn she heard another body hit the floor, but she was still seeing stars so she couldn't be sure. Beyond her control, moans escaped her mouth.

"I'm gonna kill him," Beau said.

Emily heard more rolling around on the floor.

"You can't kill him," Jimmy said, sounding out of breath. "You're the sheriff."

"Did you see what he did to her? Hit her like she was a man." He swore again, and a few seconds later, she felt his breath on her face.

"Emily." He gently touched her arm.

His voice comforted her in a strange way, but the pain continued unabated. Another moan bubbled out of her mouth. She bit her lip to stop the sounds.

"Emily, sweetheart, look at me," he said, sounding worried, almost desperate. "Let me see."

"No no no no no." She shook her head violently and whimpered.

"Honey, you've gotta let me look at it," he insisted. "C'mon."

She cupped her hand over her throbbing eye and opened the other to look at him. "It really hurts."

Alarm tightened his features. "I know it does, but we have to see if you need a doctor."

"Oh, God, I hope not." She couldn't imagine anyone *touching* her eye. "Please don't touch it," she said. "*Promise* you won't touch it."

He nodded. "I won't touch it. Just let me see it."

She slowly moved her hand away from her already swollen eye.

Beau cringed and swore a blue streak. "I swear Leroy's going to the county jail as soon as he wakes up."

"Wakes up?" she echoed and tried to lift her head.

"I put him to sleep," Beau said. "Don't get up. Jimmy's wife is taking you home while I get Leroy locked up."

She felt a strange panic. "Home?"

He looked at her with an expression of complete and absolute possession. "My home. She'll stay with you until I can get there. Get her some ice, Jimmy." He lowered his head and kissed her forehead. "Honey, I'll be back just as soon as I can."

Beau had Leroy's carcass tossed in the county jail in record time considering it was a weekend. He had to resist the urge to pound him into the ground. When the sorry Fitch brother awoke, however, even he was appalled with himself. "Geez, I hit a lady! I can't believe I hit a lady."

Beau still wanted to hurt him, but with Leroy behind bars, his first concern was getting back to Emily. It had scared the spit out of him to see her hit the floor. His heart felt as if it had been ripped to shreds. He was lucky Jimmy had been nearby, or he might have come terribly close to killing Leroy.

A wholly primitive and overwhelming response, it

alarmed Beau, because it had sent him momentarily out of control. He was going to have to do something about this, he thought, as he walked through his doorway. He was not rational about Emily.

He nodded toward Thelma, seated on his sofa. "How is she?"

"Resting in your room." Thelma rose. "I gave her a little bite to eat, plenty to drink, and something to work on the swelling. Do you want me to stay?"

Beau shook his head. "No. Thanks for coming."

Thelma smiled and opened the door. "She's a sweet one, Beau. Don't let her get away."

Watching her leave, Beau balled his fists and remembered trying to hang on to the butterflies of his boyhood. His chest felt heavy. He swore under his breath. He rolled his head, trying to relieve the tension in his neck, then walked into his bedroom.

Her one eye met his as he sat down on the bed. She held an ice pack over her injured eye and gave a weak smile. "I never realized proximity to a small-town sheriff could be so adventuresome."

He shook his head. "Emily, we can't go on this way."

Emily felt her heart stop.

He gave a heavy sigh. "I can't keep doing this."

Her whole system went into shock. She couldn't speak.

"The timing sucks. We both know that."

A shaft of pain cut right through the center of her, and she had to bite her lip to keep from crying out.

She swallowed hard. "Why? What—" Her voice broke and she couldn't force any more words.

He rose from the bed and began to pace. "I can't keep doing this. I'm like a crazy man. I was ready to *kill* Leroy Fitch. I wanted to kill him. Bad timing or not, I've gotta do something about it."

Her eyes began to tear, stinging her injured eye. She shut them both and took a deep breath. "If you're going to dump me, why did you bring me to your house?" She heard the quaver in her voice and hated it. "You could have just let—"

"Dump you!" he shouted, making her head ring. "Who said anything about dumping you?"

Confused, she clutched her aching head. "You said you can't keep on doing this. You said it's bad timing. What else could you mean?"

She felt the bed dip under his weight. "You're not getting away that easily," he told her. "You blow into town, knock me to my knees, and you think I'm letting you go?"

Still confused, Emily peeked at him with her good eye. "Well, you've been so distant the last couple of days."

"Because I've been scared spitless you were gonna leave. I don't know how you did it, but you filled up my empty place when I didn't know I had one. I sure as hell don't want you to leave."

She felt the first sweet balm of tentative relief. She swallowed over unshed tears and bottled-up emotion. "What are you saying?"

Beau reached for her hand. "Sweetheart, I love you

more than I ever thought I'd love anyone. I want you beside me at night and in the morning. I want you with me when the going gets tough. I want to make babies with you. I want to be the man who's with you when you try everything you've always wanted to try, but never have before.''

His face was as solemn as a lifelong promise. ''Emily, I want to keep you. And I want you to keep me.'' He swallowed as if he was dealing with his own set of nerves. ''I want you to marry me.''

Emily blinked. Her heart was hammering a mile a minute. She couldn't believe it. Her ears had heard his words, her mind had processed them, her soul mirrored them, but she couldn't believe it.

''You can say something now,'' he said roughly.

''I'm stunned,'' she managed. ''We both said it was too soon.''

''Will time make you more sure?''

''No,'' she said, then quickly added. ''I'm already sure. I just didn't think you were.''

He shook his head and gently pulled her to him. ''Is that a yes?''

''Yes,'' she whispered instantly, her heart full, her mind still trying to catch up. He kissed her, his mouth making the promise again as he tasted her.

She tried to make her brain work. ''Do you want to wait a little bit?''

''No,'' he said, pressing his mouth against her hair.

''Wow.''

''Wow what?'' He slipped his fingers under her chin and looked at her.

"When I tracked you down tonight, I thought I was going to have to convince you to keep seeing me." She met his amused gaze. "I was going to remind you of the satin sheets."

"Heavy artillery." His mouth eased into a sexy half grin. "That would have worked."

"And then I was going to remind you that I still wanted to light your cigar."

He chuckled. "Emily, I'm surprised at you. Don't you know a man's supposed to save some pleasures for his wife?"

Epilogue

Beau and Emily were married one month later under the big weeping willow tree next to the Methodist church. She wore a new long white gown and everyone swore she looked like a princess. Emily didn't seem to notice, though, because she was so focused on Beau.

It wasn't First Presbyterian in Roanoke, and the reception was not held at the posh Hotel Roanoke. But the people who counted were there: Beau's family and friends, and Emily's mother, stepfather and two best friends, Maddie and Jenna.

Just as Beau and Emily left the reception, a motorcycle whizzed down the street, distracting his bride. Beau covered her eyes with his hand and muttered, "One fantasy at a time." Emily just grinned at him.

Later that night they made slow, sweet love on black satin sheets, and with very little instruction from her new husband, Emily did a mighty fine job lighting Beau's cigar.

*   *   *   *   *

75¢ off

your next Silhouette series purchase.

If you enjoyed these two stories from Silhouette, visit your nearest retail outlet and take 75¢ off your next purchase!

75¢ OFF!

Your next Silhouette series purchase.

Visit Silhouette at www.eHarlequin.com
PSNCP-USCOUPON
© 2001 Harlequin Enterprises Ltd.

Silhouette®
Where love comes alive™

75¢ off

your next Silhouette series purchase.

If you enjoyed these two stories from Silhouette, visit your nearest retail outlet and take 75¢ off your next purchase!

75¢ OFF!
Your next Silhouette series purchase.

RETAILER: Harlequin Enterprises Ltd. will pay the face value of this coupon plus 10.25¢ if submitted by customer for this product only. Any other use constitutes fraud. Coupon is nonassignable. Void if taxed, prohibited or restricted by law. Consumer must pay any government taxes. Nielson Clearing House customers submit coupons and proof of sales to: Harlequin Enterprises Ltd., 661 Millidge Avenue, P.O. Box 639, Saint John, N.B. E2L 4A5. Non NCH retailer—for reimbursement submit coupons and proof of sales directly to: Harlequin Enterprises Ltd., Retail Marketing Department, 225 Duncan Mill Rd., Don Mills, Ontario M3B 3K9, Canada.

Coupon expires April 30, 2002.
Valid at retail outlets in Canada only.
Limit one coupon per purchase.

52603541

Silhouette®
Where love comes alive™

New York Times **bestselling author**

JOAN JOHNSTON

**keeps readers on the edge with her sensual
Hawk's Way series.**

Hawk's Way Brides

THE UNFORGIVING BRIDE
THE HEADSTRONG BRIDE
THE DISOBEDIENT BRIDE

"Joan Johnston does contemporary Westerns to perfection."
—*Publishers Weekly*

Available at your favorite retail outlet.

Where love comes alive™

FREE Refresher Kit!

With two proofs of purchase
from any of our four Silhouette
"Where Love Comes Alive"
special collector's editions

FREE
Refresher Kit!
✂
One Proof
of Purchase

Special Limited Time Offer

<u>IN U.S., mail to:</u>
Silhouette Quiet Moments
Refresher Kit Offer
3010 Walden Ave.
P.O. Box 9020
Buffalo, NY 14269-9020

<u>IN CANADA, mail to:</u>
Silhouette Quiet Moments
Refresher Kit Offer
P.O. Box 608
Fort Erie, Ontario
L2A 5X3

**YES! Please send my FREE Introductory Refresher Kit so
I can savor Quiet Moments without cost or obligation,
except for shipping and handling. Enclosed are two proofs
of purchase from specially marked Silhouette "Where
Love Comes Alive" special collector's editions and $3.50
shipping and handling fee.**

Name (PLEASE PRINT)

Address   Apt. #

City   State/Prov.   Zip/Postal Code

FREE REFRESHER KIT OFFER TERMS

To receive your free Refresher Kit, complete the above order form. Mail it to us with two proofs of
purchase, one of which can be found in the upper right-hand corner of this page. Requests must be
received no later than March 30, 2002. Your Quiet Moments Refresher Kit costs you only $3.50 for
shipping and handling. The free Refresher Kit has a retail value of $25.00 U.S. All orders subject to
approval. Products in kit illustrated on the back cover of this book are for illustrative purposes only
and items may vary (retail value of items always as previously indicated). Terms and prices subject to
change without notice. Sales tax applicable in N.Y. **Please allow 6-8 weeks for receipt of
order. Offer good in Canada and the U.S. only.**

Offer good while quantities last. Offer limited to one per household.

598KIY DAEY